Patricia Carrick,
beautiful and brilliant,
came out of a mill town
to create a financial
empire, risk it for
a reckless love
and continue an
American dynasty.

5

THE CARRICKS

THE
CARRICKS

Brooke Miller

A DELL/JOAN HITZIG MCDONELL BOOK

Published by
Dell Publishing Co., Inc.
1 Dag Hammarskjold Plaza
New York, New York 10017

Dell ® TM 681510, Dell Publishing Co., Inc.

ISBN: 0-440-01413-1

Printed in the United States of America
First printing—August 1982

BOOK ONE

CHAPTER ONE

'SALMON SKIES'

SAN JOAQUIN VALLEY, CALIFORNIA, SEPTEMBER, 1873

IT was called "The Gilded Age."

But there are those who claim that the golden apple was rotten at its core.

After the guns of the Civil War were stilled, America ran hellbent for progress, and Heaven help anyone who stood in the way or faltered in the quest. The Western frontier was gobbled up by every kind of settler, from miner to farmer to rancher.

By 1900 America would proudly lead every other nation on the globe in the production of meat, gold, silver, coal, oil, steel and iron. We would have more miles of track, more feet of telegraph wire than anyone else.

But the price we paid was a kind of corruption that chewed at our heart. State governments were owned, lock, stock and barrel, by giant corporations. Politicians were the lackeys of a new breed who called themselves financiers. They had no loyalty to any specific product—they were "money men."

The hoop skirt and the crinoline gave way to the bustle as the country which gave the world the type-

writer began to see laborers struggle to share in the
gold of the gilded age. The conflict between those who
controlled the resources and those who worked them
would be violent.

In September of 1873 Jay Cooke's precarious banking empire toppled like a tangle of jackstraws. Panic
ensued, a panic which the incompetent Ulysses S.
Grant—who had just doubled his own salary that
spring—could not control. America tumbled headlong into a Depression that would continue, on and
off, for nearly thirty years.

Patricia Carrick put the newspaper down and shook
her head. She was surprised she could cry after all
these years. There was no reason the newspaper should
have taken all that time to come to her attention.
For Heaven's sakes, a person could go from Oakland
to Boston by train if he wanted to. The paper should
have gotten here quicker.

The wedding announcement and story took up a
page and a half:

"World Famous Actress Weds Wealthy Industrialist"
The description of Marshall Macauley's marriage to
Violette Larson Ouan was, evidently, the social event
of the year. People came from every corner of the
country to celebrate. . . .

Every corner but Patricia Carrick's. . . . She and
her older brother, Joseph, used to joke that someday
Mr. Macauley would come West, pluck the red-haired
beauty from the ranch and carry her off into the sun-
rise. But then he married that Marguerite Travers
woman and then. . . .

Patricia got up and went to the mirror over the
hat rack by the door. The tears she shed for the love

that could never be made her cheeks shiny. She dabbed the salty traces away with the corner of her apron. "For thirty you're a fine-looking woman," she said. Her green eyes, the color of shamrocks, still blazed. Her luxuriant red hair still framed her face with a corona of flame. Her child's body—the body shamed and abused by the despicable Francis Macauley—had flowered into womanhood with a full bustline and a narrow waist.

Francis Macauley. Eighteen years later, her nightmares still brought the phantom of that terrible man to her side. When she was awake she found the company of men disturbing. Many men had courted her, and she knew she should settle down like her sisters, but she could never imagine lying down and enduring for love what the vile man with the flowing black hair had done for twisted sport.

"Ah," she said, tossing her head to the side to end her ruminations, "I have enough to do taking care of this place." She stepped out onto the dusty porch and wished the heat would leave the valley. The silver waves shimmered skyward over the thousand acres of farmland which Marshall Macauley's money had bought. She smiled again. She and her brothers had repaid his generous loan after only ten years.

They lived in the San Joaquin Valley, hammering and carving their existence from that piece of real estate which lies between the Coast Range and the Sierra Mountains. Victim of flood or drought, a constant battle of extremes, the Valley measured 200 miles long and fifty miles wide.

It was not until adequate irrigation could be provided that the San Joaquin began to attract the attention of investors.

And adequate irrigation meant one man: Simon Yarrow, owner of land, owner of a banking empire, owner of railroads, keeper of the lives and souls of thousands of men and women who fought to stay alive. Had there been no state government at all, there would have been only Simon Yarrow, a modern king.

A dust cloud on the road that ran past the Carrick farm announced a solitary rider making good time. "Maybe it's Joseph back for an early supper," she thought. She stepped into the kitchen of the small frame house to see what she could do to hurry up the cauliflower and the shepherd's pie. This was the best supper she'd been able to put on the table in weeks. Times were hard and people were talking depression. Wheat prices were low—"Lower than a pregnant dog's belly," Joseph said. They would get lower still before the economy collapsed entirely.

The rider spurred his mount through the ramshackle gate and headed directly for the farmhouse. Patricia's younger brother, Alexander, had always said he'd fix the gate.

"Good afternoon, Miss Carrick," the rider said. "Wonder if I might trouble you for a cool drink of water."

Patricia nodded slowly and went back inside to fetch the dipper from the cool room. Grant Yarrow didn't look much like his father, but he had that easy grace born of knowing that he could buy and sell the world at his own price. He was dark, good looking, single, in his mid thirties and as shameless as any man had a right to be.

He lounged in the scant shade of the front porch when she brought the water to him. Wherever he sat he seemed to own that spot. He was always at ease even when he had no right to be. "Thank you, Miss Patricia." His deep voice emphasized the "Miss" a mite more than Patricia liked. His laughing mouth smiled more than she approved.

Patricia leaned against the front door frame and watched the far horizon for signs of her brothers, Joseph and Christopher and Patrick. Mary Margaret and Mary Elizabeth were married to farmers across the valley.

"You're not half sociable, are you, Miss Carrick?" Grant said.

She shook her head. Looked at him. He was a big man. His shoulders were wide and square. His biceps barely squeezed out of the sleeves of his blue work-shirt. "Work!" she thought to herself, "The man has never done a stitch of work in his life."

"Water here's good and sweet," he said. "My father has always admired your piece of the valley."

"He can keep his admiring to his own greedy self," Patricia said. "My da's dead on this farm and my brother's killin' himself to keep it."

Grant Yarrow leaned his head back and laughed. "If I had a horse like you, I'd take even money I couldn't break her."

Patricia looked him square in his pale blue eyes and said, "You'd die trying."

He stood up. "But such a sweet death," he said. "Thank you for the water. Would you tell Joseph I'd like to see him?" He took a step forward and stopped. He handed her the now-warm dipper.

"What would you be having to do with Joseph?"

"You don't approve of me, do you, Miss Carrick?"

"It isn't important whether I approve of you or not," Patricia replied.

He nodded. "Is it because I love too many women or because I don't work for a living? Or because I gamble entirely too much? Or because a lot of young women in the valley would like to hogtie me and live a life of ease?"

"Like I said, it isn't important," Patricia replied. She took the dipper from him and started to turn away. Suddenly he caught her by the shoulders and held her before him. He was breathing heavily.

"I consider your opinion very important to me," he said. His mouth smiled, but his eyes bored through her like shafts of lightning. He pulled her slowly, inexorably closer. She could smell his man-scent, feel the submerged power in his forearms, hear his deep voice echoing against the wall behind her.

"I think you're a self-important, opinionated son of a bitch who uses people and then tosses them aside. You're just like your father only you don't have his nerve or you'd have made something of yourself a long time ago."

Grant Yarrow pulled her even closer, just beginning to feel the crush of her body against his chest. She was a real woman, a challenge. He leaned forward and took the kiss he had no right to take.

Patricia tried to pull back from the insistent mouth, but she was powerless.

When Grant had drunk deeply enough of her, he stepped back and laughed. "Tell your brother I'd like to see him. I'll be back," Grant called. He mounted his stallion and galloped down the road.

She watched his ride away, fighting the realization that she was very much in love with him. She touched her lips gently and felt the fire he had ignited.

* * *

"Pie was near perfect," Joseph said with a smile. "Nice to put my teeth down on some real food for a change." He let his grey-green eyes range across the table. There were eight hired hands now, plus his brothers. Once there'd been a dozen. He forced a smile and looked over at his sister. "Are you getting prettier, Patricia? Have you made a pact with the devil? While the rest of us get older and uglier, you get more beautiful?"

"Something like that," she said. Joseph was always singing her praises in front of the hired hands. Always trying to find a suitor. She looked down the table at the exhausted men, each with his face in his food, each trying to inhale as much as possible in the shortest amount of time. They were boys, not men. Not like Grant Yarrow . . .

Joseph picked up a napkin with the metal hooks which had long ago replaced his hands—replaced them after the cruel carding machine had snatched them from him. He hardly ever thought of Adam and Francis and Charles Macauley, the three men who had ordered his punishment for trying to organize the people at the mill back East. Sometimes he'd wake in the middle of the night, his forehead sweaty, his arms across his eyes to try to block the memory of the metal teeth which scraped his wrists to the bone . . . ,

"There's word come that Yarrow wants to hike the water rates again," Alexander Carrick said. At twenty-eight, he was muscular, handsome, a private person who came and went without saying where he had been or where he was going.

"What fer?" one of the hands asked. He sneaked a look at the beautiful and aloof woman at the head of the table.

"He's trying to pay for the damn fool railroad he's putting in," Christopher Carrick said. He pushed back from the table and rolled a cigarette effortlessly with one hand. An expert rider, Christopher prided himself on doing everything with consumate skill. Patricia was proud of her curly-headed brother and dreamed of his becoming a real power in the region.

"That damn fool railroad," Joseph said, "will open up the whole valley and make our land worth double or triple. We'll be able to move our produce out at a much lower cost. That'll give us a better profit."

Patricia laid down her fork and wiped her lips. "Grant Yarrow was by," she said.

Joseph looked over in her direction and shrugged. "And?"

"Said he wanted to see you," she said slowly.

Joseph nodded. Cleared his throat.

"What do you have to do with that scum?" she asked. To cover her anxiety she stood up and began to clear the table.

"I saw Grant coming out of the Chatfield barn last week," Christopher said with a laugh. "Chatfield's got horns just like the Devil's." Some of the hired men guffawed.

They stopped laughing when Joseph shot them a look that said a lady's present. He turned to look at his sister. She was clearly suspicious. He smiled. "Grant has a gelding he wants to sell me."

Patricia nodded. "What you going to buy it with? We haven't any money."

"He'll give me terms," Joseph said. "Why are you

so all-fired curious? I see Grant Yarrow all the time in town. I don't hold the father's greed against the son."

"—Someone's riding hard," Patrick called from his place by the front window.

Joseph led them out the door as a young boy reined in his hard-ridden mount.

"Is it time?" Patricia cried to him when he dismounted.

Breathless, the child could do no more than nod at first. Then, "Trouble," he said. "Come quick."

Patricia turned to Christopher. "Saddle Shamrock as fast as you can."

"Yes, ma'am."

"I'll go with you," Joseph said.

"I don't think there's anything a man can do to help a woman birth a baby. I'll go back with Steven here. Patrick, you see to cleaning up. I might not be back until tomorrow some time."

Steven Lacey, Patricia's nephew, looked frightened. He was his mother's son. Mary Margaret's fine features had predominated, showing none of the heavy nose and mouth of her husband, William. "Quickly, Aunt. She was screaming bad."

Patricia mounted her horse, wheeled for the gate and galloped down the valley.

CHAPTER TWO

THE Lacey ranch looked as if no one had farmed it in a year. The earth was caked hard under the horses' hooves. Underbrush had begun to creep unhindered across the yard. Birds claimed the vineyard for themselves.

Patricia reined in hard, pulling Shamrock's head around. She was off and headed into the weather-beaten house before young Steven had even reached the gate.

Mary Margaret's screams were shrill, punching the hot still air like thunderclaps. "The baby's dead! My baby's dead!"

"Sister!" Patricia cried. The scene was wrought from the nightmares of some foul artist. In the darkened bedroom Mary Margaret lay across bloody sheets trying to reach for the still lump of flesh in her hired man's dirty hands.

"It won't breathe," the bewildered old man said. "It won't breathe."

"My baby's dead! William killed him! Oh, Jesus.

16

Oh Lord. . . ." Mary Margaret Lacey fell sideways and sobbed into the filthy mattress.

"Give him to me," Patricia shouted. "Find some clean toweling. Clean rags or such. Fetch some hot water for my sister." As she spoke she pried open the small infant's tiny mouth. Already the child was a mottled blue, his mouth filled with mucous. Patricia fixed her mouth to the child's and sucked the awful smelling liquid from his nose and mouth. She spat upon the floor, turned the baby upside down and gave him a sharp spank across the purpling buttocks.

"He's dead. . . ." Mary Margaret sobbed.

The baby did not breathe.

Patricia looked up at the smokey ceiling and said a short prayer. She pressed the infant's body, then spanked it once again.

The first cry was low, guttural, liquid. Like an old man smoking his last cigar. The second cry was fed by more oxygen. The third was louder and the fourth was louder still.

Patricia laid the child in the clean rags the hired man had brought and massaged its fragile limbs until his color had changed from blue to rose.

"How long was the child not breathing?" she asked.

"A . . . short . . . time," the hired man said.

"How long?"

"You was just ridin' up . . . a minute?"

Patricia nodded. "Good." She looked at the door and saw the tear-stained faces of Mary Margaret's four older children. "You've a new brother. He's alive and so's your ma, so you can stop your crying. Run along to bed with you."

Steven nodded and shepherded his brother and sisters before him.

The child continued to cry lustily as his aunt carried him to his sobbing mother's breast. "Here, now, Mary Margaret, quit your snivelling. The boy's gonna be fine."

Mary Margaret smiled. Her skin was as grey as the sheets she lay upon. Only the orange light of the kerosene lamp gave her any color at all. Her eyes were circled with dark rings; her once-sea-green irises had gone dark and lustreless.

The child was quiet and sucked hungrily from hiis mother's thin breast.

"You said William killed your child, Mary Margaret. Why?"

"I was out of my mind with worry. I didn't know what I was saying." She looked up into the sparkling green eyes that bored into her and envied her sister as she had never envied her before.

"Mary Margaret, I want to know why you thought he killed your baby." She looked around. "Where is William?"

"He had some business in town." Mary Margaret let her sister shift the infant to her other breast. "What with the prices and all, he's had to work double hard. William says it's them corrupt politicians in Washington. President Grant and them all. He says Grant's to blame for everything that's happened. William knows a lot."

Patricia took a warm cloth and swept it gently across her sister's forehead, down her cheeks and chin. She rinsed out the cloth and then swabbed the exhausted woman's stomach and legs. When she was finished she looked down at her again. "What has William done to you?" she asked softly.

The tears began like an easy summer shower. Mary

Margaret's lip quivered. "It wasn't always like this," she said. "At first it was fine and good."

"I know," Patricia said.

"But this last year. . . ." Mary Margaret paused to let the sob run its course. "We been so poor, so dirt poor . . . It did something to Will. Changed him."

"Why didn't you tell me and Joseph?"

Mary Margaret closed her eyes. "I was ashamed. Will started drinking real heavy. He gave up. Stopped working. Me and the young ones tried, but it was too much."

"How did he try to kill your baby?"

Mary Margaret looked down at the infant, who was now sleeping peacefully on her breast. "When I told him I was in the family way again, he went wild. He started cuffing me about, slapping me whenever he was angry. And he was angry most of the time. Then . . ." She looked up at Patricia's kind face. "Then he got terrible drunk one night and kicked me in the stomach, sayin' he wanted to kill the little bastard inside of me."

Patricia gripped the washrag tightly to keep from shouting in rage. She nodded. "Did he only do that once?"

Mary Margaret shook her head from side to side. "Often?"

Mary Margaret squeezed her eyes shut against the tears. "Every night. I hid from him. Steven tried to stop him. . . ." Her dark hair was matted on the pillow beneath her head. "He wanted the baby dead."

Patricia patted the tragic woman's hands. "Sleep now, Mary Margaret. Sleep, dear sister."

Mary Margaret tried to smile and for a moment looked like she had when they were growing up. In those days no one had thought it odd that the younger sister seemed so much older. Patricia had always been the leader, had always assumed the role of mother. "Thank you, Patty."

When mother and child were nestled in sleep, temporarily beyond the pains of waking life, Patricia cornered the hired man and demanded to know where Will Lacey might be conducting his "business." A few moments later she rode off into the night.

The cocks flew at each other in a flurry of spurs and feathers and flecks of blood. The cigar smoke hung low over the pit and the shouts of the men made it impossible for them to hear the barn door open and close. Many of the men who were there were immigrants shoved west by falling wages and rising hopes of the big score to be made in silver. All they found was poverty in a new location.

"Do her, King!" Will Lacey screamed. His face was wet with perspiration, his short was soaked clear through. "Do her, man!" His fighting cock flew spur-first at the larger, older cock, a scrawny brown killer owned by one of Simon Yarrow's track foremen. Everyone knew that King was the only thing of value Will Lacey owned. He made his drinking money with the lithe bird which could circle left or right with equal ease, duck under the most awesome onslaughts and slit the throats of his opponents.

Will smiled to see King feint left, move right, and thrust forward. He took the last swallow from a quart of rot-gut and felt the flood of relief he drank for. His mind went calm, his body stopped fighting him. The rage stopped and he felt whole. "Kill the son of a bitch, King!"

The older bird went down on his left side, blood streaking its breast. King, sensing an early victory, leaped in boldly, his claws aimed straight for the brown cock's throat.

It wasn't until King was on the descent that he saw the trap open up. The brown bird rolled left and pounced on the over-eager cock, ripping out King's throat with a blood-curdling shriek.

Will Lacey waded into the sandy pit and knelt next to the still-warm bird. "King?" He sobbed into the blood and feathers and gristle that was once the best fighter in the valley. "King, darling?"

"If you spent half as much pity on your wife and children, you might have hopes of becoming a man!" The female voice cut through the smokey barn like a scythe. Thirty or forty pairs of eyes swept quickly to where Patricia Carrick stood in her divided riding skirt, her ivory-handled riding crop held lightly in her right hand. The men eased back silently; no one was willing to stand between Joseph Carrick's sister and the man at whom she was looking with fiery hatred.

"Get the fuck out of here. No women allowed," Will Lacey said, his dead bird clutched to his breast.

"How much did you lose?" Patricia asked. She stepped closer to the pit.

Will's eyes darted from side to side. It seemed as if everyone was staring at him, smiling at him. "None of your damned business!" he shouted.

Advancing on him, Patricia slapped her riding skirt with her crop, making a loud pop with each step. "I have just seen your new son," she said in the thick silence.

Lacey smiled, curling his thick lips. "Dead, I trust. No more bastards . . ."

Patricia shook her head.

"You're lying!"

"I wish I was," Patricia said. "You tried hard enough. A man who would strike a woman is the worst kind of coward, Will Lacey. A man who would try to murder an unborn child is lower than that." She raised her arm and brought the crop down with a slicing blow across the side of Will's face.

King fell to the bloody sand as his master raised his arms to try to ward off the attack. The bird's blood mixed with his master's as Patricia chopped at him again and again opening up bloody welts across his head and shoulders.

The bystanders laughed to see a six-foot man laid open by a five-foot woman who was filled with the wrath of god. One man tried to take wagers on the outcome, but no one would bet against the beautiful redhead.

Will reached up and grabbed at the whip, just snaring it. He tugged forward, yanking Patricia off balance. She tumbled towards him, narrowly missing the left cross he aimed at her chin. She let go the crop and brought her knee squarely into Will Lacey's groin, knocking him over double. As soon as his face bent down, she brought the other knee up into his chin, sending him soaring up out of the pit and onto the rough-hewn board seats.

He didn't move.

It was quiet. Patricia scanned the faces around her until she recognized someone she knew. "Mr. Bailey, will you help me get Will on his horse?"

John Bailey was in his mid-thirties. He owned the drygoods store in town. He'd come courting a few years ago, but Patricia had told him she was not going to get married. "Yes, Miss Patricia." He called to a couple of his friends and they carried the unconscious man to a mare outside. "Would you like an escort, ma'am?"

"Thank you, no, Mr. Bailey. I can manage from here."

"Yes, Miss Patricia."

With the help of the hired man, she put Will Lacey to bed in his barn, saw to the mother and newborn, and kissed each of her nephews and nieces good-night. It was after midnight before Patricia Carrick returned home.

Joseph was not asleep. Nor was he alone. Four other men from the valley sat around the table in the kitchen. "Lathrup had a whole field go dry," one of the men said.

"That's precisely why we must organize," Joseph said. "Simon Yarrow can starve us out by cutting off all our water."

"He won't have to close off the canal. All he'll have to do is raise the rates till we can't pay. Same thing."

"If we band together, though," Joseph said, "we can stand up to him."

"Lathrup's land was like powder," another man said. "It made me sick to see it."

"We'll go see Yarrow in the morning," Joseph said.

The men nodded, then said their good-nights and disappeared into the darkness.

Patricia looked at her older brother. If anyone, it was he who had grown more handsome. His eyes flashed, hinting at the raw energy that lay behind them. "You lost your hands for trying to organize the men at the Macauley mill," she said. "What will you lose now?"

Joseph drained his coffee cup and laughed. "I guess I'll have to hobble around on peglegs, eh?" He rose and kissed his sister good-night. "Just because you're Irish-born doesn't mean you have to be gloomy, darling."

Patricia watched him go upstairs and wondered if he was right. She also wondered what business he could have with Grant Yarrow. He didn't need a new horse.

Grant Yarrow. . . .

CHAPTER THREE

FROM his vantage point on the hillock, astride a stallion the color of a stormy night, Simon Yarrow could see the rail crew's work engine chuffing and puffing closer to the floor of the valley. He turned in his English saddle and could see the lacework of the Valley Canal and Irrigation Company, the arteries through which flowed the precious water that was the Valley's life source. "I could make this bowl into a desert if I cared to," he said to himself. He thought that the word "lifegiver" might look well upon his tombstone—no, mausoleum. That would be grander.

The air was sweet at this time of morning. Simon Yarrow was fifty-five, solid like a side of beef, a few inches taller than six feet. Beneath thinning brown hair, small brown eyes bore out upon the landscape, missing no details. His thin line of a mouth turned down at the corners.

It tickled Simon Yarrow to think that the Valley was only part of his empire. His railroad interests covered the West, his banks had California sewed up, his shipping concerns reached across the Pacific, down to South America and around The Horn. But the project which took most of his time was a secret enterprise known only to a select few of the inner circle. Here and in Washington Simon Yarrow had spoken of the growing "mongrelization" of the country. Workers, mostly foreigners, had begun to organize into groups. They spoke of bargaining for their wages. They spoke of withholding their labor.

If the workers were allowed to organize, the country would be destroyed. That was an article of faith for Simon Yarrow. He dedicated his life to preserving the rights of capital. If men had to be killed in this sacred war, then so be it. If laws had to be broken to maintain the status quo, then that was too bad. Financiers could organize too . . .

Simon watched the rider come up the hillock. He smiled. "You're up earlier than usual, Grant," he said. "Or have you not gone to bed yet?"

Grant Yarrow drew in his reins and leaned forward in his saddle. " 'Fraid it's the latter. I was coming home from a little nocturnal visitation when I saw you up here surveying your kingdom."

"It is a kingdom, isn't it?" his father said.

Grant nodded.

"You visiting anybody I'd know?"

"Chatfield woman," Grant said. For once he was not telling the truth. He'd met with Joseph Carrick out by the San Joaquin River bend. They'd argued about what Joseph and his fellow farmers were about to do. Grant had pleaded for more time. He told Joseph he'd sent word to Washington to get the government to intervene, but there was no stopping the farmers. They'd been pushed too far.

Simon laughed loudly and reached over to clap his

son on the shoulder. "Great Jehovah's nipples, son, but your taste gets better and better! I wouldn't mind a piece of that roast myself!"

"I'm sure her husband would be glad to work out something for you," Grant said. "He's scraping to make his water payments as it is. For a discount, who knows what he'd agree to."

Father and son laughed in the warm morning air. "Grant," Simon said, "I wanted to talk to you about your sister."

Grant's dark eyes hooded over. "About what, father?"

"Diana. . . ." The older man looked off into the shimmering distance. The words were slow in coming. "Do you think she's seeing some man in the valley?"

"Depends on what you mean by *seeing*, father."

Simon's voice exploded. "You know damn well what I mean by seeing! Like you were seeing Chatfield's wife! That's what I mean by seeing!"

Grant's mount stirred uneasily, forcing his rider to rein in sharply. Grant took off his widebrimmed fauncolored hat and wiped his forehead. "I don't know what Diana is doing, father. She's twenty and she's a Yarrow." He smiled. "We've got hot blood."

"Not Diana! Not Diana!"

Grant put his hat back on and nodded. "I'll talk to her."

"If she's seeing someone, I want to know who it is."

Grant nodded again, turned his horse towards home and waved to the foreman, Smith, who was riding up the hillock.

"There's a group of farmers want to see you, Mr. Yarrow," he said.

"Which ones?"

"The Carricks and Lattimer and them."

Simon Yarrow pulled at his chin. Nodded. "Get Johansen and Digby just in case."

"Yessir."

Joseph Carrick stood with Neal Lattimer and two other farmers who had been at his house the night before and waited for the arrival of Simon Yarrow. A few yards away the canal sluiced the precious water towards the thirsty earth. "Here he comes," Joseph said. It was hot.

"He's got riders with him," Lattimer said. A husky man, he'd moved his wife and family out from Kansas and settled only a year earlier.

"Mebbe we got him scared," one of the others muttered.

Simon reined in his horse and looked down at the four men who had gathered to talk to him. Joseph Carrick was strong, he thought. Strong inside and out. It didn't matter whether he had those hooks or not. The man could be a formidable adversary. He was a natural leader. "Good morning, gents," Simon said. "Mr. Smith here tells me you want to parley."

Joseph stepped forward and craned his neck to look up into the burly man's face. He had to shade his eyes with his forearm to see against the morning sun. "Yes, sir. It seems to us that the Valley Canal and Irrigation Company's latest rate hike is not reasonable." Joseph's Irish accent still colored his words as he spoke evenly and slowly. "Meaning no disrespect, sir, but profits are marginal as it is. We cannot pay $2.50 an acre and show any profit at all."

Yarrow nodded and smiled. He turned to Smith

and his other mounted henchmen, then looked back down at Joseph Carrick and the other farmers. "And do you all feel that $2.50 is unreasonable?"

"I've got payments," Neal Lattimer said.

The others nodded in agreement.

Simon looked down at his kidskin riding gloves and said, "It seems you gents may have a point. $2.50 is hardly a reasonable price for water hereabouts. Just this morning I was saying to Mr. Smith that I thought $2.50 was unreasonable. Wasn't I, Mr. Smith?"

Smith nodded, unsmiling, his face knife-thin. "Exactly that, sir."

"So," Simon Yarrow said slowly through a smile, "from today on the price is $4.00 per acre. That seems much more reasonable to me. How about you, Mr. Smith?"

"Much more reasonable, Mr. Yarrow."

Neal Lattimer bolted forward, causing Yarrow's stallion to rear. "You bastard! You have no right to treat us that way! We're folks just like you!"

Simon struggled to keep his high-strung mount under control. "Lattimer, get back there!"

But the young farmer had gone beyond reason. His wife was sick, his children were bone-weary from working his acres. Four dollars an acre would make him a slave to the man on the inky black horse. He reached up for the bridle; the stallion bucked and reared.

Smith and the others moved in to try to restrain the animal and get between Lattimer and their boss. Joseph reached out with the backs of his hooks to stop his friend, but Neal kept forcing the animal backwards, hoping to throw the hated man to the ground.

Steel hooves flashed in the bright sun. One clipped Lattimer's shoulder, tearing his shirt, but still he pressed forward.

"Kill him! Kill him!" Simon shouted over his horse's panicky cries. And then, suddenly, the stallion went over backwards, scattering men and animals in all directions.

Joseph tried to wade forward amidst the screams of horse and owner, but Smith had cut him off.

Simon Yarrow lay pinned beneath his horse, his legs useless under the weight. "Smith! Get him off!"

"Lattimer, get back!" Joseph shouted.

Neal leaped across Yarrow's horse and locked his hands around the big man's neck. "You won't starve us out!" the hysterical farmer cried. "I won't let you!"

The shot was not loud.

The bullet parted the air neatly, pushing itself quietly into Neal Lattimer's throat. Neal looked surprised for a moment, but even when he realized that he'd been mortally wounded, he did not stay his assault on the man on the ground. When his strength gave out and his lungs filled up with blood, he caved in and fell to the ground next to the man he hated.

Joseph looked at Smith as the foreman put away his forty-four. "You'll hang for murder!"

Smith smiled at him. Shrugged. "He was tryin' to kill Mr. Yarrow."

It was quiet as Yarrow's men helped their master to his feet. The stallion stood panting nearby. The farmers gathered around their fallen comrade and covered him with a saddle blanket.

"Four dollars!" Yarrow said. "I oughta make it

more!" He mounted his skittish horse and rode angrily away.

"No judge around here'd convict Smith."

Joseph nodded. "I wonder what'll happen to Lattimer's family."

CHAPTER FOUR

JOHN D. Rockefeller was thirty-three. Standard Oil of Ohio had been in existence for three years. Andrew Carnegie and his partners had inaugurated a steel works in Pittsburgh. The average yearly salary of a worker in the United States was a few dollars over four hundred a year. The cable car was introduced in San Francisco, and the winter was bitterly cold.

The frigid air swept from the west, over the mountains and down into the San Joaquin.

Alexander Carrick spurred his horse forward into the foothills. His rifle was slung across his pommel. Game was getting scarce; it was always a big day when he could bring home meat for supper.

The harvest had been fair, but, after the bills were paid, the family had come up with barely enough to put aside for seed next spring.

The mare was eager to follow the path cleft between the two big hills that were shaped like a sleeping Indian. She had taken the trail so often she knew long in advance where every sharp outcropping of rock was located. She knew where every gopher hole could trap a fetlock.

The little cabin had been built ten or fifteen years before. The boards were silver and didn't stop much of the wind that curled through the dell. There was only one window, but that had been boarded up for several years.

Alexander smiled to see the roan already grazing nearby. He dismounted and let his own mare munch easily at the tufts of grass that surrounded the place. Then he entered the cabin.

"Alex!" she cried. Her long blonde tresses were in disarray, a riot of luxuriant hair. She had already taken off her riding jacket. Her white blouse was partially undone, exposing the tops of her sumptuous breasts. She breathed quickly through her ripe full lips. She had a distracted quality about her. She was unfocused, always on the paperthin line between energy and hysteria. "Oh, God, please, Alex, ride me as hard as you can!"

The handsome young man embraced her roughly, pressed the breath from her, and placed his searing lips upon her own, his tongue a pitiless explorer.

"Oh, God," she murmured, overcome with passion.

Alex threw her down roughly upon the pallet on the floor.

"Ride me hard! Ride me as hard as you have ever ridden!" she cried.

Alex smiled and shrugged. Began slowly taking off his clothes. "Perhaps, Diana, perhaps."

"I beg you." She unlaced her blouse and fairly forced the man to bury his face in the wealth of her breasts. "Bite them, please! Oh, I'm dying!"

She snatched at his belt, tore at his shirt, threw her

arms around his neck and tugged him closer. "God, I want you. I must have you!"

Free of clothes Diana Yarrow guided her lover's beautiful shaft into her. She shuddered once, then again. "Ride me harder! Rougher! Now!"

Alex rammed into her, relentlessly matching her steaming passion with his own. Four months ago, when they had first begun this forbidden affair, he had been gentle, following the lead of his own soul. But Diana would not have it. Gentleness was weakness. Gentleness was teasing. Her appetites were fed by deeper, darker springs.

He grasped her breasts hard and kneaded them with strong brown hands. Still his groin pounded itself on her. He could feel the typhoon's release welling up from the soles of his feet and then suddenly the door of the shack slapped hard against the wall and shuddered.

Alexander Carrick rolled off of Diana Yarrow and leaped for his rifle.

A man stood in the doorway. "You're crazy, brother," Joseph said. He looked down at the sweaty, disheveled form of Simon Yarrow's daughter. She was beautiful, a wanton. Sex seemed to rise from her like fog on a spring morning.

"You're mixing in where you have no business, Joseph," Alexander said, covering his lover and himself with a blanket.

Joseph nodded. "Anything that affects my family is my business. Simon Yarrow finds out that you been ploughing his fields, he'll burn us all out."

Diana smiled strangely, her mind considering private thoughts that followed her own interior logic.

Something told her that this Joseph Carrick would be a much more exacting, and therefore satisfying master, than his brother.

"Get dressed, brother. We're going home." He turned for the door and said, "Begging your pardon, Miss Yarrow, but I got my obligations that come first."

Diana nodded and smiled again. "Of course you do, Mr. Carrick. I'm sorry we had to meet in this manner." She ran her hand down between her legs under the blanket.

"I'm not leaving," Alexander said.

"Of course you are," Diana replied cheerfully. "Your brother is right. It wasn't fair of me to jeopardize you this way." She winked at Alexander so that only he would know their lusts had only begun to be slaked.

After supper that evening Joseph told his family he was going out to meet with some farmers from the southern end of the Valley. Patricia warned him to be careful, kissed him on both cheeks and watched him ride out of the lanternlight.

A half hour later Joseph reined up in a grove of cottonwoods and tightened the muffler around his throat against the cold.

"Am I on time?" a voice called from behind him.

Startled, Joseph turned quickly. Then he smiled. "Close enough," he said.

"It's getting harder and harder to get loose," Grant said. "Emma Chatfield wants to know where I'm going, my father wants to know where I'm going. I tell you, my life's not getting any easier."

"I know. Mine neither. And Patricia thinks something's up. What did you get from Washington?"

Grant shook his head and leaned forward in his saddle. "Nothing, I'm afraid. I'm going to have to find a reason to go east and look after things myself. Something is up and I can't figure out what it is. All of a sudden we're entertaining Senators and high muckity-mucks from all over. It's like my father's running for office." He paused. "I need time if I'm going to be able to help you people."

"We haven't got any time," Joseph said.

"If you people move now, my father will wipe you all out! He has the firepower and he has the law! Over half the judges and sheriffs in this state belong to him!"

"We got people starving, Grant. It's now or never."

"Look, Joseph, I overheard my father and Smith talking about hiring the Pinkertons. You go up against him and you'll be slaughtered."

"Better than dying one by one like sheep," Joseph replied. "I wish it were otherwise. Thanks." He stopped. "By the way, Patricia's gone and gotten all kinds of suspicious about you. Keeps asking me what I know about you."

"For her sake we better keep our friendship secret. The less anyone knows, the better. My father has spies everywhere."

Joseph nodded. "I'm not worried. Your father's gonna be surprised when every one of his farmers joins up with us."

"I hope so." Grant tightened his reins. "Did you tell Alexander he'd best keep his hands off my sister?"

"Yeah, but I don't have much hopes his blood'll cool down. Or hers."

Grant laughed. "Family trait. All I can do is warn

him. My father will kill anybody who's caught with her and that's a fact."

The two friends spoke a few moments more and then rode off in opposite directions, each locked inexorably in a role dictated by fate of birth.

CHAPTER FIVE

PATRICIA Carrick excused herself past an overdressed schoolmarm—all flounces and ruffles—and walked into the Stockton Bank. She held her head erect, ignoring the admiring glances she drew from the idlers on the street outside.

"Miss Patricia?" John Bailey called.

"Good morning, John."

"You're looking especially pretty today," he said. He fingered his Texas-style hat, spinning it around and around in his hands. He looked down at the floor when he spoke.

Patricia smiled. "Thank you, John."

"How's your family doing?" he asked. The morning sunlight, filtered through the dusty panes of glass, shone on Bailey's blonde hair, making it resemble a sheaf of wheat.

"Fine," she lied. "How about yourself?"

"Can't complain. I opened a new store in Modesto," he said.

"Congratulations. I wish you well."

John Bailey looked at the startlingly beautiful

woman and wished the rest of the world would allow them to be frozen in this single moment. He would willingly have traded everything he had earned for a life with Patricia Carrick. He cleared his throat. "I'd like to call on you Sunday if I might." He spoke more quickly. "I know you told me you had no intention of marrying—"

"It would be nice to see you, John."

He beamed. "It would?"

Patricia nodded. He was a handsome man. He was well-favored, pleasant and well-spoken after a fashion. "Perhaps you might want to come after dinner?"

John's face sank. He did not want to wait that long. Then he smiled. "I was able to get some very fine venison. Perhaps I might bring that out early and visit while you cook it up."

Patricia laughed. John was like a little boy. The idea of serving venison appealed to her. It had been a bad, bad winter. Planting had not gone well. In New York City there'd been a riot in Thompkins Square, the police setting upon the men at a labor gathering. It was lucky nobody'd been killed. Yet a few miles away from the riot, in Staten Island, socialite Mary Ewing Outerbridge could talk of nothing but lawn tennis. "That would be very nice of you, John."

He smiled. "You still haven't changed your mind?"

"About marriage?"

"Yes, ma'am."

She pursed her lips. "No, John. I don't think so. I have responsibilities."

He nodded. "Just so. We'll eat the venison like old friends."

"I'd like that, John. Thank you."

"See you Sunday, then?"

"Yes. Much obliged." Patricia grinned and continued into the bank while John watched her go. She wore her simple full skirt with all the dignity of a woman from San Francisco all decked out in bustle, yards of silk and a parasol.

The teller directed the flame-haired woman to the officer seated at the desk in the rear of the bank. "Yes?"

Patricia looked around to make sure she wouldn't be overheard. "I would like to enquire about a loan."

The bank's officer smiled and laced his pink fingers together on the blotter before him. He did not ask the stunning woman to sit down. "Yes?"

Patricia cleared her throat. "Your bank does give loans, doesn't it?"

"The Bank of Stockton gives loans, yes."

Patricia sat down without being asked. "Then I'd like to talk to you about a loan."

"I don't understand," the officer said. Four years younger than Patricia Carrick, he found himself confused by her forthrightness.

"Let me see if I can make this clearer to you, Mister, uh, Mister?"

"Braintree. Mister Braintree."

"Mr. Braintree, my brothers and I have used up all last year's profits getting our crops in. We expect to do all right this year, but we won't be getting in any cash until harvest. So, to get through the summer, we'd like to borrow some money against what we expect."

"Miss?"

"Carrick. Miss Carrick."

"Miss Carrick, The Bank of Stockton has never had such a request."

"You don't lend farmers money?"

Braintree leaned his head to the side. "We do. If the farm is ten thousand acres or better. If the owner has good credit and clear title to the land. But we have never lent money to uh, uh, to a woman. You have me at a disadvantage."

The blood moved quickly to flush her face crimson. "You don't lend to women?"

"Not directly. To their husbands."

"Mr. Braintree, I am willing to suffer your bank's arrogance because we need the money very badly. However, I want you to know that if I owned a bank, I would trust the average woman long before I would flip a peso to some sodbuster who slaps you on the back, buys you a drink and goes belly-up the next day."

Braintree laughed a high-pitched laugh. "Excuse me, but the picture of you owning a bank tickled my fancy."

Patricia pulled a face and then placed both hands on the man's blotter. "Let me ask you: if my brothers came and asked for a loan of, say, two hundred dollars, would you give it to them? If I promised to stay out so as not to embarrass you any further?"

"How many acres do your brothers own?"

"A thousand."

"Our minimum is actually five thousand."

"Could you make an exception?"

"The Board of Directors could."

"Who are they?"

Braintree laughed aloud, causing the tellers to look in shocked silence at the outburst. "Mr. Simon Yarrow is the Chairman."

"Thank you for your time, Mr. Braintree."

"Not at all, Miss, uh, I'm sorry. . . ."

"Carrick. Just one of the little folks who don't belong in your fancy bank." Patricia rose and walked out past the curious tellers and the few customers lined up to do business. She felt outraged, ashamed, powerless.

With her head down, Patricia pushed out onto the street and nearly bowled over a man on his way in. "Oh, I beg your pardon," she said.

"Miss Carrick? It was my fault for not looking where I was going," Simon Yarrow said. He doffed his hat and gave a small bow.

When she saw who it was, Patricia recoiled as if she had stepped in one of the piles of manure on the street.

"Is there something wrong?"

Patricia Carrick shook her head. She could not find the words to speak her hatred for the man who stood before her. His water rates were starving whole families out of the valley. His railroad crews rode roughshod over everyone. He was the single most important man in northern California, and now one of his banks stood between her family and survival.

Yarrow smiled. "I see you were in our bank."

"I was."

"Were you well taken care of?"

"I can't say as I was, Mr. Yarrow."

Simon's face went sour. "Why not?"

"It would seem that your bank has a policy regarding women that I find offensive."

Simon Yarrow laughed aloud. He clucked his teeth and leaned up against the hitching rail behind him. The woman was spirited. That was excellent. She was beautiful . . . like one of those dancers who posed stark naked for the photographers in New York. Simon possessed quite a collection of those tintypes. He bowed lower than before. "Well, the laws are fairly tricky on that," he said. "Since you can't own property, Miss Patricia, you can't own collateral. If you default on a loan, we'd be left high and dry."

"If you'll excuse me. . . ,"

"I'll walk along with you if you don't mind," the older man said. "I'd like to make things up to you."

"Nothing to make up. Good day." She began walking up the street.

"Oh, but there is," Simon said, following alongside her. "How much were you asking for?"

"Two hundred dollars," she replied, without breaking stride.

Yarrow reached out and touched her shoulder to stop her progress. Patricia pulled back. "Two hundred dollars?"

"Yes."

He smiled and edged slightly closer. "As President of the bank, I am empowered to make special loans for special purposes."

Patricia looked up into the brown eyes which glimmered with secret thoughts. "I thought I had no collateral."

Simon looked around, then lowered his voice. Leaned even closer. She could smell the tobacco on his breath. "There are certain pieces of property which some women have clear title to," he said.

"You said women couldn't own property."

"The property I am speaking of," Simon said, "is the property you were born with."

"I'm a Mick, Mr. Yarrow. I was born with nothing but tragedy. I think you'd best make clear what you're driving at."

Simon Yarrow put both hands on her shoulders and held her rigidly. "I can make that loan directly to you. No, I can make it an outright gift. All you need to do to pay me back is to be very nice to me." He paused. "Deny me nothing. For one week." He smiled and let go her arms.

Patricia nodded. "That would make me a whore for a little less than thirty dollars a day, Mr. Yarrow."

"Three hundred? I'm not an inflexible man."

Patricia flushed scarlet. "No, but you are a vile and disgusting one." She drew in her breath and brought her hand up so quickly that the older man was caught off guard. She slapped him as hard as she could, making a loud sound and bringing the blood to his cheek. "I'll have nothing to do with you, your bank, or anything else connected with you!" Before he could say anything more, she had left at a fast walk, her anger unrelieved by the painful slap she had delivered.

Simon Yarrow touched his burning cheek. He watched the woman walk away and knew that her punishment would have to be very special. No woman had ever done that to him. Even if it took years, he would get his revenge.

CHAPTER SIX

It took an hour for Patricia to do all the shopping she had to do. She only had five dollars to spend and she spent it as wisely and carefully as anybody in town on that Saturday morning.

It took more than an hour to recover from the insulting and clumsy seduction attempt by Grant Yarrow's father. She still burned with rage to think that the man thought he could treat everyone as chattel on his estate.

She made her way carefully to the livery stable at the end of the long main street, her packages clutched in her arms. Joseph said he'd meet her at noon and they would head back to look after their ailing brothers. Alexander and Christopher had the fever and chills.

But she didn't find Joseph out front where he usually waited. In fact there was no one out front. She walked around to the back. No one was there either.

She stopped and listened to the gentle wind that drifted across the baked earth yard. Voices—hushed voices—toyed with her imagination. They seemed to be coming from every direction. No, from the back of the livery stable.

A small window, high up, looked into the back room of the stable. Patricia stood up on a sack of feed bags and peered inside.

". . . if you wait, the men from Washington will be here investigating what's going on. I have their word on it . . ."

". . . if we wait we'll all be dead . . . ,"

". . . when did they say they'd be here?"

". . . I say we do it now!"

". . . we could take over the whole irrigation system if we do it right. . . ."

"Nobody'd be fool enough to stop us!"

Joseph stood up in the middle of the gathering and the voices quieted down. He was tall. The thick shock of red hair on his head made him stand out like a ship's beacon. His angular good looks made others than Diana Yarrow wonder about him as a lover. He looped his hooks under his belt and looked at the forty-five men who looked to him for leadership. Each of them had a wife and children who were hurting badly.

"It's pretty much like we said. There will be an investigation of how Federal lands were divided up. And there'll be an investigation into the irrigation contracts. In the meantime we face an increase to four and a quarter an acre." He paused and took a deep breath. "And we know that'll finish us all off." He paused again. "Yarrow is tryin' to ruin us all, buy up our land at auction, just like he did with Lattimer's, and run the whole valley. Every politician from here to Los Angeles feeds off of Simon Yarrow. And he feeds off of us."

"What do we do?"

Before Joseph could answer, Patricia watched as the front door blew open and the purposeful meeting erupted into chaos. A dozen club-waving Pinkertons rushed in, breaking heads, shins, arms, elbows—anything the unsuspecting farmers put up for self-protection.

From the right side another dozen Pinkertons sallied out from the grain storage room, catching them in a tragic pincer movement.

Patricia watched in horror as Joseph slashed and sliced his way through the grey-clad officers, using the back of his hooks to try to even the score. She saw him trip and fall. A barrel-chested Pinkerton raised his club and brought it down.

"Run for it!" they cried.

Patricia heard hoofbeats behind her and looked to see two dozen mounted Pinkertons galloping down the alleyways, cutting off all avenues of escape for the doomed farmers. "Burn it down!" their leader cried.

Patricia jumped down from the stack of grain bags and tried to reach the front of the stable. A horse barrelled past her, knocking her into the side of the building. She hit, glanced off and rolled into the dirty alley as a second horseman leaped over her. She covered her head, then rolled to the side and got up to run just as a horseman plucked her, kicking, from the ground and galloped off with her towards the main street.

"Put me down, you devil-hound!"

"Not yet, my darlin'!" he cried.

Patricia tried to twist around to see her attacker, but the voice was familiar. Too familiar. "Grant Yarrow, you put me down, you son of a bitch!"

"I am saving your life, my darling!" His strong hands lifted her over his pommel like a bag of oats and he spurred his stallion out of town.

"My brother! My brother Joseph!" she screamed.

"No way you can save him, lass. They would have killed you, too."

The ride was long. After an hour on the trail Patricia stopped trying to break Grant's strong grip. He stopped and let her sit astride the horse, her skirts tucked beneath her. "Where are we going?" she asked.

"Someplace where you'll be safe." He spurred the mount off the trail and across the high ground. "My father's men are watching all the roads."

"For what?"

"Friends of your brother's."

"What about Christopher, Patrick and Alexander?"

"Your farm's being watched as well but no harm's coming to them. Yet."

"I don't believe this is happening."

"Believe it, my pretty young one. Believe it."

Three hours later they topped a rise overlooking a low squat farmhouse and some dilapidated buildings. A small dairy herd and some indifferent chickens wandered about the yard. "I'm not about to set foot in that house," Patricia said.

"Your choices are somewhat limited, Patricia Carrick." He held her firmly as he galloped down the backside of the rise, scattering chickens among his stallion's hooves.

Emma Chatfield stood in the doorway, her hands on her wide hips. Her thick black hair was piled high on her head. A willing smile glittered under huge bright blue eyes and a small nose. Emma was one of those people who are born knowing that life is too short to waste with the finer points of etiquette and morality. She curtseyed low. "I see you brung royalty," she said.

"You know each other," Grant said. "Saves having to introduce you."

Emma laughed. "Unh-hunh. Miss Carrick don't approve of us Chatfields."

"I don't know your husband," Patricia said. Every joint and muscle in her body ached.

"My mistake," Emma said.

Grant took Patricia by the arm and propelled her through the weatherbeaten door and into the kitchen of the Chatfield house. "Sit over there."

"I will not!" Patricia said. "I demand that we go back and see after my brother. He may be hurt and bleeding to death."

Grant turned to Emma, paying no attention to the furious Irish woman. "We have to keep this one under cover for awhile. I figured since your old man was gone North until Friday, we could hide out here until tomorrow."

Mrs. Chatfield beamed.

"I'm not staying here," Patricia announced, heading for the door.

Grant's move was a sudden blur of color, surprising in its grace and speed. He stood in front of the door, his arms across his chest, his smile both calming and challenging. "For your own safety, my lovely, you are my prisoner for the evening."

Patricia threw herself forward, pounding on his strong chest, clawing at his face. He ducked, parried the blows and held her tightly in his steel embrace. "Let me go! Let me go! I have to see to Joseph!"

Grant signalled to Emma Chatfield and together they took the struggling woman to the spare bedroom. It was a small room. The rose-print wallpaper was hanging in strips. The wood-frame bed was hard and dusty. "Emma, just to keep Miss Carrick from running off at night, would you be so kind as to take her gown from her?"

"Delighted, Grant."

"No!" Patricia screamed.

"I'd take your word you wouldn't try to escape, but I'd be a fool." Grant tipped his hat and left the room.

Emma pushed her sleeves up her arm. She was six or seven inches taller than Patricia and had her by a good thirty pounds. "We can do this easy or we can do this hard," Emma said.

The green in Patricia's eyes flashed as she rolled up her own sleeves. "I'm a Carrick. If you aim to get this dress off me, you'll have to kill me first."

Emma shook her head and leaped across the space, catching Patricia by the waist and knocking her backwards into the washstand. The ewer and bowl crashed to the floor in a shower of pottery. Patricia hit the wall broadside. Her breath popped out of her with a rush.

"Easy woulda been better," Emma said as she clung to the smaller woman's shoulders and rode her to the dusty floor. Astride her victim like a circus rider,

Emma plucked at the hooks and eyes on the back of Patricia's bodice.

Patricia rolled 180 degrees, hoping to toss the heavy woman to the side. The flip was quick, but Emma was quicker. Patricia wound up with Emma pulling at the neckline of the pale blue gown, exposing the clean white shift and part of Patricia's chest. "I don't wanta tear it, lovey," Emma said over the sound of her adversary's grunts.

"Go to hell!"

Outside, in the narrow hallway, Grant Yarrow leaned against the wall and lighted a thin black cigar. The sounds intrigued him, and he thought seriously about walking in, but some last shred of decency stopped him. He sighed for the waste.

And he thought about the small scrappy Irish woman on the other side of the door. Each time he saw her he was drawn more and more to her. She stirred parts of him that he had thought were long since dead.

"You bitch!" Patricia yelled with whatever breath was left. She stood in the middle of the floor, shaking, her shift clutched to her.

Emma Chatfield smiled and held the two halves of the pale blue gown that had once been whole. "My God, but you are a fighter." She turned and left the room.

Patricia heard the key turn in the door. She heard the sound of Emma and Grant talking, then walking away.

She hurried to the single window that looked out on the bored and scruffy farm animals. It was nailed shut. "I'll break the window and let myself out," she thought. "After that whore of Babylon's asleep."

She sat down on the edge of the bed and wept for her brother, wherever he was.

Patricia awoke in the dark. What was it she heard? A laugh. High pitched. Then silence. She walked quietly to the far wall and listened.

Another laugh. Muffled talk. A woman's voice. A man's voice.

Bedsprings creaked.

And then a scream.

Patricia froze.

The cry came again. It sounded as if Emma Chatfield was being murdered.

Again the cry pierced the walls. As much as she hated the woman, she didn't deserve that. And then just as Patricia was about to begin pounding on the wall to try to stop the horrible act, she heard a man's shout.

"Oh, my God, Emma, but you are the best!"

"Ohgodohgodohgodohgod! Grant I love you!"

Patricia balled her fists in rage and stormed to the window that stood between her and freedom. "That damned son of a bitch," she said to herself. "That awful, rotten, sodden, nasty, vile, whore-mongering, adultering son of a bitch!"

Emma shrieked again and laughed. The springs in her bed shrieked along with her as if she were breaking a wild horse on the mattress.

Patricia took the towel from the washstand, wrapped her hand with it, tapped the window once, tapped it again, and then put her fist through it, praying that the sounds of sex would cover the sounds of escape.

The wooden window frame was rotten, like most of

the house, and she was able to pry out the other pane without having to shatter it.

In a few seconds she stood in the moonlit farmyard, her white shift aglow. Quickly she ran around back and headed for the barn where she could hear the cows munching gently.

"Easy, my pet," she whispered to the brown mare who stood shivering in the gloom. "We won't need a saddle, will we?" she said. She pushed the barn door open on squeaky hinges, leading the horse by its bridle. "We'll see that whore-son bastard hung for what he's done," Patricia whispered as she swung easily onto the mare's back. "Easy, girl."

Patricia walked the horse around the side of the barn and cried out aloud when she felt the hot grip on her left ankle, tugging her down to the ground. "Help!"

She dropped to the ground with a thud, her shift around her waist.

"I'm glad I didn't ask for your word of honor," Grant Yarrow said. He stood, with his hands on his hips, staring down at the beautiful runaway. The pale blue-white light of the moon sculpted her creamy thighs and legs. The curve of her buttocks slipped below the waist of her ruffled shift.

Patricia stared at the dirt and said, "You wouldn't know about honor." She turned and looked up at him. "Jesus, Mary and Joseph, you're naked!"

"I can't help it if you choose to run away when I'm rutting like some animal! I grabbed a towel back there, but I lost it. Get up and get back to your room! You have ruined an otherwise perfect evening."

Patricia turned away from the man who looked like one of those statues she saw in the drawings about

Greece. Except the statues wore leaves. . . . She stood and walked back to the house, staring straight ahead. The man was an animal and yet she was in love with him. She thought she must be crazy.

Emma Chatfield stood in the doorway in a silk robe that didn't even attempt to cover her breasts. She smoked one of Grant's cigars and smiled in the lamplight. "I gotta say your timing is real bad," she observed.

Patricia held back the tears of rage until she was once again locked in the spare room, her window boarded shut.

CHAPTER SEVEN

DAWN'S sun burned the mists away, leaving in their place a hot dry wind that spoke more of summer than spring. The bugs signalled one another in hoardes. Clouds avoided the pale blue skies as if they were loathe to give shade to man or beast.

Joseph Carrick opened his eyes slowly, then snapped them shut again to ward off the pain the pinpricks of light gave him. He waited a few minutes before trying again. The pain was less this time, but still too much to bear and so he shut his lids quickly.

"I have some soup for you," the feminine voice said.

He didn't recognize it. But his nose told him there were a number of smells in the room. A woman's strong perfume. Lilac? Lily of the valley? He didn't recognize the voice. The soup was barley?

He opened his eyes and saw her. She looked like an angel. Her blonde hair surrounded her head like a halo. Her eyes were the color of Italian seas.

"Hello," she said.

"Who are you?" he asked.

55

She raised her eyebrows. "Diana Yarrow."

"Who am I?"

She shrugged. "Joseph Carrick." She laughed. "You don't have to play games with me. I brought you here. Saved you from father's wretched men."

"I forget, I guess. Joseph Carrick?" He picked up his arms and stared at the hooks which were bound to the stumps of his wrists. "Did they do this too?"

"What are you tryng to pull?" Diana asked. She put the bowl of soup down on the floor of the line shack where she and Alexander had spent so many afternoons.

"I don't remember," Joseph said.

"You don't remember who the hell you are?"

Joseph started to shake his head, but the pain was too much to bear. " 'Fraid not."

Diana was quiet as she spoon-fed Joseph the soup she had prepared on the small cook-fire outside. It must have been the blows he took on the head, she thought. She wondered how long the condition would last. Was it permanent? Or would he snap out of it by suppertime?

Joseph slept through much of the afternoon while Diana rode home and pretended to be the dutiful daughter.

As dusk was easing its way through the surrounding hills, Diana returned.

"Hello, Diana," Joseph said. He was sitting up against the far wall, finishing off the chicken breast she had left for him. The light from the lantern tossed high shadows onto the ceiling.

Diana closed the door carefully, relaxing after the metal latch dropped with a click into its keeper. She was wearing a tan riding skirt, soft black boots, a wide cincher belt and a white silk blouse with full sleeves and a matching scarf. Her eyes snatched the lantern light and reflected it with her own added brilliance.

"How do you feel?"

"I don't hurt anymore. Just my shoulder. The headache's gone."

"And your memory?"

He shook his head and shrugged. "Guess that'll come with time," he said. "I get flashes sometimes."

Diana smiled. She knelt next to him and unbuttoned his shirt to examine his shoulder.

"I don't think it's anything serious," he said. He could smell her perfume. Lily of the valley. Her regular breathing broke the silence of the onrushing night.

She peeled his shirt down his lean and wiry body. "I better wash it," she said in a throaty voice.

Joseph watched her move from him to the canteen and back again. She took a handkerchief, wet it, and laid it gently across the raw flesh. "You are very beautiful," he said.

"Thank you," she replied. Her hands trembled as she wrung out the cloth.

"Are you engaged to anybody?"

Diana laughed. She would have agreed to marry the devil himself if she could have found the man to satisfy the enormity of her desires. She shook her head.

"That's odd," Joseph said. "A woman as beautiful as you."

Diana could not believe that she was blushing. She who had done everything, humbled every good-looking man in two counties. . . .

Joseph reached up and outlined the edges of her flushed face with the back of his right hook. The metal caught the flickering lanternlight, casting a glow over the strange contrast of hard steel and yielding flesh.

The hook traced the soft contours of her cheek and Diana could not breathe for the ecstasy of the moment . . . suspended in time. Drifting. When the steel dropped down to her chin Diana moved everso slightly and kissed the metal hand. It was warm, smooth, frightening. Lightning bolts cracked in her shoulders, sending showers of sparks down into her thighs. She was powerless to stop the progression of events. It was as if she were hanging above herself, watching. Usually she was the actor.

The hooks unflipped the white silk scarf and flicked the whalebone buttons from the safety of their buttonholes. The hooks stopped for a moment at her cincher belt, then ran the gamut of fasteners and freed her from its confines.

Diana moaned as a shudder coarsed through her like the earth tremors she'd felt in San Francisco.

"Stand up," Joseph said quietly.

Diana rose majestically, as if she were the sun. She had no choice in the matter. She watched, fascinated, as the hooks on the ends of the man's wrists stripped her naked—slowly, gently, without hesitation. Joseph laid her carefully on the pallet which had been prepared for him. Then he removed his own clothes and very gently eased himself into the beautiful blonde woman.

Diana's eyes flickered open. The man on top of her was being gentle. For a moment she considered telling him—no, ordering him—as she had ordered his brother, to be as rough as he could. But she stopped herself because she had suddenly become aware of waves of hot pleasure that undulated from the soles of her feet to the roots of her hair. Each wave seemed larger than the one before it. She had never felt anything like this. It was as if every part of her body had finally decided to join her in her lovemaking.

She passed out when the red and blue and black explosions turned to violet.

In the light before dawn, when the air is as soft as a whisper, Diana awoke in the curve of Joseph Carrick's strong right arm. For a few seconds she could remember nothing—as if she had caught his amnesia— but then she shivered as she recalled the earth-shattering love they had shared.

In short, it was as if the entire universe had come to a single finite point for Diana Yarrow. Everything before this point, everything after it, would be measured from it. Her usually scattered mind had miraculously come into focus.

The focus was Joseph Carrick. He was the center of her universe.

Joseph woke slowly, barely aware of Diana's loving strokes. He parted his lips and found, as reward for his efforts, Diana's extended nipple between them. He smiled and they made love.

Once again, they scaled the heights of passion; and Diana knew a rapture more intense than any she had ever dreamed possible. Her mind was made up.

"Do you feel well enough to travel?" she asked.

Joseph nodded. "Why?" he asked.

"We're going south," she replied.

"Fine by me. What for?"

"I love you, Joseph."

He pulled her close to his face with the crook of his forearm. "And I love you," he said without guile.

Diana trembled.

CHAPTER EIGHT

PATRICIA Carrick slid down from her horse into the arms of her younger brother Christopher. "You all right?" he asked.

She nodded. "Have you seen Joseph?"

"No."

"Then he must be dead," she said. She bit down hard to try to keep the tears for later . . . when she could allow herself to weep.

"What happened?" Alexander asked when they had gone inside.

Patricia told her three brothers what had happened in town. She omitted any reference to Grant Yarrow or Emma Chatfield. That morning Grant had bought a horse, given it to Patricia and told her it was safe to go back to her farm.

"I hid out in Mr. Peachtree's warehouse," she lied, "until now." Her brothers followed her from room to room as she gathered up some clothes and a towel.

"What happened to your dress?" Christopher asked, pointing to the clumsily patched tear where Emma had won the strugggle.

61

"When the Pinkertons ran me down," Patricia replied, "I fell against some barrels."

"Oh," Christopher replied. "Where'd ya find the needle and thread?"

"In my reticule," she replied. She cast him an impatient glance. "Heat up a bath, will you? We're going to pay a call on Mr. Simon Yarrow."

Patrick slapped his palm against his pistol and said, "Now you're talking, Patricia!"

Simon Yarrow's businesses took him to four different locations: New York, Washington, San Francisco and the San Joaquin Valley. In each of the locations Simon Yarrow had built himself a giant home worthy of a foreign consulate. In New York his block-long granite mansion erupted along Park Avenue with typical Yarrow gall. In Washington a castle sat astride the landscape like a brooding presence. In San Francisco he'd borrowed from every conceivable historical period in a riot of architecture. In the San Joaquin, the Yarrow farm buildings were spread the length and breadth of a small valley. Built in the Mexican hacienda style, they included a rambling walled-in ranch house, stables, barns and equipment sheds that housed the most modern farm machinery his millions could buy.

It was cool and green in the valley. Shade trees sheltered the hitch rails, the stone walkways, and the pools.

At the outer gate Patricia and her three brothers were stopped by six guards wearing the grey cotton shirts of the Pinkertons. The Carricks were solemn, angry, curt. "We're here to see Simon Yarrow," Patricia said.

One of the guards nodded and rode to the main house to see if his employer would see Joseph Carrick's sister and brothers. He returned a few minutes later.

"Leave your weapons at the gate and follow me."

Patrick looked to his sister. She nodded once. He and his brothers handed over their guns.

Simon Yarrow stood on the top step of the front entrance, his thumbs looped in his wide leather belt. His expression was blank. His eyes moved quickly, surveying everything. Smith stood next to him, one pace back. "Miss Carrick."

Patricia got down from her horse before speaking. "I've come for the body of my brother, Mr. Yarrow. For proper Christian burial."

Christopher noticed a momentary flicker in Simon's thick-lidded eyes. He looked over at his sister.

Alexander scanned the balcony that ran around the second story of the hacienda and wondered if he might catch a glimpse of Diana.

"Why would I have Mr. Carrick's body, ma'am?" Simon asked.

"It was your men who clubbed him to death."

"No one is dead, ma'am. There was some sort of fight in town, but it had nothing to do with me. But there have been no corpses that I know of. Do you know of any dead men, Mr. Smith?"

Smith shook his head.

"Then where is he?" Patrick asked, putting his foot on the second step of the stairs leading up to Simon Yarrow.

"I assure you I don't know." In point of fact Simon now had thirty men looking for Joseph Carrick and

he had fired the men who had let him slip through
their fingers.

"I think you're lying," Patricia said.

Smith took a half step to the side to clear his field
of fire in case anything started.

Simon Yarrow shook his head slowly. "Miss Carrick,
that's the second vile insult you've flung at me in as
many meetings. Take care—I'm a dangerous man to
offend. I'll ask you and your brothers to leave my
property now."

Patricia stared straight into his eyes and thought
she saw the fires of hell blazing within them. She
turned and mounted her horse.

"Perhaps, Father, we might help Miss Carrick and
her brothers look for Joseph."

Patricia snapped back around and looked at Grant
Yarrow, looking as if he had just dressed for a dinner
party, standing next to Simon.

"That's a good idea, Grant," his father said.

Patricia's eyes narrowed to two small green fires.
"Hell will freeze before Carricks take help from Yarrows. Let's go."

"As you wish," Simon said sourly.

The next few moments exploded in a fireball of
chaos. Patrick leaped up the stairs for Simon. Smith
whipped out his six-guns, and Grant pushed him back
so that he couldn't fire. Just as Patrick was about to
make contact, Grant angled between his father and
the hot-headed Irishman, catching him a glancing
blow and knocking him sideways down the verandah.

"Señor! Señor!" A guard shouted. "Miss Diana!"

The people on the front steps froze as if in a living tabieau.

Diana rode her horse slowly and quietly from the

main gate. Alongside her rode Joseph Carrick.

"Joseph!" Patricia cried. She turned her horse and rode quickly to him. He smiled. "Joseph?"

"Good afternoon," he said cordially.

Diana reined in her mount and looked up at her father as if to challenge him.

"Go up to your room, Diana. I will talk to you later."

Diana shook her head.

Simon Yarrow's face hardened to steel.

"Only my husband can tell me what to do now," she said.

"What?"

"Joseph, what happened?" Patricia asked.

"Joseph Carrick and I were married today, father."

"Impossible!" Simon staggered backwards, his face as pale as hers.

"Oh, Joseph, what is the matter with you?"

Diana looked over at Patricia and smiled. "I'm afraid your brother has lost his memory, Miss Carrick."

Grant looked at his sister and knew she was telling the truth. About everything. She had finally found the ultimate means for getting back at her father: the man who had made her life miserable with his overbearing ways and his possessive jealousy. "May I be the first to congratulate you, Diana."

"No you may not!" Simon bellowed. "I won't have it! I will not have it! I'll have it annulled!"

"Father, I am twenty-one now. There isn't a God-damned thing you can do about it."

Simon's gaze took in the scene before him. His temples pounded. His hands felt cold and clammy. He bit down hard. It was inconceivable that his daughter would soon bed down with this hook-handed mick who made a living scratching at the earth. These steel claws would rake the silk-white skin. . . .

He cleared his throat. "Diana, tell Mr. Davis to make up the east wing for you and your, uh, husband."

Grant looked at his father and wondered what was going on inside the steely exterior. He looked at Patricia and wished he could ease the pain that was etched upon her beautiful face. He saw something very strange in Alexander Carrick's expression. The young man was pale. His mouth was stretched into a tight line. His hands appeared to hold one another down. He kept staring at his brother, then at Diana.

"Do you not know us, Joseph?" Christopher asked. "Not at all?"

Joseph shook his head.

"I believe it is called amnesia," Grant said, "this forgetfulness. It need not be permanent. Another shock could restore your brother to his normal state."

Patricia shook her head. "Bless you, Joseph. I hope you'll be happy," she said.

"Thank you—what is it?—Patricia?"

"Patricia," she replied. She turned her horse and walked it slowly out of the compound. Her three younger brothers followed closely. They said nothing when they picked up their weapons.

Out on the trail, free of the watchful eyes of the Yarrow people, Patricia wept openly and without shame. Her brothers stared straight ahead.

Back in the hacienda Joseph Carrick took a bath, attended closely by his new wife. He was sorry he'd had to deceive his brothers and sister, but if he was to end the terrible reign of Simon Yarrow, it was worth it.

CHAPTER NINE

SAN JOAQUIN VALLEY, CALIFORNIA, MAY, 1874

MEXICAN lanterns swayed in the cool breeze from the mountains, making the lights flicker like Simon Yarrow's own Milky Way. Above the lanterns the real stars played hide 'n' seek with heavy-bottomed clouds in from the Pacific.

Simon Yarrow looked down the wide table which groaned with the weight of food. The breeze ruffled his thinning hair. He tried to comb it back with his hand. Damn. Diana liked eating out of doors, "al fresco" she called it. That's what came of too much learning.

He tried not to look at Joseph Carrick. The man was what most women would call good-looking. But, hell, he was almost forty. He was just a poor dirt farmer with too much family and too few dollars. And besides that, the goddamned mick didn't even know who the hell he was.

The real pain came when Simon eyed his daughter, Diana. Diana *Carrick,* God take her! The lantern light sculpted her beautiful features. Her skin seemed to glow with an inner light. Her eyes never left her new husband's face. You'd think she worshipped him like some kind of god!

Simon Yarrow cringed at the thought of Joseph Carrick splitting his daughter with his goddamned Irish prick!

The host signalled for the Mexican guitar player to finish the ballad and be quiet. Then he rose very slowly.

Grant saw the pain in his father's eyes. The man was making a superhuman effort . . . that was plain. But he could not read the full agony behind those hard brown irises.

"Lady and gentlemen," Simon said in his deep bass voice. "This is an occasion that only comes to a father once in his lifetime: the giving away of his daughter to her husband."

Grant applauded politely. Diana sat back in her chair, unsure what her father would say next. She sipped slowly from her goblet.

"I want you two to be very happy."

"Here, here," Diana said. She thought she saw her father wince everso slightly.

"I had planned to have a big wedding, invite half the valley, my friends from back east and so forth, but my impetuous little daughter here kind of jumped the gun on me." He smiled and sipped more wine. "I guess I'm disappointed you two jumped over the broomstick instead of having a big proper wedding, but there isn't much I can do about it." He looked at his daughter's low-cut bodice, the bountiful push of breasts, surging upward. . . . Her eyes were a bluer green tonight. "Well, anyway, this is a toast, not a sermon. I give you Mr. and Mrs. Carrick. May their lives be long and happy." He drained the contents of his goblet and threw it against the white-washed wall. A long blood-red stain marked the point of impact.

Grant joined the toast and flicked his glass after his father's.

Joseph rose slowly. He cleared his throat. "I'd just like to thank you all for taking me into your family. To your health." He drained his glass.

Diana watched with amusement the faces of her brother and father, trying to plumb the depths of their own secrets. She had never felt as good, as powerful. This had been too long in coming.

After dinner was over Grant took Joseph to the billiards room and Simon asked Diana if she would care to take a moonlit stroll about the grounds. She said, "Certainly", and kissed her husband a temporary good-bye.

The billiards room was large, stonewalled, with a wide fireplace at one end and a spectators' gallery at the other. Over the mantel were Conquistadores' swords and a shield with the Yarrow coat of arms emblazoned on it. "My father had the coat designed privately," Grant said as he placed the balls on the perfect green field. "We Yarrows aren't entitled to more of a coat than we can wear." He banked a neat shot, letting both balls click just slightly.

"May I give it a try with my hooks?"

Grant smiled. "I'm sorry. Certainly."

Joseph wedged the cuestick in the right hook and slid it smoothly in the curve of the left. He matched Grant's shot.

"Evidently your condition has allowed you to remember how to play billiards," Grant said with a smile. He handed Joseph a cheroot.

"A friend of ours, Marshall Macauley, had a billiard table in Pennsylvania. He taught me. He was a first-rate player," Joseph replied after allowing Grant to light the long black stick of tobacco.

Grant grinned. He clapped Joseph on the back. "I thought that amnesia act was a mite thick," he said, "but did you have to go and marry my blasted sister as well?"

Joseph shrugged. Looked serious. "We already said a lot of individuals might get hurt. We've got to think about the long run."

Grant nodded, and flicked the ash from his cheroot. "Try not to hurt her."

Joseph nodded and made his shot, enjoying the double-click. "Diana is a very special woman, Grant; you don't have to worry there."

"At least she's not kiting around the valley anymore."

Joseph's gaze went hard and level. "I hurt my brother Alexander, you can be sure."

"What exactly happened between you and Diana?"

"I woke up in that line cabin to the southwest. I looked up and there she was. She'd hired some Mexican farmhands to snatch me away from the Pinkertons while I was knocked cold. Next thing I knew she'd proposed to me, for God's sakes. I fell in love with her. I didn't remember Alexander. We were married on an impulse and on the ride back I suddenly regained my memory. It was too late to turn back."

Grant shook his head and whistled. "You rode right into the leopard's den and that's a fact. Does Diana know you're faking it now?"

"No. I didn't know what else to do. Except now

I'm in here, I can't think of a better way to get the goods on Simon Yarrow, can you? Your shot."

Grant missed an easy shot. He shook his head.

Clouds had covered the moon. A cooler breeze overtook the night, turning it uncomfortable out on the perfectly trimmed grounds. For a few minutes Diana and her father walked without speaking. They strolled out through the gate which was manned by two guards.

When they were five hundred yards away from the hacienda's walls, Diana said, "I'd like to go back now."

"Just a few more steps," Simon said.

Diana was quiet.

They stopped in a small grove. "Has he touched you yet?" Simon asked. His voice wavered.

Diana looked away as the moon came back out to wash the valley in luminescence.

"I asked you a question," Simon said.

Diana turned back to face her father. "Why would you ask such an improper question?" she asked.

"Because I am your father and I have a right to know!" His voice had risen . . . unsteadily. His breathing was rough and choppy.

"Those affairs are private between husband and wife!"

"Don't you dare raise your voice to your father!"

"You were never my father! You were my lover!"

"I was both, damn your eyes!" He paused. "Damn my soul!" Simon Yarrow sank down on his knees in the grove in the moonlight, his head forward, his chin on his chest. "I was your father, doomed to be in love with his own daughter."

Diana looked down on the pitiful man and shook her head. "It was wrong. It was your fault. Your sin."

"But you were so beautiful . . ." He looked up and saw her radiance above him. "You looked like your mother."

"That is no excuse. I was twelve years old. Mother had been dead for those same twelve years. You had no right."

Simon stood. "You had just finished your bath. Your young body was flowering. I was lost. You loved it as much as I."

Diana looked away. "I did. . . ." Her voice was a single slender thread of sound.

"See?"

She turned back to face him again. "But now I have a real man, not a man who would violate a child! His own daughter!"

"What has he done to you, Diana?"

"Everything! In his arms I can forget your nasty grunts. I can forget my own shame. I can just love and be loved."

Simon reached out and grabbed her bare shoulders. His strong hands pinched her flesh, binding her like a wheelwright's bands. "Say it isn't so. Say you haven't fucked with this man yet!"

"But I have, father. And I have loved every minute of it."

The sounds that came from Simon Yarrow's mouth had their origins in the bottom of his soul. They were the sounds of pure pain, like some animal who, for the first time, confronts the reality of his own death.

Diana tried to back away as the hated hand tore at her dress, shredding the silk from her breasts. But he was too strong. He squeezed her shoulder with one hand while cupping her left breast with the other.

"Stay with me here now. Lie with me here," he groaned. "Please, Diana. I'll show you what's best for you. You're not like other women. Your needs are different."

Diana went wild in the grove, bringing her right knee squarely into her father's groin. "No!" she cried.

Simon fell to earth, begging for air in his lungs. He could not hear his daughter's running steps over the roar of pain in his ears. He fell on his side, holding his knees to his chest.

He didn't hear the other set of footsteps until they were right next to him.

"Sir?" Mr. Smith said in the darkness.

"Help me up, Goddamn you!"

"Yes, sir." Smith put his pistol away and leaned down to help his employer to his feet.

"I fell," Simon said in a gruff voice.

"Yes, sir," Smith replied.

They walked slowly and carefully back to the hacienda. "What were you doing out here, anyways?" Simon asked.

"You asked me to get Will Lacey, sir."

"And?"

"He's waiting for you in the barn."

"Good. Help me over there and then make sure nobody bothers us."

"Yes, sir."

When Joseph saw his wife come into the billiard room he and Grant were enjoying a special cognac which Grant had insisted his father buy. Joseph was lightheaded. The first thing he noticed was that

Diana had changed her gown since going out for a stroll with her father. The second thing he noticed was that she seemed to be suppressing some incredible energy. She was flushed, unfocussed, flighty. He took her in his arms and held her gently.

"Thank you," she said.

"Any time," he said. "Where did you get the scratch on your neck?" he asked.

Diana pulled back. She swallowed hard. "A tree branch . . . in the dark," she replied.

Joseph leaned down and kissed the boiling red welts that looked as if some one had raked her with his nails.

"Could we play, Joseph? I'm already down a hundred and twenty dollars to you."

Joseph smiled and said, "Later, brother-in-law. My wife comes first." He bowed to Grant Yarrow and then led the trembling Diana upstairs to the east wing. Though he was ashamed of what he had done to his brother, Joseph knew he was passionately in love with this wanton woman.

CHAPTER TEN

PATRICIA hauled the lines in hard, pulling the mules around while trying to keep the plow from digging itself too deep into the earth. The sun was hot. Flies swarmed in tight circles.

A few yards away Alexander slapped at his face to ward off the swarm, but it was no use. The flies were persistent. They dived without regard to his attempts. He turned the plow expertly.

"Are you all right, then?" Patricia called across the freshly ploughed rows.

Alexander did not look up. "Sure."

"What's been eating you?" she called. A mule brayed.

"Nothing."

"I know you better than that." Sweat rolled down her face.

Alexander stopped, pulling in on the mules. He swiped at the back of his head. "Patricia, I am gonna tell you a secret. I don't want it to go any further than right here."

"You know my word is good, Alexander."

75

"Diana Yarrow and I were in love."

Patricia could not stifle a cry of shocked surprise.

"And what's more, Joseph knew it."

"Oh, my Lord." She looked at the hawks wheeling giant circles, smaller and smaller. "But he doesn't know who you are. He didn't do it on purpose."

Alexander looked at the fly-covered backs of his mules. "I don't know if I buy all that forgetful stuff, Patricia. Damn me for being disloyal, but there was something about that that smelled like fish." He flicked his reins and the mules pulled.

"Wait a damned minute, Alexander! You're talking about our older brother, not some medicine show huckster!"

"Sorry, Patricia, but that's how I feel." Head hanging, Alexander moved away behind the plow.

"That's it," Joseph said to Grant as they rode back to the hacienda. "That's got to be where he keeps his papers."

Grant shook his head. "Look, Joseph, we've already tried every place in my father's office, we've tapped every square inch of wall in his den, looked through the attic and come up with nothing."

Joseph clucked his horse up a bit faster. "The wine cellar is perfect. You said yourself that he doesn't let anybody but himself go down there and that he spends a good bit of time in the cellar every evening."

"There's no guarantee there *are* any papers that would help us."

Joseph smiled. "Your father's operations are so complicated he's *got* to have a list, he's got to have notes on his blackmail, on who is buried in which plot, who owes who, who in the state government has been approving his leases. He can't keep it all in his hat, I'll tell you."

Grant nodded and followed his brother-in-law.

Simon was not expected back from town for another two hours when Grant led the way down to the spacious wine cellar below the big main room.

"He has the only key I expect?"

"Yes," Grant replied.

Joseph reached out and took ahold of the padlock and chain that were wrapped about the bars of the prison-like entrance to the wine cellar. He smiled. Then he fitted the tips of his hooks into the keyhole. He turned them in opposite directions. The click echoed in the brick-vaulted room as the lock fell to the floor.

"When they took your hands, they didn't take your talents, did they?" Grant said. The two men entered the cellar, careful to close the iron-barred door behind them.

The wine cellar was composed of three major aisles, two lined with bottles and a third lined with casks of various sizes filled with wines from Simon Yarrow's own small vineyard. At first Joseph travelled down the first two aisles, checking the labels of the hundreds of vintages Yarrow had bought or decanted himself. "Where's his wine journal?" Joseph asked.

Grant looked around and then flipped open a heavy, leather-bound book that rested on a small table equipped with a lamp and candle for decanting. Joseph checked over his shoulder as they looked through the years and years of notations. "Look for some kind of a code or such," Joseph counselled.

Grant shook his head. "Damned if I can see anything."

Joseph agreed. He walked over and looked at the far wall. He knocked the bricks with the back of his hooks, but failed to find a hollow one.

"Let's try the third aisle," Grant said.

The air smelled of fermenting grapes, cool and heady. In the lamplight, the two men examined each of the casks which lined the walls.

"I don't think he'd keep that sort of material down here," Grant said.

Joseph said, "Perhaps you're right." He reached out and rapped on the cask nearest him. It made a quiet thud. He continued to walk and rap. Then he stopped. Grant looked around at the sound. Joseph rapped the third keg a second time. And a third.

"Stand back," Grant said. He reached across the top of the cask and pulled at the back. "Look at that," he said. The top of the cask lifted off, revealing a hollowed-out section.

"The bottom half is filled with wine," Joseph said. "Ingenious, your father."

The secret compartment was empty.

The afternoon sun had slanted down into the western horizon when they came above stairs. Simon Yarrow was walking in, slapping the dust of the trail from his tight-fitting black coat. "Good afternoon," he said. "I trust you gents have kept one another busy."

"Very," Grant replied. He looked at his father and felt a chill run down his spine. It almost seemed as if Simon knew where they had been and what they had been doing. When had Simon Yarrow emptied out the secret compartment in the wine cask and why?

"Something the matter?" Simon asked. He looked at the two men's faces and didn't like the expressions he read there.

"It's been a long hot day," Joseph replied.

"Where is Diana?"

"She had a bad headache," Joseph replied.

"Ah," Simon said. 'Oh, I almost forgot. One of my men got word from your sister, Patricia. She said she'd like to speak with you this evening if possible."

"Why didn't she come here?" Joseph asked.

Simon smiled. "Patricia Carrick doesn't exactly care for us Yarrows. She wanted to meet on neutral ground."

"Where?"

"She said she'd like to see you where the canal enters your property. Where it borders mine on the northeast."

"I'll show you," Grant said.

Simon smiled. "Patricia said she wanted to see her brother alone."

"I'll find it all right," Joseph said. "I'll go wash up for supper and then leave right afterwards if that's all right."

"Fine," Simon Yarrow said. "I'll have Mr. Smith draw you a little map."

"Thank you, Mr. Yarrow."

CHAPTER ELEVEN

SIMON Yarrow watched the roseate fingers of dawn steal across the shady patio. He straightened up a stack of correspondence, took out his pen knife and sharpened his pencil. He tapped the blunt end of the pencil on the massive desk, whistled a tuneless song and then took inventory of the stuffed animal heads on the walls of his office.

The first cries came a few moments later. Then he heard footfalls on the staircase and a woman's high-pitched screams. "Where is he?" she cried.

Simon rose as Diana stormed into his office, her blonde hair streaming out behind her like the figure-head on a ship in San Francisco. She was still wearing her diaphanous nightgown which clung to her figure, outlining her full breasts in the early light.

"Where is he? Where is my husband?" she said. She put both hands down on her father's desk. Her eyes were round in fright.

"Who?" Simon replied.

"My husband! What have you done with him?"

Simon walked around the desk, passed close to

his daughter and, instead of touching her, poured himself a cup of thick black New Orleans coffee. "Diana, I have done absolutely nothing to your husband. He has memory problems. Perhaps he forgot how to get back here from his little jaunt last evening."

"That is not funny. I had a sick headache last night. I went to bed early. I woke up and he was gone! Something has happened to him! I know it!"

"Perhaps he decided to spend the night at his home in the valley," Simon said.

She shook her head. "He would have sent me word. I know it. And Grant is gone too!"

Simon sipped slowly. The chickory was flat this morning. It didn't have the bite he liked. "I wouldn't get too excited if I were you," Simon said. "If you like, you can take a ride over to the Carrick's farm and ask his sister. He met her last night after supper."

Diana looked long and hard into her father's small brown eyes. "If you have killed Joseph, Father, you have killed me."

Simon's smile slipped slightly.

Patricia Carrick was just coming out of the barn when she heard Diana's horse's hoofbeats on the trail. One of her own workhorses had the colic and she was giving him a special mixture of hers that always seemed to work. Her brothers were already in the fields.

"Miss Carrick," Diana said in a high-pitched voice that was near hysteria, "I'm looking for Joseph."

Patricia wiped her forearm across her chin to catch the perspiration. There was no denying it: Joseph had chosen a beautiful woman, Patricia thought. She couldn't blame Alexander or Joseph or half the other men in the valley for lusting after this Yarrow woman. Her every pore seemed to exude promises of heaven on earth.

Diana looked down from her horse at the handsome woman who reminded her of Joseph. It seemed to her that Patricia Carrick's tight exterior hid depths which no one had ever seen. She was sure there were secrets lodged in this woman's bosom, secrets which would shock the men who knew her. Diana shook her head to clear the tears that welled up. "Please, Miss Carrick," she said, "I need your help. Joseph did not return last night. Did you meet him by the canal where our lands meet?"

"No," Patricia replied.

"Oh, my God," Diana said. "I—I—I—" She slid down from her horse in a half faint, her hands barely slowing her descent.

Patricia dropped her feed pail and caught the beautiful woman before she plummeted all the way to the ground. Without thinking, Patricia picked up the heavier woman and carried her into the farmhouse where she laid her on her own bed. After she'd put cold cloths on Diana's forehead, she ran to the front door and banged eight times on the piece of steel which hung outside—the signal for her brothers to come running.

Diana moaned on the bed as Patricia made ready to ride out to the canal. "I'm going to leave you here," Patricia said. "My brothers and I'll go looking for Joseph."

"No," Diana said, getting up. "I must go with you."

Patricia looked at the hysterical woman and shrugged. "Suit yourself, but don't you be slowing us down. We've got work to do."

Diana nodded and the five of them rode quickly towards the northern border.

They found Joseph's horse about a mile from the canal, grazing easily, moving in the guilty way runaways do—always afraid they'll be caught. Patricia took the reins quickly and they continued on, grimfaced and silent. Even Diana had stopped sniffling, sensing the tragedy that was unfolding.

The canal sluiced along unimpeded, the dark waters coursing at depths of eight and twelve feet. Patricia had no time to consider the expense of the valuable fluid, thanks to Simon Yarrow. Instead, she scanned the sides of the canal, the groves of trees and the surrounding countryside.

"Where could he be?" Diana asked quietly.

Alexander looked over at her, shook his head and scanned the horizon for any sign of his brother. She was beautiful, but now any thoughts of her were adulterous. He shook his head again and urged his mount along the side of the canal.

Patricia stopped where a rotten tree had pulled loose from the soil and tumbled into the canal. She dismounted and stared into the confused waters around the old trunk.

Her face went hard. A piece of metal caught the sunlight as the waters chuckled around it. She knew the metal well. Its color, its sheen.

It didn't take long for her to descend the banks of the canal, grab hold of a tree branch, and make certain nothing could be done.

Joseph's face was serene beneath the precious water. His thick red hair was smoothed back by the current as if he'd been laid out by God himself. His eyes were closed and he wore a faint smile in death. It looked like he had died knowing a very private secret.

Diana's scream was short and high-pitched. She collapsed in the dirt.

"How did he die?" Patrick asked.

They lifted Joseph's body from the water where he'd been trapped under the tree. "Drowned," Patricia said. She cradled her brother's head on her lap and crooned a quiet hymn. When she pulled her hand from beneath his head there was blood on it. "Ease him over," she said.

On the back of Joseph's head was a wound where he'd been struck. "Maybe somebody knocked him out," Christopher said. "Then tossed him in."

Patricia nodded. "Yeah, but the sheriff will say the mark was made when he fell in." Her voice was hard and bitter. "We can't prove anybody did this to him. All we know is what's in our hearts."

They lifted Joseph onto his horse and carried him slowly back to their farm.

The sheriff, a political appointee of Simon Yarrow's best friend, Judge Lamont, reported the death as "accidental drowning" and shrugged when the Carricks suggested that some one had murdered their brother. "If you've some proof, I'd be glad to consider it," he said.

On the morning of Joseph Carrick's funeral the heat seemed to pump out from the south and hang over the valley like a pall. The Carricks and their friends gathered around the little family cemetery which had contained only one grave before this: Michael Carrick's, their father's.

There were nearly two hundred farmers who showed up to demonstrate their respect for the man who had been Joseph Carrick and to show their solidarity behind what he stood for. Men and women wept openly as his plain pine coffin was eased gently into the dry earth.

Patricia stood with her brothers and sisters behind the priest. A hot wind ruffled his cassock as he intoned the litany of death and rebirth. None of the Carricks wept. Patricia had already done all the crying she had time for. She and her family knew they had two jobs to do. The first was to survive. To bring in a fall harvest. The second and most important was to bring their brother's killer to justice. No matter who the actual killer might be, they knew in their hearts that Simon Yarrow stood behind him.

"Requiescat in pace," the priest said through the heat. He sprinkled holy water on the casket. Patricia almost cried to think that that holy water had, most likely, come from a source owned by Simon Yarrow, the same source which had drowned her brother, the same source which was now bankrupting all the small farmers in the valley. *"In nomine patri, et filii, et spiritu sancti."*

Diana, in black, standing alone a few steps to the side, wept quietly. She was the only Yarrow to come. Alexander watched her, then crossed himself.

Patricia wondered where Grant had gone, then leaned down and took a spadeful of dirt and dropped it on her brother's coffin. Her brothers and sisters followed. Will Lacey looked as if he'd had to fortify himself to come to the funeral. His eyes were red and his hands were unsteady as he added to the growing mound of dirt on the casket.

*   *   *

That evening, after the hot sun had dropped into the Pacific Ocean, behind the mountains, Patricia and her brothers sat in their kitchen and drank from two quarts of whiskey which Joseph had bought a year or two before. "Did he die not knowing who he was?" Patrick asked.

"I guess we'll never know," Alexander replied.

Patricia liked the burning sensation at the back of her throat. "I wonder how Mr. Macauley is," she asked her glass. "Maybe I'll write him and tell him about Joseph's passing."

"Remember when Joseph got all loco because Christopher put whipped cream on his head while he was asleep?" Patrick said to the ceiling.

Patricia laughed. "I thought Christopher was a goner, I'll tell you," she said. She wiped her eyes with her apron.

"I'm glad he got married before he went," Patrick said. "I'd hate to think he didn't get his way with a lady before he died. Hell, I'd hate to die that way."

"Be quiet," Alexander said.

Patrick looked up with surprise, but, before he could say anything, they all looked to the front door. "Sounds like a carriage."

Simon Yarrow, accompanied by a dozen guards on horseback, reined his light carriage to a halt outside the front door of the Carrick home. He tied the reins to the ring in front of him and surveyed the stone faces of the Carrick clan.

"You ain't welcome here," Patricia said.

"I can understand," Simon said.

"Then get off our property," Patricia said. Her

speech, thanks to the whiskey, was thick and deep and resonant.

Simon smiled and looked at his outriders. "Well," he said, "there's a small problem with that."

"With what?" Alexander asked.

"Getting off your property."

"What do you want?" Patricia asked, suddenly aware that she was shivering even though it wasn't even cold.

"Your brother had gone into debt to hold the farm, Miss Carrick. At his death those notes are forfeit. I'm afraid you don't own this place anymore."

As soon as Simon had spoken, Mr. Smith moved his horse between the Carricks and the man who had just stolen their land.

"You bastard!" Patricia shouted. "You lying, murdering, thieving bastard!" She tried to get around Smith's horse, but he was too quick. The guards formed a solid wall between the Carricks and their employer.

"We'll get you, Yarrow!" Patrick shouted.

Simon Yarrow smiled. "You have until tomorrow at noon to be off this land."

The Carricks watched as Yarrow and his men rode off into the night. Patricia knelt in the dirt and prayed that God would strike Simon Yarrow dead. "Because if you don't, I'm gonna and I don't care if I have to spend forever in hell for it!"

At noon the next day the sheriff presided over the end of the Carricks' life in the San Joaquin Valley. Farmers came from far away to help them load their possessions into three wagons. Mary Margaret and

Mary Elizabeth wept as they bid good-bye to their brothers and sister. Will Lacey was absent. "Too hung over to come," his wife said.

"Where you going?"

"To San Francisco," Patricia said. Her own hangover throbbed in her head. "Maybe we're not cut out to be farmers."

"What'll you do?"

Patricia shrugged. "We have a hundred dollars put away. We don't know. To hang Simon Yarrow we'll need money and lots of it. Maybe we'll find a fortune in the city." She hugged her sisters again and tried not to weep.

BOOK TWO

CHAPTER ONE

IT used to be called Yerba Buena.

And it looked as if the whole city might decide to accede to gravity's demands and dash headlong into the bay.

Now it was called San Francisco and it held in its particolored embrace on its unlikely hills as much wealth and poverty as any city on the face of the earth. In the lower sections, closer to the wharves, there hung a smoky pall from the cheap coal its residents burned. On the streets that smacked more of Alpine villages than American homesteads one-storey houses huddled against the hillsides to keep from sliding off. Vast living monuments of garish architecture stood as testaments to fast money in silver and gold.

In Chinatown the prostitutes and "waiter girls" brazenly walked the streets reminding everyone that this nearly respectable city had begun as a rip-roaring open city which thrived on the violence with which gold changed hands.

San Francisco was always known for its noise, its crowds, its fast pace, its ridiculous cost of living and its absurd ease of dying. The men were rash and the women couldn't afford to bide their time. Millions of dollars were won and lost on a single piece of paper. The Stock Exchange Board was more gladitorial than businesslike, where a man with "no sand in him" could be swallowed up by morning and spat out by suppertime.

The stores were always filled with the world's treasures and business was conducted around-the-clock. Under the gaslight carriages travelled every which way, jostled by jugglers, peddlers, clerks on the town and the ubiquitous legions of whores.

The woman stood on the corner in the twilight. Her movements were quick, her face set in an insincere smile, looking as if it had been painted on by an untalented artist. Her clothes were cheap. You could see that the dark earth colored cottons had been patched and sewed more than once.

She turned and walked down past the Maison Doree and tried her smile on two drunken businessmen who had spent their day on Montgomery Street and cheated each other out of a thousand dollars in gold. Gold and silver coin was the only medium of exchange a San Franciscan would accept. Let somebody else trust paper money!

The first businessman whistled at the woman with the smile and stopped to talk to her, but, strangely, she ran off, hiking her skirts to her calves. The businessman shrugged and hurried to catch his friend to tell him about the whore who got offended when he suggested they "make the beast with two backs."

Patricia Carrick did not stop running until she reached the edge of a little park ringed by gas lamps. She was dizzy from a lack of food; she was nauseous from her run. She was terrified from what she had decided to do.

"There's nothing for it," she'd said that morning when she awoke in the dingey little one room railroad flat she shared with her brothers. They'd tossed up a blanket for privacy, but all that did was cut down the hope of a breeze through the place. Ever since they arrived in San Francisco they'd dreamed of getting out of that hell hole of a room.

But there was a depression on. Nobody was hiring anybody. They'd found occasional odd jobs that paid less than the regular two-fifty a day, but those had been few and far between. It hadn't taken long at the inflated San Francisco prices for their tiny nest egg to be exhausted.

And now Christopher and Patrick were sick.

Her palms were clammy. Her breathing was quick. Her eyes were wide around. "If I must sell myself to feed my family," she said, "then sell I must." She paused, crossed herself, and said, "if anyone will have me." She knew what the months of malnutrition had done to her body. She was thinner, gaunt in the face. Her hair lacked the confident sheen it had always had. But her face still radiated like one of the martyrs in the book her mother had kept sacred.

But other, worse visions plagued her—visions worse than the shame of prostituting oneself for one's salvation.

Francis Macauley visited her dreams, tormented her soul, occupied her mind. He was never far from her. It was Francis Macauley, the wealthy owner of the mill where her family had worked, who had repeatedly subjected her to painful rape. At the time he had been in his thirties, she a girl of twelve. He had defiled her, humiliated her, subjected her to his abominable perversions.

At thirty-two, Patricia Carrick had not lain with any man. Not after what Francis Macauley had done. Her forehead shone with a cold sweat when she remembered the painful shaft that cut her.

"But there's nothing for it," she reminded herself. She was ashamed that she had run from the businessman back by the Maison Doree. It would have been over by now and she would have had a few dollars. She could buy food for the lads. She could afford a doctor, perhaps.

She remembered the time back East in Fall River when Joseph had brought the doctor for the two little ones who died. He was too late.

She remembered Grant Yarrow. He had disappeared the night of Joseph's murder. She wondered if he was dead or alive. He had been so handsome . . .

She rubbed up her cheeks to try to bring some color to them.

"Miss?"

Patricia spun around quickly. Her eyebrows rose as she tried to smile. "Sir?" Her voice was sweet and innocent.

The gentleman was easily six feet two or three. He more a light grey suit, cut in the English manner. The top hat matched the pearl color as he doffed it. He was fat-faced, cherubic, with wings of wispy white hair that flowed around his ears. Chin whiskers of salt and pepper sprayed from beneath his thin lower lip. Jolly pale grey eyes shone with the ingestion of too many rum drinks. He swayed as if he were still aboard a ship. "I am a foreigner in a foreign land and so you must forgive me," he said. "I am English."

Patricia nodded, hoping he was doing more than asking for directions. His accent was thick.

"I have no wish to be misconstrued," he said.

"No, sir," she replied. The panic rose in her heart, its fingers squeezing the breath from her. Francis Macauley's ghost rattled his chains in her mind.

"I do not wish to be thought rude."

"No, sir." Please get on with it, Patricia thought. If it must be you, pray do it quickly and give me my money. It flashed through her frightened mind that he didn't seem like such a bad sort. He looked like a gentle soul.

"I am deeply lonely here," he said. He put his top hat back on his head and tugged at his whiskers. "I crave companionship."

"Yes, sir."

"Would you accompany me back to my hotel? If I offend you, please forgive me and I shall trouble you no more."

"You do not . . . offend," she said in a whisper. She wished she knew if she should mention money now or later. "I. . . ."

"I am prepared to remunerate you for your time on my behalf," he said.

Patricia could do nothing but nod. She wanted desperately not to throw up the water she had drunk.

"Fine," the Englishman said. "Will twenty dollars suffice for your time?"

"Twenty dollars?" She could barely speak the words. She had dreamed of five.

"Thirty, then?" he said quickly.

Patricia nodded.

The Englishman took her arm and hailed a cab. Patricia hoped she would not faint.

* * *

As the Englishman led her into his second-class hotel on Pine Street, he said, "I cannot wait until they finish building the Palace. They say it will be the largest hotel in the world. I'd like to try that."

Patricia looked at the lobby of the hotel and froze. Under the potted palms, seated on long couches, beneath long murals, were twenty or thirty guests. Some were chatting about Thomas Edison, now a millionaire at 29, and some were reading periodicals, or listening idly to the small orchestra which played country tunes. They looked up whenever someone new came in.

Eyes bore into Patricia Carrick, picked at her threadbare cotton farmer's skirt, snatched at her cracked-leather shoes, snipped at her old-fashioned straw hat and laughed at her escort. No one said a word, but everyone knew that the strange Englishman had brought a whore to the hotel.

"Mr. Price?" the night manager said. He cleared his throat.

"Yes?" Patricia's escort replied.

"It is against the policy of this establishment," he said as quietly as he could, "to allow our single male guests to entertain female visitors at this establishment."

Mr. Price smiled and brushed off his hat. "I do not plan to entertain my female guest," Price said aloud, "I plan to have my female guest entertain me! Good evening, sir." With that, he pushed the manager aside and led Patricia, blushing scarlet, up the wide staircase between the potted palms.

* * *

The gas lamps lighted the worn red runner in the hallway. Patricia clamped her teeth together tightly, thinking of her sick brothers as a way of blinding herself to the present. "Here we are," Mr. Price said. He placed his key in the door and swung it wide.

Patricia walked in slowly, her head moving from side to side as if she expected to be assaulted by the furnishings of the room.

A single gas lamp illuminated the wide double bed, the coat rack, the dressing stand, the marble-topped bureau. A painting of a Biblical scene dominated the wall between the two windows facing the street. Incredibly, it was Joseph and his coat of many colors among his angry brothers.

Patricia turned to hear the door close behind her like a tomb's stone. "I. . . ."

"I'd like a drink, that's what I'd like," the tall Englishman said. He poured a glass of rum from a bottle on his bureau and knocked it back without so much as a "Cheers!"

The small rush-bottomed chair squeaked as Patricia sat upon it. It was the furthest piece of furniture from the large white-topped brass bed.

"Come," Mr. Price said cheerfully, "give us a kiss, lass." He sat on the edge of the bed and slapped his thighs. "I put your price up on the bureau next to the rum, if that's what you're worried about."

The pile of coins reflected the lamplight.

Patricia stood and removed her straw hat, placing it behind her on the chair. She took off her shawl and hung it carefully on the back of the chair.

"Come on, dear. I won't slap you around or anything." He'd taken off his jacket and cravat. His shirt

was open to his hairy chest. He walked to the bureau
and poured himself another drink. Then he turned
and caught Patricia by the shoulders. She was a good
foot shorter than he was, but he leaned down and put
his lips to hers.

The smell of rum was overpowering. His skin was
cool and wet. His breathing was labored.

"There, that wasn't so bad, was it?" he asked as he
stood up to his full height. "You are a most beautiful
young woman. You know that?"

"Thank you, sir."

"How long have you been in the trade?" He knocked
back another glass of rum.

"Not long."

"I didn't think so," he said with a smile. "I can
tell these things." He reached out and placed his large,
brown-spotted hands on Patricia's breasts.

She started to move back, but ordered her knees to
lock and willed her legs not to move. The hands were
heavy and hot. The nightmares mixed with the reality
as Francis Macauley licked and sucked her young
girl's breasts, biting them and leaving blue bruises.
He had pinched her nipples and when she had cried
out, he slapped her.

Mr. Price smiled down at his find of the evening
and slowly unbuttoned her blouse.

Patricia thought of the doctor she could get with
thirty dollars. Not the quack who worked the poorer
quarters, but the regular doctor who lived over on
Sansome.

Price let his fingers dawdle and then pull the light
blue ribbon at the throat of the woman's camisole.
The material parted to reveal her delightful breasts.
He swallowed hard. This was always the best part.

Whores were beautiful. You could do whatever you wanted. You didn't even know their names.

It was hot in the room.

Mr. Price rubbed his forehead with his handkerchief. Then he leaned forward and began to lightly lick the big pink nipples of the nameless woman. He looked up at her face and smiled.

Patricia could taste the bile from her stomach. She didn't know when she'd last eaten. Yes, she did. It was the day before. She'd had part of the lunch she made for her brothers.

The back of Mr. Price's head was bald and shiny. She looked up at the painting by the windows. Joseph and his coat. Her own poor Joseph lay in the San Joaquin Valley on land that now belonged to Simon Yarrow.

The memory of the man who had brought tragedy to her family brought her up short, helped her forget the man who now slavered like a young calf at her breasts.

Mr. Price eased back on the bed and unfastened his trousers, dropping the front panel to reveal a thick red shaft capped with a deep purple head. He smiled a glassy smile and said. "Your turn, my sweet."

Patricia put her hand to her mouth and stifled a cry. She gnawed upon her knuckle.

"Suck on it, lass. There's a good child." He put his hands behind his head and closed his eyes.

"Suck, God damn your mick ass!" Francis Macauley shrieked. "Suck or I'll have your whole family lose their hands like Joseph!"

Patricia looked quickly for the chamber pot. She would vomit surely. She held both hands across her mouth.

The sound was high-pitched at first. Then deeper and more regular.

Patricia did not know how long she had stood next to the bed, her palms across her mouth, staring into the middle distance above the partially-clad man. But then she heard the sound.

Snoring.

Mr. Price's thirty-dollar erection lay on his silken underwear, a third the size and growing smaller. His head was turned to the side. Some spittle ran down his cheek.

He was deeply asleep, soundly passed out on the bed.

Patricia's fingers worked quickly as she laced up her camisole and buttoned up her blouse. She took her shawl and her hat and headed for the door. It was as if her guardian angel had swooped down and delivered her. She was not going to question it.

She stopped with her hand on the knob.

It wouldn't be the same as stealing.

She walked back to the bureau. He had slobbered over her breasts. He had kissed her. It was not her fault that nothing more had come of their encounter. It was clearly his. If she were a regular prostitute she would surely be paid even if the customer could not perform.

Her hands were not slow to pick up the gold piece and the other silver change. She tied it in a handkerchief and walked quickly out of Mr. Price's room. "I'll pay him back when I become rich," she said in a near-breathless whisper.

The orchestra had finished playing for the evening when Patricia walked down the staircase to the lobby.

Most of the guests had gone to bed. She walked proudly across the floor to the doors.

"Miss!"

Patricia stopped and turned to stare into the livid face of the night manager. She blushed again and tried to block out the faces of the remaining guests who stared at the brazen woman and wanted to see her get her comeuppance.

"I don't ever want to see you in this establishment again or I shall call the police!"

Patricia nodded. Her smile was as real as she could make it. "I don't ever want to see me in this establishment again either!" She turned and walked boldly out the door, her thirty dollars burning hot against the flesh of her breasts.

CHAPTER TWO

THE room was thirty feet by twenty feet. At one end there was a window looking out on a filthy alleyway, and an outhouse used by all the tenants, filled with rotting garbage and human waste. At the other end the window looked out onto the narrow street and another two-story house just like this one.

It was ten-thirty when Patricia made her tired way up the outside stairs and into the room. She moved through the darkness and got undressed for bed on the mattress on the other side of the make-shift curtain. She looked down at Patrick and Christopher. Christopher coughed his dry cough in his sleep. Patrick slept soundly.

"Patricia?" Alexander whispered.

"How have they been?" she asked.

"Fine," he replied. "Did you have any luck?"

She nodded in the darkness, glad he could not see her blush. "It was a gift from the Lord. I was walking across a vacant lot down by Montgomery and stubbed my big old toe on a handkerchief that had thirty dollars in it. Finders, keepers, I say."

"That's wonderful," Alexander said.

"A gift from the Lord," Patricia repeated. "Go to sleep now."

"Good night, Patricia."

"Good night, Alexander."

Alexander waited for ten minutes in the darkness, his fingers laced behind his head, listening to the drone of his brothers' snoring, waiting for the sound of his sister's deep and heavy sleep. When he could pick out her special sound from the others, he slipped out of bed and dressed quietly and quickly.

"Now, I'll show them all," he said to himself. "It's a chance just like this I've been waiting for."

The months of joblessness, of helplessness, of feeling less than a man, had taken a terrible toll on Alexander Carrick. And before that? The picture of Diana and his late brother married still burned in his soul.

"I'll show them all," he said to himself as he muffled the sound of the crockery top. "I'll earn my keep yet." He reached down into the big crock pot and fingered the thirty dollars Patricia had hidden there. "It's the Carrick Bank," she called it.

Alexander stole out of the house and made his way down to Chinatown. "I won't be 'Fighting the Tiger'", Alexander thought. "No Faro for me. I'll invest Patricia's gift of God in poker. I'll run it up to a couple of hundred dollars and we'll be right back up there." He smiled.

San Francisco was a gambling town. Everyone from scullery maids to millionaires gambled on a turn of a card at a green baize table, gambled on a turn of a spade at a suspected silver mine, or gambled that the stocks they were buying would zoom up like the cost of living.

Alexander stopped outside one of the hundreds of gambling dens, this one known as "Sutter Creek" and run by the Lee family. He was inspected through the peephole and admitted to the large room with its Faro tables, wheels of fortune, and dice games.

There were no women in Lee's big room. No women to notice the handsome, well-built Irishman with the sly smile who sat in at a poker table by the far door.

Alexander purchased twenty dollars worth of chips, preferring to hang onto the ten, just in case he lost and had to go back home.

He politely refused a free drink and chose instead to devour a platter of roast beef before sitting down to give all his attention to the game.

In five minutes his twenty dollars was gone.

The four other players and the house dealer looked at him. "What's your pleasure?"

Alexander was sweating. Stunned. He pulled out the last ten dollars. "Ten."

A half hour later Alexander was still in the game with his ten dollars. He'd gone as high as thirty and as low as five.

The action at the other tables became more intense as the evening wore on. Small fortunes were won and lost. Men came and went like seasons. Time raced. The pall of cigar smoke grew fatter and hung lower over the tables.

Alexander looked down at his hand. Four cards. Two pair. Aces and eights. He smiled. He looked up at the stack of chips in front of him. A fast calculation would make it about seventy-five dollars. With that much money they could get Christopher to the doctor and have food for a good long time. A couple of weeks, anyway. They'd have a chance to build up their strength and get some good clothes. It was hard going to see about work when you looked like some kind of bum.

Alexander received his fifth card face down. He flicked the corner of it, but did not look at it. That was bad luck. He stacked the last card with the other four and shuffled them for luck. Then he fanned them carefully in his hand.

Ace-Ace-Ace-eight-eight.

A full house!

He thrust out his lower lip as if he were thinking about his hand. He didn't want anyone at the table reading his face. Nobody could beat him now. From the cards he'd counted on the table, there was no chance somebody had a straight or four of a kind. He thought he could be sure of that.

"Bump her five," the man named Max said.

"See you," the man named Al said.

Alexander nodded and rocked slightly in his chair. He tried to look bored while the dealer looked at him with almond eyes. "See you and raise you ten, just to make the evening interesting," Alexander said.

The other men at the table looked just as bored as Alexander while inside they were speedily computing the odds on Alexander's fortune. A few of them had spotted him as a fair player with some clumsy luck and a patently inadequate poker face.

"Fifteen to stick?" the dark-eyed man named Ralph asked quietly.

The dealer nodded.

Ralph thrust out his lower lip and rocked in a

slight imitation of Alexander. "See that and let's make her a whole lot more interesting." He bumped the pot with an extra fifty dollars.

Alexander paled slightly. That would leave him with no money at all. If he lost.

But he couldn't lose. He cleared his throat as one by one the other players dropped out. "Too steep for me," one said.

"You just bought yourself a pot," said another.

Their eyes stopped on Alexander. He picked up his stack of chips and let them drop, one by one, like the grains of sand in the hourglass by the door, onto the pile of chips.

The man named Ralph smiled. "Guess you bought a look, 'Red'," he said. He laid his cards on the green felt.

King-King-King-six-six.

Alexander smiled. Nodded. "Good cards, mister. But not good enough." He put down his Ace-high full house and raked in the pot.

"Jesus," said one man.

"You believe that?" another said.

Ralph nodded, his mouth a single slash. An angry line.

The dealer smiled and shuffled a new deck.

At two A.M. Alexander pushed himself away from the table and cashed in his chips. "Three hundred and sixty dollars," Mr. Lee said. "A good night for you, sir."

Alexander smiled and tucked the gold coins into his trouser pockets. "A very good night, Mr. Lee." He handed the Chinaman five dollars for luck and excused himself out into the thick night air.

The last whores of the evening were working as hard as they could, no holes barred. It was too late, they knew, and it hadn't been a good night for them. Those who had pimps knew they'd be beaten. Those who had no pimps feared they'd starve.

Alexander passed one young woman who looked a bit like Patricia. It was sad, he thought, how things worked out in life. It was a gigantic crap shoot. A poker game. If you didn't get the cards, there wasn't a damn thing you could do about it.

"Fuck me, mister, fuck me for five bucks," the small redhead said.

Alexander shook his head and kept walking.

"I'll suck your goddamned cock for five. Ten for both!" she yelled.

A group of whores across the manure-filled street laughed at her persistence, knowing her pain, but preferring to feel apart from it. "Try him for ten cents!" one shouted.

The redhead grabbed Alexander by the shoulder and spun him around. She was as strong as she was frantic. She snatched at the fly of his trousers. "Come on, ya Mick bastard. I gotta eat, too, ya know."

Alexander slapped her hand away. He reached in his pocket. "I don't want to use you," he said. "Here." He gave her a dollar.

The whore smiled. "For you I got a very special prize." She took out a folded piece of heavy paper and handed it to him. "Don't open it here. It's priceless."

Alexander tucked it in his pocket and walked quickly away.

As soon as he was a few yards distant, the whore

yelled after him, "Cockless bastard!" She turned and rejoined her friends across the street. "Easiest buck tonight," she said.

They laughed after the retreating Irishman.

Alexander puffed as he walked up the street. Damned San Francisco. He didn't know why anybody had to go and build a city on these Godforsaken mountains. He turned a corner and stopped. "Only a couple of more blocks," he told his aching legs.

The other footsteps kept coming.

Alexander tried to pierce the night with his eyes, but it was too dark. The gas lamps were out around here. The poor people didn't need them.

There were four different steps. Eight legs and feet. Coming straight up the street.

Alexander turned and continued. A chilly breeze ruffled his hair. Something told him to keep low and close to the buildings along the curb. The men behind him could just be coming back from work, but he doubted it. He was carrying over three hundred and fifty dollars. In this community money gave off an odor, a spore of its own which the poor could smell from miles away.

The men got closer. "There he is," one called.

"Head him off," cried another.

Alexander ducked down an alleyway and pumped his legs as fast as they would go. That voice! The first one. He knew for sure now they wanted him and only him. It was the man named Ralph! The man he had bested at cards. He turned the corner behind his building and aimed for the wide wooden stairs.

The footsteps thundered behind him. His breath was hot and burned his lungs.

The first blow landed across his shoulders. A truncheon. Alxander went down into the thick, foul-smelling mud. He tried to get up, but there was a weight on him, a weight who was pounding his spine.

He heard voices. Ralph's voice. Hands on him. Pulling him up. He stood and lashed out, catching someone in the teeth. He felt the teeth loosen and break on the rocks of his knuckles. A man screamed out in the darkness.

More hands grabbed at his pockets, the truncheon came down on his head and Alexander saw red comets race across the night sky. Then all was night.

As he fell into the filth of the alley, he could hear his sister screaming for the police.

It was after dawn when Alexander finally awoke. He was surprised to find himself washed and cleaned. Looking down at him were Patrick and Patricia. "How do you feel?" she asked. Her face was pale, drawn, tight.

"I'll be all right." He flexed his muscles and tried to move his limbs. "All right."

"You took my money?' Patricia asked in a dead monotone.

"Yes."

"Why? For a woman?"

"No. I gambled at Lee's."

"Oh, my God."

"I won three hundrd and sixty dollars, Patty." He sighed. "The men last night were after it."

Patricia shook her head. "There was nothing on you when me and Patrick brought you up here. Except a certificate for one of them bogus mines." She held up the piece of paper the whore'd given Alexander for his dollar.

Alexander shook his head slowly. His face was a
mask of pain. His eyes were drawn shut, his mouth
a fixed line. "Oh, God, I've made a lash-up of everything," he said.

Patricia nodded slowly. Then she half-smiled. "Perhaps that thirty dollars was a gift of the devil," she
said. "We didn't deserve it."

That evening Alexander waited until everyone was
sleeping soundly. He let himself out the back door
just as quietly as he had the evening before.

When Patricia awoke at dawn to go look for work,
she found Alexander's carefully written note:

> *"Dear Family: I'm a jinx for you. I've ruined
> everything I've touched. You'll do better without
> another brother to worry about. I love you all.*
> > *Alexander Carrick, your brother."*

Patricia did not have time to weep.

CHAPTER THREE

THE dark, good-looking man's knuckles were white. Frustrated, used to getting his way, he had never come up against such a bureaucracy before. He stared directly into the eyes of the man across the too-neat desk. "I've been waiting a year."

"We've been checking on you and, uh, looking into other relevant matters, as well," the bureaucrat replied.

"And?"

"You checked out."

"What does that mean?" Grant Yarrow asked.

"Your father is a very influential man. We had to move slowly on charges as serious as yours." He paused and snipped an errant cuticle. "You're our man," he said with a smile.

"What does that mean?" Grant asked.

"It means your life is forfeit if your father or his associates find out."

"Sounds wonderful."

"And," the bureaucrat continued, "we will disavow any knowledge of your working for this department."

"I can accept that," Grant said.

The bureaucrat leaned forward. "We need to be kept apprised of every move your father and his friends make. Especially this"—he looked at a file folder—"Judge Chase in San Francisco. It would appear that he is linked to your father's organization rather closely."

"I'll do what I can," Grant said.

The sun battered the roofs of the buildings with relentless power. The heat rose in sheets. The sky, a royal blue, was empty of clouds that might at least shade the people of San Francisco.

Most everyone was still talking about the latest scandal to rock President Grant's second administration. Back in May, two hundred thirty-eight people had been indicted for cheating the government. One of them was U.S. Grant's personal secretary. And no one suspected as the Army undertook the Second Sioux War that it would culminate at a place called Little Big Horn.

In the tenement where the Carricks had lived for a year, chicanery in Washington was of small concern indeed. There were no cooling breezes. Christopher sat in the good chair, the only one of the set that Joseph had bought which they had not had to sell, and covered his pale lips with a blood-spotted handkerchief. He coughed, his shoulders shaking, his temples dotted with perspiration.

Patricia watched him with his own pain mirrored in her pale green eyes. The doctor they had seen last winter had said it all: tuberculosis. He needed to get out of the damp climate. He needed a sanitarium.

He needed many things which they could not afford.

"Do you have to go back?" Christopher asked.

"Yes," Patricia replied. She tucked her hair up under a dust cap with ruffles and a prim black ribbon. The dress itself was black with leg of mutton sleeves, a white collar and a white apron. It was a hot uniform even in winter. In summer, it was stiffling.

"I thought Joseph said you'd never go back into household service after what happened at the Macauleys," Christopher said.

Patricia nodded. "Joseph is dead. I'm lucky to have a position at all." She picked up Miss Sybil's dress which she had finished mending and packed it carefully in the dressmaker's long white box. Judge Chase's daughters were all spoiled rotten, but Sybil was the worst. "Patty, mend this and clean it. I will be wearing it tonight," Sybil had commanded with affected hauteur. Patricia had been working at Judge Chase's for only a few weeks, but already she had taken a sincere dislike to Sybil.

And yet, she was, indeed, lucky to be working. The depression which had begun at the close of 1873 had not eased substantially and most were not as fortunate. Six days a week Patricia Carrick lived, with eleven other women, in a long hot garret on the top floor of the Chase mansion on California Street. On Thursdays she went back to look after her brothers.

Patrick, still hot-headed, brooding over the Yarrows, angry at the world, had gotten a job on the docks as a stevedore. He drank too much, fought too much, and grew bitter.

"Tell Patrick there's a half a pie in the safe," Patricia said.

"You should be wearing dresses like Miss Sybil's," Christopher said.

Patricia smiled. She had to keep from letting Chris' tragedy overwhelm her. He was wasting away, day by day. She could hardly remember the swaggering Irishman who rolled his own cigarettes, could ride any horse in California, and break any heart he wanted. Patricia had had such plans for him. She'd seen him as a senator at the very least. "Thank you, kind sir. I'll look in on you next week. Tell Patrick my wages are in the Carrick Bank." She looked over at the crock pot which Alexander had robbed that fateful night last September.

"I will. Have a good week, love."

"I will try. I just pray Miss Sybil stays out of my way. They're having dinner guests tonight. They haven't entertained since I came on staff. I must run." Patricia kissed her brother's damp forehead, held his gaze for a moment, then went down the rickety stairs to the street, clutching the box that held the expensive Paris frock which Miss Sybil had busted out of, thanks to her passion for strawberries and cream.

It was a twisted mile and a half from their tenement to California Street and the heat was like a thick curtain blocking her progress. But Patricia was not about to let the weather stop her. She was calculating.

"I've saved, in three weeks, four dollars and sixty-five cents. That means in six weeks I'll have nine dollars and thirty cents." It did not occur to Patricia to think how she did figures in her head. She had always been able to do magic with numbers without paper and pencil. "In twelve weeks I'll have eighteen sixty. In forty-eight weeks, seventy-four-forty. By next year the 'Carrick Bank' will be able to send Christopher to Colorado. They say Denver is excellent for people with his condition."

Patricia hiked up her skirts to make it over the curb when, suddenly, she heard a cry. She spun her head to the side and there, in the center of the intersection, was a young girl, five years old, standing transfixed while a heavy, fast-moving carriage bore down upon her.

Without stopping to think, Patricia dropped the dressmaker's box, ran to the little girl, swooped her up, and carried her to the other side of the street just as the iron-clad wheels flashed past.

"Praise God," the girl's mother said. "Oh, thank you, Miss. She wasn't out of my sight but a moment!"

Patricia bent over, her hands on her knees, trying to get her breath. The little girl cried softly. "It's all right, little girl."

"No, it isn't," her mother said. "I'm going to take a cane to you, girl!"

Patricia looked up at the poor, distraught woman. Shook her head. "Ma'am, I did not just save your daughter's life so you could whip the daylights out of her, thank you very much."

"I-I-I-I. . . ."

"Good day." Patricia bent down and kissed the little girl on the cheek. "But if I hear you've been dawdling in the streets, I'll come back and put the cane to you myself, all right?"

The girl nodded shyly.

Patricia walked quickly back across the street to pick up the box with Sybil's dress in it. She was going to be late unless she hurried up.

The box was gone.

Patricia looked up the street and down, but she

couldn't see the thief. She started back across to ask if anyone had seen her dress box, but there was no one to ask. All at once the intersection was deserted. "Lord love us all," Patricia said to herself. "There ain't no decency left in this world." She set her chin with grim determination and walked quickly towards the Chase mansion.

"You what? You what? Lost my dress!"

"It was stolen, mum," Patricia said.

"You lost it!"

"No, mum. I stopped to help a little girl who was going to be run down by a carriage and when I looked up, the dress was gone."

Sybil Chase could not believe her ears. If this stupid new girl thought she could steal with impunity, she had just better think again. At twenty-one, Miss Chase was pretty in an ordinary way, with soft brown hair, an hour-glass figure, vacant brown eyes, a pouty mouth and a button nose. She wore too much lip rouge and made eyes at every male she saw. She hid her faults as well as anyone, including rather thick ankles and knees. "I don't know what I'm going to do with you, Miss!" Sybil screamed. "But you may rest assured I shan't let this go unpunished!"

"Ma'am," Patricia said, "please let me pay for it from my wages every week."

"Oh, you'll pay! Don't you worry about that!"

Patricia sighed to think the funds in the Carrick Bank would be depleted for a foolish frock, but she needed the job just for the family to survive.

Sybil stomped off down the front hall.

"No time to think about it, Patty," Betty, one of

the parlor maids said. "You're to go up to the Moorish Room and make it up for a visitor."

Patricia curtseyed and walked up the back staircase to the second floor. She took fresh linens from the closest and made her way down the eighty foot long main corridor. The servants in the kitchen were jibbering and jabbering about whoever the guest might be. It was relatively unheard of, owing to Mrs. Chase's condition, for the judge to entertain at all, much less have guests stay over.

Patricia swung wide the door to the Moorish Room, a comfortably wide chamber decorated in the Moorish manner, with swagged drapes, a lot of jig-saw patterns at the windows, and a gigantic bed that looked more like a fortress than a place to sleep.

It took her a full half hour to make the bed with the fresh linens and to dust and sweep. When she was finished, she took her equipment and stepped back out into the hallway. "Oh, I'm sorry!"

The figure looked as if she had stepped freshly from a nightmare. Her hair was long, yellowish white and stringy. Her skin was pale beneath layers of powder. Her eyes were a cold blue fire. "They're trying to kill me. Who are you?"

"I'm Patricia, Ma'am." Patricia had never seen Mrs. Amelia Chase before. She was always in her suite, waited on by her own personal staff of snobbish maids and an insufferable butler.

"Please help me. You must please help me. I can trust you. I can see it in your eyes."

The woman's silken nightgown extended to the floor. It was covered with blue flowers and much of her lunch. Patricia gently led her back to her bedroom at the end of the dark-panelled hall.

"They really are trying to kill me."

"Yes, ma'am. Here's your bed, ma'am."

"I need my medicine. I'll trust you if you give me my medicine."

Patricia nodded. Ever since she had come to work at the Chase mansion, she'd heard the old woman was addicted to the opium she took in her cough mixture. And she had heard that the Judge had mistresses of his own to fill the void while the rest of the family pretended Amelia Chase didn't exist. Patricia took the fat brown bottle and uncapped it. She poured out a measure and held it while her mistress gulped it down.

"There, now," Amelia said. "You're a very pretty girl."

"Thank you, ma'am."

Amelia relaxed. Her eyes clouded over and she smiled. "Send for Violet. I must dress for dinner. I haven't dressed for dinner in some time, have I?"

"No, ma'am." Patricia tugged on the bell-pull to summon Violet.

"How long have you been working here?"

"Three weeks, ma'am."

"Are you married?"

"No, ma'am."

"Ever been married?"

"No, ma'am."

"Don't."

"Ma'am?"

"Don't ever get married. They try to kill you, and that's a fact."

Violet stood in the doorway carrying a heavy brocade gown. "The master informed me you are to wear this gown, madame," she said in a tightly pinched voice.

"Too hot, too hot," Amelia said. "I'll die in that dress."

"I am sorry, madame, but the master was quite specific." Violet walked forward with the gown as if it were a holy relic.

"What do you say, Patricia?" Mrs. Chase asked.

Patricia took a step backwards. She knew Violet's power below stairs and had no intention of crossing her.

"It's not my place, ma'am."

Violet smiled.

Defeated, the fifty-year-old woman who looked seventy stood up to be dressed like a child.

The dining room was long, wide and tall. The walls were filled, chock-a-bloc, with paintings, photographs, relics and icons from the family's travels abroad. A gas chandelier sprayed light in hot abundance over the twenty foot long table and its six diners. Judge and Mrs. Chase were at opposite ends. At Mrs. Chase's right sat the handsome guest. The Chase girls, Sybil, Sophia and Elizabeth, were ranged along the other side.

"It was absolutely unforgiveable," Sybil said to the guest, fluttering her long lashes. She smiled in the midst of her petulance.

"But you look stunning in the gown you're wearing," the visitor said. "You would compliment any gown."

"You flatter me," Sybil said.

Her sister Sophia kicked her under the table for being so patently obvious.

Out in the kitchen Patricia helped Raymond ladle the soup to fill in for one of the four girls who had fainted in the heat. "Wonder who'll be next to go," Raymond said.

"I'm used to it," Patricia said.

"Have you ever served table?"

She nodded and took the tray.

"Wait, tuck your hair in your cap, love," Raymond said. "Don't want Miss Sybil lashing out at you."

"Thank you, Mr. Raymond." Patricia hefted the silver tray and made her way through the swinging door accompanied by George, who was one of the butlers.

"No," the visitor said, in his bass voice, "prices have gone up substantially."

Patricia stopped dead; the soup sloshed forward in the tureen. "Move, damn it," George whispered.

With leaden feet Patricia stepped forward into the light of the chandelier. There, blithely chatting with the judge, sat Grant Yarrow. So *he* was the Chase's company! Woodenly following in George's wake, Patricia endured while he served Mrs. Chase, their guest, the Case girls, and, finally, the Judge, who looked appreciatively at Patricia and went on speaking about shipping prices and their effect on the commodities market.

Grant Yarrow did not look at the shivering serving girl. Nor did he look at the butler. He was too busy watching his host. Perhaps he might enlist Sybil's unwitting help in uncovering the connections between Simon Yarrow and the aging judge that the people in Washington were so eager to unravel.

Finally the soup course was served. George led the

pale maid back to the kitchen. "Are you all right?" he demanded. "Are you going to faint like all those other foolish girls?"

Patricia shook her head. "No, sir."

"See that you don't."

Patricia watched as they loaded up the serving dishes for the next course. Grant Yarrow. . . .

She hated him for his name. She felt certain he knew how her brother had died.

She loved him for his dark good looks, a voice that could make her tremble, and pale blue eyes that could see her greatest secret.

"Let's go, girl! My goodness, but you are a wool-gatherer."

As Patricia and the other maids and butlers made the rounds of the dinner table she peeked out beneath her lowered brow to catch glimpses of the man who was forever stealing into her dreams. Grant was tanned and rugged looking. He wore white tie and tails, the dark mahogany of his skin a vivid contrast to his cravat. His pale blue eyes radiated. His lips curled up at the corners. Patricia did not like the way he looked at Sybil.

"My family is the most important thing to me," Judge Chase said. "You should consider starting one before time catches up to you. It has a way of doing that, you know." The Judge was in his late fifties, tall and imposing, with a full head of wavy white hair and a strong jaw. "The family is the backbone of our country," he said.

Amelia took a sip of wine and muttered, "You're a damn liar."

"I beg your pardon, Mrs. Chase?" Grant asked.

"I said my husband's a damn liar!"

The table went deathly still. Patricia and the servants waited for the stormcloud to pass over.

"She doesn't mean that," Sybil said. "Mother will ramble."

"I damn well do mean it!" Amelia shrieked. "I am surrounded by liars! They are mendacious! And they are trying to kill me!"

The Judge rose and walked slowly to the other end of the table. He put his hands on her frail shoulders. "You are not yourself, my dear. It's the heat, surely. . . ."

Amelia stood and pulled back, knocking over her chair. "No! I am myself! It's not the heat!"

"Let me take you upstairs."

"Mr. Yarrow, help me!" Amelia cried.

"Mrs. Chase. . . ."

Amelia turned to face Patricia. "You! You take me upstairs. Patricia! I trust you."

Grant looked at the maid who held the tray of green beans and stifled the urge to shout, "Patricia!" He held his napkin to his lips and watched Joseph Carrick's beautiful sister help his hostess out of the dining room.

"I'm terribly sorry," Judge Chase said.

Grant sat down, shaken. "I understand," he murmured, but his blood ran cold.

Upstairs, Amelia Chase suddenly began to weep, her thin body shaken by a storm of sadness. Patricia held her as they walked along the dark hallway. "It's always been like that," she said.

"Yes, ma'am."

"The Judge was always a womanizer. Always. He never loved anyone but himself. Always a womanizer."

"Yes, ma'am."

At the door to Mrs. Chase's suite Violet stood, her eyebrows arched, her mouth turned down at the corners. "I'll take her from here," she said imperiously.

"Thank you, Miss Violet," Patricia said, only too eager to turn over her charge.

Amelia Chase looked at the two women in the dim gaslight and stood still. "No," she said quietly.

"Mrs. Chase?" Violet said.

"I don't want you anymore. I want her." The old woman pointed a gaunt finger at Patricia.

"Mrs. Chase, I am your personal maid."

"I don't care. I want her. Patty."

Violet turned to glare at Patricia. "Very well," she said through clenched teeth. She turned and walked swiftly toward the back stairs, her starched uniform making loud, whisking sounds.

It took a few minutes to get Mrs. Chase dressed for bed. As the moments went by she began to drift in and out of a kind of twilight of consciousness. Patricia heard snatches of conversations from forty years ago, then entirely lucid observations about life on California Street.

It was difficult for Patricia to forget that downstairs, right beneath her feet, Grant Yarrow sat drinking coffee and Judge Chase's favorite Cognac. She remembered his face when he'd looked up and recognized her. He looked shocked and, she thought, pleasantly surprised. She was grateful to him for not mentioning that he knew her.

"Patty?" Mrs. Chase asked.

"Ma'am?"

"You were daydreaming?"

"Yes, ma'am."

"Could I have my medicine please?"

Patricia fetched the familiar brown bottle. Poured a measureful.

Amelia Chase drank it down greedily, then lay back on her pillows. "Would you comb my hair, Patricia?"

"Yes, ma'am." Patricia sat on the edge of her mistress' bed and unpinned the long white-gold hair.

"They really are trying to kill me," she said drowsily. "Did you know that the Chase money is really my money? At least it *was* my money. The Judge was a penniless lawyer until he met me and married my millions. My father owned six mines. He was a handsome man, my daddy was." Amelia closed her eyes with a smile. "My husband," she continued, "has a little secret at the north end of Sacramento Street. A little white house. I've seen it. I saw. . . . I spied." Her voice grew wearier and wearier. "The Judge gave her an emerald as green as your eyes. . . . I hate him. . . ."

Patricia finished combing the woman's hair. She rose and turned down the gas jet on the wall.

"Patricia?"

"Yes, Mrs. Chase?"

"You're better than all of them."

"Thank you, ma'am."

As Patricia went up to her garret dormitory, she could hear Grant Yarrow's resonant bass voice as Miss Sybil accompanied him on the pianoforte.

Later, when Grant had a moment alone with his host, he smiled and listened as the older man spoke. "The country is going to hell," the Judge said. "What the President's men were caught doing is just what we've all been doing. I tell you, Grant, it's those labor leaders! They're trying to destroy everything we've built!"

"I totally agree," Grant lied. "If only there was something we could do about it." He eased closer to Judge Chase.

"You may not have long to wait," the Judge said with a smile.

"What do you have in mind?" Grant asked.

"You'd do better to ask your father."

Grant handed the man another cognac to try to loosen his tongue. He smiled. "I'd be interested to hear about the organization from your standpoint," he said quietly.

CHAPTER FOUR

SAN FRANCISCO, CALIFORNIA, JULY, 1875

PATRICIA awoke when she heard the other girls rustling about in the airless space under the eaves. She sat on the edge of her cot and dressed slowly. Emma, one of the younger girls who had taken an instant liking to Patricia, said softly to her, "Violet's after your head, I heard."

"It was a misunderstanding," Patricia replied.

"But she's gunning for you. They said you were gonna be fired."

"I'll talk to her. It'll be alright."

"I hope so. You're my only friend in this place."

Patricia smiled and finished dressing.

"Here, take this cocoa to Miss Sybil's room," George said when she reported to him in the pantry. Patricia curtseyed, knowing the old sourpuss liked the lickspittle type, and took the wide silver tray with the cocoa pot and delicate china cup.

The morning was a cool one. She hummed a quiet tune her father had taught her as she walked down the corridor to Miss Sybil's room. Suddenly Violet stepped out from the linen closet and grabbed her,

126

almost causing her to drop the tray. "I want to talk to you, Miss Carrick." Her eyes were bloodshot, her face pale, her grip iron-strong.

"Miss Violet, I don't want to be Mrs. Chase's maid."

"Well, you are, don't you see? Her choosing you makes you her new maid."

"I'll tell her I don't want the position. And I don't. I was happy doing what I was doing."

"I'll get you for this, Carrick."

"I've got to take this to Miss Sybil. Why don't you speak with Mrs. Chase when she wakes up?"

Violet shook her head. "Maybe I will and maybe I won't speak to the old hag. But you watch out because I'm gonna get you one way or the other."

Patricia pulled away and continued on to Miss Sybil's room. She knocked softly, then went in.

The room was dark. Patricia put the tray down on the bureau and went to the windows. She pulled the heavy curtains aside, then went back to the bureau and picked up the tray.

"Oh, my goodness," Patricia said, almost dropping the tray a second time. Miss Sybil lay under a welter of brown hair, quite naked. Next to her covered by a single sheet lay Grant Yarrow.

"Good morning," he said pleasantly. "Is that coffee?"

Patricia's eyes darkened in color, her lids closing until she was looking out between angry slits. "It's hot chocolate," she said through clenched teeth.

"What is she doing in here?" Sybil moaned. "Get her out."

"Why don't you give me the chocolate?" Grant said.

"I'll give you the chocolate," Patricia said. She took two steps forward and dumped the tray into the cocky Californian's lap.

"Mother of God!" he yelled as the steam rose from the sheet over his groin. He leaped up and out of bed, unmindful of his nakedness, and ran for the ewer that stood next to the bureau. He doused himself with the tepid water, trying not to yell at the top of his lungs.

Meanwhile Miss Sybil was beginning to realize what had happened. "Get out of here!" she screamed hysterically. "I'm ruined!! You're fired! Who is that man! I'm compromised! You'll have to marry me!"

Patricia backed out of the chaos and opened the door to the hallway, knowing that she had surely done it now. They'd have to let her go, but at least she'd leave in style.

And then there was another scream. This one more urgent, more insistent. It was Violet's voice. "She's dead! I can't wake her up!"

Judge Chase strode briskly from his end of the mansion, pushed aside his two daughters who had been awakened by the commotion, and took charge. "Call the doctor."

Many hours later, the servants were assembled in the servants' dining room. The Judge had ordered it. Two detectives had come. "I wonder what they'll want from us," Emma said.

"I don't know," Patricia replied. "Just ask some fool questions so they think they're important."

A uniformed policeman appeared at the door. "Miss Violet?"

Violet left with him, amid whispers as to why she was chosen first. Ten minutes later she returned, smiling a half smile, her eyelids drooping to the sides.

"Patricia Carrick?" the cop asked.

Patricia patted Emma's hand and followed the policeman to the Judge's study.

The two detectives looked up at her when she came in. The Judge sat behind his neat massive desk. On the walls were photographs and memorabilia from his career.

The first detective asked, "Are you Patricia Carrick?"

"Yes, sir."

"What did you think of Mrs. Amelia Chase?"

"She was a troubled woman. I was sorry for her."

"Did you ever say, 'She ought to be put out of her misery'?"

Patricia shook her head and looked over at the Judge. His face was creased with worry. "No, sir."

The second detective said, "Miss Carrick, did you ever tell Miss Violet Wilson that Mrs. Chase would be better off dead?"

"No, sir," Patricia said adamantly. "I never even met Mrs. Chase until last night."

The first detective held up Mrs. Chase's medicine bottle. "Have you ever seen this bottle?"

"Yes, sir. It's Mrs. Chase's medicine bottle. Her cough mixture."

"Did you give her her medicine last night after dinner?"

Patricia hesitated. It felt as if somebody were loosening the earth beneath her feet. "Yes, sir. She asked me to." She looked around and knew that somebody was framing her. Apparently Violet's rage knew no bounds.

A uniformed policeman entered the room and handed a piece of paper to the two detectives. They read it. Looked up at Patricia. The three men whispered together. The uniformed policeman made an exit. The second detective said, "Miss Carrick, you are under arrest for the murder of Mrs. Amelia Chase."

"You're not serious!"

"Very serious. This piece of paper, a pharmacy receipt for the poison that killed Mrs. Chase, the same poison found in this medicine bottle, was just found among your personal effects on the third floor."

"Somebody put it there!"

"You'll get your chance to tell a court of law what you think, ma'am. We have the testimony of Miss Violet Wilson as well as this evidence and your admission that you administered the fatal dose to the late Mrs. Chase." The policeman's voice betrayed no sign of the fact that he knew the pretty woman was being railroaded.

"Judge, help me," Patricia said.

He shook his head. His expression was stern, full of contempt. "No, I shall not."

The door opened behind Patricia. Three uniformed policemen entered. "Let's go, miss."

Patricia looked back at the Judge. "You son of a bitch!"

"Take her, lads," the second detective said.

"Thank you, your honor," the first detective said.

The Judge nodded grimly, satisfied for the time being that his crime would go unpunished.

CHAPTER FIVE

THE cell was slippery from the human wastes which had accumulated over the years. Every morning one of the Trustys hosed down the floor, but her efforts were careless and perfunctory. Mold grew on the walls. The only light came from a kerosene lantern in the corridor outside the cell.

Patricia Carrick walked into the cell and, when the iron gate clanged behind her, she was its twelfth occupant. The inmates all wore grey smocks that buttoned at the throat and extended straight down to the ankles. It took a few minutes before her eyes adjusted to the darkness.

Two of the women were passed out in their own vomit. Another stared at a single spot on the wall, her gaze never wavering. Yet another sang snatches of patriotic songs until someone screamed "Shut up!" and she apologized.

The others turned to stare at the "new meat" who stood at the entrance to the cell. Patricia avoided their gaze and looked at the walls where ten cots had been hinged and chained. "Which is mine?" she asked a

131

nearby woman with black stringy hair and crossed eyes.

"Bunk?"

"Yes."

"Depends how strong you are."

Patricia nodded and walked around the perimeter of the room. She stopped at the furthest bunk and sat down, her elbows on her knees.

"That's mine," a loud voice called.

Patricia looked around to see who had spoken.

A tall, broad-shouldered woman with grey hair and an underslung jaw rose from the bunk where she had been sitting and sauntered over to stand in front of Patricia. "I said, you're sitting on my bunk."

Patricia stood up and looked up at the woman. "Then would you mind telling me where I might sit down?"

"They're all mine," the tall strong woman said. "I rent them out to whoever I like. I don't like you."

"What's the going price?" Patricia asked. She put her hands on her hips.

The woman laughed. Her breath was foul, her teeth rotted painfully. "Ask one of them," she said.

Patricia looked at a mousey-looking girl with blonde hair and a sorry expression on her face. The girl looked down at the slimey floor.

"Tell the new meat," the strong woman said.

"You gotta . . . beat her up."

Patricia looked at the overbearing woman. "You got a nice racket going here," she said softly.

"So far, so good," she said. "You wanta buy in?"

Patricia kept her face totally devoid of expression. "Sure," she said, smiling into the woman's eyes. Then, with absolutely no warning, she eased forward, and brought a roundhouse right hand square into the woman's uncovered solar plexus. There was a loud explosion of breath, the woman's eyes glassed over, and she went down, unconscious.

"Shit," one of the other women whispered.

"Damn," another said.

The rest just stared in silent awe.

Patricia smiled grimly. "I wish getting out of here was as easy," she thought. Her brother had taught her how to fight.

Patricia woke sometime after dawn. She had slept, on and off, for only a few hours. The bully of the cell had woken up, vowing revenge.

A Trusty came down the corridor with a garbage can full of thick gruel which she ladled into metal bowls and handed through the bars to each of the inmates. "Where's the spoons?" Patricia asked.

"Governor don't want you havin' 'em," the Trusty said. "Afraid you'll use 'em as knives."

Patricia went back to her bunk and tried to eat the bland paste by tipping her bowl, but she was only reasonably successful. Finally, she put her bowl aside with half the porridge uneaten.

"You gonna eat that?" the tall strong woman asked.

"You want it?" Patricia replied.

The woman nodded.

"As long as you and me are friends," Patricia said, extending her hand.

The other inmates watched carefully to see what the monster would do.

Slowly she extended her hand and took Patricia's as if she had never shaken any person's hand before. She smiled.

"I'm called Patricia."

"Grace."

"Have a seat," Patricia said. Grace nodded and sat down on Patricia's bed and began to eat her gruel with her fingers.

When she was finished, Grace looked at her new friend and said, "Thank you."

Before Patricia could reply, one of the turnkeys came briskly down the corridor and shouted, "Carrick! Front and center. Everyone else back away from the gate." She rapped the bars with her three foot long truncheon of white ash.

"Watch her," Grace whispered. "She's bad."

Patricia nodded and took her place by the gate as the turnkey opened it. "Out and to the left!" Patricia walked into the corridor and turned left.

As soon as they were out of sight of the cells, the guard brought her stick down hard across Patricia's buttocks. The pain was hot and intense. The blow made her stumble. "Stand up straight!" the guard shouted. Again she brought her weapon down.

This time Patricia was ready. She turned slightly and the cruel guard fell forward with the empty blow. "You think you're cute?" the guard rasped. Her eyes were narrow-set. Her hair was black, braided on top of her head. Her lips were as grey as her skin. She lashed out with her truncheon again, catching Patricia across the backs of her legs.

Patricia crumpled up like an empty sack, headlong on the cold stone floor of the corridor. When she looked up she saw the sturdy black leather shoes of the guard.

"New meat," the guard said, "you'll know me better by the time they hang you up to dry. My name is Officer Burke. You do what I say and we'll get along."

Patricia nodded.

"You got any money?"

"No, ma'am."

"I can make your time easier if you have some dough. You think about it."

"Yes, ma'am."

"Get up." Patricia stood up and Officer Burke escorted her the rest of the way down the corridor without incident. "In here," Burke said, pointing to a wide oak door.

"Grant? Grant Yarrow?"

Grant Yarrow stood tall in the small visitors' room. Next to him was a balding man with muttonchops and a permanently surprised expression on his face. "Miss Carrick. You don't look better for the wear," he said. As soon as Officer Burke had gone they sat down at the single table in the room.

"Why did you come?" Patricia asked. Her mind was whirling, making no connections. She'd had too little sleep, too little food. Why was the man she hated, the man she'd poured scalding cocoa on, sitting nicely, neatly and handsomely across the rough table from her. Why was he smiling?

"I figured you needed a friend," Grant said, "and though you may think to the contrary, I am the very best friend you've got." He pointed to the man with the impish features. "This is Mr. Frank Jervais, the best lawyer in San Francisco."

"I can't afford a lawyer," Patricia said. "So, I thank you for your efforts, but you may—" She started to stand, but Grant stopped her with a look.

"Patricia, this is hardly the time for your Irish pride to surface once again. I am retaining Mr. Jervais with my own funds because you're being railroaded."

"Miss Carrick," Lawyer Jervais said, "the circumstantial evidence against you is fairly impressive."

"Could you put that into the Queen's English?" Patricia said.

Grant leaned across the table. "It means that Judge Chase is powerful enough to get you hanged if we don't pin this murder on him and make it stick!"

"Mrs. Chase was always saying they were trying to poison her," Patricia said.

"Did she say who *they* were?"

Patricia shook her head. "I guess I understood her to mean the Judge."

"Who else?" Jervais asked.

Patricia scratched her head.

And then she remembered the story about the house on Sacramento Street, "the little secret" which Amelia Chase had rambled on about. And the green emerald. She told Grant and the lawyer what she could.

"It isn't much," the lawyer said.

"But it might give us some leverage on the Judge," Grant said. "The last thing he needs right now is a public scandal."

Patricia watched the men talk about whether she would live or die and could not believe she had come to this sorry pass. Grant stood up and walked to where she sat. He put his strong wide hands on her shoulders. "Don't worry, my little Irish shamrock. I won't let them hang you. Even if I have to borrow money from my father's banks to buy off the executioner."

Patricia stood up, flushed. "There's cold comfort in your words, Grant Yarrow. Especially when it's your father should be hanging, not me!" Her face was crimson, her breathing shallow as she let the weeks and months' worth of frustrations and anguish out at the man who was trying to help her.

Grant reached out and pulled her to him. "We'll do what we can. We'll do what we can."

Grant Yarrow did some preliminary checking with contacts in the real estate business and then set off for the northern end of Sacramento Street.

The little white house was bordered with daisies and showed signs that a very active gardener took great care with the plantings. Grant sat in a closed carriage across the street for a few hours watching the residents come and go. A knife grinder set up shop for an hour, giving Grant the opportunity to observe the woman who lived in the white house. She was tall, in her thirties, Junoesque. She was very familiar, Grant thought.

A half hour later he remembered where he'd seen the woman. "Annette Marchand, 'The Girl on the Satin Divan'!" Grant laughed aloud. At the Empress Saloon, one of the most popular in the city, patronized by everyone of importance, there was a larger than life painting of a beautiful woman on a satin divan. She was clothed in fairies' gossamer and was the subject of more fantasies than Jenny Lind had ever been. "The Girl on the Satin Divan," Grant said. He shuddered a little himself to think of the happy moments he had spent in front of the bar at the Empress admiring this real life flesh and blood woman. "If only I'd known!" he muttered.

His musings about the sumptuous model were cut short when he heard a carriage approach and stop outside the little white house. Judge Chase stepped down from the coach and gave orders for the driver to return in an hour. "An hour wouldn't be half long enough with that one," Grant said to himself.

Grant waited for twenty minutes, allowing for as much hesitation as possible, and then walked quickly to the rear of the little white house on Sacramento. The back door was locked, but the kitchen window was up to catch the slight breeze. Grant stepped through and listened.

Voices.

He stepped quietly to the door that led to the living room and put his ear against it.

". . . I said don't worry, my love. The little Mick girl is going to drop for it."

"I'm scared, Russell."

"My alibi is perfect."

"But what about me? I bought the poison! I'm an accessory. . . ." She paused, whimpered. "I wish I had never been a party to this. We could have gone on like we were."

"No, my pet. No. There are reasons. I need the money now."

Grant nodded and retraced his steps. A half hour later he was standing in front of the pharmacist who had written the receipt for the poison.

"What did she look like? The police never asked me," the pharmacist said. "They already had her. I'll tell you she was beautiful."

"Color of her hair?"

"Brown. Like a chestnut."

"Eyes?"

"I don't know. The same I guess. Brown."

"Height?"

"She was tall for a woman, I'll tell you. Maybe five-eight or ten?"

"Would you like to go for a drink?"

"Beg pardon?"

"I want you to see somebody at the Empress."

The pharmacist shrugged. "If it'll help your client, sure."

When they reached the Empress Saloon it was almost five. The free lunch had been removed and now a broad table was being laid with all sorts of wonderful free delights.

"Well, I'll be!" the pharmacist said aloud.

"What?" Grant said.

"There she is!"

"Who?"

"The woman who bought the poison! Right there with no clothes on!" He pointed his stubby fingers directly at the painting of the Girl on the Satin Divan.

CHAPTER SIX

PATRICIA sat with her back against the cold wet wall. Grace sat, with her back to her and let Patricia plait her hair. "Officer Burke runs this place," Grace said. "The Governor is 'sposed to, but Burke's got the power."

"What did you do?"

"Hunh?"

"What are you accused of?" Patricia asked.

Grace started to turn around to look with incredulity at her new friend, but she couldn't because Patricia had a hank of her hair. "You don't know who I am?"

Patricia shook her head. "I'm sorry."

Grace let her mouth pout. "I was in all the papers. They even sent a man out from New York to take my picture."

"You must have done something horrible."

"I killed my husband with a meat axe and stuffed his frigging body in a pickle barrel. We owned a little store."

Patricia frowned. "That looks much better," she said.

Grace turned around. "My husband was a bastard. Slept with all the women customers and beat me every chance he got. I finally had enough. He was coshing me with a mallet; I picked up the axe and sliced him up like yesterday's dinner. Jeeze, but I was mad." She looked up into Patricia's eyes. "I hope you ain't disappointed."

Patricia shook her head. "I don't blame you. If a man did that to me, I might just as well be in your shoes." She paused. "Won't you get out on self-defense?"

Grace laughed. "Not on your life. I already had my trial. They're gonna hang me in a month."

Patricia looked into the woman's face. Her grey hair made her look old, but she was only thirty. Her bad teeth were a legacy from her husband—he had refused to let her go to the dentist. She was going to die and she knew it. She felt she had nothing to lose. "They can't," Patricia said.

Grace smiled as best she could. "Tell them that. My old man deserved what he got. I'd do it again if I could."

"Carrick! Carrick! Get your butt out here!" Officer Burke cried from the corridor.

Grace shook her head slowly. "I'd like to get my hands on that one before they stretch me," she whispered.

Patricia tried to smile, stood up and walked out the cell door.

"Left face," Burke said. She held her truncheon in her right hand and beat a slow rhythm with it upon her left palm.

Patricia turned slowly and began walking towards the core of the jail. Each step down the long corridor took her further from witnesses, further from help.

"That's far enough," Burke said.

Patricia turned. "What is it?"

Burke's face was sour, twisted. "I don't know how you did it, sister, but you're out. I just want you to know if I ever see you again in here you're dead meat."

"I'm out?"

Burke spat on the floor. "Get your street clothes in there. Hurry your butt."

Patricia walked into the small cubicle and dressed in a daze. She hurried as fast as she could just in case it was some horrible dream or a trick that Burke was playing.

She signed for her clothes, got her locket that had once belonged to her mother, and walked out into the long slanting rays of a perfect San Francisco afternoon.

"Patricia?" a familiar voice called from a closed carriage that waited outside.

"Grant?"

Grant smiled and stepped down to extend his hand. "Your brothers are waiting for you at your flat."

Patricia took his warm strong hand and let him help her up the step and into the beautiful carriage. She felt as if she had just walked through some magical door and entered a kingdom where handsome princes slew evil witches and carried princesses off in coaches.

Grant gave his driver the address. The driver looked surprised, shrugged, and whipped up the perfectly matched team.

"How?" Patricia asked. "How did you get me out?"

"We followed your lead and discovered that the Judge's mistress had bought the poison that they gave Mrs. Chase."

"Did they arrest the Judge?"

Grant shook his head. "I had to convince him it was in his best interests to disappear for awhile. It's very complicated and not very legal, I'm afraid." He smiled, flashing his sparkling white teeth. "But the important thing is that you are out and all charges have been dropped."

Patricia could do nothing but smile. She looked out the window and took a deep breath. "Thank you," she said. "I don't think I want to know how you did it."

"You are entirely welcome, believe me." Grant watched her carefully. She was truly an exquisite woman. Her long elegant jawline, her small sculpted ears, her delicate curve of throat . . . He catalogued her beauty as if he were an art student before a masterpiece.

"Oh! We must stop!" Patricia cried out.

"Why?" Grant said, alarmed.

"Grace, the woman who killed her husband. They're going to hang her! We must stop them. You saved me! We have to save her!"

Grant leaned back and furrowed his brows. "Grace who?"

Patricia looked confused. "I don't know her last name. She killed her husband and stuffed him in a pickle barrel."

Grant smiled. "Grace the Butcher?"

"She said she was notorious."

"She certainly is. Grace the Butcher Malone. The

jury took six minutes to decide. Nobody can save her."

Patricia's face flushed with anger and frustration. "But she was just protecting herself. Her husband beat her. He pushed her too far."

Grant shook his head. "I don't think anybody can save Grace Malone."

"Please ask Mr. Jervais, the lawyer, to see what he can do. Heaven knows what kind of lawyer she had."

Grant nodded. "Yes, Miss Carrick."

"Oh, I didn't mean to order you around."

"Of course you did, but I'll be happy to have Mr. Jervais take a look at the case."

"Thank you." Patricia paused. "I'm sorry for Miss Sybil and her sisters." She looked sidelong at Grant to see what kind of reaction she would get at the mention of his latest conquest.

"They are well cared for. Their mother's estate is very substantial."

Patricia looked down at her hands. They were still dirty from that place.

"Well," Grant said, "here is where I must get out."

"What?"

"I have some business to attend to. My life is not my own. Not for awhile. My driver will take you home and look after you. Good luck, Miss Carrick, until we meet again. Please try to stay out of trouble."

"But, how can I repay you?"

He smiled. Angled his head to the side. "Don't meet some fast-talking Irishman and fall in love. Wait for me." As soon as he had spoken, he turned, left the carriage and was out of sight.

Patricia leaned out to try to see him on the crowded sidewalk, but he was gone without a trace. The carriage rolled forward, jerking her back into the seat.

She couldn't believe what had just happened to her. Who was this Grant Yarrow? What was he doing?

When the carriage stopped in front of her home Patricia stepped down, leaning on the arm of the coachman, and thanked him. He smiled, bowed, and handed her an envelope. "Mr. Yarrow asked me to give you this, Miss." He tipped his hat and drove away, leaving Patricia to watch the dust from his wheels. The neighbors craned their necks and wondered whether what they had just seen was from a dream or did not Patricia Carrick just drive up in a millionaire's coach?

Still standing in the street, Patricia opened the envelope. Inside was a bank draft for two hundred dollars and a note which read:

"I pray you will accept this help from a very good friend. Some day you will understand. I had no hand in Joseph's death. I am working to bring his killers to justice."

It was signed, "Grant."

Patricia looked down the hill where the coach was travelling and breathed a sigh. "It may be Yarrow money, but it will help Christopher and that's a fact!" she said. "The rest will go into the Carrick Bank."

Downtown, San Francisco kept up its frantic race for the Twentieth Century. Horsecars were crammed with nickel riders; handcarts, buggies, landaus and caleches bore down upon one another as if progress could be measured in near misses and collisions. A tenderloin dinner cost 50 cents.

CHAPTER SEVEN

THE fields crackled in the hot night air as a land breeze insinuated itself through the dry crops. A pale sliver of moon hung lifeless in the dome of sky. Will Lacey rolled the empty bottle down his leg and let it drop to the dusty ground. "No damn good noways," he muttered.

In the background the lights from the Mexican lanterns at the Yarrow ranch bored yellow holes in the night. A mariachi band played faintly.

Simon Yarrow had refused to see him. "Entertaining his daughter, my asshole," Will said. He knew all about Diana Yarrow. "Fucks everything what moves," he said. Will tried to stand, then fell back onto the side of the road. He leaned forward and grabbed his knees, then sort of rolled into a semi-upright position. "Fucks everything that moves," he repeated. He liked remembering Diana Yarrow.

Will stumbled a mile or so from home before he began to notice the voices inside his gin-soaked brain. At first he thought he was hearing his wife and children. Damn Mary-Margaret anyways, he thought. Always talking. Women always talked. Didn't mean nothing. Just talk.

"Hey, Will."

"Who is it?"

"Hey, Will."

"What?"

"Hey, Will."

"Spirits," he thought. "Spirits of the night. Indian hants." He quickened his pace. There was a lantern on the front porch a mile distant.

"Hey, Will."

"Hey, Joseph." Now he was hearing his own voice inside his head. Talking to Joseph Carrick just like he did the night Joseph died.

"Patricia coming along?"

"Yes, Joseph. She asked me to ask you to wait. She's lookin' after Mary-Margaret and the baby."

Joseph smiled. *"How is the baby?"*

"Cries all the time. That's all they ever do, though."

Will Lacey began to run to get away from the voice of his late brother-in-law, Joseph Carrick. The grain cracked against his trouser legs as he ran across the fields. The moon eased behind a ragged cloud.

"What's the axe handle for, Will?" Joseph asked.

"I don't have to answer," Will shouted to the night air.

"What's the axe handle for, Will?" the disembodied voice repeated.

"Please don't make me answer," Will cried.

Will stopped a few yards from his own front porch. The children and Mary-Margaret were asleep. He felt safe in the circle of lanternlight. He turned to face the night.

"What's the axe handle for, Will?" the voice of Joseph asked.

Will knelt down in the dirt and nodded. "Nothin', just in case I see a snake or somethin'," he said softly.

Joseph nodded, turned away and looked down into the swirling waters of the canal. *"When did Patricia say she'd be comin'?"*

Will saw himself again—as he had seen himself so many times since that evening—rise up on the balls of his feet, swing the axe handle high over his head and bring it down hard on Joseph's skull.

The sounds were the worst part. He could close his eyes and press on the lids as hard as he dared to make the sight go away, but he couldn't stop the sounds of the flesh and bone crushing under his blow. He couldn't stop the sound of the splashing water as the body rolled down the embankment.

Will was drained. He looked up as the moon emerged. "I must find the axe handle," he said. "If I burn the axe handle, I'll be free of the hants." The logic of it was irrefutable to him. Kill the weapon that killed the man and the nightmares would die with it.

Inside the barn Will's lanternlight sprayed between the legs of their only cow and the one remaining plow-horse. "It's here," he whispered. Will went to the feed bin and pulled it back from the wall.

The axehandle lay among the rat-droppings on the chewed wooden floor. It was covered with dust, but the blood of Joseph Carrick had long since been washed clean. Will Lacey picked it up and took it to the middle of the barn where he laid the offending instrument on the floor. He then covered it with lamp oil and set it ablaze.

"Now I'll be free," he said. His thick-rimmed eyes were wild and round. His heavy lips were constantly bathed by his tongue which flashed in and out repeatedly. He breathed intermittently, pausing when he could to catch his breath.

The flames from the pyre for the weapon which had killed Joseph were not particular. They did not care that they were now rapidly consuming the floor of the barn along with the accumulated hay and feed. They did not care one way or the other when they leaped up the barn's side walls as long as they were fed a constant diet of combustibles.

Will squatted and watched the pyre, unmindful of the heat and smoke or the agitated cries of the animals. He was doing what was right. Now he would be free of his nightmare memories.

Will did not notice anything when the full weight of the barn's central roofbeam crushed his skull.

Mary-Margaret awakened when she heard the animals shrieking. She ran to the side windows. The barn glowed a furious orange-red. The sparks had ignited the field which ran behind the barn and the fire was bearing down on the farmhouse. She ran to the children's rooms and wakened them. She told the oldest child to take them to the main road and wait for her while she went looking for the animals and Will.

"Will?" she cried as soon as she was sure the little ones were on their way to safety. "Will?"

The barn glowed as white as a new shoe on the blacksmith's anvil. The animals' shrieks were still. "Will?" she screamed.

The fire chewed up the stalks of grain wholesale, its front growing ever wider. When Mary-Margaret turned to follow her fleeing children, she saw that the fire now engulfed both sides of the narrow track, barring that escape. "Oh, God, I hope they made it," she said. "I'll go up to the north field and cut over to the road."

A few minutes later Mary-Margaret stopped to get her bearings in the dense grain. "If I cut over now," she said, "I'll make it."

But the fire had raced faster. The smoke clogged her nose as it bore down on her. She turned to the right and hoped she could make it to the Yarrow land that adjoined.

But two arms of fire raced along with her on either side, finally linking hot fingers on the Yarrow land. Every way Mary-Margaret Carrick Lacey looked there was fire. "It isn't fair!" she screamed.

Before the fire was finally put out at dawn, the greedy flames had consumed thirteen animals, twenty farm buildings and a thousand acres of crops, half of which belonged to Will Lacey and half to Simon Yarrow.

As the sun climbed higher, five orphaned Lacey children stood round-eyed and lost, surveying the blackened fields.

CHAPTER EIGHT

FIVE of them.

The driver on the tall ice truck looked at them and wondered what the hell the world was coming to. Five kids, with a bandana's worth of worldly goods among them. The oldest boy, Stephen, looked like he could handle himself on a farm, but not in this town.

Stephen repeated the address.

The iceman, a tanned giant Irishman, nodded. "It's about six miles from here," he said.

"Which way?" Stephen asked.

The iceman shrugged. "Northeast." He paused. "But that won't help ya much."

"I'm much obliged," Stephen said. He was sandy-haired, serious and strong with piercing eyes.

The iceman watched him lead the little group across the street. The youngest couldn't be more than two, he thought. "Hey there!"

"Sir?" Stephen said.

"I go near there on the way home. Hop up on the wagon and I'll give you a drop off."

"We can't pay you anything."

151

The iceman's eyes narrowed. "I didn't ask for anything."

Stephen smiled. "In that case, thank you very much."

"Yeah, yeah. Just don't let that little one piss on the ice."

The Lacey children helped each other up onto the open ice truck. The little ones squeezed onto the bench seat next to the driver, Mr. O'Connor, and the older ones sat on the burlap bags which rested right behind.

Mr. O'Connor thought they must be crazy going to that neighborhood until the eldest told him they were orphans going to stay with their aunt. Aunt, he thought. Probably a whore shacking up there with some son of a bitch.

They had finished dropping off a fifty pound block for the watercooler at the National Bank of San Francisco and a hundred pounds at the Poodle Dog and a hundred and fifty pounds at the Maison Doree. Then, as the afternoon turned cloudy, Mr. O'Connor turned his team north. They were a nice bunch of kids, he thought. He was just sorry they had to wind up in this overcrowded city of hard-luck stories.

It took an hour before the ice truck eased to a stop on the hill where Patricia Carrick lived. Mr. O'Connor put the brake on hard and dropped a brick behind each wheel. Then he helped the children down to the street. "Thank you, Mr. O'Connor," Stephen said.

"Does your aunt know you're coming?" he asked in his still-thick brogue.

Stephen shook his head. "There wasn't time," he replied.

"Stephen?" a voice cried from the rut which served as a sidewalk. "Babies?"

"Aunt Patricia!" Molly, the second oldest, yelled.

Mr. O'Connor stood aside as the mass of little ones streaked to the very beautiful colleen who held a string bag with a couple of loaves of bread in it. The children leaped upon their aunt and wept and cheered.

Patricia was nearly bowled over. She wept with the little ones and laughed with Stephen and Molly. "Where's your Ma and Dad?"

Their faces told the answer to her question.

Patricia put a hand to her mouth. "Oh, God rest their souls."

"There was a fire," Will, Jr. said.

"I'm so sorry."

"We woulda gone to Mary-Elizabeth's, but they was all sick with the fever," Molly said.

It suddenly sunk in on Patricia that they had come to live with her. She looked at their sweet dear faces. They clung to her skirt. They had no suitcases, no changes of clothes. She tried a little smile. "Well, we've got each other, don't we?" she said. And then she saw the tall brawny iceman who stood uncomfortably on one brogan then the other. "I'm sorry, sir. My name is Patricia Carrick."

He tipped his cap. "Edward O'Connor of Cork, Ma'am. Is it Missus Carrick?"

Patricia shook her head.

Ed smiled. "It was my pleasure to bring these children from the docks."

"He didn't charge us a thing. In fact," Stephen said, "he gave us this five dollar gold piece!"

Ed O'Connor blushed.

"My family doesn't need charity, Mr. O'Connor," Patricia said politely but firmly.

Ed shook his head. "T'weren't charity, ma'am. The oldest there helped me on my deliveries." He looked at Stephen and winked, hoping the boy would lie along with him. He'd given the boy the money because he'd felt so damned sorry for them all.

"That's right, Aunt Patricia."

Patricia smiled and took the gold piece. "I'll put it in 'the Carrick Bank' so I can buy you babies some clothes." She curtseyed to Mr. O'Connor. "Thank you very much, sir. For everything."

"You're welcome, ma'am." He watched as she herded the children up the alley to the back stairs. "Miss Carrick?"

"Yes, Mr. O'Connor?"

"Might I stop back sometime to look in on their progress?"

Patricia looked confused.

"To see how my little friends are faring?"

She smiled. "That would be very kind of you, Mr. O'Connor."

She'd bedded them all down in her cot and Patrick's cot and on the floor. Then she sat on the back steps and watched the moon glide skyward. Patricia's soul was troubled, her mind agitated. "Dear Lord," she said to herself, "there isn't money enough for Patrick and me, much less five babes. And then I must send Christopher money in Denver." She smiled to think that Christopher was feeling better now that he was out of the damp air. His last letter indicated that he might be able to look for work soon.

The moon eased on its arc.

Patricia knew where Patrick was. Probably drinking whatever he made on the docks. She got up and fetched "the Carrick Bank," the cracked old crockpot, and counted the contents. "Eighty-two dollars," she said, "including the five dollars from Mr. O'Connor." She knew he and Stephen had lied. The man had felt sorry for the waifs and that was that. He had a big heart, that iceman did.

"Money is supposed to make money," she thought. "But I'm sure as shooting not going to put this in any bank around here." She remembered all too well when the Bank of California closed its doors on account of William Ralston's wild speculations with the depositors' money. They'd found Ralston floating in the Bay. "Well," she thought, "it's a damned sure thing that I'm going to have to find out how to get us Carricks some more money."

She looked up at the starry heavens and wondered if Mary-Margaret and Joseph could see what had become of the little clan. Then she went to bed, nestling on the floor between Molly and Catherine.

The next morning Patricia awoke, fed the children some of the bread she had bought and put Stephen in charge. "When I come back I want to see this place spotless." She paused. "If your uncle Patrick ever comes back, tell him not to leave before I can talk to him, all right?"

"Yes, Aunt Patricia."

She kissed them all on their foreheads and left. She didn't take the trolley all crammed to the running boards with late-to-worker workers. "Rich folks can afford it," she said as she walked the hills toward the downtown area.

She missed lunch at midday as the sun stood south, a reminder of approaching winter. "Shouldn't be spending our reserves for lunch," she said.

By two o'clock in the afternoon Patricia had knocked upon no less than sixty-six different doors. Some, like those of restaurants which weren't hiring waitresses, emitted lovely smells of roast meats. Others, like those of offices which weren't hiring clerks, smelled dusty and musty, like attics.

Patricia's flimsily-clad feet moved slowly uphill as the army of fortunate workers swarmed homewards. "Can't complain," she said to herself. "I did the best I could. Tomorrow is another day."

That night she told the children she "had every expectation of getting a position tomorrow." The children cheered and clapped their hands.

Four more days passed. Patricia had found no work. On the sixth day she walked two houses down and across the street. There was a rumor that Mrs. Kierney had gotten a few sewing jobs recently. Perhaps she needed help. Men and boys were swinging their lunch-pails on the way to work. Whistles blew far away signalling the time left before the day would begin. "Mrs. Kierney?" she called.

Mrs. Kierney appeared at her front door, her hair done up in a dust cap, her features as chiselled as any Greek statue, her forehead in a perpetual frown from sixty-three years of fault-finding. "Miss Carrick, is it? And what on earth are you going to do with five more mouths to feed?"

Patricia smiled. She never ceased being amazed at how fast gossip travelled in the little community. "That's kind of what I wanted to talk to you about, Ma'am."

"I don't want any children," she said, beginning to close the door, "I've had enough of my own. Seven lived past childhood and none of them are worth a tinker's damn. Good day, Miss Carrick."

"No, Mrs. Kierney. You misunderstand. I know you do sewing. I was wondering if you ever had any extra to do, you might consider me. My niece is eleven and she can help as well."

Mrs. Kierney stopped closing the door. She squinted. "I never heard you could use a needle."

"Give me a chance, ma'am," Patricia said breathlessly.

"There's a costume ball in a couple of weeks," Mrs. Kierney said grudgingly. "I've been worked to death. I used Lily, but her eyesight's not what it was and some of my ladies are complaining." She paused to add weight to her next statement. "My ladies won't use just anyone." She paused again. "Come inside."

Patricia marvelled at all the fancy garments hung around the large workroom. "They're beautiful," she breathed.

"We do better work than London or Paris," Mrs. Kierney said. "Most of my ladies know that but the fancy folks don't. Here, let me see your work."

Patricia took the two pieces of silk she was given and lined them up on her lap. They were darts for an elegant pale green bodice designed to go with a pastoral shepherdess' costume. At first her fingers were stiff and refused to work with the precision she knew she was capable of.

Mrs. Kierney snorted through her long thin nose.

But shortly Patricia's stitches were neat, even, tight and, to a seamstress looking for help, beautiful. Patricia smiled.

Mrs. Kierney snorted and frowned. "I'll give you more work than you can do. You'll break your back and lose your eyesight in the bargain."

Patricia could hardly contain her joy. "There are five little babies over there. They're hungry and they need clothes. I don't think I have much choice, do you, Mrs. Kierney?"

The old woman made her tight face smile.

"No, Stephen," Patricia cried, exasperated. "I tell you what. Since you can't stitch very well, you'll be our cutter."

The twelve year old gleefully dropped the material and the needle and thread. He hated sewing. It was a black art that Molly could do. He was a male and males were not ever admitted to the inner circle of these arts. "Thank you, Aunt Patricia."

Patricia put her hands on her hips and looked around the apartment. Molly was already halfway through the bodice of the pale green shepherdess' costume. Will, Jr. was carrying fabric and costumes back and forth to Mrs. Kierney's across the street, and Catherine, at five years, was taking care of Charley, the two year old, and making sure he didn't mess up the work. "Charley, watch out for the feathers!"

Charley stopped himself before toppling over a basket of ostrich feathers that were supposed to go onto some sort of Sun King costume for Mr. Larrabee.

"Here," Patricia called to Stephen. "Lay out that black cotton there and put this template over it. Pin it down and cut along the edges. Cut carefully and let's see what our man of the house can do."

Stephen said, "Yes, ma'am!" and bit down on his tongue as he went about his job.

At seven o'clock that evening they were still busily at work, turning out costumes and parts of costumes, running them over to Mrs. Kierney's for approval and bringing back new sections for construction. They were bone-tired.

On the second evening Patrick Carrick showed up dirty and unshaven. He stood unsteadily in the doorway and looked at the scene. No one noticed him. He recognized the children and wondered what had become of Mary-Margaret. He saw the fancy-dress costumes and wondered what Patricia had taken on.

He was still lean, even after his months of drinking, still handsome even after all he had done to himself, all the fights he had picked. But, as he stood in the darkened doorway looking at the exhausted family working in the dim lamplight, he began to weep quietly. The tears made clean sluiceways in the dirt of his cheeks. He wept for the children, for Patricia who had suffered so much, and for himself. He had made so many mistakes.

"Patty," he whispered.

Patricia looked up from her work to see that all the children had fallen asleep at their jobs and that her younger brother stood weeping in the doorway. She rose and went to him. "Patrick, what's the matter, my love?"

"I am so sorry."

She smiled. "Me too."

He reached out and hugged her. "I tell you, Patricia, it's all gonna be different now. I'm off liquor." He paused. "What happened to Mary-Margaret and Will?"

"There was a fire. They died."

"Mary-Elizabeth?"

"Fever. Stephen said she'll be fine soon."

Patrick cried anew for his sister. "I'll be pulling my weight around here starting tomorrow," he said.

"We need you very much," Patricia said.

He smiled as he tried to make his way into the small apartment. "It looks like we'll need a new home too."

CHAPTER NINE

"CHARLEY?"

The two year old waddled forward under the eyes of his aunt and uncle and brothers and sisters. He held out his right hand. Patricia put a bright penny in it. "That's for your help on the Claridge ball gown," Patricia said.

Charley looked at the coin, gripped it tightly, then handed it back to his aunt. "Keep," he said.

"That's the smart lad," Patrick said. He put down his mug of tea and took the boy on his lap. "Some day you'll be rich if you let Patricia save it for you." Only that afternoon Patrick himself had turned over his whole week's wages to her: a grand sum of eleven dollars. Somehow, despite all his previous boozing and carrying-on, he'd managed to keep his job on the docks.

Stephen looked at the four cents his aunt had given him and smiled. "Keep," he said as he handed the coins back to her.

Patricia laughed aloud and almost startled herself with the sound. In four short weeks the Carricks and

161

the Laceys had become a small business, turning out costumes for Mrs. Kierney and nearly making ends meet. They ate meat once a week, they had tea twice a day, and each child now had a change of clothes. Patricia was saving so that soon they could buy clothes good enough to go to church in.

"Time for bed, all," she said. "Tomorrow we have to get the Shipley order. Mrs. Kierney says it's all peacock feathers—"

"—Booo!" the children cried.

"—And lacework—"

"—Hiss!" the children cried.

"To bed with you," Patrick said. He went from pallet to pallet and kissed each child good-night. Patricia followed him and then turned the lamp down low.

Patricia found her brother sitting out on the steps in the light of the stars. She sat next to him. "You've done well," he said.

Patricia nodded. "I hope business will keep up after this foolish costume ball."

"Tell them to have another."

"I wish it were that easy," she said.

Patrick finished his tea. "Things are going all right on the docks. Now that I'm not always falling in the hatches."

Patricia laughed.

"Mr. Barton said he thought I might be made hold boss next year."

"Does that pay better?"

"Dollar a day better."

Patricia's eyebrows went up. "That's two hundred and sixty dollars a year!"

Patrick nodded and then turned towards the sound of footsteps. "Who is it?"

"Only me, Mr. Carrick. Mrs. Kierney."

Patrick rose and let the exhausted old woman by. "Is there something wrong?" Patricia asked quickly.

"Not with you Carricks' work," she said.

Patricia breathed a sigh of relief.

"No, it's my fool son Tom."

Patrick, sensing he was not wanted for the conversation, excused himself and went to bed.

Mrs. Kierney sat and looked at the Milky Way with Patricia. "He was fired today."

"I'm sorry, Mrs. Kierney."

"My given name is Maude."

"Maude."

Some of the starlight winked on the tears that dotted Maude's cheeks. "He's always been trouble. Always. The cops, the neighbors. I don't know what to do with him."

"He's seventeen. Maybe he should go away. Start all over where nobody knows him," Patricia said.

"I don't know." She turned to face her new young friend. "I had him so late, you know. He's not a mean child. He just can't stop himself." She smiled. "He says he wants to be a fisherman like his poor dead father. But nobody'd take him on. Everybody knows about Tom Kierney."

"He could fish alone. On his own boat," Patricia said.

Mrs. Kierney laughed bitterly.

"Why is that impossible?"

"Where would the notorious Tom Kierney get his own boat?"

"You could invest in him."

"My darling, I haven't got ten dollars. All my money goes into material and my rotten children. I've got one grandchild who needed a fancy doctor. She wiped out all my savings."

"He could borrow from a bank. You could sign for him."

"Ha! You ever gone into one of these banks and asked for a loan? You'd think you were trying to rob the place."

Patricia remembered the day so long ago when she'd gone to try to borrow money from Simon Yarrow's bank back in the San Joaquin. She nodded.

"The only other place you can get money is from a loan shark," Mrs. Kierney said.

"You wouldn't."

"No. It's a foolish idea anyway. Tom would never be able to be a fisherman."

"What would it cost?" Patricia asked.

Mrs. Kierney shrugged. "Forty, fifty dollars to get him started. That's what he says. He knows some man with an old boat. Nets and such . . ."

"What kind of daily profit could he show, do you think, just kind of roughly?"

"I don't know. Tom uses all kinds of figures. Maybe six or seven dollars a week. Maybe twice that."

Patricia's mind whirred with the possibilities. It was a strange idea she was getting. A mad one. If she loaned the money and charged interest, the money in the crockpot might earn money.

But what if Tom failed at this as he'd failed at so many things? What if the boat sank? She and her babies would be flat broke again with nothing to show for her lunacy.

"Let's say Tom got the money, Maude. Do you think he'd be a good fisherman?"

"I don't know. I guess so. Yes."

"How does six percent sound?"

"As what?"

"If I loaned Tom the fifty dollars to go into business, I'd want six percent interest. That's four percent less than if he was able to get it at a California bank."

"That's more than fair. What happens if he can't pay you back?"

Patricia smiled. "I guess I'd be in the fishing business, wouldn't I?"

Maude laughed. "I think you're crazy."

"One year at six percent. He'd sign a paper with me so I'd be protected."

"What if the boat broaches and sinks?"

"My bank would go under with it," Patricia said slowly.

Maude thought before answering. "I hope he says 'No'," she said. "For your sake. For his sake, I hope he says 'Yes.'"

Grant Yarrow and the tall thin man from Washington stood down the platform, separated from the groups of people who waited for the train. The chilly wind cut through Grant's light cape and chilled him to the core. The man next to him spoke softly but no less intensely in the crowded station.

"Grant, we need you to stay on this case."

Grant shook his head. "It's cost too much already. I've put it in writing. I'm off the case. I'm through wasting my life playing detective on a lot of misguided politicians who think my father's ideas are valid. Get somebody else. I'm burned out. I have nothing left to give." He put his hands on the man's shoulders. "Look, I have one chance. I'm taking it."

"You mean Patricia Carrick?"

Grant nodded. "I can't do anything but think of her. I've risked my life; I thought I could get over her, but I can't. I'm a danger to anyone who works with me." He shrugged. "I'm going to ask her to marry me."

"If she turns you down?"

"I don't know."

The other man nodded and shook Grant's hand. "Well, you're no use to the Department like this." He cursed under his breath as he saw the train hove into view. "Love. Shit," he said.

Grant smiled. "Besides," he said, "in three months I haven't been able to prove anything substantive against my father. I'll send you some wedding cake."

CHAPTER TEN

THE chill blew in from the northwest. The air smelled of sea water. The thick grey clouds roiled in the sky, growing darker and darker.

Ed O'Connor looked out of place in his blue serge, like a young boy wearing his first communion suit, uncomfortable with his necktie, always seeming about to burst out of the seams at his shoulders. His sun-freckled face shone from the vigorous scrubbing he'd given it that morning. His light brown hair was flattened upon his head. He spoke with difficulty, seemed preoccupied.

"After my wife died I took to drinking," he said as they walked slowly back from Mass on the crowded street. He looked sideways at the beautiful woman walking next to him. His breath came slowly, agonizingly. "I felt sorry for myself. One time I got so drunk, the next thing I knew I woke up on a ship bound for America. I never took another drop."

"That was fortunate," Patricia said. Her mind wandered. Mrs. Kierney's work had fallen to almost nothing. The money had dried up after the successful costume ball. She'd loaned the money to Tom Kierney; he'd made four regular payments, but now he was four days late. She shook her head to clear it. "Beg pardon?" she said to the tall iceman who walked next to her.

"I was saying that these Sunday visits to see the Laceys and you have become the highlight of my week."

"The children look forward to seeing you," Patricia said with a gentle smile.

"And you?" Ed asked.

"Yes."

They walked on in silence while Ed tried to find his courage and Patricia wondered what would happen to them when her savings were exhausted this time.

Ed stopped and took ahold of Patricia's elbow. "Patricia, I would like to ask you something."

"You know you can ask me anything you like, Edward."

"What do you think of me?"

"What do I think of you?"

"As a person."

"As a person?"

"Damn me, woman, you keep repeating me."

Patricia laughed. But underneath the laugh she knew she was stalling. She was never comfortable answering personal questions. "You are a very good man," she said.

A frown emerged on the Irishman's handsome face.

"Did I say something wrong?" Patricia asked.

He shook his head vigorously, "No, no. It's just that I was hoping for something a little . . . I don't know . . . more dashing."

"Oh, I think you're dashing."

He turned and started to walk slowly again. Patricia followed along. "We've known each other for two months now, yes?"

"September and October," Patricia replied. And in two more months, she thought, she and the children and Patrick would be thrown out of their miserable one room flat unless she could find more work.

"I know that's not a long time," Ed said, "but the times are changing. People don't wait as long as they once did."

"For what?"

"To ask people to marry them."

Patricia stopped cold in her steps. Ed turned to face her. She looked puzzled.

"I guess I'm asking you to become Mrs. O'Connor, Miss Carrick."

"I . . . I. . . ."

"If you're worried about the children, I love those little mites. I'd want them to come along as well. I've always wanted a family and this one is ready-made."

Patricia's ghosts rattled their chains in her soul. Francis Macauley's face drifted past the canvas of her mind. To lie with a man as his wife?

Ed O'Connor stood closer. "I'm not getting any younger . . . I wouldn't make any demands on you."

It was obvious what he was saying; here was a man who wanted nothing more than companionship and the warmth of a family. "I don't know what to say," Patricia said.

"I've been lonely a long time. I never thought I'd meet another woman who I'd want to grow old with. Until I met you, that is." He paused. "I'm not a wealthy man, but I've saved a bit, I own my own house, my own business, and I expect to be able to provide for you and the wee ones as well as the next man." He smiled. "People will always need ice."

Suddenly it all seemed so right. Patricia had spent her whole life doing for other people. She was mother and father to her brothers and sisters. She was mother and father to her nieces and nephews. She had always taken care of others and here was someone begging to take care of *her*! Her shoulders dropped down, she sighed. It was as if for the first time in her years she admitted how dead tired she was—dead tired from being responsible for everyone else's welfare.

"Patricia?"

"Yes, Edward?"

"Don't answer if you don't want to now. I don't mean to press you, but I do want you to know how I feel."

Patricia nodded. "I can give you my answer now, Edward."

"Don't answer if it's 'No' ", he said with a half-smile.

She shook her head. "Yes, Edward. I will marry you." A cold wind blew across her face. She shivered.

Edward O'Connor of County Cork beamed like a bonfire and looked right and left as if he were trying to find someone to share the news with. "You will?"

Patricia nodded.

"I am the luckiest man in the world! If I were a drinking man, I'd probably wind up in Australia!" He laughed, reached out and picked the pretty redhead off the ground, swinging her in a wide circle. Suddenly he realized what he'd done and almost dropped her in embarrassment. "I'm sorry! I'm sorry! I didn't mean to be forward, ma'am!"

Patricia caught her breath. The feeling of being held in the strong man's arms had made her blood rush and her skin tingle. "You are forgiven, Edward."

"I forgot myself. When can we set the date?"

"The banns have to be read."

"Of course."

"Christmas."

"Christmas?"

"Now, who's repeating who?" Patricia laughed.

Early the next morning Patricia took care of the children, left Stephen in charge and walked down to the waterfront with her brother, Patrick. The breeze had shifted to the northeast, bringing a slanting cold rain along with it. When they reached the docks Patrick said, "Are you sure you don't want me to go along with you?"

Patricia shook her head. "I lent him the fifty dollars; it's my responsibility."

"Be careful, sister. It's dangerous down here."

"I can take care of myself."

He kissed her on the forehead and then strode off to make the morning roll call. Patricia shivered in the raw air and then walked down the street towards the area where the fishermen docked their boats.

"Hey, girlie!" a stevedore yelled. He grabbed the crotch of his trousers and gesticulated at her.

Patricia looked straight ahead and never broke stride.

"Lookit her!" a sailor said to his fo'c'sle mate. He reached out for the beautiful woman. Patricia moved quickly and slapped him sideways before he knew where the blow had come from. A group of hangers-on laughed to see the aggressive sailor get his deserts.

"I got fifty bucks says you'll suck me off!" the sailor yelled after her.

Patricia did not look back.

Most of the fishing fleet waited in the harbor to see what the nor'easter would bring. The rollers came in from the bay, bringing an angry darkgreen water against their boats, slapping them, rocking them and putting seaspray over their gunwhales.

It took Patricia half an hour of asking and walking before she recognized the boat her money had bought. It rocked and bounced against the far dock. Tom Kierney was not on board. She turned and walked back to one of the fishing shacks on the beach. Smoke poured out of the stack on the flimsy roof.

Seven fishermen sat in the small space around the stove, trading stories and telling about waves that towered over their boats. "I'm looking for Tom Kierney," Patricia said.

"Tom?"

"Answer up, lad."

Tom Kierney sat against the far wall, his oilskins open to let in the warmth. The men watched him, then looked at the wet, angry-looking woman in the doorway.

"I want to talk to you, Tom."

"I don't want to talk to you," he said sullenly.

"Do you want it here in public or out there?" she asked.

Tom shook his head. A sneer ourled upon his upper lip. "All the same to me."

"You're five days late on your boat payment," she said. Patricia fought to keep her face from giving

away her inner terror at facing down this insolent
bastard while six of his cronies watched.

The men's eyes opened wide. "So?" Tom replied.

"So? So, in two more days I take your boat."

Tom smiled. "How you gonna do that?"

"I have the papers, Tom Kierney. The papers you
signed. I'll get the sheriff and that'll be that."

"You wouldn't!"

Patricia knew she didn't have enough money to
afford the legal proceedings, but if the bluff worked
. . . She smiled and put her hands on her hips. "Then
I'll auction off the boat and all the other gear to get
my money back." She paused. "Think about it. I'll
be outside for five minutes. If you don't come out
with the money before I leave, you better keep an
eye out over your shoulder."

As soon as Patricia had left, the shack erupted in a
welter of talk. "Who the hell was that?"

"That lady's a firebrand, ain't she?"

"Christ, I'd hate to tangle with her."

"You bes' pay up, Tommy-boy or you'll lose your
tits, sure as shit."

"Whooooeee. . . ."

"She loaned you fifty?"

"She a shark?"

"Six percent."

"*Six* percent? I'll take a little of that!"

"Just don't come up short on her."

Outside, Patricia waited in the shelter of the roof,
out of the slanting sheets of rain. She prayed that
Tom would buy her act and pay up.

Four minutes after she walked out, Tom Kierney
shrugged his way outside, and held out the four dollars and fifty cents. "Here," he said.

Patricia stood straight and tall. Her eyes bore in on the boy. "If you'd had a good excuse, a reason for not paying one week, I could have understood. But you just plain didn't pay. Don't do it again, Tom."

"Yes, ma'am." He smiled, a bit relieved the ordeal was over. "Ma'am?"

"Yes?"

"There's one of my friends in there asked if you'd lend him ten until next month. His lines were cut and the rest are shot."

Patricia paused. It was strange. Suddenly the crock pot was behaving like a bank. She'd always joked about it. But the sewing was gone now. She had nothing to fall back on. "Is he a good risk?" she asked.

Tom nodded. "Better'n me," he said with a grin.

Patricia thought. "All right. Tell him to come see me this afternoon."

"Yes, ma'am. And ma'am?"

"Yes, Tom?"

"I'm sorry about trying to stiff you. It won't happen again."

"Good. How's the fishing going?"

"Except for today? Real good."

"I'm glad." Patricia turned and walked off into the rain.

CHAPTER ELEVEN

WHEN Patricia returned from the docks, she was soaked clear through to the marrow of her bones. The rain sluiced down the dirty streets and soaked her flimsy shoes. Her hair straggled down, wet and cold on the back of her neck.

She looked up as she rounded the last corner and stopped short.

Grant Yarrow's carriage stood at the rough curb; his team of greys chomped in their wet feedbags. His driver huddled under his oilskins.

Patricia turned to go back in the direction she had come from, but a strong cry stopped her on the spot. "Patricia!"

Patricia turned back to face the sound. She swept the damp hair from her forehead with the back of her wrist.

Grant Yarrow, wearing a dove-grey morning coat and dark striped trousers, stepped to the muddy ground with his English riding boots. "I'm getting frightfully wet, Patricia. Would you be kind enough to sit for a moment in my carriage? I would like to offer you something in the way of a proposition." He smiled. The rain pelted his broad shoulders.

Patricia walked slowly up the hill and let the incredibly powerful man lift her effortlessly into his carriage.

The leather seats smelled of wealth and luxury. The thick carpet on the floor was immaculate. Patricia shivered as he wrapped a lambswool blanket around her shoulders. "You'll catch your death if you walk around like that in a storm," he said. "What were you doing out on a day like this?"

"Collecting," she said.

"Ah." Grant sat back on his side of the carriage. The rain dotted the roof like guns. He liked looking at Patricia Carrick. He had carried with him a mental picture of her and now, like an artist, filling in detail and touching up certain areas, he examined her closely.

Patricia caught him staring with rapt attention and shifted uneasily. "You have a proposition?"

Grant cleared his throat. "First, let me tell you that we were able to get your friend a stay of execution. Grace the Butcher Malone. Jervais is trying to get a reversal or a new trial."

Patricia smiled. "Thank you."

"But that is not why I'm here," Grant said.

"I have children waiting for me," Patricia said. "Thank you for what you've done for Grace."

Grant put out a hand to stop her from leaving. The rain pelted on the roof as he pulled her to him and kissed her full and hard on the mouth. Patricia didn't know whether the horses were moving or the earth had shifted. She felt as if she were floating.

Grant pulled back and put a hand to his forehead. No preparation could have helped him deal with the waves of passion that took hold of him. He shuddered. "I want to marry you," he whispered.

Patricia looked up at him. She felt feverish. She knew she shouldn't have walked all that way in the rain. It was suddenly hot and stuffy in the carriage. The smell of damp leather was overpowering. Her mind drifted in a confusing maze, ungrounded, undirected. Nothing made any sense. "I can't marry you," she said.

"Can't or won't?" Grant replied in a flat voice.

"Both."

"What does that mean?"

Patricia looked at him beneath her lowered lids. Her head had begun to ache, to throb. This was all going so wrong. Nothing matched. It was like a puzzle where some willful child had stolen half the pieces. "I'm engaged to be married next month."

"I beg your pardon?"

She looked up and tried to form the words as clearly as she could. "I'm engaged to be married next month. To a fine upstanding man who loves my babies and will be a good provider."

Grant closed his eyes. He nodded. He opened his eyes and did not read the longing in her face. "Well, then, you certainly don't need me," he said quietly. "I, uh, wish you every happiness, Patricia. Please forgive me for taking up your time." He leaned across the space, narrowly missing her, and opened the door.

It seemed to Patricia that the world was whirring too quickly one moment and too slowly the next. She willed her body to move out of the carriage, but it refused to work with its accustomed ease. And then, too soon, she stood on the street in the rain watching his carriage clatter down the hill.

"My God," she cried, "what have I done?"

When Patricia opened the door of her apartment, she felt as if she were coming down with the ague. She was feverish. A chill shook her. The children were playing a game in the middle of the floor with Ed O'Connor. "Ed?"

"Hello, my love," he said, getting up awkwardly. "I hope you don't mind. I couldn't work in all this weather, so I stopped by. You look drowned."

She nodded. Her brain reeled. "Ed, I must speak to you."

"And I to you, my love. I spoke to the Father this morning. He'll read the banns this Sunday. He thinks we'll make a grand couple." His shining face beamed.

Patricia motioned to her nieces and nephews. "Listen, babies, I want you to go down to Mrs. Kierney's for the rest of the morning. I'll come and get you later, all right?"

They nodded and flew down the stairs as quickly as they could.

"What's the matter, darling?" Ed asked.

Patricia laced her fingers together. "I can't marry you, Ed. I want to, but I just cannot. I am deeply sorry."

The big man looked as if he had been knocked out even though his eyes remained open. His jaw went slack.

"You're a good and fine man. You deserve better."

"No, no I don't. I want you and that's all."

"Ed, I can't."

"Look," he said, forcing a smile and taking her

small hands between his, "you're just feeling feverish, maybe you're getting a case of nerves. Once we're married, it'll all be different."

Patricia pulled back. "Ed, I can't marry you if I love another."

It was quiet. Ed O'Connor breathed out slowly. "Did you love him yesterday when I asked you?"

"I didn't know I loved him when I said yes to you."

Ed shook his head. "Women," he muttered. He looked down at his scuffed leather work shoes. "Good lord, woman, are you certain?"

Patricia nodded. She shivered with a chill.

"I hope I will be allowed to visit the children," he said softly.

"Of course," she said. "You're the father they never had."

He nodded. Cleared his throat. "I hope you'll be happy," he said, his voice thick.

Patricia did not have time to savor the irony of having turned down two near-perfect men in one hellish morning. Instead, she turned and ran down the stairs and toward the city to try to find Grant Yarrow.

The desk clerk at the posh Occidental Hotel looked at the wringing wet woman with the pale face and the wild eyes and said that she could leave a message for Mr. Grant Yarrow if she chose, but that Mr. Yarrow's comings and goings were most haphazard. Patricia took the pen and paper from the man and wrote carefully, trying not to drip rain on her efforts.

"I have reconsidered, if you will have me.
Patricia Carrick."

She smiled, folded the note in quarters, and watched as the clerk put the note in Grant's box. "Do you have any idea where I might look for him?"

The clerk was beginning to tire of this obviously lower-class woman's presence. "We don't keep a watch over our patrons, ma'am."

Patricia nodded. She turned and walked back out into the rain. "Maybe he went to have a drink. He was angry with me," she said. She walked down to the nearest saloon.

"I'm very sorry, Miss," the manager said, "but we cannot allow unescorted, uh, ladies into the Crystal. I'm sure you understand."

"Yes, of course. I was just looking for Mr. Grant Yarrow."

"Mr. Yarrow was here earlier."

"When?"

"A half hour ago."

"Do you happen to know where he was going?"

The manager looked down at her. "I suppose he was going to do some more drinking."

"Was he tipsy?"

"After all he had, miss, it's a wonder he could walk at all. I've never seen a man put back that much and live to talk about it."

"Where should I look?"

"Chinatown," the manager said as he walked abruptly away.

Patricia's fever abated somewhat as she pursued Grant Yarrow from saloon to saloon. She had no time for the hot flashes and the cold chills. She knew she was just behind him. She'd find him, apologize, and nurse him back to sobriety.

The tall Chinaman nodded, his queue dancing in the lamplight. "I have seen such a man," he said.

Patricia almost clapped her hands with joy. She had spent the entire day and part of the evening chasing him from bar to bar. "Where did he go?"

"He was very drunk," the Chinaman said.

"I know, I know, but where did he go when he left?"

"To the *Emily W.*," the Chinaman said.

"I've never heard of that bar," she said.

The Chinaman smiled, then shook his head from side to side. "The *Emily W.* is not a saloon," he said. "It is a ship."

"I don't understand."

"The sailing master of the *Emily W.* was signing on deckhands. Your friend was very drunk, a little dirty. He signed on the *Emily W.* as a deckhand."

Patricia felt the grip of fear take ahold of her guts and wrench. "Where is she docked?"

"At the end of Water Street."

"Thank you very much." Patricia ran out into the street, got her bearings quickly and headed for Water Street. "I'll get him off there before they ship out," she said. "They'll understand, him being drunk and all. I'll tell them he's worth alot more to them here in San Francisco than as a deck hand."

The rain had stopped a few hours ago, but she had not dried out when she found the end of Water Street and asked a young boy with a model boat where to find the *Emily W.*

The young urchin lifted a dirty sleeve and pointed West. "See them lights?"

"Which ones?"

"Out there on the horizon. The *Emily W.* Shipped out a coupla hours ago." The boy watched in surprise as the wet-looking woman collapsed at his feet. "Jesus, lady," he murmured. "Are you alive or dead?"

BOOK THREE

CHAPTER ONE

PATRICIA stared at the ceiling, her mind a blank white canvas. The fever had broken only a week earlier, but when she drifted back to consciousness and left the nightmares and fantasies of her disease, she pushed all thought from her mind. It was far easier than dealing with the realities.

Grant Yarrow was gone.

She was alone, most likely, forever.

The family was nearly broke.

Patricia rolled over on her cot.

"Patricia?" Patrick said.

She did not look up.

"Patricia?" he called again.

She closed her eyes.

"There's a man here to see you. Says it's urgent. I told him you had just gotten well and were very sick, but he said he had to see you and that was that."

Patricia opened her eyes.

"He wouldn't take no for an answer," Patrick said.

A short, barrel-chested Irishman pushed his way through the blanket curtain that hung across the apartment. He was bald with fat cheeks like a chipmunk. "I'm terrible sorry, Miz Carrick, but I had to speak with you."

Patricia pulled the blanket up to her chin while her brother tried to wrest the determined man from her bedroom.

"Miz Carrick, I need money! I need two hunnert and fifty dollars by tonight!"

"Come on, pal," Patrick said, "out of here!"

"Wait," Patricia called. Her voice was dry. She hadn't spoken in two weeks except to mutter in her sleep.

Patrick spun around, surprised, dropping his grip on the barrelchested man.

"Wait," she repeated.

"Thank you, Miz Carrick," the man said. "My name is Michael Kelly from down the way. I run a little pushcart with vegetables. You've bought from me sometimes."

"Your tomatoes are too dear," she said.

"That's what *you* say. You should see what *I* have to pay for them!"

Patricia leaned up on her elbow while her brother plumped up a pillow behind her. "You need two hundred and fifty dollars by tonight?"

"Yes, ma'am."

"Why did you come to me? I haven't seen two hundred and fifty dollars all at one time since I don't know when."

Michael Kelly paced the small space. "I didn't know who else to talk to."

"Take it one step at a time," Patricia said. Her pale white skin grew rosier as she spoke.

"I have the pushcart. I want a store. I can get a perfect location on Market Street and quadruple my inventory and my sales. But the stickler is I put down a binder for a hundred dollars. If I don't come up with the balance by midnight tonight, I lose the store and the binder." He looked down at his squat square fingers. "The hundred was my life's savings."

"Why did you put it all down?" Patrick asked.

Michael Kelly looked up. "Because I thought I could get a bank loan for the balance. I was sure I could." He sat down on a crate Patricia used as a bureau. "You ever been to one of them banks and tried to get a loan if you don't have money?"

"What's your cart worth?"

"Forty dollars, maybe."

"What's your custom, your trade worth?"

"I dunno. Another forty maybe."

Patricia smiled. "Your tomatoes are still too high." She pulled the blanket around her shoulders. "Patrick, what's in the bank right now?"

"A hundred and three dollars."

"We have to come up with a hundred and forty-seven dollars by midnight. Leave me get dressed. Michael Kelly, go out and sell your vegetables and let me and mine take care of getting your money for you. If we succeed, you'll have a year to pay us back at six per cent per annum. Fair?"

Michael nodded his bald pate rapidly.

"Well?"

The two men looked at the beautiful woman dumbly.

"Well, get the hell out of my room so I can get dressed."

When Michael had left and Patrick was leaving for the docks, he asked, "How are you going to raise all that money by midnight, Patricia?"

She shrugged and hugged young Charley to her. "I haven't the slightest idea. Get to work or you'll be sacked."

Stephen laughed and laid out the material for a dress which Mrs. Symington had ordered. "All right, babies," he said, in a perfect imitation of his aunt, "Let us get to work or I'll want to know the reason why!"

Patricia finished her tea, wrapped herself in a shawl and headed out to the neighborhood.

Her first stop was at Mrs. Impellettieri's. "Good morning, Mrs. Impellettieri," she said. "I wonder if I might have a chat with you."

When she left, she had five dollars.

Her next stop was at Mrs. Rodruiges' house. When she left, she had seven dollars.

By noon she was a hundred dollars short. "Mrs. Kierney," she said, "can you get all your ladies together after supper tonight?"

"My sewing ladies?"

"And any others you can possibly find."

"What for?"

"I need a hundred dollars."

Mrs. Kierney smiled. She nodded. "I'll try."

"Please. The Carrick Bank is in desperate need."

At eight o'clock Patricia, Patrick, and Michael Kelly walked into the crowded sewing room of Mrs. Kierney and looked at the fresh-scrubbed faces of thirty women. "Oh, the saints preserve us," Patrick said as

he felt the eyes of five single women pick him apart
and find him perfect for their purposes.

"Ladies, many of you know me," Patricia said. "I
speak plain when I say I think we have a good man
here in Mr. Michael Kelly. He has come to me for a
loan of $250. He wants to open a green grocery down
on Market Street. I need a hundred dollars. These are
my terms." When she had finished outlining the per-
centages paid to the bank and the return on the
money to the women in the room, she said, "Each of
us will, in a sense, own a part of Mr. Kelly's store. If
we don't like the way he's running it or if," she
paused, "his tomato prices are too high, we can have
a hand in changing things."

Michael Kelly squirmed.

"Until he pays us back," Patricia concluded.

"And what if he doesn't?" a woman asked.

Patricia smiled. "It's like I always say. Then we're
in the vegetable business."

"If the store burns down?" another woman asked.

"Mr. Kelly will carry insurance on the contents and
the building as well." Patricia looked around. "Well?"

"I'm in," a woman said.

"Me too," another piped up.

"I've got five dollars," one called.

"Look at this," Michael Kelly whispered to Patrick.
"Look at this."

"Don't get excited until we count up the totals."

The room was airless and quiet as Patricia totalled
up the piles of money and the paper receipts in front
of her on the sewing table. She cleared her throat.
"We're five dollars and fifty cents short."

The women in the room let out a collective groan.

Michael Kelly looked as if he'd been stepped on. Patrick stepped forward. "You never asked me if I wanted to chip in on this," he said.

"I thought all your money was in the crock."

He shook his head. "Ever since I stopped drinking I've kept ten dollars in my pockets for a real bash . . . just in case, ya know . . . and I never had much use for it." He grinned sheepishly and put the gold on the table.

The women in the room applauded lustily. Patricia embraced her brother and Mr. Kelly. When the jubilant noise finally abated, Patricia said, "Ladies, Mr. Kelly and we are in the vegetable business. And you just call on me if the damned tomato prices start creeping up!" She laughed aloud.

CHAPTER TWO

SECRETARY of War William Belknap was impeached for taking bribes.

Alexander Graham Bell was given a patent for an invention that would permit people to talk over wires. Melville Bissell invented a carpet sweeper and James Gordon Bennett helped bring polo to the United States. Wild Bill Hickok was killed, Colorado was admitted to the Union and General George Armstrong Custer marched 225 cavalrymen to their deaths at Little Big Horn.

It was the worst and best of epochs. President and Mrs. Grant were only two of the more than eight million visitors to the Centennial Exposition in Philadelphia.

Very slowly the depression began to ease.

Very slowly. . . .

The small beautiful redheaded woman named Carrick had looked at herself that morning and said, "Today's your birthday, woman, and you're thirty-three years old. You don't look at all bad for the miles you've put on." But she didn't have too much time to think about the fact that after all she'd been through she was still enough woman to turn most heads—men's and women's—when she went by. The men were instantly attracted and the women always wondered how the Carrick woman got brains *and* good looks.

There were the children, the nephews and nieces. They had to be fed before they went off on their part-time jobs. They sold newspapers, did odd jobs, ran errands, worked stacking produce at Mr. Kelly's, shined shoes, and helped Mrs. Kierney. Their small incomes were duly noted and placed, by their choice, in the Carrick bank.

But today was a special day above and beyond it being Patricia's birthday. It was payday. Patricia did her paperwork and then, after lunch, just before quitting time, she set herself up behind a trestle table thrown across two barrels down on the docks. A few women had already gathered under the soft warm sky in the easy-going breeze to watch this unique event.

When the whistle blew the men lined up at the shipping company paymaster's and received their carefully accounted pay. Then they turned and headed slowly down the docks to where Patricia Carrick sat under the gaze of a dozen women.

The first man in line put down three dollars, then tucked his thumbs in his belt loops and beamed broadly. "I'd like an accounting, Ma'am, if you don't mind," he said loud enough for all to hear.

Patricia smiled. "You've earned one dollar and twenty-five cents since you began investing with me last month, John," she said without looking at the journal she'd bought three months ago.

"That's one dollar and two bits I didn't even have to sweat for," he said. "Thanks, ma'am." He touched his cap and took the balance of his weekly pay to where his wife stood a few feet away.

"Next?"

"Ah, Miss Carrick," the next man said, "you don't want a fellah to have a good time."

"Walter," she said, "you have enough left to have a good time and still feed your little babies." She entered his amount in her ledger. "If you'd rather leave the full amount in John Casey's pub, be my guest."

Walter blushed then shook his head. His wife thanked God for Miss Carrick's brilliant idea of taking small sums from their paychecks and investing them before the men could squander the money. The returns in just these few months had been wonderful. And Miss Patricia wasn't at all like those snobs down at the regular banks.

Patricia looked up in time to see William Riley leaving the line and trying to duck around a stack of barrels. "William!" she yelled.

William's face appeared around the corner. "Yes, ma'am?"

"Were you thinking of going back on your promise to your lovely wife Noreen and your six babies?"

He squinched up his face. "Of course not. Can't a man even relieve himself without everyone following him?"

The crowd laughed and Patricia continued to take in the sums of money.

It was seven-fifteen before Patricia and her brother, Patrick, could climb aboard the rickety wagon they'd borrowed, and head away from the wharves. "What was the take today, my darling?" he asked.

"Seventy-six, forty-five," she replied with a smile. "That's counting Joe Cucci needing five back for his oldest daughter's first Communion dress." She looked up at the sunset glowing across the western skies. "That's enough to give the young Collins boy what he needs for his carpenter's tools and still have plenty to lend Lucky Barlow her father's passage from Brooklyn."

"You look tired."

"Ah, but I feel good."

"Because the crock pot is full?"

Patricia shrugged. "The babies finally have church clothes." She paused. "But it's more than that. It's looking around and seeing the good that sharing the money can do. Those that have are lending fairly to those that lack. I was part of that."

Patrick laughed. "You were all of that, my love."

"Well, anyway, we're finally just about making ends meet."

"Martin Cable said you oughta open a proper bank," Patrick said as he turned the team around the last corner.

"And angels should fly on my shoulders and you should be president of the United States," Patricia said.

"I think I'd make a fine President," Patrick said.

When the wagon rolled to a stop outside Michael Kelly's greengrocery, Patricia slipped down off the wagon to greet the proprietor of Kelly's grocery. It seemed to Patricia that every time she saw him he'd added another inch or so to the burgeoning spare tire around his middle. "Saints alive, what did you have for lunch, Michael?"

"Some pasta at Mama Bastiglione's," he replied,

patting his huge girth. "How did you do this week?"

"Well," Patrick replied, taking the bag of money down from Kelly's borrowed wagon.

"Thank you for letting us use your safe, Michael," Patricia said.

"Thank you for letting me use your money," he said with a laugh. "Your crock pot was getting a little crammed." He escorted them inside the closed store and pulled open the safe door. Patricia leaned down, put the bag inside, then swung the steel door shut. "Besides," Michael said, "I wanted to talk to you about another loan."

"For?" Patricia asked. She leaned over and took a carrot from a nearby bin. It was cold and crisp.

"I want to expand."

She tapped his stomach with the end of her carrot. "It looks as though you've expanded as much as you could."

"No, not me, the business," Michael said earnestly, ignoring her jibe. "I want to get some wagons to get into the wholesale end of the business. Meet the farmers and buy direct. And I want to get some push-carts out on the streets to distribute to areas that are further away from the store here." He reached out and picked up an old straw basket. He began to fill it with some fruits and vegetables. "I think I'll need five hundred."

"That's alot," Patricia said.

"The business is doing well. I'm almost paid off six months early."

Patricia munched on a tomato. "I don't know if I could take a big loss if something were to happen to you or the business," she said. "The tomato's first-rate."

"All my merchandise is first rate," he said, "and nothing will happen to your five hundred."

"It's not my five hundred. It's the five hundred of all my investors."

"I know that."

Patricia took the basket and handed it to her brother. "Let me see what I can do, all right?"

"I'm willing to pay a higher percentage. I think the sooner I get into the wholesale business as well as the retail, the sooner I'll be a rich man." He handed her a ripe plum. "And you'll be a rich woman."

"Ha!"

On the way back to their apartment Patrick asked her where she would ever get five hundred dollars. "Beats me," she said. "But the Carrick Bank didn't get where it is by *not* lending money."

That evening, as Patricia, her brother, and her five nieces and nephews sat around the table finishing up supper, they heard a noise that sounded as if someone were scratching at the door.

"Answer the door, please, Charley," Patricia said. "So what did Mr. Chalmers say about the way you polished his shoes, Will?"

Will flushed a bit, then smiled. "He said he'd pay me a nickel for polishing the shoes and another penny for polishing his white socks."

The group laughed aloud as Charley escorted four children into the lanternlight at the table. Suddenly it was very quiet.

Patricia stood up slowly, her hands on the solid round table, her face white and strained. By force of habit she smoothed her hair with the back of her wrist. "I. . . ." She tried to smile.

The four children were Harry, twelve, with sad eyes and a narrow face; Nancy, ten, with a curious expression held in check by her shyness; Eric, nine, like a coiled spring loosely held in place; and Ben, eight, pleasant-faced and slow-witted.

"Welcome, children," Patricia said.

"Hello, Harry," Stephen said.

One by one the children of Patricia's two sisters spoke to each other or embraced. Patricia looked up at the door, hoping against hope that her sister or her husband, Harry Gardiner, would suddenly appear. But they didn't.

"It was the fever," Nancy Gardiner said.

"Mum and dad lasted a long time," Eric said.

"But they died," Ben said.

Patricia looked out over the heads of her nine nieces and nephews and caught Patrick's eye. He smiled sadly. "I do think," Patrick said, "that we shall require a bit larger establishment, don't you?"

Patricia hugged four children at once without caring whose they were.

CHAPTER THREE

THIRTEEN months had passed—exciting months, as Patricia looked back on them. President Grant was out of office, but nobody expected the corruption to stop just because one bewhiskered crook had taken the place of another. America was big, brassy, growing and almost without morals where power was concerned. Government repeatedly backed big business to quell the growing labor unrest in Baltimore, Pittsburgh, Chicago and St. Louis. The spirit of dog eat dog ruled the day.

Patricia was exhausted.

Michael Kelly's greengrocery looked more like a kindergarten than a business. Children ducked under the wooden trestles, tagged one another and dived back under a flat of radishes, only to reappear seconds later behind a bin of potatoes. Their mothers chatted animatedly about prices, in-laws, and what one might reasonably expect from the second cousin of one of the Molly Maguires who was executed the year before. Michael Kelly himself had no time for chit-chat; he was far too busy making sure that Stephen

Lacey, tall and strapping at fourteen, knew exactly what to buy from which farmers. Next to him on the bench of the wagon sat his cousin Harry, a boy who had finally learned how to smile.

"Lissen, Harry," Michael Kelly said, "don't let Stephen buy too much lettuce. I don't make enough on lettuce. It spoils easy and I don't make enough."

"All right, Uncle Michael," Harry said with a twinkle in his eye, "no lettuce."

"I didn't say 'No Lettuce'! I said 'Not too much lettuce'!"

"Right, uncle," Harry said. He turned to Stephen. "Come on, Stephen, let's go buy some lettuce."

Michael would have pulled his hair out if he'd had any left. Instead, he stalked over to where Will Lacey, Jr. was loading up a push-cart to peddle over at the fancy homes on Nob Hill. "You got everything?"

"Yes, Uncle Michael," Will replied.

"You sure?"

"Sure."

"You got onions?"

Will shook his head.

"I thought you said you had everything."

"I had everything but onions."

"Go get onions!"

"Sure, Uncle." With a smile and a shrug Will hightailed it over to the newly expanded bins where Michael Kelly stored bushels of different varieties of onion.

"And don't bother taking garlic up to Nob Hill," Michael said when Will had his onions.

"They don't know how to eat?"

"Just get going."

Will smiled and pushed the heavy cart with the aid of Molly, his sister, and Nancy, his cousin who proceeded to boss him more vigorously than Michael Kelly. "Watch out!"

"Not there!"

"Hurry up!"

The noise never stopped. Except in one corner, behind the fruits, where Patricia Carrick had her desk, a corner which had become known as The Carrick Bank. It housed a desk and Michael Kelly's safe and Patricia's big leather-bound book where she entered her friends' deposits and withdrawals and loans.

The Carrick Bank was no ordinary bank. It was not chartered by the state of California. Neither was it one of those federally chartered institutions. The Carrick Bank was run on faith and the good will of Patricia Carrick. Since her first loan to Tommy Kierney—who now had two fishing boats and two employees—she had not lost a single cent on a bad loan. Nor had she taken more in interest than the local banks. In fact her interest rates were always one or two percent below the competing institutions. The name—The Carrick Bank—had begun as a joke, ribbing the serious world of banks and bankers who ran the state and the country as if it were their own private club. The immigrants who trusted their money to this unauthorized, unsanctioned "bank" took pride in the fact that they were denying their few dollars to such as the mighty Simon Yarrow who controlled vast empires of wealth.

Patricia looked up and saw a thin, black-haired woman with three children and an infant. "Sit down, Mrs. Bateo, *come vai, oggi?*" Patricia said.

"Abbastanza bene, et lei?"

"*Molta bene*. What can I do for you?"

The thin woman looked embarrassed for a moment, then looked up at Patricia. "Enzo and me, we want an American *nomme* for the *bambino*."

Patricia bit the end of her pencil and wished the sun would come out from behind the clouds outside. The women made Michael keep the windows spotlessly clean. They didn't think anybody wanted to buy vegetables in a place with dingy windows. "Why an American name? Why not Mario? I've always liked Mario."

"But this is our *bambino* born here."

"But you are still *Italiana* and proud, no?"

Mrs. Bateo nodded.

"Well, then, how about Andrea Marco Bateo?"

Mrs. Bateo smiled. Her children nodded. The infant suckled at her breast. "Would you stand for this Andrea Marco?"

"I would be honored," Patricia said, mentally computing that Andrea Marco Bateo would make her sixth Godchild: two Italian, three Irish and one Swede.

"This Sunday?"

"*Mille.*"

"*Mi piacere molto.*"

Satisfied that her day's business had gone well, Mrs. Bateo rose and swept proudly out of the store, her children tumbling in her wake.

The next client was Mrs. Lutz, who came with her husband's weekly payment on his wheelwright's shop. After her it was Mr. Balducci with ten dollars he wanted to invest for a year. After him it was a woman whose husband drank. "What can I do?"

"I'll talk to him," Patricia said.

"He won't talk to a woman."

"I'll send my brother, Patrick. He used to drink."

"He won't talk to him either."

"If he won't talk, throw him out."

"But I love him."

"It doesn't matter, Mrs. Gerald. If he won't do anything to help himself, you must get out or he must. Otherwise you'll burn yourself out like a candle. And your children will suffer right along with you."

"Yes, ma'am."

Close on the heels of Mrs. Gerald came a young woman with a very personal query. Her voice barely above a whisper, she leaned forward and said, "My boyfriend always wants to, you know . . ."

Patricia nodded.

"I think I do too. What do I do, Aunt Patricia?"

Patricia leaned back and sighed. "What do you think you should do, Peggy?"

"I don't think I should."

"Then don't. You've got to listen to yourself, lass, not some boy who's even more confused than you are. Are you ready to have a family? Unmarried and all?"

She shook her head.

Patricia smiled broadly. "You knew the right answer all along, didn't you?"

Peggy nodded. "Yes, but now I can tell Ronnie that Miss Patricia Carrick said I shouldn't. Thanks, Miss Patricia!" She flew out of the store with a relieved rush, leaving Patricia suddenly exhausted.

"What's the matter?" Michael Kelly asked while picking grapes too rotten to sell.

"I think playing God is very tiring," she replied.

"I wouldn't know. I just sell fruits and vegetables."

"All of a sudden I'm a big deal, I don't feel like a big deal," she said. She ran the backs of her hands across her face. "I just want someone to take me and hug me and ask me what I want."

Michael blushed. "That's not my style," he said.

Patricia laughed.

"How about Ed O'Connor?" Michael asked. "He's always over at your place pretending he's playing with the children."

"I wish he were the right man," Patricia said.

Michael Kelly shrugged his shoulders and wished the woman who had put him in business and kept him there were as happy as he was. As he went about his duties he wondered if she would ever find the fulfillment she craved. He watched the long stream of men and women come with problems and leave with loans, good advice or honest sympathy. "That woman is a saint," he said to himself.

At seven o'clock that evening Michael Kelly finished locking up the store-bank and waited at the front door for Patricia. "You run along," she said. "I'm behind in my housecleaning. I'll lock up."

"All right. Is Patrick going to come for you?"

"No. I'm all right."

"Good night then. And don't worry about playing God. Somebody has to do it and you're the best candidate I know."

"Thank you, Michael Kelly." As soon as he was gone, Patricia turned up her lantern and reached down in a special compartment in her safe. She pulled out a sheaf of papers and began going through them. "My goodness," she said, "but I haven't touched these in years."

As she bent over the old dusty papers and notes Patricia was not aware of the man who stood outside the greengrocery. He was tall and lean. His hands were dug deep in the pockets of a seaman's jacket.

"Look at this," she said to herself, "it's the certificate the whore gave brother Alexander for a dollar." She wished she had heard from Alexander. She and Patrick rarely spoke of him. She suspected he was dead long since.

The shadow of the tall man in the seaman's coat passed slowly across the window, but Patricia didn't notice it.

"The Grendel Mine?" she said to herself. "Five shares?" She started to toss it into the wastebasket when she stopped herself. She smiled, then reached for the newspaper on the far edge of her desk. She flipped it open to the business section and the page where daily quotes on silver could be found.

There was a time, a little earlier, when all of San Francisco had gone mad for silver mines. Maids and waiters invested in wildcat schemes and some—very few—became rich overnight.

The man outside was satisfied that the pretty redhead was alone. He looked over his shoulder and then put his hand on the knob. It turned quietly.

Patricia looked up, thinking she'd heard something. "Michael?"

The noise stopped.

Patricia used her fingernail to look at the fine print of the column which gave the mining stock quotes. "Bright Star Mine, $257; Cable, $453; Drake and Mason, $139; Frye—" She stopped. "Michael, is that you?"

The sailor edged around the side of the potato bin and stopped. He held his breath when the woman called out.

"Is somebody out there?"

Patricia shook her head and decided she must be going just a little daft if she was hearing things. But, just to be sure, she leaned back and closed the safe, turning the big knob with her foot. Then she went back to the business pages.

"The Grendel Mine . . . oh, that couldn't be the same one. This must be a forgery. Why else would a prostitute have five shares to give Alexander?"

There it was: The Grendel Mine, $1,940!

"Keep your hands in front of you on the desk, ma'am," the voice said. It was quiet, steel-edged.

Patricia looked up with a jolt. One second she had been wondering if she had close to ten thousand dollars. Now she was looking up into the barrel of a Naval issue pistol. "Put it down and leave."

The man was tall and pockmarked. His eyes shone with a quiet fire in a fixed stare. His lips were scarred. His clothes were dirty. He shook his head. "Sorry, Miss Carrick."

"Do I know you?"

He smiled, then stopped himself. "I'm the man who's gonna take all the money in the Carrick Bank."

Patricia looked quickly at the safe, then back at the man in the sailor's jacket. "It doesn't belong to me. This isn't a real bank. The money belongs to all my neighbors."

The man nodded and smiled. "I don't rightly care. Now open that safe nice and easy, and give me all the gold and silver you got. I don't want no greenbacks."

"I'm not going to give you a penny," she said. Her voice was calm, steely.

The pistol barrel flicked out quickly, catching her across the top of her scalp. The pain burned hot. "Open up or I'll plaster the wall with your guts," he said.

Patricia fought against the pain, pulled open the safe door and reached in to where the canvas bag held the coin. There was eight hundred fifty dollars in the safe. The rest of the investors' money had been loaned out. Even at that, however, a loss like this meant disaster. It would take years to earn back what this man was taking.

"I'll have that," he said, reaching across the desk. "Feels heavy."

"It's over eight hundred dollars," Patricia said.

"Good," the man said. He levelled the gun at Patricia's forehead. "Now, maybe you and me can walk into the back."

"What for? You have the money."

The man smiled, revealing chipped, blackened teeth. "You're a fine looking woman. They say you ain't never been fucked proper."

Her voice was quiet, tight. "No," she said.

"This piece says 'Yes'," the man said cruelly. He waved the gun a few inches from her face. "Stand up. Now, walk to the back of the store."

Patricia did as she was told, hoping for an opening, some avenue of escape before the man carried out his threat. Her hand grazed by the cool vegetable bins. Up ahead, there was a small wrecking bar which Michael used to open the crates. She walked slowly.

"Right here's good enough," the man said. He put the canvas bag of money down on the floor. As he did so, Patricia reached over and took ahold of the short black iron bar and held it behind her skirts. "Come over here," he said, fingering the crotch of his old serge trousers.

Patricia took the steps carefully. If she moved too early, he would see her and defend himself. If she moved too late, he could pin her arms to her sides. . . .

And then, as he reached out to grab the collar of her blouse, she brought the iron up and down in a fast-moving arc. The man stepped back, dodging the blow, turned like a dancer, took her arm and slammed it against his knee.

The iron bar went clunk against the soft wood floor and Patricia followed it, her skirts billowing out behind.

Outside Michael Kelly's store a woman pushed against the partially opened door. Hearing no answer to her cautious call, she walked into the gloom. She could hear a man's rough voice in the rear of the big store. Then a woman's cries.

The stranger moved quickly and quietly towards the sounds.

The man stood over Patricia, unbuttoning his belt. "You're a pretty piece," he said. "You're gonna learn about a real man."

All of a sudden, he pitched headlong across the bins of beets, his eyes registering a curious grin. Then he didn't move.

The woman stepped out from behind him, holding the bag of gold and silver money like a weapon. "He'll be unconscious for awhile," she said in a gruff voice. The woman leaned down and picked up the robber's gun which had slithered across the floor.

"I owe you my life," Patricia said in the dim light.

"And I owe you mine," she said. "Don't you remember me?"

Patricia stared closely at the woman's face. "Grace Malone! Oh, my God!"

"The very same. I been on hard times. Thought I'd ask if you had any work."

"Why didn't you come before this?"

"Thought you'd already done enough for me."

Patricia stood up and embraced the woman who had saved her. "Not half enough," she said. "Not half enough."

CHAPTER FOUR

SAN FRANCISCO, CALIFORNIA, JULY, 1877

THE police didn't leave until after midnight. The crowd of a hundred and forty didn't leave until an hour after that.

Patricia sat in the lanternlight of the grocery across her desk from Grace Malone. "You're looking much better," Patricia said.

Grace smiled, revealing a brand new set of false teeth. Her hair was pure white now, and she had lost her belly. "You'd be surprised how being out makes you look better."

"When did you get out?"

"Awhile back. Lawyer Jervais worked a long time for me. They almost hanged me twice, but he kept whacking at the case and finally got the whole thing reversed on some kind of legal mumbo-jumbo."

"I'm glad to see you."

Grace nodded energetically. "Likewise."

Patricia sighed. "And if you hadn't come when you did. . . ."

"Well, maybe that'll help pay my debt to you."

"You don't owe me a thing." Patricia paused.

"Grant Yarrow paid lawyer Jervais. I'm just glad to see you." She rose.

Grace looked anxious. "Uh, Patricia, could you put me up for tonight? Maybe I could sleep here?"

"You're coming home with me," Patricia said. "I'm hiring Grace the Butcher."

"As what?"

Patricia looked around. Then back at the tall strong woman. "Protection."

Grace laughed.

"I'm serious. After tonight it looks like just having a safe isn't enough. I carry a lot of money from the wharves. I make pickups and I make loans. I think I need a woman who will scare the pants off any of these boys who think they can snatch our cash."

"You're fooling."

Patricia shook her head. "I can only afford to pay you room and board at first, but when we make more profits, we can afford to pay you a proper salary."

Grace's pale blue eyes were awash with tears. "I'm your woman, Patricia Carrick. Anybody want to mess with you, they'll have to get through me."

"Heaven help them. Let's go home." Patricia Carrick locked the doors on Michael Kelly's grocery and the two women set off.

Patricia and her brood had moved downstairs to the second floor where they had four bedrooms, a living room and a kitchen. The walls were wainscotted to shoulder height, then painted plaster above. The gasjets were few and far between. In one room there were six boys. In another there were three girls. Patrick and Patricia had taken the remaining two, sleeping alone luxuriously for the first time in years.

The two women had gone four blocks before Patricia suddenly stopped.

"What's the matter?" Grace said, startled.

"In the excitement I forgot!" Patricia said.

"Forgot what?"

"The stock certificate! Tomorrow we have to take it to the bank to see if it's real." Patricia did a quick dance step and twirled her skirts wide around her. Then she stopped. "I don't want to get my hopes up. I mustn't get my hopes up."

"How much is it worth?" Grace asked.

"Nearly ten thousand dollars."

Grace stumbled on the sidewalk. "Holy mother of God. Don't get our hopes up."

As they entered the Carricks' apartment, Patrick woke up and stared at Patricia's companion in sleepy bewilderment. "What happened?" he asked. "What time is it?" He wiped the sleep out of his eyes.

"Two o'clock," Patricia said.

"Two o'clock! Are you all right?"

"I was robbed, but we caught the robber," Patricia said. "This is Grace Malone."

"Grace the Butcher Malone?" Patrick replied, startled.

Grace smiled. "The very same."

"Good grief," Patrick said.

Patricia brewed a pot of tea and told Patrick what had happened. By the time she'd finished, he was speechless with rage. "I'll kill the son of a bitch!" he said.

"Patrick, keep it down or you'll wake the babies."

"How many children do you have here?" Grace asked.

"Nine," Patricia replied.

"Saints preserve us," Grace said. She drank her tea.

"So, Patrick, I've hired Grace here to protect the bank's assets."

"She's going to knife all the robbers and stick them in pickle barrels?"

"Only if I have to," Grace said slowly.

Patrick blushed. "I'm sorry. That wasn't fair."

Grace smiled as Patrick poured her another cup.

Patricia smiled. "Patrick, can you take the day off tomorrow?"

"For what?"

Patricia quickly told him about the stock certificate the prostitute had given Alexander. "I want you to go with me and Grace to the bank to see if it's real or not."

Patrick shrugged. "I'll lose four dollars. Is it worth it?"

"I don't know," Patricia said. "Probably not."

They were up at dawn, sitting at the breakfast table staring at one another. Grace was dressed in some of Patricia's best Sunday clothing, but she was too big for most of it. Patrick sat in his blue wool suit, sweating and itching. Patricia made pots of tea as if it were the only meaningful activity she could find. The children came and went, talking quietly so as not to disturb the adults who were in this strange mood.

Nine o'clock finally came. The three of them walked slowly into the First San Francisco Bank and Guaranty Trust Company, an imposing stone building which had been designed to resemble a medieval fortress in order to convince its customers that their assets were safe within.

The interior of the main banking room was done in marble. The floor was wide and cool and spotless. A giant chandelier hung like the sword of Damocles over the tellers' cages. A row of stout oaken doors marked the special sanctuaries offstage where only the privileged might enter—where Presidents and vice-presidents presided over vast fortunes. "Sure don't look much like our bank," Patrick said with a nervous grin.

The bank guard, in a grey uniform with a Sam Browne belt and pistol, spotted them as soon as they stepped foot upon the marble floor. He knew they didn't belong. They were dressed like North Beach Italians. He made his face a blank and walked swiftly to head them off. "May I ask what you wish here?" he said officiously.

Patrick's eyes narrowed and he started to take an angry step forward but Patricia held his arm tightly. "I would like one of the officers to examine a stock certificate for me," she said.

"She would," Grace said in a quiet malevolent voice.

"I'll take it to one of the tellers," the guard said.

Patricia smiled. "Perhaps you didn't hear me, sir. I would iike one of the officers to look at it." Patricia's palms were sweating. After all this, if the Grendle Mine certificate was bogus . . . She couldn't let herself think . . .

"May I see the certificate?" the guard said.

Patricia reached into her reticule and held the piece of heavy paper up for the guard to see but not to take. "May I see the officer?"

The guard huffed and turned and disappeared behind one of the stout doors.

"I'd like to get my hands on that one sometime," Grace said.

"Get in line," Patrick said.

Patricia looked around the room with the kind of awe you see on the faces of people at Chartres Cathedral. She listened to the carefully modulated voices, watched the swift and efficient way the male tellers walked to and fro, their leather soles clicking discreetly on the marble.

Mr. Breckenridge walked out of his office with the guard, trying not to laugh at the strangely dressed trio standing in the middle of the banking floor. "May I help you?" he said. He wanted to remember what they looked like so he could tell Burton Crocker about them over lunch at the club.

Patrick pointed to his sister. "She wants to know if this piece of paper is worth anything."

Mr. Breckenridge looked at the petite Irish woman. She was beautiful in a lowerclass sort of way. "Yes?"

Patricia held out the paper.

Mr. Breckenridge took ahold of it and put his pince nez on the tip of his nose. "The Grendel?" He readjusted his glasses. "The Grendel?" He looked up at the trio. "You have five shares in the Grendel?"

"Do we?" Patricia asked. "Is it a forgery or is it real?"

"How did you get this?"

Patrick started to answer, but Patricia stepped on his foot. She smiled. "It was left us by our brother," she said sweetly.

Mr. Breckenridge smiled nicely. "Why don't we go into my office? Perhaps you'd care for some tea? Coffee? I'll have Mr. Miner come in and examine the certificate. Do you have an account with us?"

"Nope," Patricia said.

"Well, we might talk about that as well. I'm sorry. I didn't introduce myself. I'm Alan Breckenridge."

"I'm Patricia Carrick."

Seated in Alan Breckenridge's spacious office on his green leather-covered chairs, the color of old treasury bills, the trio waited while a narrow-nosed man named Miner examined the certificate with a jeweler's loupe. He looked up at Mr. Breckenridge, nodded, then carefully placed the certificate on his boss's desk. "The number corresponds to the block of one hundred shares outstanding which Mr. Hickok, uh, lost in Chinatown. He, us, gave them away as payment for services, uh, rendered, I believe. Will that be all?"

Breckenridge smiled and nodded. Mr. Miner backed his way out of the office into the nether realms of the bank. "Well," the bank vice president said, straightening his neck-scarf, "at this morning's quote you possess assets of ten thousand and twenty-five dollars."

"Ten thousand and thirty dollars," Patricia said. "Five times two thousand aught six."

"Yes, quite," Breckenridge said. "Now, may I ask if you'd care to liquidate your assets or place the certificate in one of our surety boxes?"

Patricia smiled. "Neither."

"I beg your pardon?"

"I should like a loan against the stock."

"A loan?" The man's Adam's apple quivered outrageously.

"Yes, a loan."

Mr. Breckenridge fought to control his features. He was aghast at the gall of the woman who sat in his chair as if she belonged there! "Might I ask what you expect to borrow?"

"As close to face value as I can."

"Oh, my Lord. For what?"

Patricia rose, taller, it seemed, than her normal height. "I want to start a bank."

Mr. Breckenridge had not meant to laugh outright, but he couldn't stop himself.

CHAPTER FIVE

THE odd, uncomfortable looking quartet sat anxiously on the hard, straight-backed chairs in the pale yellow hallway. The dust of the road was still on them after the ninety-seven mile trip across the valley to Sacramento. Michael Kelly cleared his throat, looked as if he might speak, then sat back again. He spun his dark fedora in his hands.

Patrick looked up and down the hall, smoothed his cap on his knee, then cleared his throat too.

Patricia leaned back and closed her eyes, happy that she was sitting still, not on Michael Kelly's jouncing wagon.

Grace Malone smiled with a thin smile and thought that if anyone messed up this trip, she didn't know what she'd do. After all, Patricia Carrick and her friends had spent close to two months working out the details of this deal. If the State Commissioner of Banking decided against giving Patricia her charter for a state bank in San Francisco, then Grace thought she just might have to have a talk with him. For Heaven's sakes, it took all that time to raise the fifteen

217

thousand dollars—ten from Patricia and five from Michael and Mrs. Kierney and a few others—and no one should stand in their way now.

A hefty-looking assistant stepped out into the hall-way and stared at the bedraggled group. Then he went back inside his office. A few moments later he stepped outside again. "Mr. Carrick?"

Patrick stood up. "Yes?"

"Would you bring your, uh, group in, please?"

Patrick nodded and they followed the man through a series of offices until they reached a conference room which was lined with portraits of former Commissioners. "Please sit down," a man said from the darker end of the room. He was stocky, his tie was loosened and his shirt was open at the neck. "It's hot," he said.

Michael Kelly agreed with him as they took plush seats around the table. Patricia put down a large folder she carried, wove her fingers together in front of her and waited.

"I'm sorry I kept you waiting," the man said.

"Five hours," Patricia observed easily.

The man looked at her under beetling brows. "Five hours," he said. "Some have waited longer; some have never gotten as far as you."

Patricia nodded.

The man leaned back, put his feet on the conference table and went about cleaning his nails while he spoke. "I cannot in my wildest dreams see Miss Carrick, Mr. Carrick, Mr. Kelly and Mrs. Kierney managing a bank in the state of California."

"I beg your pardon!" Patricia said, her green eyes sparkling like electrodes.

The man held up a freshly manicured hand without

looking at her. "You take offense too quickly, ma'am. I said I cannot imagine you four managing a bank, but my staff and I can find nothing amiss in your application. You have the necessary funds, your incorporation papers are all executed, and we have no reason to believe that your character is unsound. . . ."

"Thank you," Patricia said quietly.

The man turned to face her. "Quite frankly, I wish you would reconsider, Miss Carrick, there has never been a female bank president. I don't think you comprehend the incredible complexities of the banking business. Oh, I know from the letters in your file that you've run a little lending service, but we are talking banking now."

Patricia bit down on her lower lip so as not to say what was truly on her mind. This man had the power to grant or not to grant her charter.

"You are far too lovely a woman for this business," the Commissioner said.

"Thank you," Patricia replied in a flat voice. The man was a fool.

The Commissioner paused. He shrugged. "The neighborhood you propose to locate in seems appropriate for the banking services which immigrants require and therefore I cannot, in good conscience, turn you down."

"Does that mean you're giving us our charter?" Patrick asked.

The man breathed out slowly. Nodded. "Yes. And I wish you the best of luck."

The four immigrants from San Francisco shook the Commissioner's hand and walked out of his office with a charter for their own bank. As soon as they reached the street they forgot their weariness and hooted and hollered and skipped down the street in a very unbankerly fashion.

"No," Patricia said firmly. "That one is not it either." She had just finished looking at the twelfth vacant wood frame building in her neighborhood.

The real estate agent sighed again, for the twelfth time, and surveyed the motley crew which followed in his train. There was Mr. Kelly, Mr. Carrick, Mrs. Kierney, Thomas Kierney who smelled like fish, nine Lacey and Gardiner children whom he couldn't tell apart, an imposing iceman named O'Connor who kept staring at the pretty Irish woman, and assorted other women who sewed with Mrs. Kierney. At each and every building one or another of the principals in this crazy banking venture found something wrong.

"... too far from transport...."

"... too near the saloons...."

"... too old...."

"... too new...."

"... too formal...."

"I want the perfect building in the perfect location," Patricia repeated. "The street should be safe for grandmothers and little babies, but it should be near to where our people live and work."

"Impossible," the agent said.

Tom Kierney looked up at the sun and realized he'd lost a full day's catch. He shrugged. "There's a place down on Cranmer," he said.

"Oh, that's a good street," his mother said.

"I have a cousin on Cranmer," one of her sewing ladies said.

Patricia turned to the agent. "Do you have anything on Cranmer?"

He shrugged. "I don't know. I hadn't thought to bring. . . ."

"Let's take a little stroll then," Patricia said.

Ten minutes later they stood at the head of a quiet tree-lined street with a beautiful view of the water. "Ooooh, very nice," one of the ladies said.

"Must be expensive," Michael Kelly said. He took a look at his pocket watch and hoped that the lettuce shipment from the valley wouldn't go bad on him.

A block later the aggregation stopped at the corner of the street.

Patricia walked forward slowly as they all went quiet. She headed directly and unwaveringly for a small white wooden frame building. It was a single story with wide dusty windows that faced the side-walk. Double door had been hung directly in the center of the building. Across one door was the sign: "To Let."

Patricia looked back at her stockholders.

They smiled.

"That's the Carrick Bank," Patricia said to the real estate agent.

"It doesn't look like a bank," he said.

"What's a bank supposed to look like?" Patricia asked.

"Like a mausoleum," the agent replied. "Like a fortress."

She grinned. "Not this one. This one is for people." She turned back to her big family. "Well, let's get to work. I want to open next week!"

* * *

Patricia was off by two weeks. The Carrick Bank was not ready to open until the first week in October. There were problems. The safe company couldn't deliver on time. The printer had misprinted the name of the bank as Carick with one "R" and had to take back all the deposit slips, withdrawal slips and counter checks. The carting company which was supposed to deliver the furniture wanted a kickback, which infuriated Patrick, who proceeded to knock the teamster unconscious. So the stockholders all pitched in and, using Michael Kelly's wagon, picked up the desks and counters and hauled them to Cranmer Street. Then the carpenter who was building the single teller's cage didn't like what he had done, so he ripped it apart and rebuilt it.

At eight o'clock on the morning of the grand opening of the Carrick Bank the bank's president, Patricia, was sweeping up woodshavings with the help of her chief officer, Patrick, and the Chairman of the Board of Directors, Mrs. Kierney. Stephen Lacey was supervising the dusting of the windows and the president's desk.

The placement of Patricia's desk had been the occasion for another problem. Michael Kelly and Ed O'Connor had wanted her to put her desk behind a partition so that her position would be elevated. "No bank president sits right out in the middle of the room where everybody off the street can walk up and bother her."

"This one does."

"You'll go mad."

Patricia shook her head. "No. I want to be every bit as accessible as I was when I was in Michael's fruit corner. I want them to see me working so they'll know I'm on the job. I want them to be able to come right up and ask me a question or ask for a loan or whatever else it is."

Grace nodded and crossed her arms across her ample breast and that was the end of that discussion.

At eight-fifty-nine Grace Malone went to the front door and peeked out through the shiny glass. "There's people out there," she said.

Patrick stood by the vault, nervously adjusting his collar which wouldn't stay buttoned. "How many?"

"A hundred?" Grace replied.

Patricia tried to neaten up her desk. "A hundred?"

"Maybe two hundred?"

Angelo, the Italian teller Patricia had hired to translate for her, looked nervous. He pulled at his cuffs and cleared his throat. "Two hundred?"

Grace shrugged.

When the church bells sounded Patricia said, "Mrs. Malone, the Carrick Bank is open for business."

The nieces and nephews cheered.

Mrs. Kierney tried not to cry, but she broke down and blubbered into her apron.

CHAPTER SIX

SIMON Yarrow had returned by private railway carriage from New York only two days earlier. Croquet and polo were all the rage on the East Coast, but he much preferred yachting off Pt. Judith with Charlie Townsend. It gave Simon the chance to sound him out on several ventures, away from the incessant Offenbach concerts. ladies' teas and non-stop discussions of the Knights of Labor.

From what Simon Yarrow could tell, Townsend and his people in Newport were every bit as keen to keep government out of business as Simon and his friends on the board of the Southern Pacific. "If it looks like Washington is going to take steps to legislate the marketplace," Simon had asked, "what do you gents see yourselves doing about it?"

Townsend barked an order to come closer to the wind. He looked perplexed. "I don't know, Simon," he replied.

"I believe I do," Simon said.

"I'm sure we'd be interested to hear your ideas," Charles Townsend replied.

That had been a week ago. Now, as Simon sat surveying the scene, the board room smelled of expensive aromatic tobaccos and specially blended coffees. The leather-covered chairs squeaked with that special sound that comes from old money and the taste that comes with it. The Persian carpet was sufficiently worn to denote respectable carelessness and the fan-type windows let in no more light than necessary to read a contract or study a land deed. The California Bank and Trust was the largest and hence the most prestigious of the big three.

The board melting had taken several hours. Simon Yarrow, resting in the wingback chair, let the pipe smoke drift lazily over his head and on up to the exquisitely beamed ceiling which had been patterned after the captain's cabin of a ship. He tapped impatiently on the paper in front of him. "That's all well and good, Stephens. I would certainly have no compunctions about granting Wheelock and Wheelock the one million five as long as we hold title to the steamship and Lloyds carries the riders. I don't know why you're belaboring it so."

Stephens, a balding man in his mid-fifties smiled and pursed his lips. "Just doing my job, sir," he said to the man in the wingback chair. The five other well-dressed men around the heavy teak table laughed politely. One cleared his throat. "Next on the agenda is the Stacey loan. I believe you have the paperwork on it?"

The men around the table looked up at the man in the wingback chair to assess his mood on this loan. Then they turned back to face Mr. Stephens with his round cheeks, thick neck and deepset eyes. "Stacey needs one million two in order to complete the rail line through his northwest parcel and thereby connect all his land with southern California's outlets. I would suggest approving this one as well."

The man in the wingback chair nodded.

Stephans smiled. "Then that's it for the regular agenda. Mr. Yarrow?"

Simon Yarrow eased forward on the wingback chair. "I would like to excuse Mr. Kramer and Mr. Myer."

The men in question left immediately. As soon as it was quiet Simon Yarrow let his brows squeeze down on his thick lids atop his small brown eyes. "I am now speaking confidentially," he said.

"Yes, sir," the others said.

Simon stood up tall behind the end of the table and leaned upon it. "It's this little Mick bank the immigrants are all flocking to," he said.

"The Carrick Bank?" Stephens said.

Yarrow nodded. "I've been watching it very carefully over the last year," he said. "That red-headed woman has posted assets in excess of three hundred and fifty thousand after beginning with a great deal less."

"The dagoes and the micks trust her," Stephens said.

"Surely they do," Yarrow said. "Indeed they do."

"Surely a small immigrant bank like that offers us no real threat," observed one of the officers. He wished he hadn't spoken at all when he saw Simon Yarrow's face. The eyes bore in at him, the cruel mouth twisted down at the corners and the vein in his forehead pounded. The officer had seen this man drive men to bankruptcy, had known of two men taking their own lives because of Simon Yarrow's ruthless banking.

"No real threat?" Yarrow said coldly. "No, of course it offers us no threat now. But soon, if this sort of slipshod operation is allowed to continue, if these little chiggers of banks are allowed to grow, we'll find our privileged position eroded. We'll be hardpressed to capture the lion's share of the savings market and we'll find ourselves actually competing with them. I don't want to see that happen." He paused and breathed out through his nose. "You don't know these Carricks like I do, gentlemen. They are unscrupulous. They know no sense of right or wrong as we do. They don't subscribe to the gentlemen's agreements which we hold sacred."

"That Carrick woman," said Stephens, "has actually gone out and solicited depositors! I was told she went from door to door in North Beach and coaxed the cash out of the Dagoes' mattresses!"

Yarrow smiled. "Exactly my point. I am suggesting that we stop this chancre before it grows any deeper."

"How?"

"The way you get rid of any other competitor," Yarrow said. "You find his weak spot. You find his weak spot."

Stephens smiled. "Meeting adjourned?" he asked.

"Meeting adjourned," Simon Yarrow said. It was Carricks who took Diana's love. It was Carricks who would pay.

"Hurry up," Patricia said. She tried for the ninth time to make the feather headdress stay on top of her head, but no amount of engineering skill by Mrs.

Kierney could make the three ostrich feathers stand vertically on her flaming red hair.

"I'm hurrying," Mrs. Kierney said.

"Oh, bless you, not you, Maude, I mean Patrick. The man spends more time in front of a mirror than Bathsheba ever did."

"And look what happened to her."

"Maybe we ought to let the feather kind of drape down across my face."

"It's not a bad idea, love." She smiled while she bent the plume down. "Did you ever think that when you were sewing gowns for fancy-dress balls you'd actually be invited to one?"

"Not at all," Patricia replied. The mirrow reflected back the radiant image of a beautiful woman wearing a long cream-colored gown in taffeta, lace and silk, with elbow-length matching gloves and borrowed pearls. "Did you ever think my crockpot would have almost a million dollars in assets? And that you'd be Chairman of the Board?"

"You're the real Carrick Bank," Mrs. Kierney said. "There, how's that?"

Patricia looked at herself on an angle. "The dress is fine; it's me I'm worried about."

"You get more beautiful every day. It just ain't fair."

"Where's Patrick?" Patricia asked Molly and Nancy, her nieces who stood at the door, wide-eyed at their aunt's transformation.

"Up in his apartment," they said. The year's success had allowed Patricia and her brother to buy the building they had lived in and now Patrick occupied the room where they had begun as paupers so many years ago. Their success, based on the poorer community's trust of Patricia Carrick, combined with her unflagging love and energy, had been a phenomenon.

"Will you tell him to hurry up?"

"Yes, ma'am."

"And get Stephen for me?"

"Yes, ma'am."

Mrs. Kierney, with a mouthful of pins, surveyed the gown from all angles to see if there weren't some errant seams. Satisfied that her work, as usual, was flawless, she allowed herself a smile. "Why do you suppose Mr. Stephens invited you and your brother tonight of all nights?"

Patricia beamed. "Because the Carrick Bank is making little waves in the banking world and Mr. Stephens wants to keep an eye on us. I guess he wants to see if we have six heads and a picture of His Holiness tatooed on our breasts."

"Shame."

"Yes, but wait until Stephens and his friends at California Bank and Trust get wind of my latest scheme."

"What now?"

"I want to open a second office up in North Beach. I have so many Italian customers and they shouldn't have to walk all that way down here. I have already written to Sacramento to ask about it."

Stephen, a handsome young man at sixteen, stuck his head in the door. "Yes, ma'am?"

"Did you do your homework?"

"Yes, ma'am."

"What about Harry?"

"He's stuck on his maths."

"Poor Harry," Mrs. Kierney offered.

"Poor Harry, my foot," Patricia said. "If he's going to go to college with Stephen, he'll have to stop being poor Harry and be 'Hardworking Harry'."

Stephen nodded and left.

"Can I ask one more question?" Mrs. Kierney said.

"Of course."

"You told me why Mr. Stephens asked you to his fancydress ball but you didn't tell me why you accepted."

Patricia sat back and laughed. "Because," she said, "I'm just as curious to see if Stephens has six heads and the Archbishop of Canterbury tatooed on his breast."

The California Bank and Trust's long-term success had been very good to Elijah Stephens. His proximity to men of wealth and power had given him access to every conceivable opportunity for making money. He did well.

The Stephens mansion on Nob Hill had been built in the style most notable in the San Francisco of the later nineteenth century—which is to say every style imaginable. A Norman crenellated tower rose up on one end, followed by a mansard roof and gables, strangely unbalanced by a pagoda-like tower that told the viewer's eye that the building was more or less finished. In between all of the above there was a liberal sprinkling of classic columns, Victorian cutout gingerbread and a few Gothic arches for good measure.

"Is this splendid enough for you?" Patrick asked as they were helped down from their hired carriage.

Patricia nodded and continued to stare at the entryway festooned with flowers of every hue. The home was ablaze with lights—gas lamps, candles, and Mexican lanterns. She thought of the misery she had left in her own neighborhood and wonderd how much tonight's party would cost banker Stephens. A footman took her shawl as she and Patrick made their way inside.

"Good evening Miss Carrick, Mr. Carrick, I am so glad you could honor us with your presence," Elijah Stephens said in the receiving line. "May I present my wife, the Marquesa dela Pingaterra?" She was Patricia's age, dark and beautiful with blue-black hair, scarlet lips, anthracite eyes and neatly arched brows. When she spoke, her Spanish accent made her words seem musical.

"Please, call me Anna," she said. "Elijah likes to use my title, but in America we don't have titles anymore, do we?"

"Only cattle barons," Patricia replied.

Anna laughed.

"And my daughter," banker Stephens said, "Miss Carlotta Stephens. Mr. Patrick Carrick and Miss Patricia Carrick."

Patrick looked up into the coal black eyes of the most beautiful young woman he had ever seen. She smiled as he tried to get his tongue to say the words his brain had decided upon. Carlotta was an eighteen year old carbon copy of her mother—with one exception: Carlotta's smile was a challenge to every man who looked upon her. Her eyebrows rose, a laugh came to her throat and she turned her head to the side as if she were a bullfighter daring you to step closer. "My pleasure," Patrick said.

Patricia gave him a gentle nudge to move him

along the receiving line, but he was never fully conscious of anyone else again. When he had finished bowing to Mr. Stephens' mother, an old dowager with an ear trumpet, he looked over his shoulder at Carlotta. She was looking right at him. He turned away quickly.

"I hope you aren't going to walk into that waiter with the tray of glasses," Patricia said to her smitten sibling. "Thirty-two is a little old to be mooning like a calf."

"Did you see her? Wasn't she magnificent?"

Patricia nodded. "She was all of that and a thousand pounds of trouble to boot."

Patrick took a glass of champagne from a silver tray which cruised past him. "What makes you say that?"

"Women's intuition. Some women are sharks. Some are dolphins. Carlotta is definitely of the former persuasion. Take my word on it."

Patrick smiled and looked back at the receiving line. "Damn," he muttered.

"What?"

"Every time I look at her she's looking at me," he said.

"Shark," Patricia said.

A tall thin man came loping up to Patricia and her brother and introduced himself as Wainwright Peabody. "I'm on the board of California Bank and Trust," he said. "I've been watching your progress with great admiration."

"And I've been admiring your assets for many years," Patricia said.

Wainwright Peabody looked at her for a full five seconds before he realized she was making a joke. He laughed in a high nasal voice. "A joke. How droll!"

"Yes," Patricia said.

"Excuse me," Patrick said, sidling off across the foyer when he saw Carlotta break free of the receiving line.

Wainwright Peabody cleared his throat. "May I introduce my fiancée?" he said.

Patricia Carrick turned her head and looked right into the vacant eyes of Sybil Chase, now a few years older, her brown hair pulled back in a bun, her pouty mouth still looking as if she might cry if she didn't get her way, and, Patricia presumed, her ankles still as thick as ever. Though Patricia winced at first, it was obvious that Sybil did not recognize her as the serving girl who was accused of murdering her mother. She would hardly have expected a mick maid to turn up at banker Stephens' home in such exclusive company.

"Miss Sybil Chase, Miss Patricia Carrick."

Sybil smiled blandly. "How do you do?"

"Quite well, thank you," Patricia said.

A curious look edged its slow and relentless way across Sybil's vapid face. "Haven't we met?" she asked.

Patricia smiled. "Yes, Sybil, we have."

"Where was it? At the Cotillion?"

"No, I don't think so. We didn't go this year."

"Was it at Simon Yarrow's dinner dance in April?"

"I hardly think so."

"Then where on earth have I seen you?"

"I think the last time was when I spilled the hot chocolate on Grant Yarrow. If memory serves me, you were rather indisposed then." Patricia gave a half smile.

Sybil Chase's face underwent a most curious transformation as it dawned on her that her fiance had just introduced her to a maid! And a maid who was dressed better than anyone else at the ball! And a maid who had seen her lying naked in bed with Grant Yarrow! She put her gloved hand to her mouth to keep from screaming at the top of her lungs. "Really?" a quiet little voice said.

"We may have seen each other briefly after that when the police accused me of poisoning your mother," Patricia said as if she were talking about a recipe or the weather.

"My God. . . ." Sybil muttered.

"You two *do* know each other," the confused Wainwright Peabody said. "How droll."

Patricia looked at him. "No, not really. Not really droll at all. Please excuse me." Patricia walked across the room and into the ballroom where one of the four orchestras was beginning to play for the dancers. Her eyes darted from couple to couple until she picked out Patrick dancing with Carlotta Stephens. She frowned, then turned and recognized the Commissioner of Banking. "Good evening," she said.

"Miss Carrick. We are well met. I understand your institution is doing rather well."

She laid a hand on his forearm. "Mr. Commissioner, my bank has done better than any other institution, state chartered or national, in the country and you know it." She took her hand back.

He nodded.

"Shall we dance?" she said.

"I have never had such a charming offer," he replied.

"Don't flatter yourself. I want to ask you about my request to open a branch."

He sighed and took her in his arms for the first waltz.

"You dance very well," Carlotta said. Her voice was soft, sounding like all the voices of rich women which Patrick had heard as they disembarked from the ships he unloaded. There was a kind of ease in speaking, an effortlessness, that made him want to lean closer to listen. Her perfume was different. A fragrance he had never smelled before.

"Thank you," he said, immediately hating himself for not being more imaginative. "You do too." Now he really thought he'd become a total bore.

"What is your job at the Carrick Bank?" she asked, winking over his shoulder at one of the swains who had spent all summer in her pursuit.

"I supervise the tellers."

"Oh, I thought you had only one teller," she said.

"It's not all that hard," Patrick said.

"That must be very exciting," she said.

"Oh, it is."

Carlotta smiled. "I had always thought I'd go into banking like your sister, but father says I have no head for figures."

"It's not all that hard," Patrick sair.

"Perhaps you could teach me," Carlotta said.

Patrick paused. "I'd like that very much," he said. He had never known the feelings that overwhelmed him. All his life he had been focused on the simple facts and acts of survival. He had kept his thoughts to himself, had lived most of his waking days inside his own private world. Suddenly that world had been entered by a woman who smelled like a bouquet and looked like a dream. Moreover, it seemed as if she was genuinely interested in him!

On the far side of the ballroom stood Elijah Stephens. His smile matched his daughter's. He looked over at Patricia dancing with the Commissioner of Banking and frowned. Perhaps there was a way of keeping her from getting her branch in the North Beach. If he did not stop her, Simon Yarrow would be very very angry. Stephens wondered why one of the most powerful men in the country should care about a little Irish woman . . . even if the little Irish woman had turned out to be an outstanding banker.

CHAPTER SEVEN

PATRICIA sat at her desk an hour before closing time and tried to make sense out of the figures. The handwriting was excellent. That wasn't the problem. But the balances were off. Just as she found where the error in addition was, a young mother and father came into the bank and looked around. Patricia waved them over. "Mrs. Flynn? Mr. Flynn? How are you to-day?"

"Fine thanks, Miss Carrick."

Patricia spied the babe asleep in Mrs. Flynn's arms. "And that is Dennis?"

"Yes," the father said proudly.

"He's a fine braugh of a lad," Patricia said. "How can we help you today?"

"We just need to cash my paycheck, if that's all right, ma'am."

"Certainly." Patricia reached into her desk drawer. "And I'd like to give young Dennis a little present to welcome him." She handed the proud parents five silver dollars.

"Oh, we couldn't," Mrs. Flynn said.

"I insist," Patricia said with a smile.

"It's too grand," Mr. Flynn said.

Patricia put her arms around the parents and walked them towards the tellers' cages. "I tell you what. Take these five dollars and open a savings account for Dennis. Then, as he grows up, the money will be earning interest for him. Every once in awhile you could put a few dimes or dollars in the account and by the time this young gent is finished growing, you could have enough to send him to Yale or Princeton." The first Princeton-Yale football game was played that fall.

The Flynns grinned and nodded. "That's a grand idea."

"Patrick? Would you be so kind as to open a savings account for young master Flynn here?"

Patrick looked up from his desk. "You bet, Patricia. Could you folks step over here?"

Patricia went back to her figures. The teller had made an error of seventy-five dollars. Plus he had reversed two numbers while entering them. She shook her head. The branch office would open in another month and she'd need tellers she could trust not to make silly errors like these.

After they closed for the day, Patricia walked home with her brother. "I'm going to have to let Amadeo go," she said.

Patrick looked shocked. "Why?"

"I cannot afford to have a teller who keeps making such simple errors in arithmetic."

"I thought you told me I was in charge of tellers," Patrick said.

Patricia looked straight ahead. "That was before you began courting Miss Stephens. Now I don't know what you are." As soon as the words had slipped from her lips she was sorry she had said them.

Patrick stopped on the sidewalk in the growing dusk. "I am still your brother!"

"Really? I never see you. It's hard to tell."

"That's not fair! I'm thirty-two. I'm not a child. It's time I got married."

"Carlotta Stephens is not going to marry you!"

"Who says?"

"I do. I know who she is and what she is. I don't know what she's up to, but I don't like it!"

Patrick's face was flushed. His eyes burned. "I don't care what you like! I am in love with Carlotta!"

"Oh, Patrick, are you sure you just haven't had your head turned?" Patricia retorted in exasperation.

Without bothering to answer, Patrick stormed off, moving too quickly for his worried sister to catch up.

He wasn't quite sure what he would say when he turned up on the front steps of the Stephens mansion. Over the past month Carlotta had invited him on a number of occasions to go with her to various functions: the opera, dinner, and so forth. But they had always been in large groups in public. They had never had more than a few moments alone. During those times Patrick found it impossible to say, simply, what he felt. In fact, he wanted nothing more than to say, "Carlotta, I adore you and I want to marry you."

He found it impossible to say because he knew she would never say yes. He was a rugged-looking red-haired Irishman who had a part interest in a bank for immigrants. She was an heiress, a princess whose social position was as distant from his as a hawk from a starling.

"Who shall I say is calling?" the butler asked.

"Patrick Carrick."

"Please wait in the foyer," the butler replied with a brief bow. He turned and left silently.

Patrick stood with his hat in his hands, swirling it slowly while his eyes took inventory of the armor which hung on the stone walls. He walked slowly to a sideboard which must have measured twelve feet in length, handcarved in the seventeenth century. His fingers caressed the smooth rich wood.

"Patrick, how delightful!" the voice said from the gently curving staircase at the head of the foyer. The architect had told Mr. Stephens that "the staircase is a stage where one makes entrances and exits. That stage must be as dramatic as possible." His words were borne out as the incomparably beautiful Carlotta Stephens swept down the long gentle curve wearing a yellow silk gown whose neckline dipped shockingly low to caress the easy curve of her full breasts. Her long black hair was curled and piled atop her head.

"You look beautiful," Patrick said. He craned his neck to see her as the late afternoon light caught her through the stained glass windows.

"I was having my portrait done." She smiled. "It's such a bore. Come up and watch. Do you have time? I need company tonight."

"I would be honored." Patrick followed her up the stairs, down the main hall and into what had once been the family playroom. Now its forty by fifty foot space had been given over to a canvas drop cloth, easel and divan upon which the artist had posed Carlotta Stephens in her brilliant yellow dress.

Patrick shook the painter's hand and then took a chair and a glass of sherry. He watched spellbound as the young man's brushes searched for and found every soft line and arch in Carlotta's face.

"Do you think it a fair likeness?" Carlotta asked.

"I don't know much about paintings," Patrick said, "but yes, I do."

"Monsieur Ladoux thinks I am too vain," Carlotta said. "I asked him to make my chin less predominant."

The artist blushed and hurried to catch the last of the light.

"I think your chin is perfect," Patrick said, "on and off the canvas."

Carlotta shot him a glance that heated his soul. "You have become a flatterer," she said. "I always liked to think of you as my rough Irishman whose nature precluded insincerity."

"I don't follow," Patrick said.

Carlotta laughed. Her voice trilled the upper register. "You are the only man I know who isn't a fawning flatterer, Patrick. I admire that. You are direct, blunt, sincere. You haven't learned how to lie yet like the others in my circle."

"I always try to tell the truth."

The painter nodded to his subject. "*Je suis fatigué.* That is all for today."

"*Merci beaucoup, Monsieur Ladoux.*" She sat up from her reclining position on the divan and took a glass of sherry from Patrick. As the young portrait painter cleaned his brushes and put away his paints, Carlotta told Patrick everything she had done during the past few days. The Irishman was enthralled by each detail because, no matter how mundane, they all concerned Carlotta.

When Monsieur Ladoux had gone, Carlotta smiled and said, "I am so glad you stopped by, Patrick. My mother and father have gone away for the week and I am so bored I could scream."

"I am glad I stopped by too," he said. He looked into her eyes and wished the divan were smaller.

She reached out and took his hand. "I like to think of you as a friend," she said. "I have so few friends. Everyone wants something from me. But you, you're different."

Patrick felt the glow in his hand as if he held a hot coal from the hearth. "I'm very happy to hear that," he said.

"But you haven't told me anything about yourself! How has your week fared?"

Patrick shrugged. Then he began to speak slowly about the arrangements for the new branch office in North Beach and how difficult it would be to work in two places at once.

"Surely your sister will make you the manager of the branch," Carlotta said. "She could do no less for someone as talented as you are."

"We haven't talked about that yet," he said.

"Well, I'm sure she will."

Patrick stood and spoke, warm from the sherry, flushed from the intimate moment, and said, "I must fire my new teller, Amadeo. It is so difficult getting good help."

"Father says the same as you," Carlotta said. She reached up a hand and gently tugged Patrick onto the divan next to her. "Have I told you how handsome I think you are?" she asked.

Patrick shook his head.

"Well, you are. If I were to paint your portrait it would be as a Greek god."

"For sure I'm no Greek," Patrick exclaimed.

Carlotta laughed aloud, covering her full mouth with her soft hand. "No, I mean the statues of the most perfect men." She got up and went to a small bookcase across the room, returning with a large volume of plates of Greek and Roman statuary. "Like Adonis," she said, flipping open to a well-thumbed page.

"Oh, my God," Patrick said with a blush.

"He's wearing an acanthus leaf, love," Carlotta said.

As she spoke, Patrick looked at the book and up at her hair so close to him. She smelled of roses.

"See where his muscles bulge beneath the surface of his skin? They look like bundles of wires, each stringing to a different part of his body. Look at his chest, like yours, so chiseled where it comes out then cuts back in again. And the ripples in the stomach. The long lean calves. A woman would be a fool not to worship a god like Adonis." She turned, inches away from his face. She could feel her own breath ricochet back upon her face from his.

Carlotta leaned forward and brushed her tender lips across Patrick's cheek, chin and, finally, lips. The book of photographs slipped from her hands and fell to the floor.

Patrick's hands entwined her back and locked her in his strong arms. Her lips pulsed against his own. Finally, she pulled back in disarray, her breathing irregular, her eyes distracted. "I should not have done that," she said.

Patrick smiled and shook his head. "There is every reason in the world why you should have done that," he said.

"You are so strong," she said. "I feel like one of mother's glass figurines. Vulnerable. Fragile. You could shatter me with your love."

Patrick reached out a second time and clasped her head softly but firmly between his large hands. He pulled her to his lips again and drank as deeply as he dared.

"I want you," he whispered in her ear.

"Oh, my love, my Irish love," she replied softly. "I have no defenses against you. You are too strong."

Patrick reached behind her and began to unfasten the hooks which bound her gown. It was as if he had been made for this one moment. Suddenly all his inexperience, his unsureness, melted away and he became a powerful force for the culmination of love.

In a few moments he had slipped Carlotta Stephens from the brilliant yellow gown which she wore in the portrait a few feet away. He then untied the laces of her camisole as she swooned on the divan and begged for his release.

Her breasts were firm and tipped with rose. Her stomach rose and fell as she waited for him. She cried out quietly, stifling the scream as he entered her and made her his own. "Oh, Christ," she said as the first of her climaxes uprooted her. "My dock worker, my lover," she whispered. "My Adonis."

When they had each taken their fill of each other the room was dark and they dressed in silence. Finally, after she was satisfied that she did not look as disheveled as she felt, Carlotta lighted a gas lamp by the door and smiled at herself in the mirror. Then she turned to look at the handsome man whose ruddy face was still flushed from the loving exertions of a few minutes earlier. She had had many lovers, but this one was certainly one of the best. "Would you care for a little supper, my love?"

Patrick Carrick nodded. He took her in his arms once again. "What would you say if I asked you to marry me?"

Carlotta's face went serious. She clung to her lover and said, "It's too soon to speak of such things." She placed a finger across his lips. "Just love me as you have."

He started to say something, but she stopped him with a kiss.

CHAPTER EIGHT

THE grand opening for the North Beach branch was set for December tenth. It had taken longer than anyone had expected, but now Patricia called the branch opening, "The Carricks' Christmas present to North Beach."

Most important, before the little branch opened in a storefront by the wharves, Patricia had to teach Patrick everything she could so that he could take over as manager. She could not believe the change which had come over him since he and Carlotta had begun their affair. He was more serious, more reliable, more mature. He had even become a better banker. It didn't matter to him that they could not always find the occasion to make love; it was sufficient for him to be near this ravenhaired eighteen year old.

Patrick lied to his sister whenever he went out because he knew how much she distrusted and disliked Elijah Stephens' daughter. But the important thing was that he was the manager.

"I would have been nervous if you hadn't found

Chandler Gates," Patricia said on the night before the branch opened.

Patrick smiled, finished his tea and decided not to tell his sister that their new star teller for the North Beach branch was Carlotta's cousin. Some day he would tell her everything, but first he had to prove himself.

The tenth of December dawned bright over the Bay and the sun literally burst off the bells of the brass horns gathered for the grand opening. By eight in the morning there were three hundred residents huddled around the storefront which read: THE CARRICK BANK, North Beach Branch. Two photographers had their tripods set up and were busily measuring out the proper amount of flash powder so as to freeze forever the faces of the important people who would open the doors for the first time.

Patricia, with Grace Malone always nearby, Mrs. Kierney in her newest dress, her son Tommy, Mr. Kelly and Ed O'Connor, the nine nieces and nephews and the stockholders all grinned and jostled in front of the frosted glass doors. Mr. Linus Comstock, the Commissioner of Banking, posed with the pair of gold-painted scissors he would use to cut the big red ribbon. Chandler Gates smiled as he put an arm around Patrick and wished him luck.

At nine o'clock Mr. Comstock snipped the red sash and the North Beach Branch was open. At five o'clock that same day the branch had taken in thirty-six thousand dollars in deposits. Patricia came down from what she liked to call "The Head Office" with Grace Malone and looked at Patrick and Chandler Gates' daily sheets. She beamed like a lighthouse. "You boys are quite the team," she said. She embraced Patrick

and shook his new teller's hand warmly. "If Grace
and I don't watch out, your branch will outstrip us
downtown."

"Nothing would give us greater pleasure," Patrick
said with a laugh. He clapped Gates on the shoulder.

Gates, a tall thin man with deep blue eyes and a
round nose which held thick glasses, said. "It was a
very good day. Miss Carrick. These people here on
North Beach really trust you and you're serving them
well."

"Thank you, Mr. Gates. What say we all go out and
celebrate with a little spaghetti dinner?"

Patrick thought about begging off so he could see
Carlotta, but he quickly changed his mind when he
saw his sister's eager, expectant face. This was her
triumph. Family loyalty held sway.

Christmas, 1878 was the most joyous event in Patricia's life. She wished that her father and her brothers Joseph and Alexander could have shared the
bounty that had finally come to the Carrick family.
They had never before had a Christmas ham, nor the
wherewithal for presents. Patricia cried herself gently
to sleep on Christmas night for the beauty and fragil-
ity of life.

In April of 1879 Elijah Stephens called his daughter
into his study at the mansion. "Yes, Father?" she said.
She was tired; her face was pale and drawn.

"How would you like to take a little vacation?" he
asked.

Carlotta smiled. "Where?"

"I have just bought a home in the Napa Valley on
the lake and I haven't even laid eyes on it. I thought
perhaps you might like to take a look at it."

"Isn't that strange that you should buy something sight unseen?"

Elijah Stephens rubbed his chins and smiled benignly. "Not really. I doubt if you would understand finances and deals such as this one." He stood and walked behind his desk. "Perhaps you might like to take your friend Mr. Carrick with you for company."

"Unchaperoned?" Carlotta said with a laugh.

"The servants would go with you, of course."

Carlotta raised her brows and wondered what her father was up to. But those thoughts were quickly cancelled by the thought of spending time virtually alone with the big strong Irishman who made her feel like a woman. She went and stood behind her father, linking her slender arms around his girth. "I'll see if Patrick can get the time off from his bank."

Elijah Stephens grinned and turned to kiss his daughter. "I'm told it's a most romantic spot."

"Father, if I didn't know you better, I'd think you had become a match-maker."

Elijah shrugged. The trap was set, ready to spring shut on the infernal Irish woman.

Patrick moved cautiously. There was no way in the world that he could tell his sister that he had planned to go away to the Napa Valley for a week with Carlotta Stephens. When Carlotta had asked him, he'd jumped three feet into the air, turned and come down with a whoop and a holler. A week alone with the woman he loved!

"Something on your mind, brother?" Patricia asked.

"Last time I was talking to Linus Comstock," Patrick said, picking at the remains of the roast on his plate, "he said I should come up to Sacramento to talk."

"About what?"

"Patricia, he's the Commissioner of Banking. What do you think we'd talk about?"

"Banking. But why?" Patricia poured herself another glass of water and looked over at Grace Malone, who was just finishing her coffee. "You just caught me by surprise is all."

Patrick smiled. "I'm sorry. I thought I'd take a week in Sacramento, get in good with Mr. Comstock, and establish myself with some of the men on the Banking Committee." He looked up at her. "It's not always easy being the brother of 'that Carrick woman'."

"Who'd do your chores?"

"Chandler Gates could mind the store," Patrick replied. "He's qualified."

Patricia nodded. "I guess it wouldn't do any harm to have you putting your oar in up there. It might be a help when we open our third branch."

"Third branch?"

"Of course. We're going to see what happens when I try to open a branch down in Los Angeles."

"That'll sure rip the tops off the boys at the California Bank and Trust, won't it?" Patrick said.

Patricia nodded. "Well, you make your plans and just keep me advised, all right?"

"Thanks, Patricia."

A rumor is a little like a fire. It begins with a single spark and then, if it finds enough tinder to feed upon, it can grow into a major conflagration which no one, not even the arsonist himself, can put out.

This particular rumor began most simply.

It was in O'Casey's pub, eight blocks from the "home office" of the Carrick Bank. A man with a black leather eyepatch leaned against the bar, his legs crossed, a slouch hat down on his forehead, and talked to his new acquaintance. "Ya can't trust 'em, ya know."

"Ya don't know what you're talking about."

The man with the eyepatch smiled and ordered another round. "Well, now, if you're so smart, riddle me this: you put your money in the bank. The bank lends me your money. What if you want your money back and I ain't paid it back yet?"

The new acquaintance smiled like a firstgrader with the right answer. "They got a lot of people's savings. Not everybody asks for their dough back at the same time. See. They don't loan it all out. Just part of it."

The man with the eyepatch leaned closer. "And what if they does?"

"Does what?"

"What if everybody asks for their dough back at the same time?"

"That won't happen."

"What if it does?"

The new acquaintance looked dumbfounded. "I dunno."

The man with the black leather eyepatch smiled, revealing blackened stumps of teeth. "I'll tell ya what happens. It happened to the Reynolds Bank and about a hunnert banks back east. The first people to get their money out do all right. Everybody else loses everything." He paused. "That's what happens."

Later that night the new acquaintance, still pondering the question, staggered home. He had talked to three other men after his conversation with the man with the eyepatch. They had all been as stunned as he was. On the way home he took a walk past the Carrick Bank and looked at it in the moonlight. He leaned against the lamppost and spoke quietly. "Money? Are you in there?"

No one answered except the wind.

A half hour later the man in the black eyepatch and a dozen others met in the livery stable on Market Street. There they reported to a well-dressed man. "You shoulda seen 'em when we told 'em their bundles could go into the privvy," the man with the eyepatch said.

"You'da thought you'd cut their balls off," another man said.

The well-dressed man smiled. "I want you to ease back on things for now," he said. "Tomorrow night go to different places and start again. Meet back here at midnight."

"Yes, sir."

Elijah Stephens' man paid off the rumor-arsonists.

CHAPTER NINE

PATRICIA looked at the daily sheets from both branches and screwed up her face in a frown. She hadn't slept well in a few days. She had a vague sense of uneasiness, the nameless feeling that life's wheels were far beyond her control and that they were rolling inexorably closer.

"What's the matter?" Grace Malone asked from her spot by the door.

"Fewer savings, more withdrawals," Patricia replied.

"It's like that sometimes," Grace said. "Ain't it?"

"Yes, but this doesn't feel the same. I wish Patrick were back."

"When's he due?"

"Five days."

Grace sauntered over to her boss's desk. "Telegraph him back," she said.

Patricia smiled. "I'm being foolish. I haven't got anything to go on. It'll turn around. I guess it's the summer coming and people not feeling like putting money away. Spring fever."

Grace watched her boss and thought she ought to follow her instincts. Women's intuitions, except where men were concerned were usually right, but Grace didn't want to meddle. She'd said her piece.

The door to the bank opened. A cautious Mr. and Mrs. Flynn poked their heads inside. Mrs. Flynn carried her baby with her. "Mr. and Mrs. Flynn! How are you?" Patricia asked, glad to be able to take time away from her worries.

"Fine, Miss Carrick," they said.

"Your Dennis is looking handsomer and handsomer," Patricia said, leaning in close to see the baby. "He is definitely going to break hearts."

"Thank you, Miss Carrick."

"What may we do for you today?" Patricia asked.

The Flynns looked sheepish and started to head back for the front door.

"Is it so private you cannot tell me?" Patricia asked.

Mr. Flynn turned back to face the woman who had always treated him so well. "We changed our minds."

"From what to what?"

His wife looked at the floor. "We was gonna take our savings out."

Patricia walked forward and put her hands on their shoulders. "There's nothing to be ashamed of. It's your money."

"Thank you, Miss Carrick, but we'll stick with you," Mrs. Flynn said.

Patricia's face went white. "I don't think I understand."

"There's talk," Mr. Flynn said.

"What kind of talk?" Patricia asked. Slowly and

relentlessly her worst fears were taking shape and pressing closer and closer.

Mrs. Flynn looked to her husband for the answer.

"There's talk that you can't cover the savings," Mr. Flynn said. "I didn't believe it," he added quickly.

Patricia looked over at Grace and the two new tellers behind their cages. "No bank can cover all its savings," Patricia said.

The Flynns looked shocked.

"Your savings and Dennis's savings are out in the community, helping other families build homes and businesses."

"What if everybody wants their savings back?" Mrs. Flynn asked.

"Why would everybody want their savings at the same time?" Patricia asked.

Mr. Flynn shrugged his shoulders. "I dunno. A disaster maybe?"

"Where did you get the word, 'disaster', Mr. Flynn?"

He looked sheepish. "It's just what they're saying. If there's a disaster or something."

"Only God knows when there's a disaster," Patricia said. "But if you want your savings, you're welcome to 'em."

"No, it'll be all right."

Grace Malone opened the door and five people walked in, avoiding Patricia Carrick's steaming gaze. They lined up at the withdrawals window and stood waiting anxiously.

"More folks looking for a disaster?" Patricia said so that they could hear every syllable.

A tall heavy-set woman looked embarrassed. "It's all me and Reggie got."

Patricia looked over at her nephew, Eric. "Go see Mr. Gates in the North Beach Branch and ask him if people are withdrawing funds there, too."

"Yes, ma'am." He took off at a run.

"Grace," Patricia said, turning to her guardian angel, "tell Hilton at the First Federal Bank that we may have to dip into our savings to cover a little problem here."

"I'm gone."

Patricia turned to look at the Flynns. "If I were you I'd look inside my heart and ask myself where the disaster really is. Somebody's been spreading rumors about banks failing and you people have fallen for it."

That was ten-fifteen on the morning of Friday, May 14, 1879.

At eleven-fifteen Gates sent word from the North Beach branch that there was a line of forty people waiting to withdraw their money. At that same hour Patricia was standing outside the "head office" looking at a line which extended out the doors and half-way down the block.

"Please, listen to me," she shouted.

"We want our money," a man in a black leather eyepatch said.

"Right," said another man near him.

"You'll all get your money," Patricia said. She turned to Grace and spoke quietly. "Tell Hilton I'll need fifteen hundred anyway. No, better make it two thousand on our draw."

"Will do," Grace replied.

"Wait." Patricia looked off and saw Eric churning his short legs on the pavement, out of breath, and red-faced.

"Mr. Gates says he needs a thousand and maybe more," Eric said.

"All right. Add that and get Hilton at First Federal to send the money by carriage."

Grace left quickly, pushing her way through the curious bystanders.

"... what is it?"

"... Carrick Bank's got trouble...."

"... trouble is a disaster...."

"... what if a disaster?"

"... we're getting ours just in case...."

Patricia went from person to person in the line, pleading with them to have faith in her bank. "It's your bank as much as anybody's," she said. "You're all investors."

"We're sorry, Miss Carrick. You've always been good to us, but we can't take the chance on losing our fifty-seven dollars, I'll tell ya."

It was the same story with each of the panic-stricken people who stood uneasily on line. Panic had grown, fed by the rumors, a fire of its own. The men and women knew Patricia Carrick. They knew that she was as trustworthy a person as any in the land. But the flames of doubt fanned by the men sent by Stephens scorched all rational thought. These were men and women who had begun with no cents whatsoever. The threat that they would lose the few dollars they had saved was overpowering.

At one o'clock Michael Kelly had heard of the run on the Carrick Bank. "This is madness!" he shouted to the hundred and fifty people who jostled for places in line. "You know me! You know the Carricks! You can trust that your money is safe!"

"Who says!"

"I say!" Michael replied. "I'm one of the bank's largest depositors! I'm not running to take out my sixteen thousand!"

"You can afford to lose it!" a dirty-looking stranger yelled.

"None of us can afford to lose any money," Michael said, "but nobody's *gonna* lose any!" He turned aside to Patricia. "How much longer can you hold out today?" he asked quietly.

"Until closing," she said. "I think. If it goes on next week. I don't know. I've got funds backing up the North Beach branch. I'll have to wait until Gates reports in."

Michael Kelly wiped his bald dome and put his hat back on. "What got into everybody?"

"Damned if I know. Somebody talked about a disaster and that was it."

"Disaster! *This* is a disaster." He walked over to one of the couples he'd known the longest and tried to reason with them. They looked away.

At three o'clock Patricia closed the doors and told the thirty people left that they could come back Monday if they still felt inclined to. They gave her a hard time, but it was no use. She stood firm on the bank's right to close for the weekend.

It was a morose group which sat in the main office at five that afternoon. "Did you wire the Commissioner of Banking to ask Patrick to get home at once?"

"Yes, Patricia," Grace replied.

Patricia looked at Michael Kelly, Mrs. Kierney, the rest of the board members, and Chandler Gates. "I don't mind telling you that what we are looking at is a tragedy. A tragedy engineered by somebody outside.

The rumors started night before last. Ed O'Connor there was able to track them down to O'Casey's Pub."

"Let's get whoever started them," Michael yelled.

Patricia put up a hand to quiet him. "That won't change anybody's mind. No, we have to see this thing through. I've called in the demand notes."

"Jesus," Michael said. "That'll cripple half our borrowers."

"You think I wanted to?" Patricia said. She slammed her fist down on the ledger. "I had no choice. We are being swamped here! We have until Monday to try to reverse this thing. If they come back in the same hoards as they did today, we're finished."

None of them noticed the light tap at the door at first. Then Grace heard it and looked out into the early darkness. "Yes? Oh, Mr. Hilton, come in."

Mr. Alan Hilton, still dressed in his banker's morning coat, entered cautiously. "I trust I am not coming at an inconvenient time?"

"Right now all time is inconvenient," Patricia replied. "Come in, sir."

"May I speak with you alone?" he said.

"Anything you have to say you can say in front of my board," Patricia said.

Alan Hilton, a medium-sized man with a grey face at twenty-eight years, cleared his throat. "I cannot extend you any more credit."

"Credit?" Patricia said.

"Yes."

"But we have cash on deposit with the First Federal!"

"You used to," the grey-faced man said.

"Where in Hell did it get to?"

Mr. Hilton held out a handful of interbank withdrawal slips. Patricia examined them. "Patrick Carrick withdrew two hundred and ninety thousand dollars?" she whispered.

"So it would seem," the man replied.

CHAPTER TEN

THE newspapers chewed up the story as if they were ferrets loose in a henhouse. The headlines competed with each other:

IMMIGRANT BANK GOES BUST!
BANK PRESIDENT'S BROTHER ABSCONDS WITH FUNDS!
CARRICK THIEF!
CARRICK BANK CLEANED OUT BY MANAGER!

Beneath the headlines the smaller, but no less incriminating text, described in hungry detail how Patrick Carrick's signature was found on the withdrawal slips for close to three hundred thousand dollars over a two month period. The reporters seemed to relish telling how rumors had gone abroad causing a run on both branches of the upstart bank. Now, it seemed, there was no chance of the remaining depositors ever seeing their money again.

The story concluded by informing one and all that Patrick Carrick, aged thirty-three, six feet one inch, with red hair and beard, weighing one hundred and eighty pounds, was wanted for embezzlement. What the story did not include was that three of the four newspapers covering the story had floated loans from the California Bank and Trust Company and that Simon Yarrow had personally contacted each of the editors, reminding them of their civic duty to warn the public against unscrupulous bankers.

At the house on Meachum Street where Patricia had lived since first coming to San Francisco six years ago, a crowd of fifty or sixty kept a silent angry vigil outside. Inside Patricia looked down from her window at the unmoving people who had once trusted her. Behind her, Ed O'Connor, Grace Malone, and Michael Kelly drank their tea. Only the clicks of cups on saucers could be heard. "It's still too hard to believe," Patricia said quietly. Outside the spring sun warmed the Saturday morning air and created one of those days where everyone's first impulse is to breathe deeply, thank God they're alive, and go forward with the idea that maybe life isn't so terrible after all.

Michael Kelly looked at the newspapers for the fifth time as Mrs. Kierney came in.

"Anything?" Patricia asked.

"The hotel said Patrick never arrived. Mr. Comstock wired he had no idea Patrick was even on his way to see him," Mrs. Kierney said.

Patricia nodded.

"What do you think?" Ed O'Connor asked.

Patricia smiled ruefully. "Well, let me tell you what I don't think."

"What's that?"

"I don't think my brother is a thief," she replied.

The words came quickly, the result of so deepfelt a conviction that there was no stopping them. "You live with someone for so long, you grow blind to their assets and liabilities sometimes. But Patrick is not a thief. Family loyalty meant more to him than anything else."

Mrs. Kierney looked at the others, cleared her throat and said, "What about that Stephens woman?"

Patricia's green eyes grew hot and hard. "I don't think she could have blinded him to family," she said carefully.

"It wouldn't be a bad idea to check and see if she's in San Francisco," Michael Kelly said.

"Good idea," Patricia said.

Michael put down the papers. "I'll go right now."

"You don't think Patrick stole it, do you?" Patricia asked.

Michael shook his head. "Nope, but it don't much matter. Have you seen the faces of those people out there?"

"We all have." Patricia walked Michael to the door and thanked him.

"We can't open on Monday, can we?" Mrs. Kierney asked.

"Not without a miracle," Grace Malone replied.

Patricia came back from the doorway. She clapped her hands. "All right! We have forty-eight hours to find my brother! I want everyone who's still on our side to fan out and look for him! He may have gone on a bender for all we know. Maybe he's sick somewhere. Or maybe he's hiding out and trying to get word to us. At any rate it's better for us to find him than for the coppers. Come on now. We've had our

time for feeling low. Now it's time for action!" She
sat down with a map and quickly drew grids upon
it, outlining areas for search.

Patrick eased his leg up and over Carlotta's smooth
brown thigh. He marvelled at her olive skin—how soft
it was and yet how firm—one of the wonders of her
beauty. He let his hand trail across her flat stomach,
imagining he could feel the downy hair which grew
there. He breathed in deeply and could still smell the
roses admixed with the luxurious essences of their own
lovemaking. He smelled the back of his own strong
forearm and smiled. His skin and her skin had become one. He could not tell the difference.

Carlotta's dreams were troubled by jagged shapes
which could not be forced to fit, by whisps of truths
too terrifying to face during her waking moments.
Finally her mind pushed them down into the depths
again and she was allowed to rest quietly in the
arms of her lover.

Patrick watched his woman fret in her sleep, saw
her blue-veined lids struggle to open, then relax
again. Her breathing became heavy and deep. He
wondered what had distressed her so.

On Nob Hill the policeman nodded abruptly and
pursed his lips. "You say, Mr. Stephens, that you did
not learn of Mr. Carrick's crime until this morning?"

Elijah Stephens leaned back at his breakfast table
and tucked his dressing jacket tighter around his
wide stomach. He was proud of the way he looked.
A portly man was a prosperous man. Everyone ap-
preciated that fact these days. He was glad the two

detectives could see him in this informally luxurious setting. He had been wealthy for many years, but it still gave him a thrill to have the lower class "catch" him in all his splendor. "Yes, when I read the daily papers," he said, pointing to the garish headlines. "I am shocked, of course, but my first responsibility is to the banking public."

"You know where we can find this Patrick Carrick?"

"Yes, I am sorry to say. He is in the Napa Valley with my daughter. I am most distressed." Without any further ado, he told the intent policemen how to locate his new home in the valley.

"We'll telegraph the authorities there," they said.

"I trust you will be able to keep my family's name out of the affair?"

"We'll do our best, Mr. Stephens."

"That's all I can ask," he replied.

"I got Gussie Logan who said she saw Patrick leave the railroad station in a closed carriage with a dark-haired woman," Ed O'Connor said before noon.

Patricia grimaced. "All right. Which direction did they go in? That was probably Carlotta Stephens."

"North," Ed replied, "but that don't help much."

"Yes, it does. If we can get to him before anybody else does. Was he sober?"

Ed nodded as the door burst open and Michael Kelly stood there with his shirttails hanging out. "I ran up the street. I couldn't wait."

"What is it, Michael?"

"Stephens wouldn't see me, but I met up with Flossie Borden, his cook. She hates the son of a bitch—

begging your pardon—and she said that Miss Carlotta was up North in the Napa Valley. He bought a new house up there."

"It's a big valley," Ed said. "Where?"

"She didn't know."

"Jesus!"

Michael held up his hand and struggled to catch his breath. "But I found his driver, Charles. I'm friends with Charles' cousin, Jack Taylor, the tanner across the bay."

"Save us," Patricia said.

"And he told me where it is on the lake up there."

"Ed, arrange to get us across the bay and let's get going. Grace, let's change into clothes where we can do some hard travelling."

Her nipples grew slowly, standing up like dainty soldiers at attention. Patrick's tongue encircled them one at a time and, instead of surrendering, they grew all the more taut, all the more rigid. Then he took her, and Carlotta cried out. It was a single pure note, a call denoting an avalanche of sensations which no man had ever caused in her. She had, for the first time while making love, lost all control.

She blacked out.

At the bottom of the pit that covered her Carlotta heard voices. Familiar . . . laughing . . . self-satisfied . . . haughty.

She thought she could play both ends against the middle. So easy . . . so very easy.

She would play her father's little game—banking and bankers were so silly when you got down to it—and she would play her own game—loving the man who made her body feel like a storm-tossed ship in a typhoon.

What did it matter about Chandler Gates? What really mattered was her craving for the thick-muscled Irishman who sent her to uncharted regions of rapture.

All that talk between Chandler and her father was just so much silliness and who cared whether the Carrick Bank went under—whatever that meant? What difference did it make if Chandler had those samples of Patrick's signature?

Very slowly the pieces started to turn in her sleeping mind. They were putting themselves together, attaching themselves to meaning.

Patrick was being set up! The bank would go under and she had been blind to it because she loved him so much! How ironic, she thought. All she cared about was having him. It didn't matter about anything else!

She looked up at her handsome lover. Covered her breasts with a sheet. "Chandler Gates brought samples of your signature home," she said.

Patrick smiled, then looked dismayed. "What for?"

"I don't know. I didn't care then," she said. "I do now."

Patrick got up and looked out at the lake which shimmered in the heat. His mind was bothered, ajumble. He looked back at his woman. "Did your father ask you to pursue me?"

She smiled. "He just thought it would be nice for us to get to know one another."

"Does he know we're here for the week?"

"Certainly. It was his idea. Come back to bed."

"How well do you know Chandler Gates?"

"Not well. Daddy told me to introduce you to him and to encourage you to hire him as a teller. I just thought he was doing Chandler a favor."

"How often was Chandler at your house?"

Carlotta pursed hr lips. "After he went to work for you, quite often. He and Daddy spent a lot of time talking boring old banking in his study. I usually went to bed." Carlotta looked confused when she saw the angry expression on her lover's face. "All I cared about was you," she said softly. "Please come hold me."

"It didn't strike you strangely that Chandler and your father wanted samples of my handwriting?"

"I don't understand anything about banking! All I'm good for is loving!"

Patrick began putting on his clothes as quickly as possible. "I've got to get back. Something's wrong at the bank. I don't know what it is, but I can smell the stink from here!"

Carlotta tried to hold him, but he flung her to the bed. "Please," she begged.

"Get dressed! You're coming with me."

Suddenly there was a loud knocking at the bedroom door. "Miss Carlotta? Miss Carlotta," her maid cried, "there's men here to see you."

Carlotta put on her robe and ran to the door. "What men, Sophie?"

"Sheriff. They want to talk to Mr. Patrick, but his bed ain't been slept in."

Carlotta's face went pale. She looked back at Patrick. Then back at the door. "Tell them I'll be right out."

"Yes, ma'am," the frightened girl said.

Carlotta took a quick look in the mirror, shot her

lover a frightened glance, and went out to talk to the sheriff.

As soon as she was gone, Patrick eased out the ground floor window and edged his way around the side of the house until he could squat just below the livingroom window. The voices were loud, insistent.

". . . embezzlement. Look at the papers yourself."

"I don't believe it."

"Ma'am, I have a warrant for Mr. Carrick's arrest."

"He's not here."

"May I ask where he is?"

"You may, but I don't have the slightest idea. He went out riding last evening and I guess he didn't return."

"Is it usual for him to go out riding in the dark?"

"No, sir."

"You didn't think it strange?"

"Yes, but he told me to mind my own business."

"Which horse did he take?"

"The pinto."

"Which direction did he go in?"

"Towards the main road."

"You're telling us true?"

"Sheriff, I am not in the habit of lying!" Her face was flushed, her voice loud and angry.

"Sorry, ma'am. We're just trying to do our job. We won't trouble you anymore. But just in case he comes back, I'll leave a few men on the place." He tipped his widebrimmed hat and left.

The dust choked the dry roads as Patricia, Ed O'Connor, Grace Malone, and an exhausted Michael Kelly tried to hang onto the lurching carriage. They had been travelling most of Saturday and now the late afternoon sun spread out on the floor of the valley, picking out the vineyards in stark relief. "There's a place up ahead where we can change the team," Michael said. "I used to go there when I was buying grapes."

"We'll have to hole up for the evening soon," Ed said.

Patricia shook her had. "No time. We have to push on."

"It won't help to kill us all," Michael said.

"She said push on," Grace said.

Patrick and a frightened Carlotta managed to get two horses saddled a half hour after the Sheriff had left. His two guards lingered down by the main road, giving them the chance to saddle up and head across the vineyards to link up with the road a mile south. "Shouldn't we use the back roads?" Carlotta asked.

"Can't take the time," Patrick replied. "Hurry up."

At dusk they had reached the inn outside Napa. Carlotta was dusty, hungry and exhausted. Patrick was impatient, eager to ride all night to reach the Bay. They reined up at the corral alongside the way station and Patrick, his hat pulled low across his features, took a look around. There was a carriage and a few horses already standing inside the corral. He helped Carlotta down from her horse. She stumbled, but he held her tight. "Take it slow." He held her arm as they walked to the front of the inn and looked through the dirty windows. "Can't see a thing," he said.

Suddenly Patrick straightened up, a gun jammed

in his back. "Turn around real slow," the Sheriff said.

Carlotta looked over her shoulder. The Sheriff stood there on the front porch of the inn with one of his deputies. Both had drawn guns aimed squarely at Patrick's chest.

"Thought you might show up here," the Sheriff said. "Sure didn't buy that story about you bein' a night-rider." He showed two gold teeth in the front as he gave a smug smile.

"I don't carry a gun," Patrick said. "You can put those away."

"Not today, Mr. Carrick. Come on easy now."

As the inn door opened behind Patrick, spilling light onto the porch, the Sheriff's attention wavered just slightly. Voices and footsteps interrupted the evening.

Patrick ducked, leaped, and caught the Sheriff and his deputy across the knees with a rolling tackle. For a moment he thought he heard his name called out by his sister, but he figured that was his mind acting crazy. He rolled out onto the dusty street and tried to catch sight of the deputy's fallen weapon.

"Put it down!" Ed O'Connor yelled.

It was very quiet.

Patrick looked up from the ground and saw in the lanternlight his sister, Ed, Grace, Michael, and Carlotta. Ed held a pistol levelled at the Sheriff's ample gut. "Put down the gun," Ed said.

Grace Malone stepped out into the street and picked up the deputy's pistol. She trained it on him and pushed him back onto the porch.

"Patrick," Patricia said, "tie these two up and let's get started back to San Francisco."

"What happened to the bank?" Patrick asked.

"I'll tell you on the way. Hurry up."

As the moon rose over the horizon, the carriage hurtled back south.

CHAPTER ELEVEN

SAN FRANCISCO, CALIFORNIA, MAY, 1879

ON Sunday evening Chandler Gates stepped back from the coal stove in his room, holding the heavy steel skillet with an extra rag because he'd let the handle get too hot and ruined his omelette. "Damn," he cried when he heard a knock at the door of his apartment. Some day, he'd said to himself, he'd be so rich he'd live in hotels all over the world. "Just a minute," he muttered. "Just a god damned minute."

The door swung wide on the newly oiled hinges. Gates' first impulse, quickly acted upon, was to slam it shut in the faces he saw in his hallway. The keeper caught and he turned the key with a reflex action, locking Patricia, Grace, Ed, and Michael out of his rooms. It didn't take a genius to know that he had to run for it. He could later claim that he thought the Carricks would do him bodily harm, but right now it wouldn't do to be caught by them . . . not until after banking hours tomorrow.

Chandler Gates turned with balletic grace and leaped for the window which let out onto a small roof and down to an outside staircase.

The window was blocked. A man stood in the darkness with a slouch hat pulled low across his face. "Get back, you son of a bitch!" The barrel of the pistol was big. It caught the gaslight. He'd never seen a barrel that big. It looked like a cannon.

Gates fell back into his room as the man stepped over the window frame and, holding aim on the snivelling bank teller, unlocked the front door. "What are you going to do to me?" Gates whined. "I didn't do anything. Just because Carrick stole—" He was cut off by a hard slap across the face by none other than Patrick Carrick himself.

The scene looked like some strange kind of medical operation: Chandler Gates sat on the floor, surrounded by Patricia, Patrick, Ed, Michael, and Grace. "We're not here to hurt ya'," Patricia said, "unless you get rude or you forget to tell us the whole Gospel truth. Understand?"

Gates nodded.

Patricia smiled and patted him on the top of his sandy hair. "First off, Mr. Gates, where were you last Thursday night?"

"How can I remember things like that?"

"How much did we take in over the counter on Thursday?" Patrick asked.

"Nineteen thousand and fifty," he replied without thinking.

Patricia grinned. "Then what did you do Thursday night?"

"I went to the theatre."

"What did you see?"

" 'The Orphan'."

The room was hot and small. Ed O'Connor went

to the coal stove and closed off the vents to try and damp down the heat.

"How well do you know Mr. Stephens?"

"Who?"

"How well do you know Mr. Elijah Stephens of the California Bank and Trust Company?" Patrick asked.

Gates fixed his cravatte and stroked his throat. It was no use lying about that. "Well," he said, "as you very well know, Mr. Stephens is my uncle." He expected surprise on the faces of the others in the room, but he saw none. "However," he continued, "my uncle, as you might expect, is a very busy and very prominent man in San Francisco. He certainly does not have time to socialize with a teller from the Carrick Bank even if he is his nephew." He smiled and cleaned his glasses with a handkerchief.

"We understand," Patricia said. "We're just trying to get the answers to a few questions." She looked over at Patrick who still held the oversized Navy pistol. "When did you last see your uncle?"

Gates shrugged, tugged his sideburns, then waggled his hands while thinking. "It's been at least a month, maybe more. . . ."

"Are you absolutely sure?" Michael Kelly asked.

Gates nodded, pleased with how he was doing under pressure.

Ed O'Connor opened the door to the apartment, revealing Carlotta Stephens standing in the hallway. "Good evening, Chandler," she said, almost apologetically.

"G-g-good evening, Carlotta," Gates stammered, clearly nonplussed to see her.

"Please come in," Patricia said. "We were just asking Chandler when he'd last seen your father."

Carlotta smiled. "That's easy. Thursday night last. They spent two or three hours in father's study."

Chandler Gates looked at the faces that faced him. "Ohhh," he said, "I forgot. . . ." His voice dwindled away as the final realization sunk in. He wasn't going to be able to talk his way out of this one.

It dawned in a cold slow drizzle. By eight o'clock the rain had disappeared, leaving an uneasy humid fog which hung in the air like a shroud.

The crowds had begun to gather long before dawn. Sixty families had slept out on the sidewalks in front of the main office of the Carrick Bank rather than take the chance of being too late.

Each of the thousand-plus depositors tried not to think of the headlines which stained the front pages. Whether the poor people could read or not they knew what was said about Patrick Carrick and they knew that what was printed was true. They hoped that Patrick had not stolen *their* money. They hoped that Patrick had stolen somebody *else's* money.

By a quarter to nine the sun began to parboil the water in the atmosphere. The crowds surged forward and to the side like undecided waves mixing from estuary and ocean. A fight broke out when a man imagined another family was trying to cut in in front of him. The wives had to be pried apart by those around them. By the time the fight was over, six people had cut in in front of the feuding families.

At nine o'clock one hundred policemen were dispatched to watch over the crowd.

At nine fifteen the crowd began chanting, "We want our money!" and the bank had still not opened.

"There they are!" were the first three words, shouted

by the man in the black leather eyepatch. "Let's get 'em!"

"There they are!" the crowd yelled.

A large closed coach made its slow and relentless way through the clots of people and police. At the reins, up on the box, sat Patricia Carrick. Next to her was her brother, Patrick. Someone threw a rotten tomato. It splattered on the knee of Patricia's long calico dress. A policeman waded into the crowd and relieved a balding man of a basket of spoiled vegetables.

". . . Get 'im!"

". . . he's got 'is gall, hey?"

". . . There's the bastard! Lynch him!"

Patricia held her face quiet and immobile. Inside she still raged. It was all she could do to keep from roaring like an animal which has been wounded. In all her days she could not remember being as furious. God had made men strange—this she knew—but she had in no wise been prepared for the depths to which they could sink.

When they had faced down Elijah Stephens just before dawn, he had smiled and cooly said that everything Chandler Gates said was a lie.

"But, uncle!" Chandler cried. "I gave you the money!"

Elijah turned and shrugged his shoulders, looking to the two detectives as if to say, "Who's to account for a poor demented relative?"

"But I gave it all to you!" Chandler screamed. Patrick had to hold him back to keep him from tearing his uncle apart.

"It must, I fear," Elijah said, with his hands nestled warmly in his dressing gown, "be your word against mine. The word of a poor relation against the word of the president of California's leading banking institution."

"But you have had conversations with your nephew, sir?" the taller detective said.

Elijah smiled and nodded. "The boy was beside himself. He had, I think, gotten rather heavily involved in gambling in Chinatown. I consoled him, tried to show him the straight and narrow. It was, as you can see, no use."

"But uncle, you told me we had to get rid of the Carrick Bank unless the whole industry was to become degraded!" Gates wept salty tears. His eyes darted back and forth.

Elijah Stephens shook his head.

"Well," Patricia said, "no matter who's lying here, Patrick is off the hook. But we are still out the three hundred thousand." She sat down heavily. "And our depositors will cut our throats tomorrow."

"Today."

She nodded. The grey light of dawn had crept through the gauzy curtains. She looked at Chandler Gates. "I'm sorry for you, you pathetic piece of pusillanimity." She faced Elijah Stephens. "But you are plain and simple the devil incarnate." She sighed, shrugged her shoulders and headed for the door.

"Wait," a melodious voice called from the door to the dining room.

Patricia turned and looked deep into the dark flashing eyes of the Marquesa dela Pingaterra. She stood tall and patrician, her silken hair tied back in a long braid. In her slim hands she held a leather valise.

Elijah Stephens' face was the color of milk. He

started to step forward, but his feet would not move. "No," he croaked.

"I believe this is yours," Anna Stephens said, holding the bag out to the red-haired woman who looked as if the world had shaken loose from its moorings.

Patricia took ahold of the bag, amazed at its weight. She opened it quickly. Then looked back at Mrs. Stephens.

"Elijah kept it in the attic. He thought I didn't see." Her voice was soft.

"Why?" her husband suddenly cried.

Anna Stephens, the Marquesa dela Pingaterra, answered simply. "Honor," she said.

The next few moments flashed like a nightmare, a dream that made no sense until it was done. While everyone's attention was diverted to the bag holding the money and the husband whose wife had just informed upon him, Chandler Gates had eased forward to the banker's desk. His hand took fated hold of a long silver letter opener.

Gates flew forward as if he had come hot from Hell on a mission of horror. No one could stay him by the time they saw his trajectory.

The letter opener, clutched in his hand, entered his uncle's right eye and pierced his brain in less time than it took to fall to the floor.

Patricia, atop the coach in front of her bank, remembered the incredible pain she read on Elijah Stephens' face. The rest was screams and scufflings.

It took a full five minutes before the crowd could be made to be quiet. Patricia and her brother rose to stand atop the coach where they could be seen. Patricia began.

"Friends," she said, "the crisis is over."

"Says you," the man in the leather eyepatch cried.

"Yes," she said in an exhausted voice. "I do. The crisis is over. It was created by banker Stephens and, we suspect, others in order to try to ruin us. The bigger banks wanted to keep you and me as small as possible. Look what they did!" She searched for the faces of her friends, the mothers and fathers who'd asked her to be godmother of their children. "They turned you against me, they turned us all against each other! They made us break faith!" She paused. "They made you think your friend and my brother Patrick had stolen from you! We must never let them manipulate us like this again!"

Patricia sat down, tired. "Inside this coach is enough money to cover every last one of your deposits. We floated a loan from the bank we use because, when they heard the truth, it restored their faith in us. Anybody who wants his money can come and get it. But don't bother coming back when you learn that the Carrick Bank is here to stay!"

"Make an aisle there," Patrick yelled abruptly. "We'll be taking the money inside. We'll open in a half hour." He jumped down, nearly landing on the nearest depositors who stepped back quickly. Patricia followed him.

The doors of the Carrick Bank opened at ten-fifteen on Monday morning. The first woman in looked around, then left. Another ten minutes went by.

"Strange," Grace Malone said.

At ten-forty a man came in and deposited sixty-two dollars.

Five minutes later a man and wife redeposited a hundred and twenty-five dollars.

By the end of the day the Carrick Bank was back in business and the crisis had, indeed, ended.

"Are you angry?" Ed O'Connor asked the woman he still loved above all others.

Patricia shook her head. "If it was my life savings I'd feel the same," she said. "But I don't want to look backwards. I want to look forwards. We're stronger now than we've ever been."

BOOK FOUR

CHAPTER ONE

TWENTY-FOUR short months had chased one another off the calendar. Fortunes had been won and lost. Billions of dollars had changed hands, moved from one country to another, one bank to another, one cartel to another. Men had died seeking a moment's rest from the race for wealth.

President Garfield had been elected. Some thought it didn't matter who was in the White House. Business ran government, not the other way around. Whatever business wanted, business got.

George Eastman had finally succeeded with his roll film idea, Thomas Edison amazed everyone with a display of three hundred incandescent lamps and there was more and more agitation against the trusts and monopolies which controlled the destinies of so many people.

Women of fashion wore hats with giant plumes and sported gloves in pink, grey, or lilac. Men still wore beards and heavy black suits. Most wives were afraid of the new gas stoves, preferring the safety of the old cast iron coal and wood-burning monsters that dominated most every kitchen in America. Cattle prices were so high that ranchers began selling shares in their herds and putting up barbed wire wherever they chose.

In San Francisco everyone talked about the Palace Hotel, the biggest in the world, as the rich got richer and the poor dreamed of one big break.

The Carrick Bank thrived, building on top of the near disaster that had tested it. Patricia learned more each day as the assets of her friends and neighbors grew in this fertile environment. She had a knack for selecting the best, if not always the safest, investments in an economy that was treacherous. Only a few months into 1881 she'd had to send Patrick to New York to act as her middleman with the big investment houses. He'd gone, happily, thrilled with the chance to show what he could do on his own with his new wife.

The morning dawned hot down by the wharf.

The man's skin had a leathern look, tanned by suns upon suns, remorseless in their constancy around the Horn. His gait up and down the streets was uneven, broad, a bit sideways—as if he were unsure of which way the earth might run at any minute. His clothes fit tightly on his tall muscular form—broad shoulders, a wide back that tapered down to a narrow waist. His right hand was thrust up over his right shoulder grasping a small sea bag. His name was Yarrow. Grant Yarrow.

A streetwalker, late returning home, stopped and stared at the man and wished she had met someone who looked like him when she was a girl. He looked over at her and smiled. "Hi, sailor," she said to him as she let him pass.

"Good morning," Grant said in a deep resonant voice. "How are you?"

"Can't complain," she said. "You looking?"

He shook his head. "I'm already spoke for."

She shrugged. "Guess this ain't my day."

The sailor turned up Meachum Street and was astonished to see that it had not changed one jot. The wooden frame buildings were scabrous, in need of paint. The dirty street was still covered in manure which, in turn, hosted acres of black flies. Dirty children played tag in the alleys and mothers hooted out of windows for them to be careful.

The man stopped and lowered his seabag to the ground. An old woman smoked a pipe on the stoop and tried to hold onto a squirming two year old granddaughter who had slipped out of her diaper. "I'm looking for Patricia Carrick," he said. His voice quavered just a bit.

The old woman puffed and squinted. "What for?"

"I'm an old friend."

"She moved."

A look of concern passed across his face. "When she got married?"

The old woman shook her head. "She never married."

The sailor smiled a broad grin. "You sure?"

The old woman yelled across the street. "Yo, Bertha!"

"Yeah, Babsie?" came a voice from one of the flats.

"The Carrick woman ever get hitched?"

"Her? Never! You got any corn flour?"

"How much you need?"

"Half a pound?"

"Anytime!"

The sailor waited eagerly but politely until the important matters were taken care of. Then he asked the old woman if she knew where Patricia Carrick had moved to.

"Menlo Park? I don't know. Micks come and micks go and most of 'em like to ferget they're micks. You might ask at one of her banks."

"Her what?"

The old woman made a face. "You really aren't very smart are you?" she observed.

The sailor's handsome face went through several expressions before landing in confusion. "I've been at sea for five and a half years," he said. "I don't know anything that happened. Patricia Carrick manages a bank?"

"You just are plain ignorant. Patricia Carrick *owns* three banks in San Francisco and two in Los Angeles and one in Sacramento. And all I can say is that hers are the only banks what are fair to us and don't give us short shrift."

Grant shook his head. "Where can I find one of her banks?"

The old woman pointed the way and gave explicit directions—the kind of directions you might give a five year old child. She had no faith that this sailor would ever find his way there.

"Much obliged," Grant Yarrow said as he set off in the direction she'd pointed out.

As soon as he was out of earshot she said to her granddaughter, "He's a sure good looking man, but the sea's stolen his wits."

Her granddaughter belched and slid off her lap.

Grant had to wait for a half hour before the Carrick Bank opened. When he walked into the airy, well-lighted, spacious wooden building he couldn't help but look around in wonder. Patricia's big desk sat squarely in the middle of the floor where most banks had nothing at all. There were pretty paintings of San Francisco on the walls. Of the four tellers, two were women.

"May I help you?" a deep female voice asked.

Grant turned quick to face the sound and said, "I'm looking for Miss Patricia Carrick."

"She's not here right now. May I help?"

Grant shook his head slowly. "I don't think so. When will she be in?"

"Two weeks."

"Two weeks?"

"That's right."

"May I ask where she is?"

"May I ask who's asking?"

"Grant Yarrow."

"Grant Yarrow? You're Grant Yarrow?"

"Yes, ma'am."

The woman let out a whoop and flung herself forward, locking the sailor in a bear's embrace. He blushed and waited until her outburst had subsided before he asked who she might be. "I'm Grace Malone! It was you and your lawyer friend who saved my onions!"

Grant smiled and stepped back still somewhat wary that the huge woman might feel another fit of gratitude. "Well, it sure looks as if everything worked out all right for you."

"You just better believe it, Mr. Yarrow! Oh, wait until Patricia hears you're back!"

"Where is she?"

Grace put a heavy hand on Grant's shoulder and led him over to Patricia's desk where they sat down. "She's in New York City."

Grant's face dropped.

Grace nodded. "Yep. She took her niece Molly, who's marrying Tom Kierney, so she could pick out her trousseau. She also had bank business and she wanted to see Patrick, who's in New York managing investments and such. I'll bet you didn't know he married Carlotta Stephens, did you?"

Grant shook his head. If he had been to the Moon for five years he would have known as much. He looked at the cathedral ceiling in wonder. "How did she manage all this?"

Grace beamed with pride, thrusting out a barrel chest. "By being better than anybody else and by taking on the people nobody else wanted." She leaned forward. "Banks like the California Bank never even suspected that all these little immigrants had hundreds and thousands of dollars saved up and stored away in shoeboxes. Patricia went out and found the deposits the way you'd look for silver or gold in the ground."

"That's fantastic."

"Sure is."

"I'll bet my father wasn't pleased."

"None of them other banks was. They tried to ruin us."

Grant nodded. "Can you tell me exactly where Miss Patricia is staying?"

"The Astor."

"Thanks." He stood up and waited until she'd thanked him several more times and pumped his hand another dozen times before he asked, "Do you think I could float a small loan from the Carrick Bank?"

"Anything you want is yours," Grace said. "Hell, I owe you my life!" She slapped him on the back. The tellers, who had been eavesdropping laughed.

Patricia held the gown up in front of her as she stared into the mirror. "Good Lord," she said. "Another birthday and I still look all right for a dowager. Thirty-eight years old isn't all that old," she mumbled. "Is it?"

"Beg pardon?" Molly said from the other room in the Astors poshest suite. She popped her head in the door to her aunt's dressing room. "Did you call me, Aunt Patty?"

Patricia looked at the beautiful young woman who was on the verge of turning nineteen. Molly Lacey's light brown hair caught the late afternoon light and radiated it back tenfold. Her pale, ice blue eyes seemed to go on forever. Her heart-shaped chin, her high cheekbones and her unassuming beauty balanced on the line between childhood and maturity. "No. But seeing as how you're here, which gown should I wear and where are Stephen and Harry?"

"The blue and on the two-fifteen from New Haven." Molly always felt a bit in awe of her aunt. Not just because Patricia Carrick was suddenly famous and wealthy. Even when they were poor she had sensed both the power and the unassailable beauty of this flame-haired woman whom most men admired but dared not cast their nets for. Patricia Carrick was like one of those paintings in the museum. Men looked, sighed, made little whimpering sounds, shrugged, and moved on to more accessible goals.

"I hope their final grades were worthy of them," Patricia said. "Yale men." She laughed and threw down the pink and the light green. "That's silly somehow."

"What is?"

"Harry Gardiner and Stephen Lacey, both paupers at birth, hobnobbing with the nabobs in New Haven. If a fortune teller had predicted that five years ago, I'd have split a seam laughing. You really think the blue?"

Molly nodded. Then she stepped aside as her aunt slipped easily into her gown. It seemed as though everything Patricia did was effortless. "Aunt Patty, do you know what love is?"

"I beg your pardon?"

Molly smiled. "I didn't mean it that way. I meant, do you know when you're in love and when you're not?"

"I should hope so." Patricia looked at her young niece and cocked her head to the side. "You don't know if you love Tom?"

"One minute I think I do and the next minute I just do not know."

Patricia walked over to the tray table which room service had left for tea and finished her cold cup of oriental blend. "I don't know if marriage is supposed to be a love affair," she said slowly.

Molly blushed. "But what if Tom is wrong for me? What if we end up hating each other?"

"Tom is a good man. He'll be a good provider. We just financed his ninth fishing boat. I swear he'll be a millionaire by the time he's thirty." Patricia put her cup down carefully. "But you don't care about his money, do you?"

Molly shook her head. "I want to be sure I love him, that's all."

"Well, I'm not going to let my favorite engaged niece marry somebody she doesn't love."

"But I *do* love Tom. I think. I want to be sure."

Patricia laughed and looked at her hair in the hand mirror. "Certainly is hard to come by, but," she said as she took ahold of Molly's shoulders, "there's an excitement that comes from *not* knowing. The only thing that's sure is dying." She kissed her forehead. "Now let's get going to dinner or we'll miss the two Yale men."

CHAPTER TWO

NEW YORK CITY, JULY 1, 1881

It was raining. Patricia and Molly waited with Stephen and Harry until the Astor staff had found a closed carriage before setting off to Delmonico's for their joyous reunion dinner. Stephen and his cousin had both grown tall and handsome. Their aunt said, "What choice did they have? They're Carricks still and all, aren't they?" Stephen was the more reckless and dashing of the two. Harry was, at bottom, just as adventuresome, but he was the more private. In some circles in New Haven they were known not always affectionately as "The Battling Micks."

Five minutes after the carriage sloshed downtown carrying its laughing foursome, an exhausted Grant Yarrow, rumpled and unshaven from his long trip across the continent, stepped past the doorman at the Astor Hotel. The doorman shrugged and figured he'd let the desk clerk handle the problem. After all, the desk clerk was getting paid to deal with that kind of stuff.

"May I be of assistance, sir?" the manager asked,

brushing past the desk clerk to try to steer the poorly dressed man out of the luxurious lobby.

"I understand Miss Patricia Carrick is a guest here."

The manager was impressed by the man's manner of speaking, but his dress indicated a class of society which the patrons of the Astor had no wish to be reminded of. "I'm sorry, sir, but I am not at liberty to discuss the Astor's clientele."

"I was told by Miss Carrick's assistant in San Francisco that I might find her here."

The manager looked from side to side. The half dozen bellboys were marshalling beneath the message board, sensing the possibility of an altercation. To tell the truth, they enjoyed hustling the unruly from the hotel as discreetly as possible. "Yes, uh, quite so. Yes," the manager said, "Miss Carrick is staying with us this trip." If the truth be told, the manager wasn't all that happy having the nouveau riche Irish woman and her niece as guests.

"I'd like to speak with her. I am a friend."

The manager looked back at Grant. "Yes, I'm sure." He smiled. "Well, I'm sorry but Miss Carrick is out for the evening sir. Perhaps you might want to return tomorrow?"

Grant looked disturbed. "Is she out of the city?"

"I believe she went to dinner."

Grant looked around the lobby. He spied a chair beside a tall palm. "I'll wait until her return."

"But she may be hours," the manager said.

Grant smiled. "I don't mind. I can catch up on some sleep."

"You can't sleep here, sir."

"How about here?" Grant walked around one of the marble pillars and plopped himself into a red velvet upholstered wingback chair. "This is just right." He picked up a newspaper from the end table beside him and settled in for an extended stay.

The manager could find no words to eject the shabbily dressed man from the lobby. "Will you force me to have my staff bellmen throw you out bodily, sir?"

Grant grinned from over the top of the paper. "Will you have me tell my employer that you wouldn't allow me to wait here for her to deliver a very confidential and very important message?"

"What employer? What are you talking about?"

"I have news for Miss Carrick from her bank manager in San Francisco. It's urgent that I speak with her."

"Why didn't you say so in the first place?"

Grant went back to reading the paper. President Garfield was going to make a speech in upstate New York tomorrow. "You didn't ask me," Grant replied.

Exasperated, beaten at every turn, the manager strode quickly back to the wide main desk with its marble top. He was happy in the sanctity of his sharpened pens and flawless register.

At Delmonico's the air was filled with laughter. The wine stewards could hardly keep up with the demands the gourmands made upon the generous cellar. Harry laughed as Stephen told their aunt about the absolute necessity of dropping paper sacks of water into the balcony of the students below them in Bingham Hall as those hapless fellows were trying to impress the town girls who walked upon the green.

"They threatened to thrash us," Stephen said, "but when they looked at Harry's insane gleam, they thought better of it."

"But what have you learned?" Patricia asked.

Harry picked up a small bit of bread and put it on his tongue. "We have learned," he said, "that it is better to be a Belmont than a Lacey or a Gardiner, that Fence is better than St. Anthony's, that Skull and Bones is far far better than Heaven itself and that anything is better than Sheffield Scientific."

Stephen laughed and finished his wine.

"You two aren't becoming snobs, by any chance?" Molly asked.

Harry and Stephen looked at each other and couldn't stifle the laugh. "Oi," Stephen said, "oi don't t'ink nuffin' cud moik us snobs, Moll."

"Why isn't uncle Patrick here?" Harry asked.

"He and Carlotta had to go to Long Island to close a deal he's been working on," Patricia replied.

A tall man with a razor-thin moustache stopped at the table and bowed low. "I'm terribly sorry to disturb your dinner, Miss Carrick, but Mr. Macauley wanted to make sure that you got his dinner invitation for tomorrow night and the theatre afterwards?"

Patricia nodded.

"He especially wanted me to ask if your niece would care to attend."

"Yes, she will be with me." Patricia looked forward with great anticipation to seeing the man who had helped them so many years before.

"Excellent. I shan't take any more of your time."

As the man left, another took his place at Patricia's elbow. "Sorry, Miss Carrick, but a cable from London came to our office."

Patricia read the flimsy paper quickly and handed it back to the man. "Tell them I haven't made up my mind on the mortgage market yet."

"Yes, ma'am." The man left as quickly as he had come.

Stephen watched his aunt with the cool detachment of a young man who knows precisely what he wants. He admired what she had become. People came to her, asked her questions, she replied quickly and without effort, and they went away again. It was as if she were the center of a maelstrom—quiet and assured—and he envied her that. He also envied her her power. He smiled. "What say Harry here and I go to Europe this summer, Aunty?"

Patricia smiled and reached across the table with a strong hand. "What say you get your fannys to San Francisco where you'll clerk for Grace Malone?" Her smile and her grip left no doubt as to where and how the two boys would spend their vacation.

"I like San Francisco, don't you, Harry-lad?"

"Love it," Harry replied. "Especially working for the butcher."

"I'll tell her you said that," Molly put in.

"I'll pay you five dollars if you don't," Harry replied.

At midnight the carriage returned to the Astor. Harry and Stephen were politely and a little drunkenly humming Yale songs. Molly was shaking her head in amazement and Patricia was laughing at anything and everything. It had been such a long life, she thought. And now she was beginning to enjoy her "babies" more as entertaining friends than as heavy responsibilities . . . which was not to say she wouldn't spank them if they needed it.

The doorman swung wide the portals as Harry made elaborate shushing gestures which Stephen and Patricita imitated with abandon. They crossed the lobby and made their shushing way up to the second floor.

The manager smiled and bowed as they passed, but he made no effort to awaken the sleeping man behind the far pillar.

At two AM Grant Yarrow awoke with a shudder. He looked around and saw that the lobby was empty. Then he saw the clock above the front portals. He leaped up and ran to the desk. The night manager, a shorter, pleasanter man, looked up at him. "Where did you come from?" he asked.

Grant pointed back at the pillar. "I—where's the other man? With the lacquered hair . . ."

"Mr. Parks? He went off at one. Can I help?"

"Is Miss Carrick back? I was waiting for her."

The man turned to check the pigeon hole. The keys to her suite were gone. Inside, a note reminded him to awaken the Carricks at nine. "Yes, they are all in."

"But I asked Parks to wake me."

The man shrugged. "I guess he forgot."

Grant slammed his fist into his palm. "He forgot all right." He turned. "I'll be back."

"Yes, sir."

At ten o'clock that morning Grant Yarrow, as good as his word, returned to the Astor. The lobby buzzed with major domos, chauffeurs waiting for their charges, assistants taking notes, and callers queueing up at the front desk. "May I help you?" a desk man called across to the disheveled man who had started up the wide staircase.

Grant turned and looked down on the twenty or so men and women who looked up at him as if he were a fly in the aspic. "No," he said. He turned and took the stairs three at a time. Three bellboys made tracks across the space and climbed after him.

Grant knocked on 201 before the hard-charging bellboys could round the corner of the thickly carpeted hall. A maid opened the door and gave a little yipe when she saw the man who looked as if he had spent the night sleeping on a park bench . . . which he had.

"Who is it, Ella?" called a voice from the living room.

Ella bounced lightly off the door as Grant strode past her. The bellboys stood, confused, at the threshold.

Patricia looked at the shape as it seemed to explode into the living room. She instinctively pulled back, causing the seamstress to drop the hem.

Grant Yarrow stopped and stared. The red-haired woman who had warmed his thoughts while he sailed every ocean on the face of the globe stood on a small footstool wearing a wedding gown of tulle and satin. Pearls seeded every inch of the bodice. Hundreds of buttons cinched up the long sleeves. A diamond tiara dripped lace from the top of her head.

The bellboys huddled behind Grant goggle-eyed.

"Jesus H. Christ," Grant said, "this is the way I left you the last time!" He turned and started to bowl over the bellboys like tenpins.

Patricia's relieved laugh stopped him before he could make good his escape. "It's not for me!" she yelled. "It's for Molly! *She's* the bride!"

"Stay still," the seamstress said with a mouthful of pins.

"Ah," Grant said. "You can't blame me for not knowing what to think."

Patricia shook her head. Then she looked over at the bellboys. "Thank you, gentlemen. I won't be needing your help this time."

"Yes, ma'am." They bowed their ways out.

Patricia looked at Grant in absolute stoney silence. Despite his three-day growth of beard and his cheap suit he was clearly the most handsome man who had ever chased anybody across a continent. "The bodice is too tight," she mumbled.

"It wasn't too tight a minute ago," the seamstress said curtly.

"I can't breathe," Patricia muttered.

"Not my fault," the seamstress mumbled.

Suddenly the floor looked miles away, the footstool was a veritable tower. "Would you care for dinner?" Patricia asked. "I mean breakfast?"

Grant shook his head. Crossed his arms and leaned against the wall to admire the reality of his long vision.

"Molly isn't feeling well after last night," Patricia said. "We're about the same size."

"It fits very well. You should be the bride."

Patricia's head shook from side to side as an instinctive response. She stopped. Shrugged. Blushed. "Who'd marry a worn-out woman like me?"

Grant struggled to find his throat closed off against words. It would have been so easy to say, "I would marry a worn-out woman like you and be ecstatic!"

Instead, he said, "Oh, I don't know. You'd be surprised." He paused. "You own banks now, eh?"

Patricia nodded. "I guess I'm married to my career." She looked down at the carpet. "Did *you* ever get married?"

Grant shook his head. "I've been aboard one ship or another for five years," he said.

"Why so long?" she asked.

Grant shrugged. "I didn't know what to do with my life. The sea was so simple. You live or you die. When you turned me down . . . I think I went a bit off. It's all right. My mother left me some land in the Napa Valley. I think I'll grow grapes. Make wine."

"Don't say wine around here this morning."

"Had too much last night?"

Patricia nodded. "Why did you want to see me?" Her heart pounded itself against her ribcage.

Grant's eyes were hot and his temples felt tight. He was about to answer when the maid came into the room and announced the arrival of Benjamin Macauley.

"Please stand still, ma'am," the seamstress said.

"How can I stand still when I've got two visitors and my stomach feels like I've swallowed poison? I haven't seen Mr. Yarrow in five and a half years!"

Benjamin Macauley was twenty-one years old the way some men are forty. His eyes gleamed with a wisdom he had not earned. Rather, he had inherited it as a result of the pains suffered by his mother and father in his upbringing. Violette Larson, the world-renowned stage actress and Marshall Ma-

cauley, the financier, had undergone the hellish tor-
ments only the completely passionate will ever comprehend. The product of their illicit love was Benjamin Macauley, now a dark-haired young millionaire
who wore clothes with the same ease with which
he wore his skin. He was tall, well-built and slender
with a clean-shaven face framed by dark curls.

Benjamin looked at the stunningly beautiful woman in the wedding gown and instantly wondered if
she were in the habit of bedding younger men. If she
were, this errand for his father could be far sweeter
than anything he had even known in the business
world. Before he could launch into his greetings, a
slight motion off to one side caught his eye. He looked
over and saw an unshaven, rudely dressed man in his
early forties lounging against the wall. This bit of
incongruity was only matched by the sense that something was going on between the woman in the wedding gown and the man in the three dollar suit. Benjamin grinned to think that Miss Patricia Carrick was
the type to take on workingmen lovers. There was
more than met the eye here at the Astor and that was
for sure.

"Good morning, Miss Carrick," he said with only
the slightest trace of irony in his voice.

"Good morning, Mr. Benjamin Macauley," she replied. His tone had not been lost on her, but Patricia
was damned if she was going to explain to some
twenty-one year old why she was standing in a wedding
gown looking goony-eyed at a man who looked like a
chimneysweep.

Benjamin gave the maid his hat and walked in to
admire a bit more of the woman in the gown. "My

father and mother send their very best regards and look forward to seeing you this evening."

"I can't wait," Patricia said. "The last time I saw Marshall Macauley I was twelve. He risked his life and reputation to help us get out of Fall River and then out of Pennsylvania. He was a giant among men. We Carricks owe him everything."

"Papa warned me that you might try to give me the key to the city," Benjamin laughed.

"Anything we have is yours, Benjamin," she said. "I'm very sorry. This is Mr. Grant Yarrow, Mr. Benjamin Macauley, the son of our great benefactor."

Grant shook the handsome young man's hand and decided he shouldn't feel jealous of this handsome pup. But he couldn't help feeling as if this Macauley boy was looking at Patricia the way he might size up a good filet.

Molly Lacey walked in from her bedroom, her hair perfectly coiffed in braids on her head, her new frock from Stewarts pressed and frilly, her eyes aglow despite the hangover which the wine had engineered. "Good morning." She stopped when she saw Grant Yarrow. "I . . ."

"This is Mr. Grant Yarrow," Patricia said.

Molly curtseyed before the handsome older man, then turned to face Benjamin Macauley. She wobbled slightly. He reached out and took her arm. "By your leave," Benjamin said.

"Thank you." Her eyes were cast on the floor as her face flushed crimson. "I don't know what happened," she said in a faint voice.

"Wine is what happened," Patricia said. She looked down at the seamstress. "Are you finished, dear? I have business to conduct here."

The seamstress looked up. "It's no nevermind to me, Missus. I'm not the one being married."

"Neither am I," Patricia said, feeling a bit flushed herself, knowing that Grant was listening to every word. "Molly, let us change clothes and you can play the blushing bride."

Molly looked curiously at Benjamin and then followed her aunt to the bedroom to exchange clothes, leaving Grant Yarrow and Benjamin alone.

"What sort of business are you in?" Benjamin asked.

Grant smiled. "I *was* in shipping. Now I guess you could say I'm at rest." He laughed. "What is your line of endeavour?"

"Investments," Benjamin replied. "That and trying to sample every one of life's delicacies."

Grant nodded. "A noble ambition. I once was an expert in that field myself. It palls after a few decades."

Patricia returned quickly, decked out in a simple pale green dress, her hair pinned up randomly, carrying a leather envelope full of papers. She smiled. "Grant, do you want to stay while Benjamin and I conduct our business?"

He shook his head. "I'll return later if that's all the same."

"How about luncheon here?"

He smiled. "I'll be back at one."

Patricia and Benjamin were just finishing up the last details of the cooperative venture with the Macauley Company and Lazard Freres when Grant returned, clean-shaven and wearing a brand new ready-made suit. Molly sat in a corner doing needlepoint, her eyes never leaving the young businessman. "Perhaps Miss Molly would care to see some of the sights of the city while she's here," Benjamin said.

"Oh, I'd absolutely love to," Molly said without waiting for her aunt to respond.

"If you wouldn't mind," Patricia said. "That's very kind of you."

Benjamin packed up his briefcase, bowed and took his leave with Miss Carrick's niece.

Patricia and Grant went downstairs to the court restaurant and ordered a light lunch. Neither spoke until after the waiter had gone to make their salads.

"Was it a profitable morning?" Grant asked.

"I hope so," Patricia replied.

"Your success is breathtaking," Grant said.

"Some lucky investments," Patricia said. "And some very loyal friends."

"My father not among them, I take it?"

Patricia's face turned to stone. "He tried to ruin us. I have no direct proof, but we're sure it was him. I'm sorry for being so blunt, but I'd kill him with this knife if he came in here now."

"I wouldn't stop you. I haven't had anything to do with him for years. I hear he just keeps getting richer and more powerful."

"That he does."

They looked off at the other diners. Grant looked back at her. She was so enchantingly beautiful he forgot the words he'd practiced in the park. "This is a very pleasant spot," he said.

"Yes," she said.

"I have a question I'd like to ask you," he said.

She smiled uncertainly. "I'll try to answer."

Just then the waiter returned and placed the salads

in front of them, then came back and ground pepper on top. "Is everything satisfactory?" the waiter asked.

"Yes," Grant muttered distractedly.

"Good." The waiter left.

"The salad is good," Patricia said after sampling a leaf of lettuce.

"Um-hum." Grant looked up at her. "Patricia, I very much want you to—"

"I'm sorry, Miss Carrick, I told this gentleman that you were dining, but he insisted," the maitre d' said.

Patricia nodded and greeted a neatly dressed man with a large envelope. "What is it?"

"I need your signature on the bonds."

Patricia looked at Grant. "I'm sorry." She scribbled her signature on the heavy papers and bid the man a curt good-bye. "I really am."

"Yes," Grant said.

"You were going to ask me a question."

"Yes."

"An omelette for the lady and a crepe for the gentleman," the waiter said, easing the hot plates before the diners. He waited until they had each sampled a bit before leaving.

Grant began to laugh. He put down his fork and held his napkin to his mouth.

"What's so funny, Grant?"

But before he could answer, a dark-suited man ran into the restaurant screaming at the top of his lungs, "The President's been shot!"

"What?"

"President Garfield's been shot!"

Dumbfounded, Patricia and Grant could only stare at each other speechlessly.

CHAPTER THREE

THE train swayed from side to side as it crossed from one line to another outside Chicago. Molly Lacey sat at the rear of her aunt's private car and watched the rails converge into pinpoints on the brown and gold horizon. She kept thinking of the handsome man named Macauley. The single perfect afternoon in the park had made her life a cauldron of contradictory and impossible emotions.

Benjamin had said to her, "The only sight in New York I want to see is the beautiful woman from San Francisco."

"Pardon?"

"You are the most magnificent woman I have ever seen," he said.

Molly blushed and leaned back in the carriage. She could not stop the world from turning upside down. The man had spoken, had said she was beautiful, had caught her completely unawares.

He took her gloved hand between his own. "I'm rash, I'm rude, I'm unpredictable, and I'm in love with you," he said.

"You can't. . . ." she said softly.

"Yes, I can. I can do anything and I can fall deeply in love at first glance."

"I'm engaged to be married."

"That," he said, "doesn't make you any the less desirable to me."

Molly turned to look out the window. "What is that building?"

"I don't know and I don't care," he replied. "Would you care for a tot of brandy?" He flicked open a beautiful teakwood bar at the front of his carriage. Before she could answer, he poured her a thimbleful and pressed it on her.

"I think you're toying with me," she said.

"Of course I am," he said. "Isn't it wonderful?"

"What am I supposed to say? I think you better take me back to the Astor."

"What are you supposed to say? You're supposed to say nothing, just throw yourself into my open arms." He laughed and swung his arms wide.

Molly put a hand to her face and laughed at the spectacle he was making. "You're not serious . . ."

"Try me." His voice was suddenly husky and low. He leaned forward and kissed her gently upon the lips in a solemn, well-calculated gesture that sent hot rivets coursing through Molly's heart. "Is that serious?" he whispered.

Molly nodded.

His hand traversed her arm and touched her neck with fire. She leaned forward for the second kiss.

The train switched again, making her feel increasingly uneasy as she put miles and miles between herself and Benjamin Macauley. She knew he was a fraud, a lover in love with love, but she couldn't stop thinking about him. He was so different from Tom Kierney.

"Molly?"

"Yes, Aunt Patricia?"

"We're going to have dinner now."

"I'm not really hungry."

Patricia knelt on the carpet next to her niece and looked at her. "What's the matter, girl?"

"I just don't feel all that well."

"Would you like to see a doctor?"

Molly shook her head. Then looked up to see Grant Yarrow enter the car. Patricia had invited him to return to California with them in her private car.

"Maybe I'll take a nap while you and Mr. Yarrow have dinner," Molly said.

Patricia nodded and she and Grant went to the table. The crystal tinkled as the train vibrated across some rough trackbeds. "I can't believe what has happened to this country," Patricia said. "Two times I've seen presidents struck down. I only pray that President Garfield survives."

Grant nodded. "May I be perfectly blunt?" he said.

Patricia looked up surprised.

Grant dropped his heavy fork on his plate. "I know that the president has been shot, that the whole country is in shock, that the Stock Exchange could go insane because of it, and that we should all be praying mightily for Garfield's speedy recovery, but that doesn't change the fact that if you don't marry me, I'll get up from this table and jump off this car into the wilderness."

Patricia tried to swallow the piece of lamb but somehow her throat refused to function normally.

"Well, since you're not talking," Grant continued,

"let me add that I know there will be insurmountable problems. For instance, you are now wealthy and I am on my uppers. My father is certainly not going to leave me any of his money. People, including me, will say I married you for your money. Another problem is all your nieces and nephews think you are their private preserve and mother and patron saint and all that. I propose to change that because I am probably the world's worst sharer of loved ones. Then there's the fact that I think you work too hard. Empire building is admirable enough, but you need more time to play. Thus I would have to force you to delegate more responsibility to others." He smiled to see the laugh building on his lover's lips. "Moreover, so that you don't mistake my intentions, I have found a priest aboard this train who, thanks to a bottle of the best brandy I could buy in Chicago, is most willing to marry us right away."

"Grant. . . ."

"Spare me anything but your assent. I couldn't bear anything else." He drank the last of his wine and slammed down his napkin. "What do you say, woman?"

Patricia stashed her fears as far down as they would go. She strained to clear her throat. Then, "What car is the priest in?"

Grant Yarrow stood up, hooted at the top of his lungs, kissed her full on the mouth and went running out of the car.

Molly ran in, her hair half brushed for the night. "What happened?"

"I'm not sure," Patricia said, "but I think you'd better wait right here with me so that I don't go to pieces."

* * *

The priest had already sampled a fair amount of the expensive brandy by the time Grant hustled him to the rear of the train where Patricia's car had been coupled on in New York. He was a short squat man with a head shaped like a bullet and long sideboards of alternately grey and black hair. "Good evening, ma'am," he greeted Patricia somewhat blearily.

Patricia looked across the man's shoulders at Grant Yarrow who stood tall and immobile in the center of the private car. The lamp swung near his face from the ceiling. Patricia looked back at the priest. "Mr. Yarrow says you can marry us."

The priest laid a finger alongside a nose that looked like a topographical map with its ridges and lines. "What? Oh, well, it isn't the normal thing, but the wild west has made many exceptions. Standards one might follow in the city won't hold up out here, you know." He leaned against one of the heavy easychairs for balance as the train highballed down the straight stretch of track. "When was the last time you took confession?"

"Last Sunday," Patricia replied.

"And you?" he asked Grant Yarrow.

Grant cleared his throat and mumbled.

"Beg pardon?"

Grant mumbled a date again.

"I didn't hear that," Father Crotty said.

Molly piped up quickly, "He said five and a half years ago, Father."

"Thank you, Molly," Grant said through clenched teeth.

"You're welcome," she replied brightly.

"Well, that won't do at'all," Father Crotty said,

THE CARRICKS

313

taking a leather wallet from his coat pocket. "Step this way," he said. He led Grant to the far end of the car and there, as the darkened scenery vanished, he heard confession.

Five minutes later Father Crotty and Grant were smiling down on Patricia. "You two will have to do something about the civil side of this thing," the priest said, "but in the eyes of God you'll be hitched up all right and proper. Would you join hands, please?"

Molly called Stephen and Harry from their rooms and the two young men stood wide-eyed as they watched the woman who meant so much to them get married by a funny-looking little priest who smelled of expensive brandy.

Patricia watched as if this were all happening to someone else. "I've always been such a level-headed sort," she said to herself.

"Not today," her inner voice replied.

"But why?"

"Because you love Grant Yarrow. You have loved him ever since you met him."

"Patricia?"

"What?"

"Say I will."

"I will."

The voices around her buzzed for a little while longer.

"Congratulations."

"What?"

"We're married."

Patricia looked up and saw Grant Yarrow's most precious face coming closer and closer.

Grant smothered her kiss with his own, and a desire

she had never known before washed over her. When he let her breathe again she was overjoyed to see shining faces surrounding her. Molly, Stephen and Harry grinned with unabashed joy as they saw their aunt, who had always been so in control, so articulate, almost intoxicated with happiness.

"Is Grant your uncle now?" Patricia asked giddily.

"I doubt it," Stephen replied. They laughed.

"Well, who could he be?" Patricia asked.

Harry looked at the strong build on the man who had stolen his aunt's heart and said, "He can be anybody he wants to be. I won't go up against him." They laughed again.

Shortly a porter arrived with some champagne and some biscuits and thus the wedding party idled away the better part of an hour laughing and singing and telling tales of when aunt Patricia lost her temper and showed her red hair to the roots. The priest turned out to have a most impressive tenor voice which he used to thrilling advantage on every Irish song any of them had ever heard.

At one in the morning Father Crotty excused himself back to his car, blessing the Carricks and Grant Yarrow. He was followed in short order by Patricia's niece and nephews.

As soon as Grant and Patricia were alone, sitting on the settee, facing the windows, he put a strong arm across her shoulders and just let the rhythm of the train be as eloquent as any poet. Miles and miles went by. Every once in a while a light would be visible in a town as they thundered along, but, for the most part, it was a deep purple dark. They could see themselves reflected on the glass, a handsome couple comfortably entwined, sensing no urgency.

To Patricia it seemed as if they had always been sitting here just like this.

Grant felt no need to make the evening go any faster than it was going. Something in him told him long ago that Patricia Carrick, for all her physical beauty, was not one to be taken like a conquest. He had bedded many women in his life. This one would have to be earned, not won.

At three o'clock they spoke. "I have always loved you, Grant," she said.

"And I you," he replied. He smiled. "I didn't realize it at the time. That's all."

"I knew it."

"You mean that everytime you were spitting fire at me you were loving me?"

"Not exactly. But almost."

Grant remembered the time he had had to hide her out at Emma Chatfield's house. That was probably the time he really knew he loved this woman. He turned slowly and kissed her soft lips. She sighed.

at four o'clock the dark purple skies were leavened with grey and the morning stars popped brilliantly onto the vaulted heavens. "Would you make a wish?" she asked.

"On a morning star?"

Patricia nodded.

"Yes."

Patricia wrinkled her nose. "Well, what is it?"

"You're not supposed to tell your wishes or they won't come true."

"You can tell them to your wife," Patricia said. She liked the way that sounded: "your wife."

Grant kissed her nose. She scratched it because it

tickled. "I wished that someday you will be proud to bear the name Yarrow."

"I am," she said quickly.

He shook his head sadly. "No, I can see it in your eyes when you hear it. Though you love me, you cannot forget the pain my father has given you. I hope that you will be allowed to forget."

Patricia took his head between her hands and kissed him on the mouth, drinking as deeply from his well of strength as she dared. When she had finished she brushed his cheeks with her soft eyelashes.

"You have not told me your wish," he said.

"I wished that you would take me so very gently to our bed now."

Grant kissed her, rose from the settee, picked her bodily from it, and carried her down the car to her master bedroom.

Patricia lay quietly on the top of the bed and breathed slowly while Grant slipped her from her clothes. A small lamp burned in a wall sconce, tossing shadows onto the ceiling. Grant's movements were deliberate. There was no wasted motion, no haste. As soon as he had removed her clothes, he covered her with a silken sheet. When he was naked, he eased under the sheet with her and lay for a few moments in the semi-darkness, letting her become accustomed to his presence.

It was during those precious moments that Patricia was able to bid good-bye to Francis Macauley, the man who had so cruelly used her when she was a little girl. The nightmares, the terrible memories slipped away, replaced by the strong and tender and caring man who only now let his hands seek hers. He kissed each of her fingers, licked between them just lightly, and then sought the firmness of her breasts.

Fearing she was doing the wrong thing, but somehow driven by unconscious commands, Patricia reached out to Grant Yarrow and guided him into her. Grant breathed a slow sigh.

They were one.

CHAPTER FOUR

No one expected the reporters. But when the train pulled into the station, twenty or thirty newshounds pushed, shoved and jostled one another on the platform in order to get interviews and photos of the surprise wedding couple of the year. When the son of one of America's most powerful men married the woman who had turned banking on its ear, this was news!

Patricia first got word of the reporters presence when she and Grant were having coffee with Molly, Stephen and Harry. She wore a smile; her skin glowed like the dawn; she chattered; she looked at Grant with gigantic adoring eyes; she reached out and touched him every few minutes to make sure he was still hers. She told jokes she remembered her father telling.

"Missus Yarrow," the conductor said, "there's reporters out there to talk with you and the mister."

"About what?"

"About you being married," he replied.

"How did they find out?"

"Telegraph, I reckon."

"Oh." She looked around at the others. "What do we do?"

"Talk to them," Grant said. "It's harmless and painless. It's easier to answer their questions than to run away from them."

Patricia nodded. "I guess. Well, let's go."

Molly followed her family out to the platform, hoping that Tom Kierney hadn't come to welcome them home. She looked at her aunt, absolutely delirious in the arms of the man she loved. And what of her? She now knew she didn't love Tom Kierney. How could she? She was confused, infatuated with Benjamin Macauley. She could think of no one else even though she knew he would never grow up, never take love seriously.

The reporters ranged themselves out across the platform with the photographers taking the choicest spots with their tripods, their tall conical hoods, their flashbars.

"Miss Carrick, will this marriage—"

"Mrs. Yarrow," she corrected.

"Mrs. Yarrow, will this marriage mean any changes in the philosophy of the Carrick Banks?"

"Why should it?"

"Well," the reporter went on, "Simon Yarrow's philosophy of banking is elitist at best."

Grant stepped forward. "I'll answer that. My bride married me, not my father. Simon Yarrow's doings are *his* business, not ours."

"Mrs. Yarrow, will you be meeting with your new father-in-law in the near future?"

"I doubt it," Patricia replied quickly.

"Why not?" another reporter asked.

"Because there is no love lost between us. That's

all I'll have to say on that subject. Suffice to say his principles are not mine."

The reporters buzzed with this quote from the outspoken woman. Grant smiled and tightened his grip on her shoulder.

An older man, carrying a heavy black camera, made his way, by means of a well-used elbow, to the front rank of photographers. His eyes ranged quickly from face to face as if he were afraid of being recognized. He hid his own face by looking down into the viewfinder. His weathered right hand reached down into his coat pocket and pulled out a small nickel-plated handgun.

"Mr. Yarrow, when did you last speak to your father?"

Before Grant could answer, there was a flash from the front rank of photographers, an explosion, and a scream. The handsome man who had married Patricia Carrick seemed to be trying to reach out into the crowd. Then he collapsed, ripped across the middle by a giant red stain.

The reporters ducked for cover or ran behind the baggage wagon. The braver photographers stayed their ground to catch sight of the beautiful redhead who lay on the platform clutching her new husband to her breast. In the background the man with white hair and a beard dropped his camera and ran up the platform. Someone yelled, "There he is! Stop him! He killed Grant Yarrow!"

Stephen and Henry ran after him.

"The bullet is lodged up against his spine," the surgeon said in a half whisper. He was young, well-trained, more expert than most of his older colleagues at the hospital. "What that means," he said, "is that Grant Yarrow is paralyzed from the waist down."

"My God," Patricia whispered. She reached out and took Stephen Lacey's arm for support.

The young doctor rubbed his face with his hands. He'd been up for too many hours now. He didn't know how many since they brought in the new patient. "I'm not about to say the paralysis is permanent. But right now I can't go in after the bullet for fear of killing him."

"It'll kill him worse to be paralyzed," Patricia said.

The doctor nodded. "He may regain the use of his limbs without the surgery. It's one of those things. There are cases like your husband's in the literature from the war."

"May I see him?"

"Of course. For a short while."

Patricia followed the doctor down a long pale green hallway. The plaster had only recently been repainted and still smelled of fresh paint, making her nauseous. The nurses and orderlies came and went with their own starched, impersonal efficiency. Patricia did not pay any attention to the presence of the new electric lights which hung from the ceiling on their long serpentine wires.

The young doctor stood aside apologetically at the door to Grant Yarrow's room. Grant's new bride walked in cautiously, slowly.

Grant's dark hair lay limp upon the clean white pillowcase. It looked as if he had just lain down after swimming in the bay. His forehead was bathed in sweat.

Patricia looked over to the doctor. "Is he in pain?"

"Some," the surgeon replied.

"Grant?" Patricia whispered near him. She leaned down and kissed his feverish lips. "Grant?" She sat down on a chair and held his hands in hers. "Dear God," she prayed silently, "please let this man live. Amen."

The lips near the redheaded woman's ear began to work slowly, laboriously. The breath came out unevenly.

"What, my love?" Patricia said.

"Ch--ch . . ."

The doctor said, "We had better let him get his rest now."

"Wait," Patricia said.

"Chase," Grant whispered.

Patricia turned and looked at her husband. "Chase? Stephen and Harry chased him and lost him."

Grant's head moved from side to side with infinite care. "Chase. Chase was the man."

"Judge Chase?" Patricia said.

Grant's nod was slight. "I saw him as he fired." His voice was raspy, clogged with breath. "He had a camera." His eyelids fluttered under the exhaustion of holding them open. "Get Judge." His breathing became heavy and deep.

Patricia walked back down the hallway alone. Up ahead, in the lobby she saw Henry, Stephen and Molly standing next to an older woman dressed in black, with a veil covering most of her face. It wasn't until she was within six feet of her that she realized to her astonishment that it was Diana Yarrow, whom she hadn't seen in years.

"How is he?" Diana asked.

Patricia turned to her niece and nephews. "You

babies go on without me." They didn't move. "Go along now."

"Yes, ma'am." She kissed each one good-bye before turning to speak with Grant's sister. Diana looked much older than the twenty-eight turns of the calendar she had lived through. Her eyes were a duller blue-green than Patricia remembered. Her skin was a paler, pastier white. She had begun to paint her lips larger than they actually were. Her blonde hair was tied down in a tight bun.

"How is my brother?" Diana asked.

"He's alive," Patricia replied. "He's paralyzed. The bullet is lying next to his spine."

"Jesus. . . ."

"How did you get here so quickly?"

Diana smiled an ironic smile. "I was in the city when the newspapers came on the streets. Buying a wedding trousseau." She laughed a flat laugh. It was an effort for her to stand there talking to her brother's wife. The frightening nausea of her morning sickness was made all the worse because the child she carried was her father's. "May I see him?"

"Grant is asleep."

Diana started to say something—all manner of things tried to frame themselves in her mind, but none of them would come forth. She turned and walked towards the door.

"Diana?" Patricia said.

"Yes?" Diana replied.

Patricia shook her head. "Nothing."

Diana left the hospital.

It was not until that evening at home that Patricia read in the papers that Diana was engaged to marry Ambrose Parker, senator from California and, next to Simon Yarrow himself, the most important and powerful man in the state. Patricia wondered why such a young woman would go on to marry a man in his late sixties.

That evening Patricia Carrick Yarrow sat down with the head of a private detective agency and hired him to begin looking immediately for Judge Chase.

CHAPTER FIVE

SAN JOAQUIN VALLEY, CALIFORNIA, AUGUST, 1881

"DAMAGED goods," Ambrose Parker said. "Damaged goods."

"I won't have you talking about my daughter that way," Simon Yarrow said. He made his shot. The billiard balls clicked crisply together.

Parker smiled and chalked his cuestick. "Yes, you will." His small brown eyes were heavily lidded with layers of fatty tissue. His nose was crisscrossed with blue and purple veins. His double chins wobbled like wattles when he spoke. A leonine mane of white hair capped his tall frame. "You will take any kind of shit I want to dish out and you'll call it French cooking."

Simon's hands were white as he held tightly to the side of the billiard table. To think that this slimey operator was in a position to ruin everything Yarrow had struggled to create. In a land of corrupt politicians Ambrose Parker was a veritable king! The man seemed to know everything Simon Yarrow had ever done, everyone Simon Yarrow had ever known.

Ambrose Parker's hold over Simon Yarrow was complete. He held in his possession enough material

on the wealthy financier and land baron to have him
hanged for treason.

Senator Parker laughed to see Simon miss a shot.
"I heard that that Carrick woman bought a house
in Menlo Park and is moving your son out there tomorrow."

"I have no son."

Parker smiled. "Ah, yes." He made his shot. "She's
turned the whole bottom floor into a hospital for him.
He's still an invalid from the waist down." He followed up that shot with another winner.

"I have no son."

Parker looked up and tapped his host on the chest
with a bony forefinger. "Yarrow, the trouble with you
is you get too involved emotionally. I've spent a lifetime divorcing myself from feelings. That way I
never become too upset to do what's right."

Simon Yarrow lighted his fifth cigar of the evening.
Outside the last stragglers were packing up and going
home. The wedding and reception had gone on too
long. Dawn would be rolling across the hills in another couple of hours. In another half hour or so
Diana would be lying in bed with this corpulent
senator.

Diana! The only woman Simon Yarrow had ever
really loved. And now she carried his child within
her body. Simon smiled a sick smile. At first, after
Joseph Carrick's murder, Diana had resisted him.
But he'd beaten her down, taken her will from her.
The morphia had helped. Now she was his. All his.

Senator Parker won the game and was setting up
the balls when Diana walked into the billiard room
wearing her silk dressing gown. "Will you two be
playing games all night?" she asked.

"Mrs. Parker?" the Senator replied.

Diana looked behind her as if he were addressing someone else. Then she looked at him.

"Mrs. Parker," the Senator continued, "I well realize that as the apple of your father's eye you have been used to having your own way in most things. Now that you are my wife, however, we had best get the rules straight."

"Senator," Simon said.

Parker raised a hand to stay his host's protests. "Please, sir, I am speaking to my wife." He smiled. "First, you will bear in mind the words in the service read today. You are to 'love, honor and obey.' To me the whole thing is for you to realize that you are to obey me in everything. I shall warn you that any breach in the observance of that oath will be most severely and, yes, harshly, dealt with." He smiled. "Am I making myself clear?"

"Senator, I feel a misunder—"

"—Simon, you will cease this interruption at once!" Ambrose Parker walked across and stood directly in front of his bride of eight hours. "Do you understand what I have said, woman?"

Diana nodded anxiously.

Parker slapped her across the face. "Do you understand what I have said, woman?"

"Yes!"

"Do not raise your voice at me, woman!"

Simon Yarrow strode across the room and started to put his hands on this detested adversary.

"I wouldn't do that, Yarrow!"

Simon stopped in his tracks. "I will not stand by and watch my daughter abused! If you harm her . . ." Simon said.

"You'll what?" Parker concluded.

Simon stood there in the middle of his own billiard room and felt as if the entire world had been snatched from him. He could not afford to go up against Parker.

Parker laughed and took Diana by the arm. "Let us go to our wedding couch, my love."

Diana looked over her shoulder as the man pulled her rudely forward. Her eyes widened. She had never seen her father look so small.

In their room the Senator quickly removed his clothes, revealing a body that was stronger than Diana might have suspected. His eyes burned malevolently as he stripped her of her negligee. "Since we are both such old hands at this, my blushing bride," he said, "we can dispense with the romantic folderol. Turn over."

"No."

The slap came swiftly, stinging her face and raising a welt. "You can learn quickly or you can take your time." He smiled. "Bear in mind that I got my start in this state breaking horses for the cavalry." The second slap came equally as quickly, forcing Diana to cry out in pain and turn over as she had been ordered.

But the pain of the slap was nothing compared to the pain she felt when he bore relentlessly at the tightness of her anus. She cried out as he battered his way through and speedily spent his cruel seed. Then he turned over and went to sleep.

Diana watched the dawn come as she wept for all that her life could have been with the man named Carrick.

CHAPTER SIX

MARSHALL Macauley sat at the front bay window of his
mansion on Fifth Avenue and watched the chilly
fall rain dot the leather roofs of the carriages as they
traversed the intersection. At fifty-four Marshall still
had the long lean look of his youth. His black hair
was peppered with grey at the sides, giving him the
aspect of a matinee idol. His eyes had seen a great
deal over the years, but they continued to burn with
the intensity he had always enjoyed. Wherever he
went he could be sure to turn the heads of women
young and old.

In those fifty-four years Marshall Macauley had
seen the dissolution of his family; he had saved the
Carricks from bondage to his brothers; he had saved
Joseph Carrick and his father from the gallows; he
had grubstaked the Carricks to their new lives in the
West; he had lost his first wife in a vicious murder
and, finally, he had been allowed to marry his one
true love: Violette Larson, the world renowned stage
actress.

By the man's elegantly tapered hand was a letter

from Patricia Carrick. The contents had disturbed him, judging by the furrowed brows and the down-turned lip.

"Grant continues to improve in spirit if not in body," she wrote.

Marshall looked over at the tall slim bureaucrat who stood quietly by the bookcase. "Why would Chase want Grant Yarrow out of the way?" he asked.

The tall man moved closer, his hands deep in the pockets of his heavy wool suit. "Before Grant shipped out, he was working for us at the Bureau."

Marshall looked surprised. "On what?"

"I cannot go into too much detail, Mr. Macauley, but Grant was gathering information concerning his father's activities."

"My Lord," Marshall whispered. "On his own father?"

The man nodded. "It took its toll from him. His passion for Miss Carrick had been badly frustrated, and just as bad, he was figuring things out about old man Yarrow that would turn your stomach. But he couldn't get any proof—so he quit."

"Obviously Judge Chase didn't think there was any shortage of hard evidence to be had."

"Judge Chase had two scores to settle. First, it was Grant Yarrow who nearly got him hung for his wife's murder. Second, Chase was a crony of Simon Yarrow's and we suspect he was number two man in the state. Without realizing what he was on to, Grant just may have tripped over some information, some clue he might have overlooked, something that would help us incriminate Simon Yarrow in a treasonable plot."

Marshall drummed his fingers on the edge of the chair. "Why come to me?"

"You're a friend of Patricia Yarrow's. No one would suspect your visiting them in California. We want as much information as possible from Grant as to why he thinks Chase wanted him dead. The future of our country may depend on it."

Marshall nodded, agreed to travel to San Francisco, and showed the man from Washington to the door.

"Father?" Benjamin Macauley called from the living room.

"Yes?"

The handsome young man with the engaging smile walked into the foyer. He wondered what had made his father look so worried. "How are you, father?"

"Can't complain. You?"

Benjamin nodded. "Fine."

There was a pause between them, as physical and tangible as the oriental carpet that separated them. Marshall loved his son deeply, but he was clearly exasperated by the young rakehell's behavior. "It would be so much easier," he'd said to Violette, "if he'd just hold dear the same values as I do." They'd both laughed.

"You wanted to see me?" Benjamin asked.

Marshall looked distracted. "Uh, yes." He summoned up the uncomfortable time he'd had with Jacob Stern, one of his clerks in the New York office of Macauley and Son. The man had looked so distressed—and well might he be—when he tried to broach the subject with the head of the firm.

Marshall cleared his throat. "How well do you know Jacob Stern's daughter?" He tried to remember her name, but it eluded him.

"Rachel?"

"Yes."

Benjamin grinned. "Not well enough," he replied.

Marshall laced his fingers in front of him. Shook his head. "You've got the poor man beside himself with worry."

Benjamin shrugged. "Have you ever seen her, father?"

"No, I haven't."

"You have missed a treat for the eyes. She has dark black hair, a deep brown skin that's as smooth as whipped cream, a form that's more to look at than any dancer in any of mother's shows. A smile that speaks volumes—"

"—I'm sure that's as it may be—"

"Father, if you're about to tell me not to see Rachel Stern anymore, you might just as well tell me not to breathe." He laughed aloud. "She is out of a dream!"

"You said the same thing of Hillary Newton and Francine Drury and Molly Lacey."

"And I meant every word of it." Benjamin looked at his father. "Father, what can I say? I was born out of a great love affair. Therefore I am filled with more love than any other man. I can't help it."

"You are filled with something, but I'm not sure it's love."

"Father . . ."

"Benjamin, all this may be true. You may be God's gift to women, but you are causing me problems."

"Such as?"

"When the Chairman of the firm gets visited by a clerk, when I can't go to the Eagle Club without

Nelson Drury collaring me, when Laird Newton tells me you're going to marry his little Hillary—and there's precious little about 'little Hillary'—then I find your behavior untenable. Am I getting through?"

"I'll fall in love with total strangers from now on."

"Benjamin? What about these girls?"

"They love it."

"And when the light of their lives moves on like some rutting dog, how do they feel?" Marshall walked over to his son and placed both strong hands on the boy's shoulders. "I'll tell you. They feel cheated. You seem to promise them you are more committed than you are. You know you're a moth and I know you're a moth, but they think you're a prospective husband!"

Benjamin smiled to see his father work so hard to protect him from himself. He never felt quite so much love from the man as when he bawled him out for something. Marshall was never comfortable taking his son down a peg. Benjamin embraced his father. "Very well, father, I shall try to make amends." He paused. "But I do wish you'd take a look at Rachel Stern."

"She's only seventeen!"

"And quite old enough to be married," Benjamin replied.

"Jacob Stern does not want his daughter marrying a Christian if it's all the same to you, my boy."

"I'm not good enough?"

"You're not Jewish enough! Stay away from her."

"God, but she's beautiful."

Before Marshall could reply to his son's rapturous outburst a uniformed butler appeared carrying a silver tray. He walked to Benjamin and stood erect while the younger Macauley took the telegram from the salver. The butler waited while Benjamin tore open the envelope and read the contents:

"Arriving from California tonight at nine."

It was signed, "All my love, Molly."

"Will there be a reply, sir?" the butler asked.

Benjamin shook his head. "No, uh, no, Briggs."

"Very well, sir." The butler made a noiseless exit.

"What is it?" Marshall asked. "You looked worried there for a moment."

Benjamin tried a smile. "Nothing, father." He looked up at the clock on the mantel. It read six o'clock. Three hours before the Lacey girl would show up at the Station! Right at the hour he was supposed to be having a private supper with Rachel Stern! This would tax a magician's powers! "Have we finished our man to man talk, sir?"

"As long as you promise to leave Rachel Stern alone."

"It looks as if I had better, sir," he replied. He turned the big knob and let himself out.

Marshall shook his head. "I can trust that boy—in anything that has nothing to do with women. I am afraid he is an incorrigible lover." Marshall grinned. "He gets it from his mother, damn me." He went to his office and sat down to write a telegram to the Yarrows.

"Am I disturbing you?" a melodious voice asked from the secret doorway that opened alongside the bookcase in his office. Violette Larson stood with a hand on the lock. She was dressed in a clinging silk dressing gown, her long auburn tresses hanging free, her green eyes glimmering in the low light, her delicious form filling every important part of her gown.

She prided herself in making a mockery of the calendar which said she was fifty-five years old. Last season she had played an Ophelia which the critics hailed as "a most bewitching performance. It looks as if Violette Larson has made a pact with the devil, for she looks not a day older than nineteen."

"You can never disturb me, my love," Marshall replied. As far as he knew, only his wife and he were aware of the passageway that led from his den upstairs to the boudoir. Even Benjamin was unaware of the means by which his parents regularly enjoyed their own very private assignations while the "outside" world thought she was resting for her performances and he was working on his papers.

"What did the young lover say?" she asked.

"He said he'd never see Rachel again."

"Hah!"

Marshall shrugged. "What can I tell you? I figure Jacob Stern will have to put a minie ball in Benjamin's buttocks before the boy will understand that some people take their daughter's virginity extremely seriously."

Violette frowned. "I hope it won't come to that, love."

"You ever try corking a tea kettle?"

Rachel sat in the far corner of the restaurant, afraid that she would see someone she knew. She comforted herself by telling herself that no Orthodox Jew would be caught dead in this kind of place. The smell of the sausages frying in the kitchen would be enough to make them faint. As it was, it made her queasy. She looked up at the doorway each time someone came or went, but she missed Benjamin's entrance for she didn't know he was there until she felt a hand on her arm. She looked up in fright.

"Hello, my little love-bird," Benjamin said. He liked what he saw. She was even more beautiful than he had told his father. Her hair was the color of a raven's wing, her eyes darker still. Her skin was softly tanned, her figure an hourglass of perfection.

"I began to despair," she said.

"Never despair," he replied, kissing her ungloved hand.

She sighed and felt a wave of relaxation sweep her under in its tow. "I love you."

"And I love you," Benjamin said, "but your father has gone and put grease on the rails, my love."

"Father?"

"He spoke to my father—"

"—Oh, God!"

Benjamin shrugged. "Father has forbidden me to see you again."

"I'll die!"

"Hush, hush," Benjamin said. "Do you think that will stop us? Never." He squeezed her hand, oblivious to the other diners around him.

"Oh, but I love you," Rachel said. She reached up and stroked the jet black curls across his forehead.

"But we shall have to be more circumspect and we shall have to wait."

"Wait? Wait for what?"

Benjamin leaned closer. "Right now we are being watched. I'll have to leave as soon as I can. We are under suspicion and we'll have to be on our best behavior for a week or so until we can earn back the trust of our families."

Rachel looked sad but she nodded obediently.

Benjamin looked at his pocket watch, a beautiful gold hunter his mother had given him when he graduated from Princeton. "I'll slip out right now. I'll get in touch with you the usual way when I think it's safe, all right?"

"I'll miss you so."

"And I you," Benjamin said. He leaned forward, kissed her on the cheek and wished life was simpler.

At nine his carriage pulled up in front of the train station.

CHAPTER SEVEN

As the steam billowed around his shoulders, the conductor leaned against the car and watched the young nineteen year old walk quickly past him carrying a red and brown carpet bag. He wished he were about fifteen years younger . . . he'd show that little western beauty something! He turned away ruefully, wishing that the fates had dropped the light brown hair, the ice blue eyes, and the trim figure into his life instead of the dumpy woman who stuffed her face whenever he was on a run.

Molly dared not look from side to side for fear of attracting unwarranted advances from the strangers who flowed on both sides of her towards the gate at the end of the platform. She was traveling alone; she shuddered to think of what Aunt Patricia would do to her when she found out. Only whores traveled alone . . . She had sneaked out of the house in Menlo Park, boarded the train and bought a ticket for New York. She felt dirty, hot, and tired. But she was buoyed up by the thought that soon she would fall into the comfortable, sweet-smelling arms of her lover.

Molly had a perfect mental image of Benjamin Macauley. She even remembered his voice, the way it seemed to single her out and caress her with its tones.

"Are you meeting someone?" a handsome traveler asked.

"I am being met," she said in a husky voice.

"Too bad," the man said, hurrying up with his leather valises.

Molly blushed to think that he was the twentieth or twenty-first man who had spoken to her since she boarded the train. It was frightening, but she had just enough resources to last until. . . .

He looked exactly like her mental image. Right down to the coloration! His cheeks were red and healthy. His eyebrows were dark arches over his piercing black eyes. "Benjamin!" she shouted.

Some of the travelers around her stared then gave her room as she threw herself into the arms of the striking looking young man.

"Molly, you foolish, lovely girl!" he said into the perfumed freshness of her hair. He did not smell the soot that had filled the cars as often as not. "You terrific foolish girl!"

"Oh, don't chastise me, beautiful Benjamin! I don't think I could bear your criticism. Just hold me as you are holding me now. There, oh, yes." She looked up into his measureless eyes and felt she would swoon. "What must you think of me?"

"That you are shamelessly in love with me," he replied.

"This is so," she said, oblivious to the curious passengers who strolled past her, slowing up so as to eavesdrop. "I am shameless." She thrust her arm through Benjamin's, letting him carry her bag.

"Is this your only case?" he asked.

"We can buy me clothes in New York. I don't ever wish to be an embarrassment to you, Benjamin."

"Quite so," he said.

"Father, mother, this is Miss Molly Lacey," Benjamin said.

Violette, freshly back from her evening performance of Portia, looked up from her soft white towel and then looked over at her husband. Benjamin was hardly in the habit of bringing home his conquests—especially one carrying carpet bags. The girl was surely a stunner—wilted from travel it would seem—but one of the best Benjamin had corraled in her recent memory. "Good evening, Miss Lacey."

Molly curtseyed. She couldn't get the words out that she had practiced. All her life she had heard her aunt talk about Miss Violette Larson. She had read stories about the woman in her periodicals and had snipped her photographs and pasted them in a scrapbook. Once she'd even done her hair in the twist that the legendary actress had made the rage.

Marshall rose from his easy chair in the little second-floor parlor where they never entertained and put his paper down on the deal table. "Molly Lacey? Is your aunt come back?"

Molly blushed crimson and shook her head.

"I don't understand," Marshall said, looking to Benjamin or to Violette for an explanation. Violette shrugged and took the last of the cold cream from her fingers.

Benjamin put a finger inside his collar to try to gain time and an extra supply of air.

Molly took a step forward. "May I sit?"

"Oh, please, dear," Violette said. "How rude you must think us."

Molly sat and unpinned the little straw hat with the bluebirds and the cherries on it. She placed the hat in front of her on her lap. "I'm afraid my being here is grossly improper," she said tremulously.

"I beg your pardon?" Marshall said. He cupped a hand around his ear to hear her muffled words.

Molly blushed again. "I have fallen in love with your son."

"Oh, my God," Violette said.

"A fate worse than death," Marshall muttered.

"Beg pardon?" Molly said.

"Nothing, my dear. Please go on," Marshall said, casting a frozen eye upon his profligate.

"I am supposed to marry Thomas Kierney of San Francisco. My aunt gave him a loan. It was her first loan before she was a bank. And his mother kept us alive when we could as easily have starved."

"That's a nice match," Violette said helpfully.

"Anyway, when I met Benjamin here, I knew I couldn't marry Tom Kierney who always smells like fish and who calls me his 'little sunflower'."

"There are worse things, believe me," Violette said.

"That's as may be," Molly said, "but I'm here to claim Benjamin."

Marshall stared at her in mute dismay. Then he turned to his son. "Benjamin? What do you have to say?"

While Benjamin fought for words, Violette said, "Do you mean that your aunt doesn't know where you are?"

Molly nodded and picked at the trimming on her hat.

"Oh, lord," Violette said. "We had best wire her immediately."

"Please, don't," Molly said tearfully.

"I'm still waiting to hear what Benjamin has to say, my love," Marshall said.

Benjamin smiled. "I, uh, well. Father, mother, there are two ways to examine any problem . . ."

"Which way would you have us examine this one?" Marshall thundered.

Benjamin jumped backwards. "Well . . ."

Molly turned around and looked at her equivocating lover. "You said you loved me, Benjamin . . ."

Benjamin, trapped, nodded because he couldn't think of the words to fit the chaos in his brain. Every alarm system in his head was going off simultaneously. Loudest of all was the bachelor alarm, the indicator that sensed the possible end to his footloose ways.

Violette could not help letting a small satisfied smile traipse across her lips. "Benjamin, you won the Mc-Cloud cup for debate at Princeton. What happened to your silver tongue, my love?"

Benjamin essayed a smile of his own, but failed miserably.

Before Benjamin's glib tongue could catch up with his panicky brain, there was an insistent knocking downstairs. "Who could that be?" Violette asked no one in particular.

"Rachel Stern, perhaps?" Marshall offered.

"Oh, my God," Benjamin said.

"Or Mr. Jacob Stern," Marshall said.

"Or a host of others," Violette added.

Molly looked miserable and confused.

The butler appeared on the thick cream-colored carpet and bowed. "Mr. Patrick Carrick regrets the intrusion at this hour, sir, but he would like to speak to you on a matter of the utmost importance."

"Send him up, Boynton," Marshall said. "Well, Benjamin, before this young lady's uncle gets up here, would you like to make an accounting of yourself?"

Patrick had gotten the telegram at a late dinner. Patricia was obviously beside herself for news of her niece. It read: "Molly run away stop. Think to New York stop. Ask Marshall Macauley for help stop. Send word immediately stop. Love, Patricia." Carlotta had wanted to accompany him, but now that she was pregnant, Patrick insisted that she stay home and get her rest. After all, she was carrying the first Carrick to be born in America in a generation.

Molly was always the wild one, he thought. "Takes after her aunt with her sassy ways. You'd think she was a man, right and proper." He followed the butler up the wide-treaded stairs and down the hallway to the private wing.

When Patrick Carrick was ushered into the private parlor he stood at the threshold and surveyed the sight. Miss Violette sat at a small table wearing a thick dressing gown. Her face was as pink as an angel's. Marshall Macauley, with whom he'd had a number of lucky business dealings since coming to New York, stood by a small fireplace looking quite nonplussed. Benjamin Macauley, for whom Patrick had little use —"The boy's spoiled rotten," he'd said to Carlotta— sat on the love seat next to Molly, who looked as if she'd just been playing target with a sandbag.

"Good evening, Mr. Carrick," Violette said.

"Good evening, ma'am," he replied. He turned to Molly. "Your aunt is sick with worry, little one. You should be ashamed."

Molly nodded.

"Are you all right?"

Molly nodded and attempted a smile.

Patrick looked around to see if anyone felt up to explaining what was going on.

Violette stood up at her improvised make-up table. "Mr. Carrick, we have the pleasure of being able to announce the engagement of our son Benjamin to your niece, Miss Molly Lacey."

Benjamin grinned with relief and nodded. Considering the alternatives, he was damned lucky to be getting the beautiful Irish girl on the loveseat next to him.

"We better send a wire to Patricia," Patrick said.

"She's too much like her aunt," Grant said. "She sees something she wants and she goes and gets it."

Patricia smiled and finished her tea. "Do you want some more?" Grant said no and so she cleaned up the tray by the head of his bed. Each time she looked at the immobile body of her strong husband she had to consciously stop herself from weeping for him, something he was too strong to do for himself. She bathed his forehead with a warm cloth, then wrung it out and walked over to the window and looked out at the clear night sky. "It's a beautiful night," she said.

"What stars can you see?"

"I don't know the names of any of them," she said.

"When I get well," Grant said, "I'll teach you them so you can navigate without a compass."

Patricia nodded. When he got well . . . Each day the doctor came and poked her husband. Each day Grant felt nothing. When she walked the doctor to his carriage he said, "It's possible for a spontaneous remission, but the odds are very much against it. I want to be honest with you."

"I'd like to know which stars I wish upon," she said. She turned to face him. "I hope Tom Kierney doesn't get derailed after all this. When Molly gets back here I'm gonna whip her, then hug her."

"Then marry her off to Benjamin Macauley. This could be quite the social event. I wish I could be there," Grant said. "Maybe I will be."

"Of course you will. Even if we have to wheel you down the aisle in your favorite bed!" She smiled and picked up a hand mirror and a brush so she could do her nightly two hundred strokes. She was still bothered by the report from the private detective she had hired to track down Judge Chase. She didn't know whether to tell Grant. She didn't want to bother him . . .

It seemed that just about everyone concerned with the murder of Mrs. Chase was either dead—of mysterious causes—or out of the U.S. Chase's mistress had been found an apparent suicide in New York's Hudson River. His lawyer was another apparent suicide, found in San Francisco Bay. His daughter had left the city two years earlier and was living in South Africa. At every turn in his investigation the private detective had run into the sense that very important people were hiding something about Judge Chase, something more complicated than his wife's murder. The police did not seem to be pressing forward at all. Moreover, they were resentful that the private investigator was trying to follow the leads in the Grant Yarrow shooting. "This thing stinks, if you'll pardon the expression," the detective said.

"Penny for your thoughts?" Grant said.

"Nothing worth that much," Patricia replied, tugging the brush through her lustrous hair. Suddenly she felt light-headed, faint . . . She lost her balance and switched feet to try to compensate. Then pitched sideways onto the foot of Grant's bed.

He cried out.

Patricia shook her head to try to clear it, then suddenly turned to face her husband at the head of the bed. "What did you say?"

"I said 'ouch!'"

"Why?" she breathed.

"Because you fell on my ankle," Grant said, confused.

"And you said 'ouch'?"

"Of course I said 'ouch'. Wouldn't you?"

"If it hurt I would have!"

"Of course it hurt!"

Patricia crowed with joy! "Grant, you felt your ankle!"

"I did! Of course I did! Oh, Good Christ I did!" He wiggled his toes and shouted at the top of his lungs.

Patricia hugged him as servants and children streamed into the room to see what all the shouting was about. They jumped for joy to hear that Grant might just walk again!

Simon Yarrow looked at his daughter and dared not ask how she got the bruise over her eye. She left the dining room when her new husband told her he wished to speak to her father alone.

"Simon, I have been advised that your son's wife has hired an investigator to find Chase," Ambrose Parker said.

"Jesus."

"I am going to terminate Chase. I may well need to go further."

Simon Yarrow nodded dumbly. He could not stop thinking of his daughter. She seemed to be drugged all the time.

"Then I'll be leaving for Texas tomorrow. I want you to follow up on the Carrick woman."

Simon Yarrow nodded. He had gone too far and there was no turning back.

Grant had no sooner begun to make his recovery when Patricia looked up from her needlework and caught her breath. "Holy Mother! It's you, isn't it?"

"It's I, Patricia."

"Mr. Macauley!" She stood quickly. "You didn't write or wire . . ."

"I thought I'd surprise you both," Marshall replied.

"Come across a continent for a surprise?" Grant asked.

The tall handsome man shrugged. "Well, it was a spur of the moment decision. Could I get a cup of tea?"

Patricia nodded. "You certainly could. And some scones and I made a cake! I'm so glad to see you!" She nearly ran out into the hallway.

As soon as Patricia had stepped out of the room, Marshall said, "McGriffen paid me a visit two weeks ago."

Grant's expression changed from a smile to a frown. "I quit working for him a long time ago. I'm sorry he bothered you."

Marshall shook his head. "Me too, but I can't

worry about that right now. He told me about your investigation."

"They all think there's a conspiracy to overthrow the government and that my father's one of the leaders. I think they're mad. I tried to convince them my father's just a greedy son of a bitch, not a traitor."

"From what I've seen recently, I don't think they're mad," Marshall said softly.

Grant looked at him.

"A great deal has happened since you quit the Bureau," Marshall said. "McGriffen has kept up the investigation and it appears your father's people have been very patient and very successful."

"Does he think Judge Chase came out of the woodwork because of this organization?"

Marshall nodded.

"I couldn't get anything on him," Grant said.

"McGriffen wants you to help me see if there's something you remember that might lead us somewhere on Chase."

Grant leaned back against the pillow. He let his mind drift back. "Let's give it a try," he said.

"Good," Marshall said. "Tell me about the first time you met with him."

When Patricia reappeared an hour later with a tea tray, she found the two men looking serious. "You look as if you'd been written out of a will," she said.

Grant tried to force a smile. Marshall rose and apologized but said he had to leave.

"What was that all about?" Patricia asked.

"Ghosts in the closet," Grant said in a whisper.

BOOK FIVE

CHAPTER ONE

SHE put down the letters which told of the creation of the Standard Oil trust and looked down at her stomach, marvelling at the size of it. Being a small woman, she had assumed that the baby would grow in proportion to her frame, not in some proportion known only to the race of giants called Yarrow.

It had caught her by surprise. Even as Grant lay invalided all those weeks, she knew that all was not well within her own body. But her attention had been focussed on Grant.

The first real sign was the dizziness she felt when she pitched headlong onto Grant's bed, causing him to yell out in pain.

Two days later the doctor asked her about her menstrual cycle. "You mean the curse?" she replied.

The doctor nodded.

"I've been off, but things have been pretty hectic around here," she said. "I wrote it off to Grant's condition. I'm like that. I get tense, I shut down."

The doctor smiled. "Well, you better get ready to be shut down for about nine months," he said.

Patricia smiled, preferring not to comprehend. "I'm very busy. Grant is on the mend. His surgeon says he'll be walking like normal in another week."

"And you'll be having a baby in late April or early May."

"I have a new branch opening in Los Angeles."

"You'll be having a new Yarrow opening in April."

When the reality finally sunk in on Patricia Carrick Yarrow, she sat very quietly and rocked back and forth, her arms looped across her belly. She smiled for no specific reason and stood at the window looking down on some of her nieces and nephews who were playing in the yard out back. She could not quite understand the mystery of life and growth, but some inner consciousness allowed her to enjoy her ignorance. Suddenly she felt connected to the entire universe—as if she were an extension of everything that had gone on before and everything that would follow. The fetus in her womb would become a person and join with others to march into the twentieth century. She would share in a progeny which would participate in the miracle of this great country.

Patricia got up from her desk at the bank and walked to where Grace stood. Grace was increasingly protective now that her employer was carrying a child. "When are you gonna quit?" she'd asked. "This is no place for a lady in your condition."

Patricia had smiled. "Tell that to the immigrant ladies who do their shopping, have a baby while diapering a baby, and then make supper for their hard-working husbands. I'm not about to turn into a conservatory flower because I'm carrying a child."

Grace looked up as Patricia stepped closer. "I don't see them yet. Maybe their train was late."

They were waiting on a visit from Marshal Macauley and the irrepressible Benjamin.

"You shoulda sent me with Mr. Yarrow," Grace said.

"Please call him Grant."

Grace shook her head. "I try, but I can't. He's still the man who saved me from hanging—thanks to you—and he'll be Mr. Yarrow till I die."

"I think I see them!" Patricia cried. She opened the door, threw on her shawl against the forty-five degree chill, and stepped out onto the sidewalk.

Marshall and Benjamin got down from the carriage and helped Grant, who still walked with a limp, get down after them. She was amazed how Marshall Macauley could travel across the country and look like he'd just come uptown from his mansion. They embraced warmly and went inside the Carrick Bank.

"You look, uh, extremely pregnant," Marshall said.

Patricia and Grant laughed. "Grant says that's because his son is going to be a giant."

Benjamin leaned back to look at Grant Yarrow. "If he's as tall as his father, he will be."

They spent the afternoon at the bank talking about the mortgage market. "Everyone on the east coast is wild to buy up mortgages out here," Marshall said, "but none of us knows what's valuable from what's swamp."

Patricia nodded. "My bank would be happy to act as agent for you," she said.

Marshall smiled and crossed his fingers. "That goes without saying. But I think we'll need somebody on it full time out here looking over the investment properties."

"You mean Benjamin?" she asked as politely as possible. She still didn't have a clear idea of how this handsome young man who was marrying Molly in June would fit into her life. Or not.

"No," Marshall said, "I was thinking more of Grant here."

Patricia pushed her chair back. "I think that would be too taxing on him," she said.

"Why don't you let me answer?" Grant said.

"I'm sorry, I didn't mean . . ." she stammered.

Grant patted her hands. "No offense taken. It's just that you've been treating me like an invalid longer than you needed to. I'm fine."

"But you'd have to ride up to the valley—all over—"

"I ride every day. I don't need my cane to ride."

"And I'd miss you. You'd be gone for weeks at a time."

"It'd be good for me," Grant said in the tone she had learned meant his mind was quite made up.

Patricia spread her hands wide. "Then that's it. Mr. Grant Yarrow is the Carrick Bank's vice-president in charge of mortgage investments for Macauley and Son, Incorporated, its heirs and assigns. How about sealing the deal with Grace's coffee? I guarantee you it's the worst coffee on the west coast."

"No," Grant said, "yours is."

"Who do you suppose taught me how to make coffee?" Patricia laughed.

After work they went to dinner with Molly and talked of the June wedding.

When Patricia woke, Grant was missing from the bed next to her. She lighted a lamp and looked at the clock on the far wall. It read three-forty-five. A strong wind had kicked up out of the west and was punching the lace curtains on the far wall. She got out of bed and went to close the window. As her fingers curled around the bottom of the frame she stopped.

The moon was nearly full, angling low and casting weird shadows across the silver-grey-green lawn. Two men on horseback leaned low on their saddles, slouch hats blown back by the wind. She did not recognize either man.

But she did recognize the two men on foot who were talking against the windstorm, trying to make themselves heard by the horsemen. One of them leaned on a cane. And bits of their speech tangled in the gale and traveled to her casement.

". . . Falcons . . ."

"He paid Guiteau. . . ."

"But Guiteau said on. . . ."

". . . Chester Arthur. . . ."

". . . Parker's man. . . ."

"Consarn it, I told you. What do I have to do to convince you they're serious!"

The men on horseback turned their mounts and galloped away. When they reached the main road one turned north and the other turned south. Patricia watched Marshall and Grant walk back into the house. She waited a few minutes, then closed the window.

Grant and Marshall stood in front of the fireplace taking the chill off when the door to the sitting room opened, revealing Patricia in her new cotton dressing gown and a woolen shawl which Nancy Gardiner had knitted her.

"Hello, love," Grant said. "Couldn't sleep?"

Patricia forced a smile. Shook her head. "Is this man's talk or can anyone join?"

"Please sit down," Marshall said. "We were just

going over some of the criteria for the mortgage business."

"Marshall doesn't want to lose his investors' money," Grant chimed in.

"Ah," Patricia observed. "Were the two men on horseback some of your investors?"

Marshall and Grant did not look at one another. There was a pause. Marshall rubbed the sleep from his eyes. "They had word for me from New York."

"Ah," Patricia said.

"My broker suggested I sell quickly so as not to lose my shirt. They carried the telegrams. I trust they didn't wake you up?"

Patricia shook her head. "Would you care for some tea?"

"No, thank you, I really must be getting to bed now. I'm sorry for the excitement," the older man said.

"No trouble," Patricia said. She waited while Marshall kissed her cheek and walked off down the hallway. Grant stood uneasily by the fireplace, then took the tongs and spread the logs apart so they could die out peacefully. Patricia watched him as he worked, sure that he was trying to avoid her. She waited.

"Shall I escort you back to the sanctity of our bed, madame?"

"I'd rather hear an explanation of what's going on," Patricia replied. "I heard the name Guiteau being bandied about and President Arthur's as well. And Ambrose Parker, perhaps?"

Grant picked up a pipe and lighted it from a twig which flared on the hearth. "It's not an easy story to tell."

"What is it?"

"Patricia, when your brother died—"

"—You mean when your father murdered my brother!"

Grant nodded. "I went to Washington to try to get help for you and all the other ranchers my father was oppressing. At that time I was enlisted in a special department created to investigate threats to the republic . . . from within. I'm now convinced that my father is the leader of a group of extremely powerful men who were supposedly conspiring to circumvent the Constitution, to limit our freedoms and, eventually, to seize power directly."

"And they're linked to Guiteau's assassination of President Garfield?"

"We think so."

"My God. . . ."

"I quit the Bureau in frustration. Our leads had dried up, our hands were tied by the very Constitution we were trying to protect. Most of all, I was in love with you. I couldn't think of anything or anyone else. So I quit and asked you to marry me. You turned me down and I went a little crazy."

"How does Marshall Macauley fit in?"

"He had tripped across the conspiracy in conversations with Charles Townsend of New York and Newport. Then he found that Townsend and my father were very close. He contacted the Bureau and they enlisted him to work with me to find out why Judge Chase tried to kill me."

"What did you find out?" Patricia asked.

"Judge Chase had mentioned—the night his wife was murdered—the name of Peter Myers. He boasted that Myers was a good friend. I guess he assumed that such information was safe with the son of Simon Yarrow."

"But Myers is being named to the Supreme Court!" Patricia said.

Grant nodded. "Myers is one of them. Chase wanted me out of the way before I remembered our conversation. Up to then, nobody suspected Myers of even knowing Chase or my father or Ambrose Parker."

Patricia sat in thought for a few minutes. She looked up at her husband. "How dangerous is this?"

Before Grant could answer the front door exploded with loud knockings. She shook from the shock and spun towards the sound. And then, behind her, Marshall appeared at the head of the stairs.

"What is it?" Marshall called.

Grant shook his head. "I don't know." He went forward, unlocked the door and swung it open to reveal a young telegraph runner with a leather cap. "Yes?"

"Telegram for Mrs. Grant Yarrow?"

"Mrs. Yarrow?"

"A busy night for Western Union," Patricia said.

"Beg pardon?" the boy replied.

"Nothing. Give it to me, son." Patricia took the flimsy envelope and ripped it open. Her eyes took less than a few seconds to read the words. "My Christopher is dead," she said.

"I'm sorry," Grant said softly.

She crumpled up the paper. "No message," she said to the boy.

CHAPTER TWO

THERE was nothing for it. The Denver authorities said Christopher had been murdered. There was no motive for the crime—no motive anyone could fathom anyway. Just the peculiar note found next to the tubercular patient's cold corpse:

> "Enough, this must stop."

There was no signature. There were no clues to aid an investigation.

A few days after Christopher's sealed coffin arrived in San Francisco and he was buried in the pretty little plot Patricia had picked out, a Denver detective called at the Carrick Bank for an interview with the deceased's sister.

"I don't understand," Patricia said.

"I simply asked if you knew anything about your brother's political associations," the baggy-looking little man said.

"Such as?"

The man shrugged. "Backing a candidate for President or something?"

Patricia squeezed the bridge of her nose as if to

dispel the increasingly thick fog that seemed to be engulfing her. She shook her head. "My brother was sick. He didn't care about politics. Why do you ask?"

The man shrugged again. "No reason. Well, I won't bother you anymore."

Patricia watched Grace escort the man out, then lay her head down on her blotter to try to gather her wits.

"Patricia?"

Patricia looked up. "Yes, Grace."

"Maybe you better go home for the day."

She shook her head. "Christopher never hurt anyone, Grace. His last letter said he thought he was feeling well enough to come back here and help out in the bank. He didn't mention anything about politics."

"Politics?"

"The detective asked if Christopher was involved in politics. I wish Grant were here. Any word yet?"

Grace said, "No. Tomorrow I'm sure. He wanted to see after the Baskin property up on the ridge." She smiled. "Did you see Molly's going-away dress?"

"I was too busy."

"Too busy? Now something's real wrong when you're too busy to see your own niece's going away dress."

"Maybe I'm fighting the realization that soon Molly will be leaving us."

"But you'll have your new baby."

Patricia looked down at her swollen belly and nodded. It had stopped feeling like joy of late. She was tired, her ankles felt like lead, and the child kicked out less often. The doctor said everything was fine, but she didn't agree with him. He wasn't carrying this watermelon of a child around all day.

Her normally high spirits had flagged badly after her brother's strange murder. And the knowledge that her husband was playing a dangerous game didn't help any, either.

That evening Patricia left work early and had her driver take her some by the most direct route instead of visiting among the immigrants as she usually did. When she arrived back in Menlo Park she saw a black buggy parked outside at the rail. Ben Gardiner, a strapping fourteen year old, and his sister Nancy, two years older, came out with twelve year old Catherine Lacey at a run. "Aunt Patty, there's a sick lady inside," Catherine called.

Patricia got down from her carriage and ran in as quickly as her condition would permit.

Diana Yarrow Parker sat in the parlor by the fireplace where a roaring set of logs threatened to turn the room into a small inferno. She shivered. Her blonde hair was stringy and wet, dampened from the perspiration which coursed down her face. She had lost weight in her face, chest and shoulders even while gaining precious weight in her womb. She was clearly near term in her pregnancy. Pink to the rims, darting about, her eyes reminded Patricia of the eyes of a rabbit Henry had once kept in a cage.

Diana tried to stand when she saw Patricia enter. "Please forgive me," she muttered.

Patricia turned to Nancy. "Nancy, go make up the bed in the guestroom. Ben, make a fire in the fireplace up there and Catherine, see if Miss Brophy will fill the old bed warmer from the cookstove. Move, children." She turned back to face the woman who had once been married to her brother. "Diana, is it the child?"

Diana turned her face fully in Patricia's direction. A long, ugly bruise ran down the side of her face. A plaster covered a cut over her eye.

"Oh, my God," Patricia said. "What happened?"

Diana tried a sick smile. "My husband . . . must not know where I am. . . ." Her voice was thick. She cleared her throat, but it didn't seem to help.

"Don't talk. Give me your arm." Patricia leaned down and helped the woman up. She was surprised by how light she was even while so far along in her pregnancy. "When is the child due?"

"I don't know," Diana muttered.

It took Nancy and Catherine to help get Diana in bed and send her perspiration-soaked black dress down to the laundry room. Patricia sent for the doctor and then sat at the bedside of her husband's sister as the woman drifted in and out of consciousness. She had Ben stow Diana's carriage and horses out of sight in case Senator Parker's people came looking. The bruise on the side of Diana's face—taken with the bruises that covered the length and breadth of the woman's naked body—spoke eloquently of the reason Diana had run to her brother's home. Patricia could not believe one person could bear so much abuse.

A half hour later Dianan fluttered her heavy lids and looked at Patricia. "Don't let him take the baby."

"I won't."

"It isn't his."

"It's not the Senator's?"

Diana shook her head very slowly.

"I won't let him take the baby, Diana."

"Thank you."

An hour later Diana woke again as if to make sure that Patricia was still watching over her. She smiled and drifted off again, only to wake a few moments later. "I loved Joseph Carrick very much," she whispered.

Patricia looked at the woman and did not respond.

"You never forgave me for loving him."

"Don't speak now," Patricia said.

"I must speak now," Diana said. "I'm dying."

Patricia reached out and took the woman's slender hand with its paperthin skin. "The doctor is on his way."

"Joseph was . . . Joseph was killed by order of my father."

"We knew that. Please, rest."

Diana shook her head. "Joseph was getting too close. He and Grant were getting too close to the Falcons."

"Falcons?"

"My husband and my father . . ." Diana lapsed into a half-dream state and then came back a few seconds later. "He paid Will Lacey to kill Joseph. . . ." She drifted off.

Patricia rose very slowly, her weight increased fiftyfold by the revelation that her own brother-in-law, the father of Stephen, Molly, Will Jr. and Catherine, had been the one to crack Joseph Carrick's precious skull like an egg. She went to the fireplace and pushed a log which had fallen back onto the fire. She looked at Diana and prayed that there were no more terrible secrets to be revealed.

A knock at the door interrupted her mournful thoughts. "Yes?"

Molly appeared at the door. "There's a doctor here, Aunt Patty."

"Doctor Canfield?"

Molly shook her head. "He's the new one. Says Doc Canfield was busy and sent him."

"Send him up please, Molly. And Molly?"

"Yes'm?"

"When Diana is well, I want to see the frock you bought for going away on your honeymoon."

Molly glowed.

The doctor walked in slowly, a man in his early sixties. He introduced himself as Doctor Standish and placed his bag down on the bedside table. As Patricia looked on he examined Diana, breathing through his nose with increasing difficulty. When he saw the woman's bruises he nodded, shook his head, and kept his private counsel.

When he had completed his examination he looked up and said gravely, "If I thought it advisable I'd move her to a hospital. Unfortunately it is too dangerous. For her and the child."

"Will she live?"

"I don't know. She is in a total collapse. Her color is bad, her pulse is rapid, her breathing shallow. The child may live. I can't say. I'm just not sure she's strong enough to withstand the rigors of childbirth." He paused. "How did she come by the bruises? She looks like she's been in a terrible accident."

Patricia nodded. "Yes, she has been."

The doctor looked into Patricia's eyes and saw no malice there. He nodded as well. "I understand."

"What do we do now?"

"We wait," he replied. "I'd like to ask one of your children to go tell Dr. Canfield that I'll be detained here indefinitely."

"Of course." Patricia left the room and returned a few minutes later with a tea tray. She poured cups for the doctor and herself. "You are working with Dr. Canfield now, Dr. Standish?"

"Until my ship is ready to go again," he said. "I'm a ship's surgeon."

"A strange profession for a man as—"

"As sober as I am?" Dr. Standish laughed. "Yes, I'll admit most of my profession do tend towards the incompetent. I happen to love the ocean. People—lots of people—make me uncomfortable. The ocean is the last frontier."

"I'm sorry. I didn't mean . . ."

Dr. Standish smiled kindly. "I don't mind. As soon as the *Emily W.* is ready to sail again, I'll be back in my element."

"What ship did you say?" Patricia asked.

"The *Emily W.* Do you know her?"

"I know someone who sailed on her for five years."

"Who?"

"Grant Yarrow."

"Yarrow? You are the Irish girl he spoke of all the time?"

"I hope so," she replied.

Dr. Standish smiled. "Of course! Patricia! That's the name! You must be very happy."

"Yes," she said, not completely sure of anything anymore.

Just then Ben knocked at the door and said somebody named Parker was downstairs.

CHAPTER THREE

AMBROSE Parker did not presume to stand inside Grant and Patricia Yarrow's home. Instead, he rested casually on the verandah, his wide-brimmed hat on his lap. He wore a conservatively cut suit in black worsted, a white shirt and a black string tie. His liver-spotted hands were tight and gnarled like old oak roots. He crossed his narrow knees.

"May I help you, sir?" Patricia asked. Ben Gardiner stood slightly behind her.

Senator Parker rose and smiled. "I am Senator Parker," he said.

"Yes. I recognized you from your pictures in the newspapers," she said.

"I am looking for my wife. A lady with whom you are acquainted? The former Miss Diana Yarrow? The former Mrs. Joseph Carrick?"

"I do know the lady in question." Patricia kept her face as noncommittal as possible. "But I have not seen her since the night my husband was shot. She came for news of him and we only had the briefest of conversations." Patricia made sure she did not oversell her innocence. She had seen many a loan applicant try to impress her with his or her guilelessness.

There was a long pause, during which Ambrose Parker let his eyes roam about the front yard, the easy sweep of the two acres of lawn, the riot of greenery down by the main road which fenced off the place from prying eyes, the barn over by the side yard, the towering trees that must have been standing here long long before the Indians came. Then he looked back at Patricia. She was a beautiful woman —more beautiful in the flesh than in the newspaper shots of her. There was something so goddamned sensual about a woman that strong. And yet still in all she had so many delicate features: her throat, her ears, her jawline. She sure didn't look almost forty and that was for earnest. She looked like the kind of woman who would be very surprised when she awoke in his special room. He looked up at her and smiled. "I see Doc Canfield's carriage. Is somebody ill?" he asked.

Patricia walked slowly down to the edge of the verandah and looked up at the dusk. "Will, Junior has a touch of the croup. Dr. Standish is seeing to him."

Ambrose Parker nodded. "I'm sorry to hear about the child's illness," he said. "I see somebody has taken the team from their traces. Is the doctor planning on spending a long time on this croup?"

Patricia turned and laced her fingers together. "Senator Parker, forgive me, but I am laboring under the impression that you are not satisfied with my telling you I have not seen your wife since my husband was shot."

Parker leaned his head back and laughed. "Such a nice way of putting it," he said. "No, I'm fully satisfied. I was just prolonging my visit for personal reasons."

Patricia's eyebrows went up.

"You are quite easily the most attractive woman I have laid eyes on in months," he said.

"You must have been in the wilderness, then," Patricia said. "I'm afraid I must get back to my sick child, Senator. Is there anything else I can do for you?"

Ambrose Parker put on his hat and settled it at a jaunty angle on his head. "If you do see my wife, please contact me at Mr. Yarrow's. It's most urgent. She is about to birth our first child and she's been plagued by severe mental problems. I've never seen it so bad. To be frank with you I'm afraid she may hurt herself. She has bruised herself unmercifully, throwing herself about in an effort to lose the baby. I fear for both their lives. I'm sure you understand."

Patricia's face stayed immobile while she tried to sift the truth from what this man with the fat-lidded eyes and the double chins was saying. She nodded and then watched him mount his horse and ride off the property.

"Could Diana have made these bruises herself?" Patricia asked Dr. Standish a few minutes later.

Dr. Standish looked down at the angriest of the welts upon her and shook his head. "I don't think so. This one is from a strap. She'd have had to whip herself pretty hard to raise a welt like that."

Patricia pursed her lips and walked to the window to look off in the direction Senator Parker had ridden. She turned back. "How much longer before the child is due?" she asked the doctor.

He shrugged his shoulders and sat down to scan the evening paper. "It depends. If Mrs. Parker here can manage to stay alive for another four hours, than we may see the child. If she dies first, I don't know whether the fetus can be saved." He flipped the front page back. "Look at this. Oh, I'm sorry. I talk to myself whenever I read."

Patricia smiled slightly. "It gets so that a man can't earn a living without getting himself cut up," he continued.

"I beg your pardon?"

"Here's a physician in Los Angeles who was murdered in his office. Robbed by some fool full of liquor. I tell you it's better when you're at sea. You may not be in control of your fate but you're a damn-site better off. Pardon my language."

"I don't mind. I've heard worse."

"And here's another. I tell you I can't wait to get back aboard ship. 'Private Investigator slain in office.' Him you can imagine being killed. Probably done in by some man he was following to some floozy's boudoir. Incredible how rash men can get when they want to leave hearth and home. I never married. Wonder who this Boudreau fellow was watching." He rustled the paper, looked over the top, checked his patient's condition, then looked at his hostess. She stood, pale, holding the post on the end of the guest bed.

"Are you all right? Mrs. Yarrow?"

Patricia held on tight to the post. "I think so. What was that detective's name?"

Dr. Standish reached back for the paper he'd dropped on the floor. "Henry Boudreau. Why?"

Patricia shook her head. "Nothing . . ." she lied. It *was* him, the man she had hired to try to find Judge Chase! "I was just curious."

"Perhaps you had best lie down, ma'am. You are in a family way. I don't want two patients. I'll need your help." He helped Patricia down the hall to the wide and beautiful bedroom she shared with Grant. The walls were covered with a pale blue paper. The bed was spacious and soft. "I'll call you soon as I need you," the doctor said.

Patricia lay on the bed and watched the shadows on the ceiling. She tried to put together the confusing and chaotic bits and pieces of information that whirled about her tired brain. She slept fitfully for twenty minutes before she rose and went back to the guest room. Dr. Standish looked up. "You look much better for your rest, Mrs. Yarrow."

"How is Diana?"

"The same."

"If you'd like to take a little rest, I'll watch her, Doctor."

He nodded. "It's going to be a long night." He consulted his pocket watch. "It's already nine. Thank you. If she shows any change at all, wake me."

Patricia led him to Harry's room and gave him a down comforter.

When she returned to the guest room, Diana was turning over on her side fretfully. "There, there, my dear," Patricia said.

"No time," Diana said.

Patricia thought to go and wake the doctor, but he had not had time to close his eyes. "Easy, Diana." She bathed the woman's forehead with a cool cloth.

"The Falcons . . ." Diana said. "Simon . . . Ambrose . . . If they get to President Arthur. . . ."

Patricia leaned close to the woman's face to hear the words that staggered from her mouth. "Who are the Falcons, Diana?"

Diana's eyes fluttered open.

"Your brother Grant is involved in this, Diana. We have to save Grant."

The nod was almost imperceptible.

Patricia massaged her sister-in-law's wrists. There was the smell of death on her. "Grant and Mr. Macauley. And Judge Chase," Patricia prompted, hoping to elicit more information.

Diana nodded again.

"It had to do with the assassination of President Garfield," Patricia said.

"Yes. Oh, yes. The Falcons . . ."

"The Falcons paid Guiteau?"

"He . . . is . . . their man . . ."

"Who are the Falcons, Diana?"

She rocked her head from side to side. "All over the country. Every state."

"Who are they? What are they?"

"My husband, my father . . . The heads . . ."

"What do they want to do?"

"Kill President Arthur." Diana looked over at Patricia. "Judge Chase is dead. Killed by Falcons. Buried behind the barn near the 'target rock'." There was a long pause. "They are going to take over the whole government . . . Martial law when President Arthur is killed . . . men in every state. . . ."

"When, Diana, when?"

"Soon. Papers. I got the papers. In . . . carriage. . . ."

"But *when*?"

"Nothing you can do. Parker leaving tomorrow after dinner. . . . They're going to kill Grant. The Falcons marked him. Too dangerous . . ." The cry Diana uttered was sharp. Patricia got up and went to fetch the doctor, her mind electrified by the news Diana had told her.

"We'll have to work quickly," Dr. Standish said when he had examined the sick woman.

At two in the morning, with Grace Malone, Patricia Carrick Yarrow and Dr. Standish looking on, Diana Yarrow Parker gave birth to a small male child. His cries were weak, exhausted from the difficult birth.

Patricia held the child up so that his mother could see him.

Diana's skin was grey, her eyes ringed with dark brown circles. Her mouth was a tight line, drawn back across her teeth. She tried to smile, but the effort was too much.

Dr. Standish cautioned Patricia that Diana had but a few moments to live.

Patricia laid the infant alongside Diana and leaned closer to hear the woman's last words. "Baby looks . . . like his father. . . . Simon the father . . . Forgive me, God."

Diana closed her eyes as she looked down at the the sleeping infant.

Patricia stood back and let the doctor drape the sweat-soaked sheet across the tortured woman's face.

"Do you know of a wet-nurse?" the doctor asked.

"I do," Grace said.

"Good." The doctor sighed. "She fought just long enough to save the child. She was very brave."

As soon as the doctor had gone, Patricia told Grace that they were leaving for the San Joaquin Valley.

"What for? You need your rest. We need to watch over this babe."

Patricia shook her head. "We'll put the baby with Mrs. Layton. Grant is in the Valley somewhere and there isn't time to try to find him."

"Time for what?"

"Time to stop Ambrose Parker." She grabbed Grace by her shoulders. "Grace, Grant and Marshall don't know the conspiracy is ready to strike. If we don't act now, everything is lost." She paused for breath. "And they're going to kill Grant!"

Grace understood little of what Patricia had said, but when she heard that Grant Yarrow was in danger, she didn't need to hear any more.

CHAPTER FOUR

IT was past noon before the carriage carrying Grace
and Patricia arrived on the outskirts of the Yarrow
ranchlands. They had travelled all night and all day,
first by rail, then by hired coach. Patricia had managed to sleep part of the time, but the urgency of her
mission kept pressing itself upon her, robbing her of
the rest she needed.

Patricia watched the familiar territory pass by the
window of the coach. The green hills brought back
a flood of memories, most of them of their first months
battling the land and bringing forth a crop. Joseph
had been a good farmer, dedicated to the land, teach-
ing them all to respect nature's bounty and to live ac-
cording to nature's laws.

And then it had all gone sour. Simon Yarrow's incredible greed reached across the green valleys and
over the lush fertile hills and sapped the goodness
from the land, burning and scorching whatever it
touched.

The driver got down from the box. "This where
you wanted to be?" he asked.

Patricia nodded. He went to the back of the carriage and untied his saddle horse. "We'll bring back the carriage tomorrow," Patricia said.

"No problem there, ma'am," the driver said. "With what you paid me, you can have her till Saturday." He spurred his mount and rode back towards town.

Patricia and Grace climbed up on the boot and Patricia took the reins. She wondered if, indeed, she would be bringing back the rig when she promised. "Git up," she shouted. The carriage rolled down the bumping side road that led across Simon Yarrow's land.

Senator Ambrose Parker was tired, but he felt none of the exhaustion he should have felt. It had been a long trip back from San Francisco. He had ridden hard and then slept only a few hours until lunch. But Parker smiled as he dried his face. This day had been long in coming, but it was here at last.

"There's no word of Diana," Simon Yarrow said, as he came into the Senator's room. "Rector just reported on the telegraph."

"Damn the bitch to hell," Parker fumed.

"She's my daughter," Yarrow said tightly.

"But a bitch nonetheless. Plus she knows a great deal more than she should," Parker stormed. "That is your fault."

Simon leaned against the back of one of the light blue upholstered chairs. "What do you plan on doing with Rouse?"

The words came quickly, quietly. "Discipline him."

Simon nodded.

The front yard was baked dry and hot when Parker and Yarrow emerged into the afternoon sun. Senator

Parker was dressed in a light tan suit. Simon Yarrow wore a white shirt open at the neck. A dozen men were ringed about a tall thin man who knelt in the dust with his hands tied behind him. Parker looked up at the sun. Then he checked his pocket watch. "Talmadge Rouse, you have been found guilty by your betters of insubordination. It is my unpleasant duty to pass sentence upon you."

"You ain't no judge," the sullen prisoner said.

The air was still except for the distant shriek of a hawk's meal. Then Parker looked across the ranks. "Being a Falcon means absolute obedience. Asking no questions. Doing exactly what you are told. We are too close to the ultimate victory—the salvation of our country—to let men like this man here jeopardize what we have spent almost ten long years building." He turned to look down upon Talmadge Rouse. "Lt. Rouse, you are hereby discharged from the ranks of the Falcons. Cut him loose, men."

Rouse looked up, surprised. His brows arched up. His jaw dropped. When he had been unfettered he stood up, unsteadily. His eyes darted from man to man as he began to back across the yard, expecting one in the company to draw on him. He smiled. "I'll keep my mouth shut," he said through the anxious grin. He kept backing up towards the gate. When he thought he was safe enough, he turned and began to run.

The shot pierced the air and echoed against the walls that surrounded the farmhouse. Senator Parker holstered his .44 and turned to the men around him. "There are five thousand Falcons across the country, each man ready to die for the cause." He turned and walked back into the house with Simon Yarrow.

Patricia heard the shot as she and Grace made their way down the back road a half mile from the farm. "What the hell are we gonna do against all them?" Grace asked.

"We have to stop Ambrose Parker and Simon Yarrow. I don't know how."

Grace shook her head and then gritted her teeth. "You know I'll follow you to hell."

"That's exactly where we're going," Patricia replied. "Do you have any questions about how we get in?"

Grace shook her head.

"All right. We'll stop here." Patricia got down from the box and walked around to the back of the carriage where Grace helped her climb into the luggage compartment.

"You breathe in there?" Grace asked.

Patricia nodded grimly. "Let's go."

Grace jumped back up on the box and drove the team down to the front gate of the Yarrow ranch.

When Grace got within fifteen yards of the big double gate an armed sentry came out to stop her progress. "Help you, ma'am?"

"Like to see Senator Ambrose Parker, sir."

The sentry smiled at the strange looking woman. "What for?"

"Just tell him I know where his wife is."

The sentry raised his brows, talked with his partner and then waved the carriage inside. "Rein up over there," he said as soon as Grace passed through the gates. "We'll go talk to Senator Parker."

Grace climbed down and followed the man.

It was hot and cramped inside the luggage compartment as Patricia eased the leather cover back just far enough to peek out at the ranch yard. Her heart beat quicker and quicker as if it would never slow down—just speed up until it failed.

A single man walked from the barn across to one of the bunkhouses. The sun sent long shadows from him. When he passed out of sight, Patricia eased herself down to the hard earth. The pistols rubbed against the inside of her thighs where she had them tied.

Senator Parker looked up from his sherry at the man across the table. He held his glass aloft. "To our success," he said.

The man in the dark suit with the handlebar moustache and the narrow eyes nodded. There was a rosewood box on his lap containing the tools of his trade. His name was Sandfire. He let his lips touch the sherry, but he did not drink before putting down the glass.

Simon Yarrow watched the man, Abington Sandfire, and wondered if he too would go to the gallows as the assassin of President Garfield would. The plan called for his escape, but they all knew there were no guarantees. Yarrow looked at the clock on the mantel. In another hour they would leave for the train. In four days their journey would end in Washington. In five days their man would ascend to the Presidency. In six days the Constitution would be suspended in order to preserve order.

The sentry knocked at the door.

"Come?"

"Sir, there's a woman drove in says she knows about Mrs. Parker."

Senator Parker stood up quickly. "Show her in." He looked over at Simon Yarrow. "Use the telegraph to get word to our people in town."

Grace Malone looked around the room, her small pale blue eyes missing nothing. She sure didn't like the looks of the third man.

"Good afternoon, Miss?" Parker said.

"Mary Elizabeth Coady," she said.

"Miss Coady, you have word of my daughter?" Simon Yarrow asked.

"I do. I heard on the grapevine you was looking for her."

"We certainly are."

"It'll cost ya," Grace replied. She smiled grimly with her false teeth gleaming.

"A hundred dollars?" Simon said.

"Five hundred," Grace replied.

"Agreed," Simon said. "Where is she?"

"Where's my money?"

"Miss Coady," Senator Parker said, "you are becoming most tiresome with your insistence upon remuneration. If you persist, I shall have Mr. Sandfire here lift the top of your head off with his pistols."

"And you'll never find Mrs. Parker neither," Grace said. "All the same to me." She hoped that the three men couldn't see far enough to notice the perspiration which flowed like a river down her neck and back. She knew she couldn't reach the pistol which she had hidden in her handbag. Not before they ripped her in half.

Simon Yarrow went to the sideboard and yanked open the side drawer. He took out a leather bag and held it up for Grace to see. "Here's five hundred in gold, Miss Coady. Where is she?"

Grace took the bag. Smiled. "Out in the carriage," she said.

"What?"

"Why didn't you say so?"

Grace walked quickly with the two men as they hurried out into the foyer and out the front door to the courtyard. She just managed to stay ahead of Parker and Yarrow and fling open the side door.

Simon pushed Parker aside as they both reached in and grabbed for the canvas cloth that covered the floor of the carriage.

"Hold it right there," Patricia said, rising from beneath the cloth with both pistols aimed squarely at Ambrose Parker and Simon Yarrow.

"What the hell is going on?" Simon Yarrow said.

"It seems that Mrs. Yarrow is taking us prisoner," Ambrose Parker said tightly.

"You're damn right," Patricia said.

Grace reached into her bag and took out a gun which she jammed into Abington Sandfire's back. "Move an inch and lose it all," she said.

"Now then, gentlemen," Patricia said, "very carefully get into the carriage." She paused to catch her breath. The cramps in her stomach made her want to bend double, but she couldn't afford to take her eyes off her quarry for a moment.

Simon Yarrow climbed in as Patricia pulled herself up and to the other side. He was followed by Senator Parker and Abington Sandfire.

"Hand your weapons to Miss Malone, please," Patricia said.

Simon Yarrow brought out his .44 butt first and tossed it to Grace. Ambrose did the same. Sandfire relinquished a small calibre handgun from his vest. "You can't hit all three of us with those two horse pistols," Senator Parker said. "Moreover, you'd be tried for murder."

"I can gut-shoot two of you," Patricia said across the narrow aisle, both pistols scanning the three men's stomachs. "The third might be lucky. Would you like to draw straws?" The pains were coming harder now. "All right, Grace. Let's move."

Grace nodded and pulled the curtains shut, slammed the door of the carriage and got up to take the reins. In a few seconds they were rolling past the sentries and headed south-west.

CHAPTER FIVE

"WHERE do you intend taking us?" Senator Parker asked. "Do you mind if I smoke?"

"Yes, I do," Patricia said. The interior of the carriage was hot. The swaying motion was nauseating. Th pains in her womb made her want to cry out. "San Francisco."

Ambrose Parker nodded. "Very brave. That presupposes you do not let your attention wander. Not for a moment."

"Be quiet," Patricia said. She dared not wipe the sweat from her eyes with the back of her arm for fear one of her three adversaries would take the opportunity to jump her.

"May I ask why you're doing this?" Parker continued.

"Because you are trying to work an evil plot against the government," Patricia replied.

Sandfire and Parker laughed. "Is that what my lovely bride told you?" Parker said.

Patricia did not reply.

"That's funny. We're being kidnapped on account of the insane ramblings of a sick woman."

"Diana is dead," Patricia said.

Simon Yarrow started forward as if to staunch the flow of truth from the woman who spoke it. "No," he breathed.

"She gave birth to her son and then died last night."

"May God have mercy on her," Simon said.

"And you," Patricia said.

Ambrose Parker was silent for a few moments. "I still don't know what you would have us charged with," he said.

"Treason," Patricia replied.

"Where is your proof?" Parker asked.

The carriage lurched left and then right again. Sandfire, sensing the moment, leaned forward and reached out for one of the pistols. Patricia, acting from instinct, brought down the barrel across his fingers, cracking two of his knuckles. "Ow!" he cried.

Patricia held her bead on the other two. "I think you'd best keep your hands to yourself."

The assassin nursed his fractured fingers in silence, nurturing his rage for this woman who was threatening to destroy everything.

"You still haven't answered my question," Parker said.

"I know where Judge Chase is buried," Patricia said.

Parker smiled. "That we shot a wanted felon is no crime," he said, leaning back after the carriage had struck a rut.

"I know that Mr. Yarrow hired Will Lacey to kill Joseph Carrick."

"Heresay evidence doesn't wash," Parker replied. "It would appear, Mrs. Yarrow, that you are kidnapping us unlawfully. You have nothing. If I were you I would turn this coach around and take us back to the ranch before you get in any more trouble."

It was Patricia's turn to smile. "In Diana's carriage I found a number of items which I shall make available to the Federal authorities."

"Such as?"

"They were things Diana had collected to get her own revenge on the two men who had hurt her most. There was a whole case in the boot of her carriage. The documents should fetch a pretty price at auction. A genuine letter from Charles Guiteau to Senator Ambrose Parker, dated one week before he fired at President Garfield. It talked of his plans in some detail. At the very least it was careless of you or your staff not to advise the President that this man was lurking about."

Simon Yarrow started to say something to his partner, but Parker cut him off. "That is hardly an indictment," Parker said.

"You would deny me all my surprises?" Patricia said. She had to pause for breath. The pains in her gut were increasing. "There are receipts for weapons, a list of all the important Falcons in the United States, a list of future targets, and so forth."

Parker's eyes narrowed. "Very interesting," he said.

"Where do you have these items that you say will incriminate us?" Simon asked.

"We left them with a friend. If anything happens to us before tomorrow, he'll take them to the Federal

Judge. I'm here now to make sure you snakes don't work any more destruction before the law catches up with you."

"Very wise," Yarrow replied. "Perhaps we could make a deal."

Patricia shook her head. "There isn't enough money in the world. I swore I'd get you for my brother's murder. Now I'll have the pleasure of being able to watch you hang for it." She paused. "And I guess that you had a hand in Christopher Carrick's murder as well." Patricia reached up and banged on the ceiling of the carriage with one of her pistols.

As soon as Grace had brought the team to a halt, she jumped down and opened the door. "What's the matter?"

"I can't make it all the way," Patricia said. "The baby is hurting bad."

"We can't stop at any of these towns along the way," Grace said. "Without the evidence we couldn't convince anybody."

Patricia nodded. Grabbed her stomach with both arms. "Tie them up."

"All right. Hang on."

It was when Grace, in her hurry to reach Simon Yarrow's wrists, leaned across between Patricia and Abington Sandfire that Ambrose Parker lashed out with both feet, hurling Grace onto Patricia's pistols, giving him the time to swing with a right and then a left, knocking Patricia unconscious. She fell into a long black tunnel, filled with the cries of infants. Sandfire was on Grace in a flash, flattening her with a vicious blow of his elbow across the side of her head.

"Let's get the hell out of here," Parker said.

* * *

Patricia's dreams all blended together. Faces. Names. Figures. There was Linus Comstock, the banking commissioner. Chandler Gates, the man who had tried to ruin the Carrick Bank with uncle Elijah's blessings. Michael Kelly, with his barrel chest. Ed O'Connor. She hadn't seen that magnificent ice man in a year. Whatever happened to Sybil Chase? Emma Chatfield, the wanton who had bedded Grant Yarrow so shamelessly. Was she still alive?

Alive?

Her baby. Was her baby alive?

Patricia's eyelids struggled to part. There was a strange throbbing along her left cheekline. It felt as if a hot cloth had been plastered to her face. And there were the sharp pains in her stomach. She reached out to feel the reassuring stretch of her skin as it mounded up in a distended growth. Just then the infant kicked out and she caught her breath.

The room was dark and cool. The curtains had been drawn. It was a woman's room. There were dolls on the dresser, arranged the way a young woman might arrange them long after she'd finished playing with them. The fourposter had a lace canopy that was interwoven with delicate pink and blue ribbons.

The door opened and needles of light stabbed her bruised eyes. A tall figure blotted the light. Then the door closed again. A few seconds later she could feel the weight of the person depress the mattress by her feet.

"Who is it?" she asked.

The horsehair mattress rustled. "It is I," Senator Parker answered.

Patricia pulled her feet closer to her body in an effort to avoid his nearness.

"You are in my late wife's room. A very pretty room." He paused. "The doctor says your baby will die a-borning if you don't get help soon."

"The doctor?"

"He took a look at you while you were unconscious. We didn't want our favorite guest dying on us."

"Where is Grace Malone?"

Parker shrugged. "Taken care of." He stood up and came closer. "Mrs. Yarrow, let me play all my cards at once so that we can expedite things here."

"Go ahead." The pains were duller now and more frightening.

"I couldn't care less what happens to you and your baby. But I do want to get hold of those documents which Diana stole. She was very good. She stole only the most incriminating for her safe-conduct. I want them back. I will allow the doctor to assist you in the birth of your child if you tell us where to find the papers. Otherwise, I shall simply let you scream your head off up here until you and your blasted offspring expire."

"What about the President?"

"Mr. Sandfire left this afternoon for Washington. There isn't a thing you can do to stop the events that are in motion." He smiled. "The doctor says you have one or two hours at the most. Tell us where the documents are, we'll telegraph our operatives in San Francisco, and that will be that. You'll have your doctor." He paused. "What say?"

The choices were clearly laid out. Save your child and the Republic would be no more. Save your Republic and take your baby to the grave with you.

Patricia's eyes shone brightly as she shook her head. "I can't live like you," she said.

Senator Parker's response was instinctive, reflexive. He swung out with the back of his hand, stinging her skin with the swiftness of the attack. His breathing was heavy. "Suit yourself. I shall be back to look in on you." He shook his head. "You are a fool."

A thin crack of daylight disappeared as Patricia held her knees up as close to her body as possible. After awhile that failed to ease the pain. She knew something was wrong. Women had birthed babies alone for many years . . . out on the prairie, in the mountain cabins. But it didn't feel right. It felt as if the child were struggling for life and losing.

Patricia got up from the bed and walked slowly to the window. She pulled back the thick drape and stared out through the iron grillwork at the thick dusk which had gathered in the ranch yard. She could see men moving to and fro in the lanternlight down by the main gate. It was obvious that something was afoot. Men were loading a wagon with wooden crates. Another wagon arrived in front of the barn as soon as that one was loaded. She watched the first one head out through the gat and towards Stockton.

She stifled a cry, leaned her hands on the sill for balance and waited for the pain to subside.

Simon Yarrow found her standing there when he threw back the door. His skin was pale. His eyes were cold and penetrating. He slammed the door behind him. "It's all turned to shit," he whispered hoarsely. "All, all of it." He paused to get his breath while Patricia carefully backpedaled to the bed. She held her stomach, trying not to cry out with pain. For an hour now the contractions were a minute apart with no relief. No sooner did the pains subside than they were replaced by new pains which seemed to burn with electric fire.

"Diana told me about your child," Patricia said, as if this frightful news might stop his slow advance.

"It's all turned to shit," Simon Yarrow said. And then he stopped, looked up at the beautiful woman on the bed. "It's all the fault of you fucking Irish, isn't it?"

"No," Patricia said.

"Sure it is." He sat down on the edge of the bed. "Before you came this valley was a special sort of Heaven. And then my wife died. You should have known her. She looked just like Diana."

"Help me," Patricia said. "I'm dying. Save my child, please." The pains were overwhelming now.

"And then you and your Goddamned brother Joseph came here. But I still had Diana. Until he took her from me."

"Help me."

"I still have my farms. My valley. This is my valley." He was raging almost incoherently now, his eyes glassy. "But you weren't satisfied. You wanted my land. Then you went after my bank. And now you want to stop me from taking my rightful place. Fucking mongrel scum—you won't stop until you've ruined the whole country. Unless we stop you first."

"But it was Parker who killed Diana," Patricia pleaded. "Not me." Her voice was thin, reedy.

"I came to kill you," Yarrow replied simply. "You

ruined everything." His face was a fleshy blank, like
unrisen dough. He drew a small calibre pocket pistol.

Patricia's eyes flashed about the room looking for
any way out, any weapon, any salvation. Her pulse
beat faster and faster in her ears. Momentarily her
pain was forgotten in a mad frenzy to preserve her
unborn child. "No," she said.

Simon Yarrow turned to look at her. "I knew that
we shouldn't let you micks into the valley, that you'd
spoil it for us all. I was right."

Patricia put out a hand in front of her as the
muzzle of the silver plated pistol swung slowly towards
her face. "Don't," she cried in a hoarse whisper. She
reached behind her, caught ahold of one of Diana's
dolls, and threw it at him. It bounced and fell harm-
lessly to the ground. She stepped backwards, caught
ahold of a seashell and threw that as well. Still Simon
Yarrow strode forward, enjoying his moment of complete domination.

"I've been waiting so long for this," he said.

Patricia's hand made contact with a wide round
shape, a celluloid cannister of face powder. Quickly
she took off the top and threw the half-pound at her
father-in-law.

The shower of face powder exploded across his
face, filling his eyes and nose with pumice and scented
flour. He fired two shots as Patricia swung round to
the side and kicked out at his groin. Her foot made solid contact, sending fiery and icy fists of pain up into
the bottom of his stomach. Simon Yarrow dropped
his gun and fell forward, buckled in half, breathless.

Patricia dropped to her knees, grabbed the gun and
watched it erupt in a bright orange and red shower.

The small calibre shell tumbled end over end, broke through the skin of his forehead, bit through his skull and tore his frontal lobe apart like an animal on a kill. Simon Yarrow's eyes looked heavenward and the last image etched upon them was of the woman he had wronged for so many years.

Before she could think, the door burst open and Ambrose Parker stood on the threshold looking confused. The picture was all wrong. The woman held a shining object—a gun, he thought—and suddenly it exploded.

Patricia remembered firing twice into the perplexed Senator.

Parker lay on the floor, two angry holes spilling life from his chest cavity, a third leeching from his side. Tears blotted his face. "Nooo," he cried. "Not me! Not me! Don't let me die! Get the doctor!"

Patricia eased herself onto the bed and collapsed.

CHAPTER SIX

MENLO PARK, CALIFORNIA, JUNE, 1882

THE bride wore white, a high-necked lace gown which trailed off thirty feet into the chubby hands of two cherubic children, godchildren among Patricia's growing hoarde.

The bridge's gown was made by Mrs. Kierney's women and, though the bride had not deigned to marry Tom Kierney, the old woman gave her blessing: "It's just as well, Molly girl, on account of Tom's never been any good at all except to fish and who'd want a man smelling like cod all the time?"

The groom wore a complete morning outfit and, with his handsome father as best man, the two Macauleys cut as fine a figure as anyone had seen. What none of their many admirers knew was that just before coming West to take Molly Lacey for his bride, Benjamin Macauley had bedded Rachel Stern for the first and last time. "My last fling—for awhile," Benjamin told himself as he adjusted his cravat.

Patrick and his wife smiled as Benjamin and Molly each made slight errors in their vows as they repeated them after the priest's baritone litany.

The Laceys and the Gardiners were arranged by
ages and sizes, looking on as the first of this incredible
brood got married. They wondered what it would be
like to have a fancy sister who lived in New York
with the famous Macauley family. They hoped they
wouldn't miss her too terribly. Little Catherine hated
her high button shoes and the grosgrain ribbon from
her hat kept tickling the back of her neck.

Ed O'Connor and Michael Kelly watched Molly
come back up the aisle with her new husband and
said silent prayers for her. She would probably need
them if half of what they heard about Benjamin
Macauley was true.

Molly herself was absolutely stunning as she walked
quickly up the aisle as Mrs. Benjamin Macauley. Her
skin radiated, the floral halo above her veil made her
look like one of the saints in the stained glass windows.
She liked the smiles she saw on the faces of friends
and relations—the list topped out at five hundred—
and she wondered if they wondered how she was going to tame this gorgeous hunk of a husband. She
had no doubts whatsoever.

Benjamin looked at the strangers' faces—intermixed
with friends from Princeton and New York, several
private cars' worth—and thought what a tribute it was
to Patricia Carrick Yarrow that all these people
turned out to see her niece married. The room where
the wedding gifts were stored was chock-a-block filled
with everything from fine silver to garlands of specially grown garlic. The guests themselves were executives,
ironmongers, blacksmiths, waitresses, fishermen, bankers, bankrupts, idlers, farmers, and anyone else who
had ever glowed after dealing with the redheaded,
hardheaded Irishwoman.

Benjamin smiled at his mother, Violette Larson, and gave a nod as if to say, "Not bad, eh, mom? I have the prettiest of the lot." She smiled back and hoped her son would know what real love was—one of these days. She knew she had spoiled him, knew that he suffered that peculiar sort of Narcissism which looks well on the very handsome. His sense of humor and his good looks and his money would stand him in good stead—until he was really tested by life's sharp edge. She hoped he would make the grade.

Grant Yarrow watched Molly and Benjamin walk back up the aisle and wondered how he had ever come to this place—a survivor who had married the most special human being ever put on this planet. He looked down at the infant who slept in the small basket on the seat next to him and marvelled at the mysteries of God's grace. Joseph Christopher Michael Yarrow was far too small to carry all the names he had been given, but Grant was certain he would grow into them.

Next to Grant's son lay Laird Parker, Diana's son, already growing huskier by the day. Grant thought the child didn't look much like the late Senator, but time would tell. The babe would be lucky if he never looked like the scoundrel who had almost succeeded in toppling the government. Had it not been for Patricia the Falcons could easily have come to power and demolished much of what reconstruction had accomplished. Agents of the Justice Department killed Abington Sandfire just as he boarded the trolley for downtown Washington for his appointment with destiny and Chester Arthur.

The Falcons were in disarray. Yarrow and Parker

were both dead. The others had gone underground, but the government had Diana's stolen lists. They made interesting reading. Had it not been for Patricia Yarrow, who knows what would have happened?

Grant looked down the pew and smiled at Grace Malone who wept quietly at the magnificence of the ceremony and the love that it betokened. She wept for the little girl who had once been Molly Lacey and had never picked up after herself.

But, as soon as the wedding couple had left the cathedral and stepped into the carriage for the ride to the reception, all eyes turned to the front of the cathedral again to watch the best man, Marshall Macauley, take the arm of the "mother" of the bride. Patricia looked up at the man who had always seemed part of a dream world, and thought he was still—next to Grant, of course—one of the handsomest men ever to snatch the strings of a woman's heart. She still felt tired, plain exhausted if the truth be told, but today was the happiest day of her life. She had a beautiful family; she had survived her nightmarish ordeal, and she had played a crucial role in destroying a heinous plot against the country which had had to be both mother and father to her.

When Grant and the others had finally blasted their way into the fortress that had been the Yarrow farm. they found her almost unconscious, lying next to her newborn babe, suckling it among the dead. She had hung between life and death for a week before massing all her will to survive.

And now she walked out into the clear blue San Francisco day, knowing that she had been tested beyond man or woman's endurance.

She smiled to know in her soul that she had not been found wanting. She turned back to her husband and kissed him on the mouth for **no reason other than** she felt exactly like doing it.

AMERICAN DYNASTY
Volume Three

THE
STERNS

by Brooke Miller

Scorned by her family and rejected by the man she adored, Rachel Stern surrendered everything to save a son whose exploits would astound turn-of-the-century New York. From the ashes of a forbidden love, Rachel Stern founded an American dynasty.

**An October 1982 title
from DELL/EMERALD**

07639-0

AMERICAN DYNASTY
Volume One

—THE—
MACAULEYS

by Brooke Miller

Disinherited by one of the nation's most powerful families, Marshall Macauley gambled on a ruthless country, fought for an impossible dream, and founded an American dynasty.

A June 1982 title from **DELL/EMERALD**   **06099-0**

Jennifer

BOOK ONE

Jennifer meets the handsome and mysterious playboy-entrepreneur Malcolm Boyd when she visits her twin sister Marina's Southampton beach house. While this intriguing man challenges Jennifer to research the question: What makes an ideal lover for a woman?, Jennifer and her dark mirror-image Marina explore the equally absorbing question: Can two sisters share one man?

A DELL/EMERALD BOOK $2.95 (04209-7)

BOOK TWO

The next in Jennifer's series of erotic adventures! On assignment for the mysterious Count Bessarbria, Jennifer travels to London, Paris and Biarritz following members of the Stage of the Golden Dawn. She documents their reenactment of ancient fertility rites and continues her own pursuit of the exquisite pleasures of love.

A DELL/EMERALD BOOK $2.95 (04274-7)